BETWEEN TWO WORLDS I.

"Wandering between two worlds,
one dead, the other pow er less to be
born."

- Mat thew Arnold

TIMELINE

World's End	1913 - 1919
Be tween Two Worlds	1919 - 1929
Drangon's Teeth	1929 - 1934
Wide is the Gate	1934 - 1937
Presidential Agent	1937 - 1938
Dragon Har vest	1938 - 1940
A World to Win	1940 - 1942
Presidential Mission	1942 - 1943
One Clear Call	1943 - 1944
O Shep herd, Speak!	1943 - 1946
The Return of Lanny Budd	1946 - 1949

Each vol ume is pub lished in two parts: I and II.

BETWEEN TWO WORLDS I.

Upton Sinclair

Simon Publications

2001

LCCN: 67120285

ISBN: 1-931313-02-4

Dis trib uted by Ingram Book Com pany

Printed by Light ning Source Inc., LaVergne, TN

Pub lished by Si mon Pub li ca tions, P.O. Box 321 Safety Har bor, FL

An Author's Program

From a 1943 article by Upton Sinclair.

When I say "historian," I have a meaning of my own. I portray world events in story form, because that form is the one I have been trained in. I have supported myself by writing fiction since the age of sixteen, which means for forty-nine years.

… Now I realize that this one was the one job for which I had been born: to put the period of world wars and revolutions into a great long novel. …

I can not say when it will end, because I don't know exactly what the characters will do. They lead a semi-independent life, being more real to me than any of the people I know, with the single exception of my wife. … Some of my characters are people who lived, and whom I had opportunity to know and watch. Others are imaginary—or rather, they are complexes of many people whom I have known and watched. Lanny Budd and his mother and father and their various relatives and friends have come in the course of the past four years to be my daily and nightly companions. I have come to know them so intimately that I need only to ask them what they would do in a given set of circumstances and they start to enact their roles. … I chose what seems to me the most revealing of them and of their world.

How long will this go on? I can not tell. It depends in great part upon two public figures, Hitler and Mussolini. What are they going to do to mankind and what is mankind will do to them? It seems to me hardly likely that either will die a peaceful death. I am hoping to outlive them; and whatever happens Lanny Budd will be somewhere in the neighborhood, he will be "in at the death," according to the fox-hunting phrase.

These two foxes are my quarry, and I hope to hang their brushes over my mantel.

Author's Notes

In the course of this novel a num ber of well-known per sons make their appearance, some of them living, some dead; they appear under their own names, and what is said about them is fac tu ally cor rect.

There are other char ac ters which are fic ti tious, and in these cases the au thor has gone out of his way to avoid seeming to point at real persons. He has given them un likely names, and hopes that no per son bear ing such names ex ist. But it is im pos si ble to make sure; there fore the writer states that, if any such co in ci dence oc curs, it is ac ci den tal. This is not the cus tom ary "hedge clause" which the au thor of a *ro man à clef* pub lishes for le gal pro tec tion; it means what it says and it is in tended to be so taken.

Various European concerns engaged in the manufacture of munitions have been named in the story, and what has been said about them is also ac cord ing to the records. There is one American firm, and that, with all its affairs, is imag i nary. The writer has done his best to avoid seem ing to in di cate any ac tual Amer i can firm or fam ily.

...Of course there will be slips, as I know from ex pe ri ence; but *World's End* is meant to be a his tory as well as fic tion, and I am sure there are no mis takes of im por tance. I have my own point of view, but I have tried to play fair in this book. There is a var ied cast of char ac ters and they say as they think. ...

The Peace Con fer ence of Paris [*for ex ample*], which is the scene of the last third of *World's End*, is of course one of the great est events of all time. A friend on mine asked an authority on mod ern fic tion a ques tion: "Has any body ever used the Peace Con fer ence in a novel?" And the re ply was: "Could any body?" Well, I thought some body could, and now I think some body has. The reader will ask, and I state ex plic itly that so far as con cerns his toric char ac ters and events my pic ture is cor rect in all de tails. This part of the manu script, 374 pages, was read and checked by eight or ten gen tle men who were on the Amer i can staff at the Con fer ence. Sev eral of these hold im por tant po si tions in the world of trou bled in ter na tional af fairs; oth ers are col lege pres i dents and professors, and I promised them all that their letters will be con fi den tial. Suf fice it to say that the er rors they pointed out were cor rected, and where they dis agreed, both sides have a word in the book.

Contents:

BOOK ONE

We Are the Music-Makers

1

Peace Be within Thy Walls

WHEN one has been away from home for more than two years, and has seen Paris and London and New York, one's house may be found to have grown strangely smaller, its glamour turned to dinginess. Lanny Budd walked around the outside, noting how the sky-blue paint on the shutters had faded and what the malicious sea air had done to the hinges. Inside, the upholstery was soiled, the curtains drooped drearily, the piano was out of tune—in short, the place would have to be done over. Only van Gogh's sunrise and Monet's lilypond had their glories undiminished—*ars* instead of *aes perennis*.

Lanny, still in his twentieth year, had full authority and a bank account replenished; so as he strolled he meditated upon the various styles he had observed in his travels. Would he care to dwell in the presence of French splendor, such as he had grown used to in the Hotel Crillon and the Foreign Office on the Quai d'Orsay: huge gilded chandeliers, heavy tapestries, stucco cupids on the ceiling, silk upholstery on spindly chairs? Or would he prefer the austere fashion of his father's home in Connecticut, the woodwork painted white and the old furniture cut in straight lines without ornament? Would van Gogh and Monet look well against a paneling of dark wood in the dignified English fashion? Or should he be jolly and modern, and turn the drawing-room into a child's nursery with primary colors, a frieze of wild animals chasing one another, and draperies of eccentric designs put on by batik? His thoughts moved from one to another of the villas along this Côte d'Azur; he had been in scores of them—but mostly when he was younger, and his mind wasn't on interior decoration.

Midsummer of the year 1919, and Lanny had just witnessed the closing of the Peace Conference of Paris. He had cherished a dream to help remake Europe, and for six months had worked hard, and had made a mess of it—so he believed, and his friends agreed. Now he had taken on a simpler job—to fix up his mother's home and add a studio for a new member of their family. That, at least, one ought to be able to do without bungling! Lanny's mind, in sharp reaction from world politics, was set upon mastering the techniques of architecture, carpentry, masonry, interior decoration, and landscape gardening.

II

In one corner of this estate was a small building of stone. It stood on the edge of a grove of trees, facing the west, looking out over the blue and gold Mediterranean. It had only a couple of windows and got most of its light from a skylight on the north side. The building was less than five years old, but already it was haunted, and Lanny after two years' absence had waited a while before summoning the courage to go near it. When he unlocked and opened the door he stood for a few moments looking in, as if he thought the very dust on the floor ought not to be disturbed.

Nothing had been touched since that tragic day, a little more than a year ago, when Marcel Detaze had laid down his palette and brush, written a note to his wife, and stolen away to throw himself into the hell of war. Lanny hadn't been here, and hadn't thought it wise to question his mother about it; better if she forgot it quickly. But Lanny himself wasn't going to forget his stepfather.

He came slowly into the room, looking about. The easel had something on it, covered with a cloth. The palette was on the table, face up, the colors hard and dry. The painter's little blue cap, worn and faded, lay near; also a newspaper, with headlines telling of the last German rush on Paris. A ghostly voice was saying to Lanny: "You see—I had to go." A quiet voice, for Marcel had never had to argue with his stepson.

He was gone, France was saved, and here was the studio, the

shutters closed and fastened, the shade pulled over the skylight, and a year's drifting of dust which the mistral had forced through cracks of windows and doors. Lanny opened one of the shutters, creaking on its rusty hinges, and let in the bright sunlight of the Midi. He saw that Marcel had been reading a book on military strategy—an odd subject for a painter, but of course he had been trying to understand what was happening to *la patrie* and whether she needed the life of one of her sons, already crippled in her service.

Lanny raised the cloth from the easel. There was a crayon sketch which clutched him like a hand. It was the face of a peasant, and the youth knew him at once—an old truckman for one of the flower-growers here on the Cap d'Antibes; he had taught Lanny to drive a car. Marcel had the gift of line: the slightest stroke of his pencil, and something lived and moved. In these crayon lines you saw what weather had done to the face of a man. In the wrinkles around the eyes was sly humor, in the bristling mustaches the spirit of those forefathers who had marched all the way to Paris, dragging their cannon and singing: "To arms, to arms, ye brave!" Lanny took the sketch to the light to study its fine points. Again he heard the ghostly voice: "You see—I have left something of myself!"

In back of the studio was a storeroom, and the youth unlocked the door. Along the walls were racks which Beauty, his mother, had had built, sparing no expense in her futile effort to keep a French husband at home when *la patrie* was in danger. On these racks were canvases, each tacked on its wooden frame and overlaid with dust. The work of Marcel Detaze was not bid for in auction rooms, its prices were not the subject of gossip in the newspapers, so it hadn't been worth anyone's while to break into the place.

Lanny didn't need to take any of the canvases down. He knew which shelves held the war paintings, and which the landscapes of the Cap, which the fiords of Norway, which the Isles of Greece and the shores of Africa. Standing in that dim and dusty room, he experienced a return of the strange feeling which had stolen over him amid the ruins of ancient temples, with his stepfather telling about the lives of those long-vanished lovers of beauty. Now Marcel had gone to join them; were they meeting in some Greek limbo, sharing the secrets of their techniques of painting—or perhaps fighting their battles over again? Marcel, who had stood at the second battle of the Marne, could meet the heroes of Thermopylae on equal terms. In Lanny's mind were many sentences from the book of Greek epigrams which they had read amid the ruins. "In peace sons bury their fathers; in war fathers bury their sons." Twenty-two centuries had passed, and Lanny had seen it happening in France, England, and America.

III

Over at the villa was another souvenir of Marcel, one which Lanny was inspecting for the first time. Baby Marceline had about as many months as Lanny had years, and like him she was a child of the Midi; playing about in the patio, rolling on the grass in the hot sunshine, with only a breechclout, and the rest of her brown as a hazelnut. The old family dog had presented the household with a litter of puppies, and Marceline toddled, and these raced after her, falling over themselves and she falling over them. It made a charming picture, and how the father would have loved to sit and make sketches of it! Once more Lanny thought, what a strange thing is life—and how wasteful. Marcel had learned so much, and now he was gone, and his daughter had to begin at the beginning and learn to walk, picking herself up and starting again when she failed.

She had her mother's sweet and gentle features, and her mother's natural gaiety; also, apparently, her mother's impulse wherever she was to want to be somewhere else. Lanny found it interesting to have a half-sister and to engage in child study. Quickly he realized that Marceline perceived what he was doing, and enjoyed being the center of attention. Did she get that from her mother? Lanny decided to read a book and find out what was known about heredity. Marceline had her father's odd combination of blond eyebrows and darker hair; was she developing traces of his gentle melancholy? When the puppies fell asleep and the child sat gazing before her, what mysterious processes were going on in the budding soul? Apparently she had no memory of the lovely blond being who had brought her into the world and performed the feat, almost forgotten among fashionable ladies, of nourishing her at the breast. Six months had passed since Beauty had gone away, and what Baby Marceline depended on was a rosy peasant woman who was growing larger week by week and developing a soft brown mustache. It was Leese's firm faith that to be fat was the proper destiny of all female creatures. She fed the darling *petite* at all hours, and rocked her to sleep, and fondled and kissed her, and brought many relatives to do the same—all in violation of basic rules laid down by pediatricians. But it didn't worry Lanny, because he had had the same kind of upbringing, and the soft Provençal dialect had been as you might say his foster-mother tongue.

One thing troubled him, the fishpond with a little fountain which graced the center of the patio. Marceline would lie and watch the goldfish and try to catch them, and Leese insisted that she knew enough not to fall in—and, anyhow, the water wasn't deep. But Lanny would take no chance, and got a carpenter to make a little picket fence in sections hooked together; so the baby could watch the fish but not join them. The youth wrote his mother that all was well, and she might enjoy her third honeymoon with a good conscience. He smiled as he penned the words, for he had sojourned in New England and learned that people differed in matters of conscience; but he and Beauty had their private understandings.

IV

The mother wrote long letters. She and her lover had found a cottage on the rugged shore of the Bay of Biscay; a Basque woman came in to clean up for them, and they were living *la vie simple*, a charming adventure for complicated persons. For the first time, the mother had no interest in meeting the fashionable and important of the earth; there were reasons which were never mentioned in her carefully guarded letters. The war censorship of mail was supposed to be at an end, but you could never be sure.

For the third time in her life Mabel Blackless, alias Beauty Budd, alias Madame Detaze, *veuve*, had taken the difficult role of everything in the world to a man. She was trying to be family, friends, country—plus the whole German army. She had to make her lover forget defeat and shame, poverty and ruin. In this role she was one among millions; for Europe was full of men whose lives had been shattered and disorganized, and of women trying to comfort them and help them back to normality. Don't scold them, don't nag them; don't be shocked by anything they do or say! Understand that they have been living in hell, their lungs are impregnated with fumes of that region—only be glad it isn't mustard or chlorine gas. Let them do anything they please with you and pretend that you like it; tell them anything they want to believe; sing them to sleep, and when they have nightmares wake them and soothe them like sick children. Feed them, play with them, and count it a triumph if now and then you get them to laugh.

Spain had got rich out of the war, and her leisure classes were flocking to their northern coast; it was like winter on the Riviera in old days. There were many Germans, both traders and officials, and any one of them might recognize Kurt Meissner. Beauty referred to this possibility, using her code which Lanny understood. Kurt was "our friend," and the Germans were "his old associates." A censor would have thought it was a burglar she was trying to reform, or at least a drunkard. "I want our friend to break off permanently. Help me to persuade him that he has done his full duty, and should forget the past."

Lanny, eager to oblige, would compose joyous letters about the life of art, and his friend's genius, and the happiness they were all going to enjoy. Originally it had been the younger man's idea to build a new studio as a surprise for both his mother and her lover; some day they would drive up to the gate of Bienvenu, and Lanny would take them to the new building, and hear their cries of pleasure. But now he decided that this was risky. Kurt might make up his mind to return to his own land, to help rebuild it, or to get ready for another war—who could guess what impulse might seize a Prussian artillery officer, one month after the treaty of Versailles had been rammed down his country's throat?

So the subtle Lanny Budd revealed what he was doing; a delightful adventure, constructing a studio for the composing of music that was to bring back the days of Bach and Brahms and restore the prestige of the Teutonic race in the noblest field of human activity. The masons were laying the firm foundation, and Lanny gave a sketch of the groundplan. The work was being done by those relatives of Leese who hadn't been killed or crippled in the war, and Lanny told whimsical stories about workingmen of the Midi, class-conscious and inclined to be suspicious, but opening up like flowers when you chatted with them, and especially when you tried to help on the job and let them laugh at your blunders. The artist in them was touched when it was revealed that a musician was to live here and compose; a Swiss gentleman, he was being called.

Lanny knew that Kurt was among the millions of unemployed men; for the German army had been cut to almost nothing, and Kurt's family couldn't have saved much from the ruins of war. So Lanny expounded his dream of being a young Lorenzo dei Medici and gathering around him a noble company of worthy artists. "My father gives me some money," he wrote. "I haven't earned it—and maybe he hasn't either!" Since Lanny had been meeting Socialists and other unorthodox persons at the Peace Conference, his mind was full of their dangerous phrases. "What better use can I make of money than to help men who have the gifts that I lack? My father wants me to spend it to make myself happy, and if it makes me happy to help my friends, and my mother's friends, why shouldn't I have that pleasure?"

Be careful of every word, Lanny! Kurt Meissner, in spite of his notion that he is a modern man and artist, has the instincts of a German aristocrat, and how can he face the thought of being supported by a woman, especially by the one he loves? The English have a name for a man like that, and Kurt has no mind to carry it. When Kurt writes this, Lanny has to be deeply hurt, and to argue for his mother's right to be happy too. Lanny's money is his, not his mother's, and it may be a loan if Kurt insists—every franc of it carefully recorded, so that a great musician can repay it out of the proceeds of future performances, or royalties, or salary as a conductor, whatever it may be. There is precedent enough in the lives of musicians—for the borrowing if not for the repaying!

V

The painters came and started on the outside trim of the villa. The paperhangers were working inside the drawing-room. The upholsterers took away the furniture, to do it over with soft brown cloth that would wear. The background was to be a wallpaper of cream color with an unobtrusive pattern, Lanny having decided that this would be in keeping with the austere spirit of his friend and the domestic intentions of his reformed mother.

A man came and tuned the piano; and Lanny lived again in that music to which his fancy had turned during the past couple of years, whenever life had become too complicated. A translator-secretary at a peace conference had been powerless to restrain Italians from seizing Yugoslav territory, or Turks from slaughtering Armenians; but when he sat down at the piano he was his own master, and if he didn't like the way a composer achieved his modulations he could change them. Lanny's fingers had lost some of their speed while preparing reports on the distribution of Europe's populations; but when fingers are not yet twenty years old they limber up quickly, and Lanny soon had the freedom of that garden of delights in which he planned to spend the rest of his days.

At the driveway entrance of Bienvenu were a pair of heavy gates which you could lock if you wished. At the entrance to the footpath was a light wooden door with a tall aloe, now in blossom, on either side, and a bell which you had to ring. Inside were palms and bananas, a cascade of purple bougainvillaea, the scent of narcissus and the murmur of bees; there were beauty and peace, and Lanny meant that there should be friendship and love. Good-by, proud world, I'm going home! So he had said, the day the unsatisfactory treaty had been signed. Every month Robbie Budd sent Beauty a check for a thousand dollars, and from now on Lanny was to have three hundred. Besides that, he had a thousand which he had earned his very self, and of which he was unduly proud. It was mixed up with the rest in his bank account at Cannes, but in his mind he saw it separately, a series of checks signed by the disbursing officer of the State Department of the United States.

He wanted to spend these sums to make a little happiness and order in the world. He would get a few friends around him, persons who loved the arts and were content to live with them. The fact that his mother had fallen in love with one of his best friends was an odd circumstance which would help to close the little circle. It would solve the problem of a German army officer's broken life, and at the same time would keep Beauty out of the clutches of those many fashionable persons who abused her hospitality and won her money at bridge. While Lanny wrestled with the intricacies of a Bach fugue he told himself that Kurt's serious disposition would reform him as well as his mother, and keep him from futile love affairs and other escapades that he wanted to put behind him.

VI

The carpenters were working on the new studio. The framework had magically arisen—one large room with a small bedroom and bath in the rear. Lanny would watch the work and amuse himself trying to help; then he would go and practice sight-reading for a while. When he felt the need of companionship, he would phone to Jerry Pendleton to come over for a swim, or perhaps go torch-fishing at night. They would sit in the boat on the still water and recall the Austrian submarine that had risen in the sea close beside them. The ex-tutor and veteran of the Meuse-Argonne was in much the same mood as his former pupil; he too had wanted to get away from it all—and what an unusual sort of refuge he had found for himself in the Pension Flavin in Cannes!

He had married the French nation, so he told Lanny: the sweet and gentle Cerise, the mother who owned half the pension, the aunt who owned the other half and helped to run it, and the boarders, who in this hot midsummer season were not tourists but respectable French permanents employed in banks or other offices, and who considered themselves as members of the family, entitled

to be concerned with its affairs. Jerry had to have some American
to whom he could unbosom himself, and as Lanny had lived most of
his life in France, he was able to explain matters and clear up mis-
understandings. Another peace conference!

French women of the middle class are apt to be frugal, and when
they are in business they have to be if they are to survive. And here
was a son-in-law who presented them with a complicated problem.
An upstanding, capable young American, he had plunged into a
fiery furnace and helped to rescue *la patrie*. American soldiers enjoyed enormous prestige among the French in those days; they had
come as semi-divine beings, several inches taller than the average
poilu, accoutered and equipped like no troops ever seen in Europe,
and laughing, insolent, ready to make a lark even out of a plunge
into a furnace. "*Ah, comme ils sont beaux!*" the mademoiselles had
cried with one voice.

Lieutenant Jerry Pendleton, handsome and red-headed, was now
a husband with responsibilities; but what was he to do about them?
He had no money, and there was no work to be had in Cannes.
Thousands of Frenchmen coming back from the war, all looking
for jobs; and no tourists in summertime, no certainty that there
would be any in winter. Jerry was willing to go to work with his
hands, *à l'américaine*, but that was unthinkable in France; he must
have a white-collar job, and uphold the dignity and prestige of a
pension which catered to the most respectable bourgeois. The two
anxious ladies fed him, and withheld any word that would remind
him of his humiliating position. His father owned a couple of drug-
stores in a far-off region of cyclones called Kansas, and if Jerry's
dignity was affronted, he might order his wife to pack up and follow
him across the seas—thus depriving the two ladies of their hopes, one
for a grandson and the other for a grandnephew.

A happy solution *ad interim*—Jerry would go fishing, taking a
basket and bringing back specimens of the many strange creatures
that swarm along the rocky Mediterranean shore: *mérou*, and *mostele*, the long green moray, the gray *langouste* in his hard shell, cut-
tlefish large or small, each with his own ink to be cooked in. This
pleased the palates of all the guests, and at the same time was entirely

respectable, being *le sport.* The son-in-law went with a friend who owned a sailboat, and lived in an elegant villa on the Cap, and associated with the wealthiest and most distinguished persons. While Jerry entertained his friend with stories about the boarders, the widow ladies fed the boarders upon details of a new studio at Bienvenu, the redecorating of the villa, and the sad case of Madame Detaze, whose husband had given his life for *la patrie,* and who was now spending her period of mourning in Spain.

VII

In a corner of the garage at Bienvenu were piled some forty wooden cases which had come by steamer from Connecticut to Marseille, containing the library willed by Great-Great-Uncle Eli Budd to Lanny. The youth summoned his courage and took a carpenter to Marcel's studio and set him to lining the walls with shelves. Lanny was taking this place for his own, being certain that if anywhere in the limbo of good souls Marcel was watching, he would approve that course. The studio meant more to Lanny than to anybody else, not even excepting Beauty. She had loved Marcel's paintings because they were his, but Lanny had loved them because they were works of art, and Marcel had understood this difference and made jokes about it in his fashion half gay and half sad.

After the shelves were stained and dried, Lanny had the cases brought down a few at a time, and Jerry came to help him unpack. The ex-lieutenant was no scholar, in spite of having been nearly through college; but he was impressed by the physical bulk of two thousand volumes and by Lanny's firm declaration that he intended to read them all. The old Unitarian minister had been even more learned than his heir had realized, for here was a pretty complete collection of the best books of the world in half a dozen languages: not much theology, but a great deal of philosophy, history, and biography, and a little of every sort of *belles-lettres.* Only the Latin and Greek were hopeless, Lanny decided. He had French and German, and could brush up his Italian, and soon learn Spanish, which Beauty and Kurt were now studying.

The classifying of so many books was quite a job. They moved armloads to one shelf, and then decided they had made a mistake and moved them to another. Presently there came another assistant —M. Rochambeau, the elderly Swiss diplomat who was spending his declining years in this village of Juan-les-Pins. He lived in a little apartment with a niece, and found it lonely during the summer season. He had known Marcel and admired his paintings before the war, and had stood by him in those dreadful days when the painter had been brought back from battle with his mutilated face covered by a silk mask. A man of reading and taste, M. Rochambeau could tell about these books, and where the doubtful ones should be placed. He would become excited by the contents of this one or that, and Lanny would tell him to take it home and read it.

The friends would leave, and evening fall; Lanny would stroll down to the studio and sit inside, with the pale moonlight streaming in at the door. The place now had two ghosts to haunt it. Lanny would introduce the ghost of Marcel to the ghost of his great-great-uncle and please himself with the fancy that this introduction was taking effect in the limbo where they now resided. Lanny listened to their cultured conversation, which began, naturally, with Greek art and civilization; for the youth had told Eli how the yacht *Bluebird* had taken him and Marcel to the Isles of Greece, and how they had stood among the ruined temples and Marcel had read aloud out of the anthology. Lanny had written Marcel about Eli's comments; so the two ghosts were no strangers, but exchanged freely their deepest sentiments. The young ghost, who had arrived first in this limbo, made the old ghost welcome. "Upon that far shore I wait for thee, O Callimachus, and prepare for thee a banquet worthy of thy noble deeds."

VIII

So passed the rest of the summer. The workingmen labored steadily, and the villa shone like new, and the studio approached completion. Lanny had written Kurt to inquire what sort of interior decoration might be appropriate to the music of Bach and Brahms; Kurt had tactfully expressed approval of Lanny's taste, so the studio was being done uniform with the villa. Step by step Lanny sought to lure his friend on. "That thousand dollars which I earned trying to make a just peace I want to spend for the best piano that can be found in Paris, and I want you to select it so I can be sure it really is the best."

But seducing Kurt was no simple task. Beauty's letters would reveal that the haughty one was brooding over his country's fate, and thinking of Brazil or the Argentine, where Germans were still able to earn a living without British or American permission. Lanny would have to go deeply into the psychology of vanquished artillery officers, aspiring musical geniuses, and lovers dependent upon their ladies. The money of Beauty and her son had come out of guns and ammunition used to blast the hopes of the Fatherland; how now could Kurt endure to live upon it? Lanny would make tactful references to the moral problems of a munitions manufacturer and his son. "My father refuses to let his own conscience be troubled, but he can't help knowing that mine is. It pleases him when he can give me money, because then he doesn't have to think of me as sitting aloof and condemning him in my mind. You and I can't change what has happened, Kurt; but if you believe in music and in your own gifts, why shouldn't you turn some of our money into beauty and kindness?"

Kurt of course would share these letters with his companion, and she would report to Lanny what effect they were producing. Having spent more than half her thirty-eight years managing recalcitrant men, Beauty possessed a store of wisdom. She wouldn't plead too much, and never find fault, but just make love the loveliest thing in Spain. She would reveal her own weakness and the need of a man's moral strength. She would gently refer to Lanny's needs; he was a good boy, but so easily influenced, and with a tendency to wander from one art to the next. He needed some older and steadier person to help him concentrate. For such a service many a rich man would be glad to pay, but couldn't buy it at any price. So many tutors Lanny had had, of German and Italian, of piano and dancing and the study of the encyclopedia. The least competent of them had received more than it would cost for Kurt to stay at Bienvenu.

What Kurt did for Lanny's mother would be purely incidental—and surely the dullest person who came to the home would know that!

So at last the young officer's scruples were broken down, and he wrote his parents in Schloss Stubendorf—now a part of Poland, thanks to the evil treaty—to ship him the music and the instruments which he had collected. Kurt told them that he was to be the teacher of that American boy who had been the family's guest nearly six years ago. Since the boy's mother hadn't been a guest, it was not necessary to tell about her. Kurt hoped that his parents would forgive him for living in France; he would have nothing to do with that hateful people, but would live a retired life inside the Budd estate and go on with his serious labors as at home before the war.

IX

Lanny's twentieth birthday came, and the adoring mother was sad because she wasn't with him; her conscience pricked her, and she wrote a letter full of apologies and of advice which she herself had not always put to use. Not for the first time, nor for the last, her pen turned to the subject of love, and the women who would be after her precious one, and his need of caution in such matters. So many cunning creatures hunting him with deadly arts, impossible to resist!

It went without saying that no woman could really be worthy of Lanny Budd in the estimation of his mother; least of all these modern chits, these shallow ones, bold and froward products of the war, which Beauty thought of as a universal plague that had poisoned the world. She had watched them in Paris during the Peace Conference, and reported them ravenous for pleasure, for sensation; knowing no restraint, no loyalty; greedy for attention, for worldly success— "golddiggers" was the new name for them, and a woman of the old days contemplated them with a horror which was rather comical when you recalled how far she herself had been from a model of discretion.

Perhaps it was Beauty Budd's sins returning to torment her—a not uncommon phenomenon of the moral life. While Kurt worked at his music, Beauty would sit upon the shore of the Bay of Biscay, and before her mind's eye would arise an image of a youth slender, graceful, with brown eyes forever a-shine with the expectation of new delights; with wavy brown hair worn long according to the fashion, and having a tendency to drop over into his eyes; a smile quick yet gentle, a heart kind as a girl's. Lanny, back there in Bienvenu, was nearing the age at which his father, traveling in Paris, had met an artists' model even younger than himself. Beauty knew exactly what had befallen that youth, for she had planned it; even in the moments when her heart had seemed to be hitting hard blows under her throat, she had known what she was doing, and why, and how. Women always know, and whatever happens is their fault—so Beauty insisted!

But she had really loved Robbie Budd; not merely his money or his position as the son of an old and proud New England family. She had proved it when the cruel test came, when by a little effort she might have married him and caused him to break with his stern old father. Where would you find a woman today who would make such a sacrifice? Was Lanny going to meet one on that Coast of Pleasure, where already the roulette wheels were beginning to spin and the colored bands to thump and screech? When Lanny in his letters mentioned the sloe-eyed demoiselle in the pension, the jeweler's daughter who wore too many of her father's wares; when he referred to the American females who had come down from Paris to lie in the sand and forget the war that had been won and the peace that had been lost—and how they drank too much and drove motor-cars crazily—yes, Beauty knew them, she had attended the after-midnight parties and knew what the pleasure-hungry creatures might be doing to her darling, her precocious, her incomparable son! "Remember, Lanny," warned the birthday letter, "the more attractive you make Bienvenu, the more eager some woman will be to get in there before I do." Lanny chuckled; he could have named a woman, several in fact; but he couldn't fail to be amused when his flighty mother turned Puritan—a joke which he and his father had shared on many an occasion.

X

Lanny would go back to his music. He had learned a lot of Bach by heart, thus paying tribute to Kurt's taste. Also he derived pleasure from the swiftly falling notes of Debussy's *Gardens in the Rain*, but wasn't sure if Kurt would permit himself to approve any French music. He enjoyed the strange fantasies of Moussorgsky's *Pictures at an Exposition;* having visited one exposition with Kurt, and others with his English friend Rick and with his stepfather, Lanny took all these friends with him to this odd Russian exposition. Ordinarily he didn't care for "program music," but when it was humorous and full of quaint turns, his curiosity was aroused and he wished that the pictures had come with the score.

Baby Marceline had solved the problems of equipoise, and was able to walk and even to run without stumbling. She would stand in the doorway while Lanny played, and presently, watching her, he saw that she was swaying to the rhythm. He played a simple tune with a strong accent, and her steps began to move to it; he decided then that she should discover the art of the dance all by herself. A new department of child study; it went on for weeks, while the tiny feet tottered here and there and the laughing brown eyes shone with the delight of adventure. Suddenly she began to display marvelous improvement, and Lanny was about to write his mother that they had a terpsichorean prodigy, when he learned that Leese had unwittingly spoiled a scientific experiment by taking the little one's two hands and dancing with her out in the patio. After that Lanny would put a record on the phonograph, and Baby Marceline began a full course in the eurythmics of Jaques-Dalcroze, with variations according to the free expressionism of Isadora Duncan.

There was hardly a spot in or about Bienvenu where Lanny hadn't danced. The loggia in front of the home was smooth, and Beauty had had *al fresco* parties here, and musicians had come from Cannes, and the fashionable ladies and gentlemen had taken the good the gods provided them. First it had been the waltz, and later the Argentine tango, and then crazy inventions from New York. To that loggia had come M. Pinjon, the gigolo with whom Lanny had struck up an acquaintance in Nice; he had brought his piccolo flute, and played it while he danced the farandole. That poor fellow had lost one leg in the war, and was now back with his peasant father, and on the table in the drawing-room was a little dancing man carved in wood which he had sent to his friend in the *grand monde*.

By that old piano in the drawing-room Lanny had learned old dances such as the minuet and the polonaise, and had teased his mother and some of her friends to practice with him. Here too he had danced "Dalcroze" with Kurt when the two boys had come from Hellerau. In the sad days after the outbreak of the war, when Marcel had been called to the army, Lanny had made dancing with his mother a part of their day's regimen, to keep up her spirits and keep down her *embonpoint*. There were few of those phonograph records which hadn't such memories bound up in them.

Now Lanny was beginning a new dancing life with this half-sister, this tiny mite of budding fun, this box of stored miracles. Her laughter was like bubbles from champagne when you pull the cork. Her feet were all motion, whether they were on the ground or waving in the air. Her large brown eyes watched Lanny, and her arms and legs tried to imitate what he did. If he moved slowly and repeated the motion often, she would follow him, and he was proud when he had taught her the Dalcroze motions for three-part time and four-part time. He wrote Beauty, who had learned all this from him, and was learning more of it from Kurt—for the monster of *embonpoint* was stalking her in Spain!

The Dalcroze school in Germany had been closed during the war, and the tall white temple on the bright meadow had been turned into a factory for the manufacturing of poison gas. But the seeds of joy and beauty had been scattered widely, and here were two households, one on the Riviera and the other on the Bay of Biscay, where the lovely art of eurythmics was being kept alive. There was another on the River Thames, because Lanny wrote to Rick, the English friend who had been with him and Kurt at the school. Poor Rick was a cripple and would never dance again, but he and Nina had a little boy, not much older than Marceline, and Lanny wrote about his experiments in child training and Nina promised to repeat them.

XI

Lanny thought continually about those two boyhood friends who had fought each other in the war, and whom he was resolved to bring together again. He didn't mention this to Kurt; he just forwarded Rick's letters to Beauty, knowing that she would read them aloud. Lanny's idea was to get Kurt settled in the new studio, with the new piano and all his other instruments and his music scores; then, after things were going well, Rick and his little family would come for a visit and perhaps find a villa or bungalow near by. The three musketeers of the arts would talk about the really important things of life, carefully avoiding world politics and other forms of rascality.

Such was Lanny's plan. He remembered Newcastle, Connecticut, and his stern old Puritan grandfather who manufactured machine guns and ammunition and conducted a Sunday morning Bible class. On the Sunday after the Armistice he had expounded a text from the hundred and twenty-second Psalm: "Peace be within thy walls, and prosperity within thy palaces." The grandson learned that one of the carpenters working on the place was a skilled wood-carver, and he brought this man into the drawing-room and had him cut the first half of this text in old English letters on the thick edge of the heavy mantel.

After the work was done, Lanny happened to read one of his great-great-uncle's books on ancient Greece, and learned that the poet Aristophanes had said "Euphemia 'sto," which is "Peace be here," or "Peace to this house." It was one point on which the Greek and the Hebrew spirits had met; it was a longing in the hearts of all decent people the world over. But Lanny had derived from his six months' adventure in diplomacy the conviction that the decent people were still a long way from getting what they wanted. The best that anyone could do for the present was to build him a not too costly home in some part of the earth where there was no gold, oil, coal, or other mineral treasure, and which was not near a disputed boundary or strategic configuration of land or water. There with reasonable luck he might have peace within his own walls, and perhaps think some thoughts which might be helpful to a hate-tormented world.

2

Kennst Du das Land?

THE "season" was coming once more to the Riviera; and all over
Europe and the Americas individuals and families were realizing that
it was possible once again to get passports and to travel freely, *en
prince* if you had the price. Swedish lumber merchants and Norwegian operators of whaling fleets, Dutch traders in coffee and rub-
ber and tin, Swiss holders of electrical shares, British owners of coal
and iron mines, French masters of munitions plants which had magically escaped bombing through a devastating war—such lucky persons now heard at the family breakfast table laments about damp
fogs and icy gales, and were reminded of a land where the lemon
trees bloom, in the dark arbors the golden oranges glow, a soft wind
is wafted from the blue heaven, the myrtle stands still and the laurel
high—*kennst du es wohl?*

So once more the white yachts began to appear off the little harbors of Cannes and Nice, and the long blue express trains from Paris
were crowded with passengers. Perhaps half of them were Americans, who for five years and more had been reading about Europe
twice every day, but had been denied their customary cultural holidays. Now again there were luxurious steamers, and no submarines
to challenge their crossing. Tourists took sight-seeing busses to the
war zones, visiting those towns whose names had become historic,
even though they were mispronounced. Sight-seers roamed over
battle-fields whose dreadful smells had not yet been washed away.
They peered into blasted trenches with human hands and booted
feet sticking out of the debris. They gathered trench helmets and
shell cases to be taken home and used as book-ends or umbrella-stands.

And when these thrills began to pall, there was the Côte d'Azur, the beautiful, the romantic, unscarred by war; its rocky shores and cliffs and winding valleys, its ever-blue sea and ever-shining sun. Here you wore sport clothes and strolled on fashionable promenades, staring at great personages about whom you had read in the newspapers: kings and their mistresses, Asiatic potentates and their boys, Russian grand dukes escaped from the Bolsheviks, and a miscellany of statesmen and prizefighters, journalists and jockeys, masters of industry and stars of stage and screen. In the evening you could put on your finery and rub elbows with these celebrated ones in the gambling casinos, and even hope to pick up acquaintance with them in the so-called American bars.

This latter institution had moved into what promised to be permanent exile; for at home a strange new phenomenon had developed out of the war, a throw-back to old-time Puritanism. It had begun as a war measure, to save foodstuffs, and now was being riveted upon the country by means of a constitutional amendment that could never be repealed, so everybody said. As the awful reality of Prohibition dawned upon the pleasure-seeking classes, they had but one impulse, to purchase steamer tickets for the land of wine, women, and song. When the steamer had passed the three-mile limit off Sandy Hook the corks began to pop and the joy to flow, and first-class passengers swore solemn oaths that never, never would they return to the land of the Pilgrims' pride. How often they said it made little difference, because they had forgotten it all next morning.

II

Of course not all the visitors to the Riviera were like that. People of cultivated taste came to enjoy the warm climate and lovely scenery. Up in the hills behind Cannes were villas belonging to English and Americans who came regularly each winter and lived decorous lives. Among these was Mrs. Emily Chattersworth, who had turned her estate into a home for the re-education of French *mutilés*. Marcel had gone up there and entertained them by making sketches on a blackboard, and after Lanny's return to Bienvenu one of his first duties had been to pay these poor fellows a call. He was interested in their progress, and also he wanted to see the portrait which Marcel had made of Mrs. Emily.

It had a central position in the drawing-room of Sept Chênes, and showed a tall and stately lady, with entirely white hair, standing by a small table which you could see in this room. So she had stood in the early days of the war, when she had called the American residents together and urged them to active succor of the refugees and the wounded. The face in the portrait was grave, not to say stern, and the pose and feeling of the picture were so real that the lips seemed about to open and say, as Lanny had heard them say more than once: "My friends, we have accepted the hospitality of France, and if there is such a thing as gratitude in the world, we owe it now to her people." To Lanny it was as if he heard also the voice of Marcel declaring the debt that *la patrie* was paying to the chatelaine by the agency of his fine portrait.

A year had passed since victory had been secured, and the hostess could feel that she had done her duty. The crippled men who had learned new trades were sent back to their homes, and those whose cases were hopeless were placed in government care. Sept Chênes, like Bienvenu, was done over, and the owner came to spend the winter. When Lanny heard of it he went to call, and told the great lady how much he thought of the portrait, and she in turn told him how the reputation of Marcel Detaze was spreading among art lovers. "What are you going to do with all those beautiful paintings, Lanny?"

He answered that his mother was intending to arrange for an exhibition as soon as she returned; and this brought up a subject by which their friend's mind was deeply intrigued. "What on earth is Beauty doing in Spain?"

The young man hadn't been a budding diplomat for six months to no purpose. He was prepared for the question, and smiled lightly. "She'll be home soon, and will tell you about it."

"You mean you're *not* going to tell me?"

Lanny kept on smiling. "I think she wants to have the fun."

"But what on earth? Is it something sensational?"

"Why should you think that?"

He had learned a lot about the feminine soul, and one thing was its intense preoccupation with matters of the heart. Here was this stately lady, almost sixty—he knew it to the day because her mother had once told him she had been born in Baltimore to the tramping of the Sixth Massachusetts Regiment, marching to the American Civil War. In fifty-eight and three-quarter years the infant Emily Sibley had become what the French call a *grande dame;* presiding over a *salon* and matching wits with the keenest minds in France. She had cultivated an impressive manner, she dressed with studied care, and provided for herself a semi-royal background; but here she was possessed by an itch of curiosity, revealing to Lanny the soul of a child who simply couldn't endure to be kept in the dark about what had happened to her intimate friend Mabel Blackless, alias Beauty Budd, alias Madame Detaze, *veuve.*

Lanny told her about Baby Marceline and his own researches into the development of the musical sense in infants. He told about Robbie Budd, and the progress of his oil venture in southern Arabia. This involved the fate of Emir Feisal, that dark-skinned replica of Christ whom Lanny had met at Mrs. Emily's town house during the Peace Conference. The young Emir was again in Paris, pleading to be allowed to rule his native land; his friend Lawrence had gone into hiding, for shame at the breach of trust. Mrs. Emily ought to have been deeply interested in them both; but instead she broke in: "Tell me the truth, Lanny—has Beauty married again?"

He had to resume his gay smile. "There's a reason why she wants to tell you herself, and when you hear it you'll understand."

"Such a woman! Such a woman! I never know what to expect of her."

"Well, at least she doesn't bore you," replied Lanny, his smile widening to a grin. Many others did, he knew.

III

With the coming of cold weather, Beauty and Kurt had motored to the Mediterranean coast of Spain. Beauty had been away from her baby and her home a full year, and couldn't stand it much longer. She was still afraid to bring Kurt into France; but she got him comfortably settled in another cottage, this time with a Catalan woman to do his cooking and cleaning up. Then she sent a wire to Lanny and took a train for Cannes.

Stepping from that train she looked just as lovely as on the first day that Lanny could remember. In the sunshine her hair still had glints of gold, and it wasn't gilt. She wore a light gray traveling dress and a little hat like a flower-basket turned upside down. When the youth had seen her last she had grown slender because she was too badly frightened to eat; but now her natural gaiety had come back, and all her colors—also that torment of womankind which you politely called "plumpness." Lanny would have to start scolding her again, and keep the cream pitcher on his own side of the table.

Beauty saw that both her offspring were brown and well; the baby shy, and not pleased to have a stranger seize her and cover her with kisses. To call her "*Maman*" awakened no memories and gave no pleasure. The mother was anxious; had she lost the affection of her darling forever? Lanny told her to chase the puppies around the patio, and she and the baby would be friends in half an hour; and so it proved.

Beauty inspected the new architecture and interior decoration and gave it her approval. A lovelier home could not be desired: when would she be able to live in it? She hadn't been able to write about her anxieties, and now she poured them out. Should she risk bringing Kurt here? Or should she take him to New York or some other remote place until his record had been forgotten?

They shut themselves up in her boudoir for a long conference. Lanny, manlike, was disposed to minimize the danger. The war was over; the intelligence department of the French army must have been demobilized along with the rest; there wouldn't be so many agents seeking for men who traveled on false passports, and if one were caught it would be a matter for criminal, not military, law. Officials could be reached by influence, or, in the last extreme, by money.

"But what about Leese?" argued the mother. "She's bound to recognize Kurt, and she knows that he's German."

"I've fixed that all up," said the worldly-wise youth. "I told her
I was building the new studio for my friend the Swiss boy who had
visited us before the war. Did she remember Kurt? She said she had
thought he was a German. I explained that he came from the German part of Switzerland. *La Suisse* and *la Silésie* don't sound very
different to her, and she has got the new idea well fixed in her mind."

Lanny went on to tell about Emily Chattersworth and the curiosity that was troubling her so greatly. She also had met Kurt, so it
would be necessary to make a confidante of her. Lanny drove his
mother to Sept Chênes, and left the pair together, while he sat out in
the sunshine on the piazza, reading a novel he had chosen from his
new library, Hawthorne's *Blithedale Romance,* which his great-
great-uncle had talked about. A fervor for social perfection had
seized upon the young idealists of New England before the Civil
War, and they had tried living in a colony. It hadn't worked, but it
was fun, at any rate in a book. Lanny would read for a while, and
then stop and wonder how Mrs. Emily was taking the still stranger
romance which she was hearing from the lips of its heroine.

IV

"This much I have guessed," the mistress of Sept Chênes was saying. "It's a man!"

"I seem to be built that way," replied Beauty, sorrowfully. "Honestly, Emily, I hadn't the remotest idea it could happen to me again.
I thought I was going to spend the rest of my life grieving for Marcel. But men have suffered so dreadfully in this war——"

"And you met one who couldn't live without you?" There was
mischief in the eyes of the *salonnière.*

"Don't tease me, Emily. It's a tragic story, and you'll see how helpless I was. But first you have to swear on your knees that you won't
breathe a word of it to anyone; you must really mean that, because
it might be a matter of life and death—to say nothing of a perfectly
frightful scandal. The man was a German agent."

"Oh, *mon dieu!*" exclaimed the other.

"I need your friendship as I never did before. Maybe you will decide not to have anything to do with me, but at least you will keep my secret until I release you."

"You have my word," said the older woman.

"You remember the summer that Lanny was in Hellerau, before the war. One of the boys he met there was a German named Kurt Meissner; his father is what they call the comptroller-general of a great estate, Schloss Stubendorf, in Upper Silesia, which is now a part of Poland. I don't know if you will recall that Lanny went to spend Christmas with that family."

"I believe I do," replied Emily, and added: "You've been robbing the cradle?"

"No—you may say I've been robbing the grave."

"Well, I knew it would be something unusual. Go on."

"This boy was older than Lanny, and had a great influence over him. He was serious and hard-working, in the German fashion. He was studying to become a composer of music, and he had all the different instruments and was learning to play them. He was a moral boy, and Lanny looked up to him as being a sort of inspired character, and always talked about trying to be as good as Kurt, and so on. They kept exchanging letters, and Lanny let me read them, so I knew him quite well."

"And you were falling in love with him?"

"I never thought of any man but Marcel. Kurt was Lanny's friend and I thought he was helping Lanny to be a good boy, and I used to hold him up as an example. Then the war came, and Kurt became an officer in the German army. He and Lanny kept in touch, because Lanny had a friend in Holland and Kurt had one in Switzerland who forwarded letters for them. After the Armistice, when Lanny and I met in Paris, he was unhappy because he hadn't got word from Kurt, and thought he must have been killed in the last fighting, like Marcel. Lanny wrote to Kurt's father in Stubendorf, but no answer came. He went on worrying half-way through the Peace Conference; and then one day, walking on the Rue de la Paix, he saw his friend riding in a taxi."

"A German officer?"

"In civilian clothes. Lanny knew he must be there on a forged

passport. He followed him and made himself known. Kurt tried not
to recognize him, but finally admitted what he was doing. Of course
it would have meant shooting if he had been caught. Lanny didn't
tell me, he didn't tell anyone; he just went on doing his work at the
Crillon, and keeping that secret locked in his heart."

"How perfectly awful, Beauty!"

"That went on until late one night Kurt got word to Lanny that
the French police had raided the headquarters of the group for
which Kurt was working. The poor fellow had been walking the
streets for twenty-four hours before he called Lanny; and they went
on walking on a rainy winter night while Lanny tried to think of
some place to take him. He thought of you—but you had so many
servants, they decided you couldn't hide anyone. They thought of
my brother Jesse, who is some sort of Red, as you know; but the
police were watching Jesse—this was right after Clemenceau had
been shot. When Kurt was about exhausted, Lanny decided there
was nothing to do but bring him to my hotel. After midnight I heard
a tap on my door, and there were the pair of them, and what could
I do?"

"You mean you kept that man in your apartment?"

"If I had sent him out on the street, it would have been to certain
death; and I had seen so much killing. I thought the war was over,
and we were supposed to be making peace."

"What was he doing in Paris, Beauty?"

"He was trying to influence French and Allied opinion for the
lifting of the blockade against Germany. You remember how it was
—we were so indignant about the starving of German women and
children."

"But what could a German agent do along that line?"

"He had large sums of money at his disposal. He won't talk about
it, but from hints I have picked up I gather that he accomplished a
good deal. He managed to meet some influential people. Don't you
begin to guess anything, Emily?"

Mrs. Chattersworth had been listening to the troubles of a harum-
scarum friend; it hadn't dawned on her that they might have any-

thing to do with herself. But now suddenly a bolt of lightning flashed in her mind. "Beauty Budd! That Swiss musician?"

"Yes, Emily," said the anxious culprit. "That Swiss musician was Kurt Meissner."

V

The time had come to which Lanny's mother had been looking forward over a period of six months. Sooner or later she was going to have to make a clean breast of these matters to Emily, and with forebodings in her heart she had rehearsed the scene. Now, when it actually confronted her and she saw the look of horror on Emily's face, she couldn't bear to let her speak, but rushed on desperately:

"For God's sake, Emily, don't think that I meant to do this to you! Nothing on earth could have made me do it. I hadn't an idea of it until I walked into your drawing-room and saw Kurt standing at your side. I never had such a shock in my life. I came near to fainting, and can't imagine how I managed to carry it off."

"How did this man know about me?"

"As I told you, Lanny had discussed you along with others. He mentioned a list of his friends. What Kurt did was write to Switzerland and get in touch with his superiors, and with their help he went to work on the names he had got."

"But he wrote me that he was a cousin of an old friend of mine who had died in Switzerland. How could he have known about that?"

"He tells me the German intelligence service can find out anything. That's all I know. His lips are sealed, and not even love can open them."

"But what could he have been expecting to accomplish in my home, Beauty?"

"He wanted to meet influential persons, and he did. Presumably he got what he wanted from one of them—so he didn't come back to you any more."

"How perfectly appalling, Beauty!"

"I assure you I haven't got over the shock of it yet. I tremble every time I see a French uniform."

"And you never gave me an idea what was happening to me!"

"Lanny and I debated that problem in great distress of mind. We figured that you wouldn't want to give him up to be shot; that didn't seem according to your nature. On the other hand, if you didn't report him, you'd become responsible for what he might do. So long as you didn't know, you couldn't be blamed. After you came and told me that the police had questioned you about Kurt, I never slept a wink. How we got him out of the country is a long story that I won't bore you with now."

"I can't think when I was ever less bored," replied the other. She looked into those lovely, gentle features, now so strained and anxious, and added: "I used to think of you as a sort of cross between a gazelle and a butterfly; now I'll have to call you one of the world's great actresses. I have never been so completely taken in."

"You have to find it in your heart to forgive me. I was caught up by a whirlwind. You see, I had fallen in love with the man. It sounds disgraceful, but let me tell you how it was."

"I'm not so surprised by that part. How long were you shut up in the apartment with him?"

"A whole week; but it wasn't only that, it was the tragedy of his position. You know, Emily, how I felt about the war at the outset. I hated it, and only as I watched Marcel's frightful sufferings did I begin to hate the Germans. Before the war was over, I had learned to hate them heartily. And there were Kurt and I all day and all night—he couldn't leave—at least, I wouldn't let him. Everything I believed about the war was a challenge to him. We argued and quarreled, we fought the whole war over, until at last Kurt made me see the German side. They really have a side, Emily."

"I suppose they think so." Mrs. Chattersworth's voice was cold.

"Kurt was wounded twice; the last time he had pieces of his ribs shot away, and while he was in the hospital he was nursed by a young woman who had been a schoolteacher. They fell in love and were married, and she was expecting a baby. That was the time toward the end of the dreadful food shortage caused by the blockade. The baby was born dead, and the mother contracted T.B., but she went on working; Kurt was at the front, and didn't know about it until she had died of a hemorrhage. That's the story he told me; and there he was—having lost everything, even his home—he swears he will never live in Poland. The Germans are a proud and bitter people, Emily, and they're not going to take their defeat gracefully. It's not merely the territory they've lost, the ships and all the material things; it's the humiliation, the insult of having been made to admit a guilt they don't feel. I really thought that when the Versailles treaty was signed Kurt might take his own life. And you know, I wasn't so happy myself: the world after the war didn't look lovely to me; the way people were behaving made me sick. I thought: Here's Lanny's friend whom I might help. And I did that; I've managed to get him back to something at least half-way normal. I know it seems a ridiculous love affair, but if only the world will let us alone and not have any more wars, Lanny and I between us can keep Kurt at his music. I've come to beg your forgiveness—and for your help in this task."

VI

The stately Mrs. Emily Chattersworth had not always enjoyed the secure position which was hers in France. Far back in the past, but still vivid in memory, were the days when she had been the wife of a great New York banker, whose institutions had been under investigation by a legislative committee. Then she had known what it was to read scare headlines about her husband's business and even his private life; to have her telephone wires tapped, her servants bribed, her home burglarized and papers stolen. She said nothing about it now, but remembered that she too was an exile!

Nor was the *salonnière* in position to throw stones on account of the younger woman's sexual irregularity. Emily had had an unhappy married life, and after her husband's death in France she had taken a well-known French art authority as her *ami*, gently putting aside his offers of marriage because she wouldn't trust any man's attitude toward a great fortune. Now her hair had turned white, and the band of black velvet which she wore about her throat was no longer wide enough to conceal the wrinkles; her heart was sad, because she was losing the man she loved, and, fearing that, was ceasing to love him. Now she faced the problem: was she going to give up another friend?

Emily had met Beauty at the time of the latter's unmatched loveliness, and when she was generally accepted as the wife of the wealthy and handsome Robbie Budd. Americans came to France to do as they pleased, and it wasn't the fashion to ask to see marriage certificates. It was only later that Emily Chattersworth had learned about the stern old Puritan father in Connecticut who threatened to disown his son—and meant it—if he should wed an artists' model in Paris. By that time Emily had come to know Beauty and to appreciate her natural sweetness of disposition. Also, the childless Mrs. Chattersworth had grown fond of an eager and precocious lad whom she would have been glad to have as a son.

With one-half of her mind she listened to the details of a strange love entanglement, while with the other half she debated what course she was going to take. The voice of prudence said: "A German agent will always be a German agent, no matter what he may pretend. At any rate, you can never have any peace of mind about him. The possibilities of embarrassment are endless, and will last as long as Germany and France last. While you were being deceived, you could be excused; but now that you know, what excuse can you give?"

But the voice of the heart said: "This woman is in trouble, and it isn't of her making. Am I to say to her: 'I will have nothing more to do with you or your son'?"

Aloud, the mistress of Sept Chênes remarked: "What on earth do you expect of me, Beauty? I introduced your friend to a large company in my home as M. Dalcroze. Now how can I tell them that he is Herr Meissner?"

"At present he travels as my chauffeur, and his passport reads 'D. Armand.' We will let the D stand for Dalcroze, and call him Kurt Dalcroze-Armand. If anyone remembers meeting him in Paris, you can say that he came to you as a stranger and that you introduced him by the wrong name."

"You seem to have thought of everything, Beauty."

"I spent weeks shut up in that dreadful hotel suite with nothing to do but plan and scheme ways to make some sort of future for Kurt and myself."

What Emily said at the end of the session was that she would stand by her friends so long as Kurt devoted himself strictly to music. Let the Swiss gentleman with the unusual name of Dalcroze-Armand arrive in Bienvenu as Lanny's friend and music-teacher, and stay inside the estate and work at his art. "Frenchmen will soon be doing business with Germans again," said Emily, "and I doubt if anyone will concern himself with your visitors or employees. If the police should happen to trace him, we'll have to see some of our friends in the government."

Beauty sat with her hands clasped and the tears starting on her cheeks. "Oh, thank you, thank you, Emily! You will see how hard I shall work to repay your kindness!"

VII

Fortified by this powerful support, Beauty went back to Spain, and her tall chauffeur with the bright blue eyes and abundant straw-colored hair donned his uniform and motored his mistress to the French border. That was the point of peril, and in preparation for it Beauty had donned the gayest costume ever worn by an American lady of fashion on a motor-tour. Not too *outré*, no jewels, and only a little make-up and perfume, but an effect of springtime, most agreeable in December; a jardiniere hat sprouting golden poppies, a pink crape dress hinting at hidden charms, and a full-length silver-fox coat spread on the seat at her back, ready for use when the sun dropped low and the chill of the Riviera night descended. Border guards and customs officials would know that this must be the favored one of some fabulous American magnate; and when she presented her passports and descended from the car to fill out her declaration, she enveloped them in gracious smiles, costly perfumes, and fluent French. Each one imagined himself a master of multi-millions, embracing that vision of joy, and no one had more than a glance for a chauffeur standing by a car, keeping guard over a silver-fox coat and other treasures.

When they were safe in France and darkness covered them, the chauffeur slipped out of his uniform and donned a well-tailored costume appropriate to a Swiss piano virtuoso. They spent the night in an inn at Cette, and drove all the next day and night, arriving at Bienvenu in the small hours. The gates were swung open and then locked behind the car, and Beauty's protégé was safe in a love-nest from which he was not going to emerge for many a month if his *amie* could have her way.

There was that new studio, all pink stucco with sky-blue shutters; and a new grand piano—or should one say a grand new piano? Lanny had had to give up the idea of having Kurt choose it, and had found it himself in Cannes. Those two boys—so they still thought of each other—exchanged embraces with ardor born of anxiety on the one side and of gratitude on the other. Tired and stiff as Kurt was after a grueling journey, he seated himself at the sonorous instrument and poured out the tumult of Schumann's *Widmung. Ich liebe dich in Zeit und Ewigkeit*—and Beauty and Lanny and the piano each might take it as applying to her or him or it!

VIII

That pink and white motherly hen had her three chicks under her warm wings—and how she would guard them! She had seen so much of cruelty and suffering, she had felt so much of grief and terror, that all she asked of a harsh world was to be let alone in her quiet nest; she could get along without any more glory, or whatever it was that a "professional beauty" had craved. Her smart clothes were hung in closets, where they would grow quickly out of date; but never mind, she said, fashions move in spirals, and they'd be good ten years from now. When her smart friends invited her to dances, she told them that she was still in mourning for Marcel. Naturally they would wonder about that severe and dignified-looking music-teacher of whom they caught glimpses; but if they suspected a scandal it would be sexual, not military.

Two children and a lover were three children in Beauty's eyes, and she would do everything in her power to spoil them. If they wanted anything they should have it, and if they did anything it was marvelous. She wanted them to take that attitude to one another; she would sing the praises of each to the others, and watch them all with anxious eyes. Fortunately no sign of disharmony appeared. Kurt found Baby Marceline a charming creature, and joined Lanny in his course of child study. Kurt hadn't thought that one so young could perceive musical rhythm, and when she would toddle over to his studio he did not resent the interruption, but played little German folk tunes for her to dance to, and then carried her home and laid her in her crib. Beauty understood that he was thinking of the child he had hoped for and lost.

When Kurt had visited Bienvenu in the year 1913 there had been two women servants. Rosine was now married, and had a family of her own; Leese had brought one of her nieces as maid-of-all-work, and a brother as handyman. Of course these servants gossiped about the family, as did the servants of all the other families on the Cap d'Antibes. Very soon the peasants and fisherfolk knew that the young music-master was also the lover of Madame; but nobody objected to that—"*C'est la nature.*" They took it for granted that he was Swiss, and knew that he spent his time causing thunderous volumes of sound to echo through the pine woods and over the *golfe*. Passing on the road they would stop to listen, and between hauls of their nets the fishermen would look at one another and exclaim: "*Sapristi!*"

Kurt had got all his instruments and his large stock of music. Lanny also had a supply, and they carried armfuls back and forth and soon got them hopelessly mixed. Lanny was relieved to find that Kurt did not carry the late international unhappiness into the realm of art; he was willing to listen to English and French and even to Italian music. But he had severe standards; he liked music that was structurally sound and hated that which was showy. Presently Lanny began to note that it was the great German composers who had the desired qualities and the foreign ones who lacked them. Lanny said nothing about this, because he was trying so hard to please his friend.

IX

Lanny was only a little more than a year younger than Kurt, but this had made a great difference when they were boys, and his attitude of deference still continued. It was Lanny's nature to admire other people and find them wonderful. His mother had often objected to that attitude, but in the case of Kurt she didn't; so all things worked together to make Kurt the master of this household. It was his genius which was being cultivated; it was his taste which set the standards. Beauty didn't really know anything about music, except for dancing. She liked pretty tunes, but didn't know why everything had to become so complicated and so noisy. But that was the way Kurt liked it, and that was the way he had it.

Beauty's first man had wanted her to be the most admired woman in a ballroom, and so she had spent his money upon clothes; he had liked to sit up most of the night playing poker, and so she had lost a lot of his money for him. Beauty's second man had liked to sit out on the rocks and observe the colors of sunsets and breaking waves; he had raved about the way certain men put upon canvas little dabs of lead dissolved in oil. All right, Beauty had given tea-parties for painters, and had listened to their patter, and learned to tell Manet from Monet, Redon from Rodin, and Pissarro from Picasso. Now here was another kind of genius, another strange and bewildering art; Beauty listened, and it seemed to her a chaos of sound, going on without any discoverable reason for either starting or stopping. But Lanny would cry out that it was magnificent, he had always known Kurt had it in him; Beauty decided that she had known it too.

There was a thing called a "concerto" which Kurt had been working on all his sojourn in Spain. Every now and then a new passage would be completed, and then the whole thing would be played through, up to and including that. Beauty had heard it while reading the popular magazines, while putting supper on the table, while sitting on the rocky shore of the Bay of Biscay, O. If her fingers had been physically capable of the task she could have played every note of it. It meant to her: "Thank God, Kurt is busy! Kurt is keeping out of danger! Kurt is not killing other men, or being killed by them!"

They had been able to get only a small upright piano in Spain, but still he had been able to extract a tremendous racket from it. From watching him rather than from listening, Beauty had come to understand that he was trying to find something to take the place of the war; trying to vent his rage and despair, his love for his own people, his grief at their humiliation and defeat. Watching his face while he played, Beauty lived through her agonies with Marcel, and then those with Kurt, shifting back and forth between the German soul and the French.

Now Kurt had got a man-sized piano, and could really hear his concerto, and Lanny could clasp him and hug him, behaving the way music lovers did at concerts, and which Beauty considered extravagant. The composition was supposed to have an orchestral accompaniment; Lanny could read this with his swiftly flying eyes, and would sit with the score and imagine it while Kurt played the piano part. Then Lanny proceeded to learn Kurt's part, and while he played it Kurt would sit with several instruments about him and pick them up one after another and play snatches on the violin, the oboe, or the flute. The next thing, Lanny was learning to play the orchestral part on his piano, and at the final stage the gardener came with three sturdy sons of the Midi and picked up the old piano in the drawing-room; puffing and grunting, with sweat streaming from their faces, they lugged it over to Kurt's studio and set it down beside the new instrument. So the two maestri could play both parts, and then indeed the passers-by on the road heard something; the rumble of it shook the bedrock of the Cap. But it was all right with Beauty; if they had asked her, she would have consented to build a railroad so that they might transport pianos all over the estate. Anything to keep one's male creatures at home!

X

One of the first things Lanny did was to take Kurt down to Marcel's studio. He had placed the heavy easel in the middle of the

floor, so that the right amount of north light fell upon it. There was
a large painting on it covered with a cloth, and Lanny put Kurt in
front of it, saying: "This is going to knock you over."

It pretty nearly did. When Lanny took off the cover, Kurt found
himself facing a half-sized portrait of his mistress at the age of seventeen, when she had been a famed artists' model in Paris. The painter
had portrayed her in the nude, sitting upon a silken couch, leaning
slightly upon one arm and with a light blue veil half crossing her lap.
A shower of golden hair fell over one shoulder, and bright sunlight
streamed upon it and upon the creamy white skin delicately tinged
with pink. The painter had been a lover of the flesh, and had studied
all the curves and shadows, making something luxurious and se-
ductive, causing every male creature to catch his breath. "Oh,
Lanny!" exclaimed his friend. "What a gorgeous thing!"

"I found it so," said Lanny.

"Is that Marcel's?"

"Marcel wasn't painting then. It's an Oscar Deroulé. He was a
fashionable painter of the *fin de siècle*. Robbie says it is the sort of
thing they put in high-class American bars."

"You can put it in a bar or in a church, according to how you
look at life," said Kurt.

After he had studied this work, Lanny said: "I'll show you
Beauty dressed for church." He took the cloth into the storeroom
and put it over another painting and brought it forth; he set it on
the easel, and with a proper sense of drama lifted the cover. This was
the *Sister of Mercy*, which Marcel had made of his wife during the
long agony of the battle of Verdun. Beauty wore a nurse's costume,
and in her face was all the anguish and pity that Marcel had seen
while she was bringing him back to life. Kurt, who had had the same
experience, rejoiced that a painter had immortalized the soul of this
woman they both had loved.

One by one Lanny brought out the best of his stepfather's works:
his war painting of the *poilu*, and the dreadful one he had called
Fear. Nobody was to·see that, Marcel had said, until the Germans
could see it also. Now a German saw it, and knew that what he had
suffered in his secret soul was the same as a Frenchman had suffered.

Why should either have wished to inflict it upon the other? So Marcel seemed to say, and Kurt felt himself at one with his late antagonist.

Lanny brought out samples of the earlier work: the scenes of the Cap, which Kurt could check in various weathers and at various hours of the day; those of Norway, and the Isles of Greece and the shores of Africa, fruit of the *Bluebird* cruises. After Kurt had seen a dozen or so of these, he felt he knew Marcel both as painter and as man, and was not ashamed to be his successor in love.

XI

Once every twenty-four hours a glow stole up behind the Cap and spread over the sky, and dazzling sunlight descended upon the flowers and foliage and red-roofed houses of Bienvenu. The great orb moved its appointed way over the blue Mediterranean, and sank in a blaze of color behind the dim Estérels. Then the dark half of the sky-wheel moved through its unvarying course, and streams of twinkling stars dropped into the abyss behind the mountains. Every four weeks the moon appeared as a gleaming crescent above the same mountains, and night by night grew larger until it was a great silver ball, by whose light the woods and gardens took on a new and mystical beauty, troubling to the soul. The flowers poured out their tiny jets of perfume upon the still night air, and two young musicians would sit upon the shore, watching the lights of the city across the bay and listening to the sounds of distant music, experiencing a strange awe which they sought vainly to express in their art.

Here was everything that a lover of nature could ask, and more than any philosopher could understand in the longest lifetime. The flowers in the crannied walls held all the secrets of God and man; like sun and moon and stars, they too had their appointed courses, they budded, blossomed, died, and were renewed according to age-old patterns. There was an insect world living upon the plants and upon itself, and a bird world living upon both. If you looked below the surface of the sea, you found a myriad of fantastic forms, each following unceasingly its predatory role. Who or what had been in-

terested to contrive these complicated structures and inspire them
with a determination to struggle and seek through millions of centuries? And those more powerful creatures which had a brain, and
were able to study and comprehend the others, and use them for
their purposes—yet knew no more why they did it, or thought they
ought to! "So hot, little sir?" the stars had said to Emerson; and
Lanny gave this great man's essays to Kurt, introducing him to New
England transcendentalism, stepdaughter of Kurt's German idealism.

The two budding philosophers would take long walks at night,
when no one paid any attention to them. They would wander over
the shore-paths which had delighted them in boyhood; they would
visit by moonlight the ruins of long-dead civilizations, and speculate as to what had brought them down and whether the same forces
were at work in their own heedless world—but not quite so sure of
itself as it had been a few years before! Kurt would be moved to
tell what he had experienced during the war, and Lanny during
peace-making. Across the bay lay the Île Sainte-Marguerite, where
Kurt's aunt, the Frau Doktor Hofrat von und zu Nebenaltenberg,
had been interned as an enemy alien for five years. Now she was home
again, hating the French. Kurt told about her and other members
of his family, all greatly reduced in circumstances but not in pride.

As time passed, Beauty's fears diminished, and she was willing for
them to take walks by day, provided they kept out of the towns
and never spoke German. Tourists were numerous, and the sight of
a tall man with blond hair and blue eyes no longer attracted attention. The two friends dived off the rocks, they sailed in the *golfe*
and outside it, they climbed into the distant hills covered with thyme
and lavender, and looked upon orange and olive vineyards and the
marble palaces of fashionable folk. Once again they sat in front of
that ancient monastery of Notre-Dame-de-Bon-Port and gazed at
the lovely prospect of blue and green water, the shining towns of
the Riviera, and the Italian Alps with their snowy tops. From here
the Estérels were dark red porphyry, and the horizon was a blur of
blue mountains where it was not a ring of blue sea.

Here six years earlier two boys had sat, talking with preternatural
solemnity about their lives and what they were going to make of

them. Lanny had been the more deeply impressed, and recalled what his older friend had said about the mission of art and their duty as carriers of the torch of culture. Kurt remembered it, and declared that he still held to that faith. It was profoundly true that movements of the human spirit came first, and that the events of history were consequences thereof. Very tactfully Lanny sought to encourage this mood in his friend; for history had been hard upon Kurt and his people, and it was much desired by the rest of the world that they should draw back into themselves and experience a new birth of the spirit.

In the earlier, boyhood conversation Lanny had enlisted himself as a disciple of German idealism, and now he told his friend that he was waiting to be justified in his faith. All three of the great B's of German music, Bach, Beethoven, and Brahms, were calling to Kurt Meissner to carry on their tradition. Lanny talked about them with such intensity of feeling that the German was deeply touched. The new Kurt of political bitterness seemed to fade and dissolve, and the old Kurt of moral fervor and devotion came back to life. When in the twilight they descended the slope, it seemed to Lanny that the war was really over and the soul life of Europe beginning again.

3

Double, Double Toil and Trouble

I

ERIC VIVIAN POMEROY-NIELSON had planned to devote his life to the study of what he called "theater." He had chosen that career after seeing his first children's play at the age of six, and from then on he had set out to learn all he could about playwriting and acting, stage- and scene-painting, music, poetry, and dancing. The practice of these combined arts would, of course, call for a lot of activity; one would have to go about, and stand up and show other people what to do, and stick at it through all-night rehearsals; and here was Rick, at the age of twenty-two, a war cripple with essential parts of one knee missing and a steel brace on his leg. Also with a wife and baby, and his father having to sell parts of the family estate on account of war taxes. But still, Rick wasn't going to give up his career!

"It's dogged as does it," is the English saying, and Rick had figured out a long campaign, beginning with those activities which were easiest. He didn't need his knee to work a typewriter, so he would acquire that art, and at the same time practice writing. He would make some money, and, if possible, a reputation; then he would do a play, and his father would help him to find a producer, and he could go in his own right and sit in a chair and watch rehearsals, and if his play was a success, a whole chain of mountains would come to Mahomet.

All this Rick wrote to his friend Lanny Budd, with many typographical errors; it was his first job on a machine, he said, and Lanny put the letter away in his desk, certain that it would find a place in a museum some day. Just as Lanny knew that Marcel Detaze was going to be recognized as a painter, and Kurt as a composer, so he knew that Eric Vivian Pomeroy-Nielson would become a famous name of the English theater. Almost at once Lanny's judgment began to be vindicated, for as soon as Rick had learned to do a manuscript without errors he wrote a sketch drawn from his war adventures, the simple story of a flier who started out at dawn and what thoughts went through his mind as he headed for Germany. It was authentic and moving, and was accepted and paid for by the first newspaper to which Rick offered it. Lanny was so pleased, he bought every copy of the paper he could find in Cannes, and sent one to his father in Connecticut and others to friends who had met Rick.

The baronet's son, brilliant and versatile, was also trying his hand at poetry. His own severest critic, he wouldn't send any of it to Lanny. Nobody could possibly publish it, he declared, because it was so bitter. He was one of those many heroes who were not satisfied with what they had accomplished by their sacrifices and were questioning the whole universe to know who was to blame. Was it the stupid old men who had sat in the council chambers and sent the young men out to be drowned in mud and blood? Was it all mankind, which was able to invent and build machines but not to control them? Was it God, who had made men wrong—and why? Rick quoted four lines from a poem he called *After War:*

> Are nations like the men they make?
> Or was it God who fashioned men?
> O God, who willed the clay awake,
> Will now to sleeping clay again!

Lanny was impressed by these lines and begged for the rest, and Rick with a sudden impulse sent him a large batch of verses, saying that they were hopelessly crude but couldn't do any worse than bore him. However, Lanny refused to be bored; he thought that Rick was voicing what was in the hearts of millions of people, himself included. It happened that in London, at the home of Lady Eversham-Watson, Lanny had met a magazine editor, and, without telling Rick, he sent the poem *After War* and was delighted when the editor offered to publish it and pay two guineas.

Kurt agreed that the verses were good; and Jerry Pendleton, sarcastic fellow, remarked—not in the presence of Kurt—that any German would be glad to hear that an Englishman regretted having licked him. Jerry was one doughboy who had no sorrows over the Versailles treaty, and declared that "Old Whiskers," as he irreverently called Kaiser Wilhelm, was a lot better off sawing cordwood at Doorn. Lanny's former tutor had heard a lot about Kurt Meissner, so it had been necessary to take him into the secret; but of course he didn't know about Kurt's having been a secret agent. If he guessed the situation between Kurt and Beauty, he was discreet enough never to refer to it.

II

The fact that Rick had come so near to Kurt's point of view concerning the late unpleasantness made easier Lanny's project for reconciling England and Germany. Kurt said that Rick had evidently matured into a man of judgment, and that it would be a pleasure to meet him again. So Lanny's letters to Rick and Nina began to be full of the wonders of the Côte d'Azur: the lovely flowers in their garden, the soft white sand of the beach at Juan, the delights of sailing in the bay, the health-giving qualities of ozone and sunshine. When Rick developed a cold, the pressure became intensified. More people had died of the flu than had been killed in the war—and England had lost too much of its young manhood already!

Lanny repeated the arguments which had succeeded with Kurt. What was the use of a fellow's having money if he couldn't spend it on his friends? Robbie Budd knew Rick and admired him, and had cabled offers of help when he had learned about Rick's crash. Now that kind father was sitting at home, unhappy because Lanny wouldn't spend his money; it could only mean that Lanny had been seduced by the propaganda of the Reds and was offended by the smell of munitions profits! But if Lanny should cable that he wanted to rent a villa for Rick and his family, Robbie would cheer up at once. Lanny wrote this, and then, fearing that it might not be the best argument for an anti-war poet, he tore up the letter and wrote another of somewhat doubtful ethical quality—he offered to spend for Rick that thousand dollars which he had got from the State Department of the United States, and which he had already spent for Kurt's piano! A genial device: Lanny would keep that thousand dollars in mind, and spend it over and over on anybody who had conscientious scruples against munitions profits!

Sophie, Baroness de la Tourette, had a pleasant little villa on the other side of the Cap, near Antibes, where she had stayed off and on for years. Now she had gone to visit her people in Cincinnati, and wrote Beauty that she was remaining in order to get a divorce. "The hardware business has been shot to pieces," she explained, "and I find I can't afford the upkeep of a title." Lanny sent her a cable, offering to rent the house for Rick, and she said all right, and after he had done it Rick had to come.

Lanny met the little family at the station. He saw that Rick was thinner; he was working hard, and forcing himself to take exercise. His keen features had more of the old fire in them, and Lanny realized that it was one thing to weep for the world's wrong, and another to write verses about it. Rick had always been mature beyond his years. He made jokes in his old fashion, and spoke with his customary contempt of those whose artistic standards were beneath his own. There were touches of gray in his wavy black hair; this appeared to be one of the effects of shellfire upon the human organism.

Nina was her pretty, birdlike self, only she was a mother-bird, and both husband and son were her babies. Little Alfy, as they called him, had been named after his grandfather, but was a miniature of Rick; he didn't take kindly to railroad trains and automobiles, but was trying to get loose and start to explore the wonderful new world. He had been born in the midst of war and horror, but didn't know anything about it. Was this a blessing of nature or a betrayal? His father asked the question in a sonnet.

They drove first to Bienvenu to have lunch, and on the way Lanny told about Kurt's state of mind, and asked his friends to go easy on the subject of the past five years. He told about the concerto, now finished. Incidentally he remarked, quite casually: "Kurt has become Beauty's lover." Such was the correct tone among the young sophisticates. You said it *en passant*, as if it were: "Beauty and Kurt have gone sailing this morning." Your friends said: "Oh, jolly!" or "Ripping!" and that was that.

III

Rick hadn't seen Beauty or Kurt since the outbreak of the war, and Nina had never met either of them. So there were greetings to be exchanged and curiosities to be satisfied. Little Alfy was set down in front of Baby Marceline, who gazed at him with wide brown eyes and one finger in her mouth; he took command, as he would throughout life: seeing the dogs, he toddled after them, and Marceline followed. He was going to be a baronet and a member of the English ruling classes, and Marceline was going to have a half-share of Bienvenu, a valuable property; also of whatever her father's paintings might bring. As soon as they were born Lanny had written the two mothers, bidding them start matchmaking, and in their minds they had done so; now when their eyes met there was appraisal, not merely of each other, but of the future of two families.

Lanny and Rick and Kurt at Hellerau had dubbed themselves the three musketeers of the arts. "When shall we three meet again In thunder, lightning, or in rain?" So they had asked, and here was the answer. There had been plenty of thunder and lightning, but now the uproar had died away, there was a rainbow in the sky, and a heavenly melody floating in the air, as you hear in the *William Tell* overture—or preferably in Beethoven's *Pastoral Symphony*, since Kurt Meissner will tell you that Rossini's music is somewhat meretricious. It will be to music of the highest quality that these three musketeers march forward into life, resolutely, in spite of defeats and disappointments. When Rick hears fate knocking at the door in four thundering notes it will not tell him that he is growing deaf, but that he is a cripple for life; and with the help of art he will learn to take these blows of fate and make a *scherzo* out of them, and in the end perhaps a triumphal march.

After lunch Lanny drove the new family over to their temporary home, which he had stocked up with tinned goods enough for an African safari. There was one of Leese's able-bodied relatives to act as maid-of-all-work; one of her orders would be to carry Rick's typing machine out to a rustic table every morning when the weather was fair. There he would sit alone, and his rage against human stupidity would fan itself white hot, and molten words would pour from the typewriter, all but burning the pages. Strange as it might seem, the more he lashed the damned human race the better they liked it; such was the mood of the time—all thinking men agreed that the peoples of Europe had made fools of themselves, and it was proof of advanced views to abuse the "old men," the "brass hats," the "patrioteers," the "merchants of death."

It was as if you had been on a terrible "bat" the night before, and had got into a row with your best friend and blacked both his eyes. Next morning you were apologetic, and willing to let him have the best of all the arguments. So it was that both Lanny and Rick dealt with their German friend; the Englishman talked as if it was really quite embarrassing to have won a war, and of course what he wrote about British bungling pleased Kurt entirely—only he found it difficult to understand how British editors were willing to pay money for it!

IV

One of the consequences of Rick's coming was that the subject of world politics was brought back into the family conversation. Lanny had deliberately put the subject out of his mind, and tried tactfully to have Kurt do the same. Kurt got no newspapers from home, and when members of his family wrote to him, they put the envelope in a second envelope addressed to Lanny Budd, so as to avoid attracting attention. But now came Rick, bringing with him the custom which prevailed in his father's home of discussing public affairs at all hours of the day and night. Rick took a couple of newspapers and half a dozen weeklies, and would lie propped up in bed reading and making notes. The war, however many bad things it had done, had brought it about that British politics were French politics and German politics and Russian politics and American politics. All the nations of the earth had been thrown into one stew-pot, there to simmer slowly. Double, double toil and trouble; Fire burn and cauldron bubble!

So Lanning Prescott Budd descended the steps of his ivory tower and pushed open its gold-embossed doors and thrust out his delicately chiseled nose. Instantly it was assailed by the odors of a colossal charnel-pit, a shell-hole as big as the crater of a volcano, filled with the mangled flesh and bones of millions of human beings. His ears, carefully schooled to the appreciation of exquisite music, were stunned by the screams of dying populations, the wails of starving children, the imprecations of the frustrated, the moans of the hopeless. Before his eyes stretched a prospect of desolation; shell-blasted fields, skeleton trees without a leaf, buildings that were smoke-blackened walls, their empty windows like human faces with eyes picked out by birds of prey.

The Turks were still slaughtering Armenian peasants. Civil war was still raging in Russia, the Whites now being driven in rout to all points of the compass. In Siberia a freight-train loaded with Reds was wandering aimlessly upon an eight-thousand-mile track, the locked-in prisoners perishing of starvation and disease. The Polish armies, invading Russia, were still dreaming of world empire. The White Finns were killing tens of thousands of Red Finns. The Rumanians were killing Red Hungarians. There were insurrections and mass strikes in Germany, a plague of labor revolts in France and Britain, millions unemployed in every great nation, famine everywhere in Europe, flu in the western half and typhus in the eastern.

When, in the middle of 1919, President Wilson and his staff had left the Peace Conference, that body had stayed on to settle the destinies of Austria and Hungary and Bulgaria and Turkey. It was still holding sessions, with despairing peoples waiting upon its decisions; when these were announced they were generally out of date, because events had moved beyond them. The British and French statesmen were agreed that Italy should not have Fiume, but an Italian poet with a glory complex had raised a revolt and seized the city. All statesmen agreed that the Bolshevik madness must be put down, but meanwhile it throve and spread, and mountains of supplies which the Allies had furnished to the White generals were being captured and used by the Reds. The statesmen decided that Turkey should lose most of her empire, but the Turks dissented and retired into their mountains, and who had an army to go after them? The French had seized the land of poor Emir Feisal—all but those parts which had oil; the British had these, and there was a bitter wrangle, and it looked as if the alliance which had won the war would break up before it finished dividing the spoils.

British statesmen had promised to make a world fit for heroes to live in, and now Rick's version was that they had made one it needed heroes to live in. Lying on the table in Lanny's study was one of Eli Budd's volumes, the poetry of an old-time New Englander who had been one of the patron saints of Rick's grandmothers, but to

Rick himself was no more than a name. Rick was moved by curiosity to dip into the volume, and he happened upon *A Psalm of Life*, which was to be found in all school readers. The crippled aviator declared that it "griped his guts"; anybody could write "doggerel" like that, and to prove it he composed on the spot a revised version:

> Tell me not, ye wishful thinkers,
>   That the spirit reigns supreme,
> And man's hoping is a token
>   Of the mortal's valid dream.

The modern psalmist went on to tell the world how he had "seen the Brute in action," and his conclusion was:

> I have wakened from a nightmare
>   To a living death by day;
> All my dreams a tabulation
>   Of the price my hope must pay.

V

On the first day of every month, unless it was Sunday, the businesslike Robert Budd dictated a letter to his son—a good, satisfying letter telling about the family and the business, and never failing to include some advice to the boy about taking care of himself, and learning to spend money wisely, and not letting women get too much hold on him. Lanny had saved these communications over a period of years, and if he had published them, judiciously expurgated, they might have made a New England equivalent of the letters of Lord Chesterfield.

The family in Connecticut was thriving, as it always had, and meant to; they were solid people. Lanny's two half-brothers were in St. Thomas's; they could enter younger than Lanny, because they had been trained according to a system. Lanny's half-sister Bess, who adored his memory, was reading a book he had recommended and struggling to play a piano piece he had mentioned. Esther Budd, his stepmother, was marshaling the ladies of Newcastle for the relief of war victims in Armenia and Poland. The president of Budd Gunmakers Corporation was showing his age, but could by no means be induced to relax his grip upon affairs; he had inherited a great institution and was determined to pass it on to his heirs in better condition than he had received it.

They were going to save the business, Robbie assured his son; they were making the dangerous transformation of their activities, and instead of machine guns and carbines and automatic revolvers, cartridges and hand grenades and time fuses, were producing a great variety of implements of peace. No easy task finding markets for new products, but they would do better in the boom which was surely on the way. But what a tragedy for America, and how it would some day regret the dismantling of its vitally important munitions industry! Lanny understood that to his father there was a loss of dignity and prestige, even a personal humiliation, in having to turn from the fashioning of beautiful, shining, deadly machine guns to the monotonous multiplication of frying pans, tack hammers, and freight elevators. It was possible to feel romantic about the Budd gun, which was the best in the world and had proved it in the rock-strewn thickets of the Meuse-Argonne; but who the hell wanted to hear about hardware?

However, the great plant had to go on; wages had to be earned, and taxes and upkeep, and dividends if possible. The world had munitions enough to last a decade, and the pacifists were in the saddle in America; the hallelujah shouters were proclaiming that the war to end war had been won and the world made safe for democracy. There was no philanthropist to subsidize and save an American munitions industry, built at breakneck speed by heroic labors. Far from appreciating this service, the nation had turned upon its benefactors and was calling them profiteers and merchants of death. Robbie Budd was a deeply offended munitions salesman, and the more so because his oldest and best-loved son had taken up with these critics and no longer desired to follow in his father's footsteps. Robbie never referred to this, but Lanny knew what was in his heart.

However, Robbie was a businessman, and the customer is always right. The customer didn't want machine guns, he wanted automobile parts and bicycles and gadgets of a thousand sorts, and Budd's would oblige him at mass-production prices. Also the customer would want oil, and Robbie, having many connections in Europe, had picked up a good thing in that line, and had let his friends and innumerable cousins in on it, and now was concerned to prove himself a businessman in his own right, not merely a son of Budd's. He had come to London twice during the fall and winter, and had been too busy to go down to Juan; Lanny had protested and pleaded, and so in the month of March Robbie cabled that he was on his way to Paris, and that nothing should interfere with a holiday. This sort of cablegram always marked a red-letter day in Lanny's young life. Moralists might scold about blood and profits, but none of them could deny that Robbie Budd was good company.

VI

The foreign representative of Budd Gunmakers had known for some time that he had got himself an odd sort of extra family, and he was curious to see what had been happening to it of late. Impossible to imagine a more unlikely tie-up than the butterfly Beauty and the grave and punctilious artillery officer turned spy! Add to it Lanny, product of a sexual irregularity, who didn't mind his fate, but seemed to have decided that the moralists were out of step with him. So many families were breaking up and recombining, wasn't it more sensible to leave everyone free to move without notice?

Father and son went for a long walk, as was their custom. Robbie was in his middle forties and had been leading a sedentary life all winter; for the first time in Lanny's experience he puffed a bit on the hills, but he didn't like to admit it and went on talking. He was a hearty, solid man, with brown eyes and hair—when he went swimming you saw the hair growing all over his chest. He liked having a good time, but underneath he was greatly worried about the world, which was in what he called a god-awful mess. People in Europe had been fighting for so long, they seemed to have forgotten what productive labor was. Lanny knew that his father's mind had watertight compartments in it, and there was no use mentioning the difficulty of combining peaceful industry with the mass production and marketing of instruments of slaughter. What Lanny had to do was to let his father talk, and when he couldn't agree, say nothing. All through the war, both in France and in New England, Lanny had had to practice the art of keeping his thoughts to himself, and at the Peace Conference he had perfected his technique.

He described the life of Beauty and Kurt, who were getting along surprisingly well. Beauty was much in love with her man, and had got over being embarrassed about it; Kurt was a good influence because he kept her at home—he wouldn't let her spend money on him, so she didn't spend it on herself. You could see Kurt's musical stature growing, Lanny said; and Robbie listened politely, but without much enthusiasm. Robbie had been to Yale, and had got vaccinated with culture, but it hadn't "taken"; he knew a lot of college songs and popular stuff, but left highbrow music to those who pretended to understand it. Maybe Lanny did; in any case, his father was satisfied if it kept him happy and out of mischief.

One important question: Was Kurt having much to do with Germans? Lanny answered: "No. What could he do, anyhow?" The father didn't know, but he said there would be war of one sort or another between France and Germany so long as those two nations existed. And certainly Bienvenu must not become a secret headquarters of the Germans.

They went back and had a swim with the family. There was a boat-landing with steps, and on the bottom step Lanny had had two iron handles fastened for Rick. If there were no strangers present to embarrass him he would unstrap his leg brace, and with his two arms and one good leg would help himself down into the water, where he could float around and swim with his hands. Nobody must offer to help him, or take any notice of his troubles, just let him alone and in his own way he would work them out. Meanwhile, observe the blue sky and the varicolored houses, the gray rocks and green hills of the Golfe Juan. Robbie, who had seen Rick in Paris just before he went out to his near-death, had admired his grit then and admired it now. He told Lanny that was one fellow who must have help whenever he needed it.

Also Robbie saw Beauty in her tight bathing suit, and had a good time describing in exaggerated language the ravages of *embon-*

point upon her charms. Beauty and the cream pitcher were a standing joke in that family. You might have thought it in dubious taste while millions of babies were perishing of slow malnutrition. If Beauty had had one of those little ones before her, she would have starved herself to feed it; but the little ones were in the newspapers, while the cream pitcher was on the table four times a day, including teatime. Also there was Leese, whose arts were a perpetual conspiracy against the figures of ladies who came to Bienvenu. *Bouillabaisse* with butter floating on top, *rissoles* fried in olive oil, sugary fruit *pâtés* with curlicues of whipped cream—so it went, and Beauty would tell herself she was just tasting this or that, and would go on until there was no more taste on her plate.

VII

In the evening the family sat in front of a log fire, for the nights were chilly. Mrs. Emily had been invited to join them, and they talked about the state of the world, concerning which various members of the group had special information.

Robbie told about America. President Wilson had come home from his peacemaking to find the country wholly indisposed to ratify the commitments he had made. He had spent his last reserves of health upon a tour of the nation; then a paralytic stroke had laid him low and he was a helpless invalid. If you were willing to believe Robbie Budd, the executive branch of the United States government now consisted of an elegant lady who owned a jewelry business, and whom Lanny had seen in Paris wearing a gorgeous purple gown and a purple hat with plumes; a navy doctor whom the President had raised to the rank of admiral; and a secretary whom Robbie described by a term of depreciation common among the ruling classes of New England—"Irish Catholic." The President saw no one, and this triumvirate of amateurs decided what papers he was permitted to read and sign. The Constitution of the United States might be the most perfect instrument which had ever emanated from the brain of man, but it had its oversights, and one was a failure to provide what was to happen when a president had a paralytic stroke.

However, it was an election year. In three months the Republican

party would name its candidate; no college president, but someone
who understood American business and its needs. The money to
elect him would be forthcoming—Robbie knew where it was coming
from—and in a little less than a year America would confront the
world as a new-born nation, no longer to be trifled with in international affairs. Robbie didn't think that, Robbie *told* it, and the
others listened respectfully.

The talk turned to the state of France, and here they heard a
salonnière who numbered men of affairs among her friends. Clemenceau, the Tiger, had won the war but lost the peace—at least in the
estimation of the Robbie Budds of France—and he had been ousted.
There was a new premier, Millerand, and now it appeared that he
too was yielding to the blandishments of Lloyd George. They were
likely soon to have Poincaré, which meant simply that the war with
Germany would be resumed in one form or another. Nobody in
Europe was in a mood to think of mercy—save only the Germans!
It was a very sad picture that Emily Chattersworth drew.

The mention of Lloyd George brought Rick into the conversation. Rick's father knew the key men of his country, and reported
what they were saying in the clubs. Lloyd George was the only one
of the war chiefs who still held power, and he did it because he had
no principles, but was able to say, with the most passionate fervor,
the opposite of what he said the day before. The "little squirt of a
Welsh lawyer" had wrecked his own party getting power, and now
was the prisoner of the Conservatives; useful to them because he
could talk Liberal, and that was necessary with a bitterly discontented electorate.

Lanny told a story about his English friend Fessenden, one of
the secretaries attached to the British staff at the Peace Conference.
Fessenden had noticed that through a long and tedious discussion
Lloyd George was "doodling" on a sheet of paper, and at the end
crumpled it up and threw it onto the floor. Young Fessenden res-
cued it, thinking it might be something that would be of advantage
to his country's opponents. He found that the British Prime Minister
had covered an entire sheet with repetitions of one single word:
"Votes. Votes. Votes."

VIII

Here sat these seven friends in soft-cushioned chairs, seeing one another's faces by the light of shaded lamps and the red and gold flames of burning cypress logs. Convenient little tables held ashtrays for their cigarettes and glasses for their drinks. On the walls around them were fine pictures, and shelves full of books for every taste. In one corner of the room was a piano, and when they asked him to play, Kurt produced soft music which turned time into beauty and glorified the processes of the human spirit.

Everything in the world appeared to be theirs, and yet their talk was troubled; it was as if the ground upon which this lovely home was built had turned to sand and might slide into the sea. On the center table lay newspapers telling with shocked headlines that the French and British armies had occupied Constantinople, which was threatened with revolution and might plunge the world into another war. When one said "another war" one didn't count the dozen or so small wars which were going on all the time, and which one had come to take for granted; one meant another war involving one's own land; one meant—horror of horrors—a war in which the late Allies might be fighting against each other!

Robbie Budd, newly hatched oil man, could tell them what the day's news meant. The old Turkish Empire had collapsed, and a new Turkey was going to be born, with all the benefits of modern civilization, such as oil wells and tanks and pipelines, not to mention copper mines in Armenia and potash works on the Dead Sea. The only question was, which benevolent nation was going to have the pleasure of conferring these blessings upon the Turks? (This wasn't Robbie's phrase; it was Rick's rephrasing.) The British had got hold of all the oil, but the French had got Syria and the Hejaz and were trying to control the routes of the pipelines; behind the scenes there was a furious quarrel going on, with screaming and calling of names in the nasal French language.

Now suddenly came this *coup d'état* in Constantinople. The benighted Turks didn't want to accept benefits from either Britain or France, but wanted to dig their own oil wells and keep the oil; so the quarreling friends were obliged to act together in spite of their wishes. Lloyd George was talking about a holy war, in which the Christian Greeks would put down the heathen Turks; but what effect would that have upon the several hundred millions of Moslems who lived under the Union Jack or near it?

Robbie pointed out that a certain Greek trader by the name of Basil Zaharoff had just been made Knight Commander of the Bath in England, a high honor rarely extended to aliens; Zaharoff controlled Vickers, the great munitions industry of Britain, and had saved the Empire at a net profit which people said was a quarter of a billion dollars—though Robbie Budd considered the figure exaggerated. Zaharoff was a friend of Lloyd George, and was reported to be one of his financial backers, which was only natural, considering how much money a politician had to have and how much governmental backing an international financier had to have. Zaharoff's hatred of the Turks was one passion of his life that he didn't have to hide.

"So," said Robbie, "you can see why British troops have been put ashore in Constantinople, and why French troops had to follow, even though the French government is supporting the Turks behind the scenes. Added to this is the fact that Constantinople until eighteen months ago was a German city, and German agents have been left behind there, to make all the trouble they can for both British and French. Naturally that would include a revolution by young Turkish patriots."

Robbie said this much and then stopped, realizing that he was in the presence of an agent whom the Germans had left behind in Paris. Kurt made no comment; of all persons in this room, he had had the best practice in keeping his thoughts to himself. But Lanny could imagine those thoughts without trouble, for only a couple of days earlier Kurt had received a letter from the comptroller-general of Schloss Stubendorf and had read passages to his friend. There, too, the British and French troops had found it necessary to intervene—not in Stubendorf itself, but in districts near by, known as "plebiscitary," whose inhabitants were going to have the right to decide whether they wished to be German or Polish. A bitter campaign of propaganda was going on, and a fanatical Polish patriot was organizing the young Poles to intimidate the Germans and try to drive them out before the voting took place. At any rate, that was the way Kurt's father described the events. Lanny remembered the name of Korfanty, which he was to hear frequently during the next year or two.

IX

When a fellow hasn't seen his father for eight or nine months and can't be sure when he will see him again, he naturally wants to make the most of his opportunity; so Lanny was pleased next morning when Robbie said: "I have some business to attend to that will interest you. Would you like to drive me?"

"Would I!" said the youth. He knew it was important because Robbie didn't say anything about it in the presence of the others. What Beauty didn't know she wouldn't tell!

When the car had passed the gates and headed toward the village, Lanny said: "Which way?" The father answered: "To Monty," and the son got a thrill.

"One guess!" he laughed. "Zaharoff?"

"You win," was the reply.

As a method of education, Robbie had made it a practice to tell his son about his affairs. Always he would say gravely that nobody else was to know about the matter, and never in his life had the boy let anything slip. He must be especially careful now, the father warned, since one of his pals was a budding journalist and the other a German.

Robbie revealed that he had taken the munitions king of Europe into his "New England-Arabian Oil Company." The old Greek devil had learned about it—he learned about everything in his various lines —and had sent for the American and made a proposal which it seemed the part of discretion to accept. "We're in British mandated territory, and we can't expect to operate without their protection; so we have to give a slice to some British insiders."

"Who sups with the devil must have a long spoon," quoted the youth, sagely.

"We have measured the spoon," smiled the father. "He has a twenty-five percent interest."

"But mayn't he buy up some of the other stockholders?"

"I have the pledges of our American investors, and I think they'll stick. More than thirty percent are Budds."

Robbie told about the oil business as it was carried on in southern Arabia, a wild and desolate land, the home of fanatical tribesmen, mostly nomads. You paid one chieftain for a concession, but you couldn't know what day he might be driven out. However, they had made a strike, and the clean-up would be rapid. Robbie portrayed khaki-clad young American engineers and leather-skinned drillers from Texas, sweating on a sun-scorched coast lined with sand and rocks, and living in a stockade with a watch tower and machine guns mounted on the walls. "Would you like to see it?" asked the father, and Lanny said: "Some time when you go."

The youth understood quite well that his father was trying to make the oil business sound romantic. Robbie Budd could not give up hope for the response he used to get in years past, when an eager lad had drunk in every word about the selling of machine guns and had leaped at every chance to believe that he was helping. But now, alas, Lanny's mind had suffered a sea-change; it was full of ideas about oil as a cause of war. When he learned that his father had let Zaharoff in "on the ground floor" so that he might have a British gunboat lying in the little bay near his oil wells, Lanny wasn't surprised, and didn't blame anybody, but just preferred to stay at Juan and play the piano.

"You are happy in what you are doing?" asked the father, later in their drive.

"Really I am, Robbie. You've no idea how many fine books there are in that library. It seems every time I open one I get a new view of life. I hope you don't think I'm wasting my time."

"Not at all. You know what you want, and if you're getting it, all right."

"I want you to understand I'm not going to live on you the rest of my life, Robbie. I'll find some way to put to use what I've learned."

"Forget it," was the reply. "So long as I have money, you're welcome to a share." Robbie said it and meant it, but Lanny knew that it involved giving up a long-cherished dream that these two might work together and that the son would take over what the father was building.

X

Eighteen months hadn't been time enough to replace all the motor-vehicles of France, and the Route Nationale had less traffic than they remembered in old days. They sped past famous vistas of hills and valleys, blue sea and rocky shore, and came to Monte Carlo on its high promontory. Zaharoff was still staying at the hotel where a small boy had been able to steal his correspondence; he had a large suite there, suitable to his station as Grand Officer of the Légion d'Honneur and Knight Commander of the Bath. Robbie said he owned the hotel and was a heavy stockholder in the gambling casino at "Monty," well known to be one of the gold mines of Europe.

The munitions king looked paler and even more tired than when Lanny had seen him last, in his palace on the Avenue Hoche in Paris. That had been a social occasion, but this was a business one, and the gentle duquesa and her two daughters did not put in an appearance. Robbie had come with a portfolio of documents, to give information and get advice from a one-time fireman of Constantinople who had entrusted a couple of million dollars to his care.

No manners could have been more polite than Zaharoff's, no voice more soft and persuasive; yet it seemed to the youth that there was a subtle change in the relationship of the two men: his father was now the subordinate and the other the master. Perhaps this was just because Lanny remembered so vividly the occasions when the Levantine trader had suggested the idea that Vickers might buy out Budd's, and Robbie had answered suavely that Budd's might prefer to consider buying out Vickers. Time had passed, and Zaharoff's judgment had been vindicated; Robbie's wonderful dream of the world's greatest munitions industry up the Newcastle River seemed dead forever. Budd's was having to abandon that field to a great extent, while Vickers—it was having one hell of a time, as Robbie

said and as the old man admitted, but Britain and France were going
to keep their munitions industries, both under the control of this big-
bodied Greek with the hawk's nose, the white imperial that bobbed
while he talked, and the steely-blue eyes that never smiled even when
the lips pretended to.

Lanny had nothing to do but listen while his father produced
documents and explained them. If Lanny ever wanted to drill a
couple of dozen oil wells he would know what it cost; also he would
understand that Arab sheiks, so romantic on the motion-picture
screen, were rapacious and incendiary in their attitude toward petroleum companies. Zaharoff knew that he was dealing with a capable
businessman, and what he had to say was put in the form of suggestions. He revealed his distrust of all Moslem peoples, so entirely lacking in modern business sense and in respect for vested capital. With
that frankness which had always surprised Robbie Budd's son, he
discussed the attempted revolution in Constantinople, the scene of
his youthful struggles. He defended the right of the Greek peoples
to recover the lands taken long ago by the Turks, and said that he
was insisting that the Allies should put the Turks out of Europe for
good and all. Once more Lanny sat behind the scenes of the world
puppet-show and saw where the strings led and who pulled them.

He learned that the strings reached even to that far-off land of
liberty which he had been taught to consider his own. The munitions king wanted to know about the prospects of the election of a
Republican president of the United States; he knew the names of the
prominent aspirants, and listened attentively while Robbie described
their personalities and connections. When Zaharoff heard that
the Budd clan expected to have a voice in selecting a dependable
man, he remarked: "You will be needing funds and may call on me
for my share." Robbie hadn't expected that, and said so, whereupon
the master of Europe replied: "When I invest my money in an
American company, I become an American, don't I?" It was a remark that Lanny would never forget.

4

A Young Man's Fancy

ROBBIE sailed for home by way of Marseille, and Lanny motored him to the steamer, so they had a chance for another heart-to-heart talk. Robbie wanted to know what his son was doing about the problem which was the torment of great numbers of men—a woman. Lanny said he was getting along all right; there were so many interesting things in the world, and he was holding to the suggestion of the idealistic young master at St. Thomas's Academy, that it was wiser to live a celibate life until he had met the woman who was to be his permanent mate. Robbie agreed that that was all right if you could do it. Lanny revealed that he sometimes found himself with shivers running over him at the thought of a woman, but he would look at those who offered themselves openly in public places on the Riviera and decide that he wouldn't be satisfied with them; then he would come home and play sweet sentimental music on the piano until he had tears in his eyes, and after that he would feel all right. Father and son laughed together.

Robbie had been discussing this also with Lanny's mother, and he talked a little about her attitude. To Beauty social life now presented itself as a conspiracy of mothers and daughters to trap her too eligible darling. Everywhere he went were simpering misses making eyes at him, and hawk-eyed, hawk-faced old women watching from the sidelines. Beauty knew, for she had heard them plotting against other victims. Budding females were trained for the marriage market, they were dressed for it, they learned to walk and talk and dance and flirt for it. In the presence of their highly developed arts the unhappy male creature was as helpless as a moth in a candle-flame.

"You're going to have a hard time finding one who will please Beauty," said Robbie, with a smile; "but all the same, don't fail to have her advice, because that's her department."

"What I want," said Lanny, "is to learn something worth while, and meet some woman who is interested in the same things."

"It can happen," said Robbie. "But most of the time what the woman is thinking about is making you think she's interested. And if you're fooled it can play the devil with your life."

"I know," said the youth; "I've been keeping my eyes open." He didn't feel as young as his years.

"I don't mean for you to worry," added Robbie. "When the time comes, ask yourself what you really want and if you're getting it."

There the matter rested. Lanny saw his father on board the steamer, and gave him messages for the many Budds, and hugged him hard, and then stood on the quay and watched the steamer warped out into the harbor. Waving to the receding figure on the deck he thought: What a wonderful world, what a blessed state, when one can see one's father off on a comfortable sea-hotel, and know that neither in the Mediterranean nor in the outside ocean will there be any submarines watching for a chance to send it to the bottom!

II

Three months had passed since Beauty and Kurt had returned from Spain, and nobody had manifested the least suspicion of or hostility toward a Swiss music-teacher; so gradually peace settled in the woman's heart, and there began the burgeoning of new impulses toward her fellow-creatures. What was the use of being beautiful unless once in a while you allowed others to enjoy the sight? What was the use of having a handsome, eager, and eligible son if you kept him shut up in a garden? Afraid of fire as Beauty was, it appeared that she had to play with it.

The Duchesse de Meuse-Montigny was giving a very grand garden-party; and since Beauty's costumes were all hopelessly out of date she went in to Nice and had M. Claire fit her with something worthy of the occasion. Lanny was supplied with a light worsted suit of that spring's cut. Kurt couldn't go to parties, of course, and didn't want to—he was working on a Spanish suite for strings. So there was Lanny on a smooth green lawn with a Japanese peach tree for a background, and all around him predatory creatures flaunting costumes bright with freshly discovered hydrocarbon dyes, and cheeks and hair with the same; smiling coyly or wantonly, and doing their best to say something original and brilliant to please a youth reputed aloof and unattainable. It was just after a devastating war, when young males were scarce and young females ravenous. Inside the white marble palace a colored band was thumping, and Lanny would take the would-be brides in his arms one by one, sampling their charms symbolically, and Beauty would watch out of the corner of her eye and ask questions about the one in pink organdy or the one in white tulle with yellow shoulder-bows, and seldom be satisfied with what she learned.

What did she expect? Well, obviously, any woman who aspired to marry Lanny Budd had to be beautiful. How could he endure to have her about the house otherwise? She had to be rich—not just comfortably, but something super and solid, no fly-by-night fortune based on speculation. There were heiresses all over the place, and why not cultivate them? Lanny had told Beauty of Tennyson's *Northern Farmer,* and she endorsed his formula: "Doänt thou marry for munny, but goä wheer munny is!" Also, it would be safer if the chosen one belonged to an established family, and could prove it by Debrett. Finally, she would have to be clever, almost a blue-stocking, otherwise how could she keep from boring Lanny? Even his own mother couldn't do that!

To find all this in one package was no easy matter; Beauty had been to many social affairs, and had inspected the best that Paris and London and the Riviera had to offer, but she was still looking. Her friend Emily was in the conspiracy, and at this garden-party the pair inspected new candidates and discussed them *sotto voce.* The daughter of the California shipping magnate was overgrown and flavorless, like the fruit of her native state. The French girl was real Saint-Germain, but looked anemic; moreover, the family estate was mortgaged. The one whose father was a cabinet minister used her eyes like a screen actress and, anyhow, French politicians were mostly riffraff. The English girl doubtless had more sense and better breeding than any of them, but look at that gawky figure! The inevitable Russian princess, escaped from the Bolsheviks—her title sounded so impressive, but it meant merely a country squire's daughter in Russia, and even if she had once been rich she probably had nothing now except the jewels she had been able to hide in her garters or the heels of her shoes. Also, she might be promiscuous.

Such were a mother's thoughts at a garden-party; but meanwhile Lanny was having a very good time. He loved to dance, and if delicately gowned and perfumed young things were available for the purpose, he would take them in his arms, and carry home memories which would last him many a day. He would try to set these thrills to music like Kurt, or put them into verses like Rick, and when he wasn't satisfied with his own attempts, he would turn to the masters. A *thé dansant*, a flower show, or a dinner dance would lend wings to the music of Chopin and illuminate the pages of Shelley. The sunlight clasped the earth and the moonbeams kissed the sea, and all these kissings were worth something to Lanny, even though they kissed not him.

III

A large white yacht slid into the harbor of Cannes. Its flag showed that the owner was aboard, and presently it showed that he was not. His name was Jeremiah Wagstaffe and he was a Philadelphia banker who had been involved in the scandal with Emily's husband, but since he had operated through dummies, he hadn't had to move to France. His fortune was of the third generation, and in America you can build a tremendous tower of pride in that time. Mr. Wagstaffe's tower was his wife, who held herself like a drill sergeant and looked at the rest of mankind through a lorgnette.

They were just completing a Mediterranean cruise, and with them was their niece, Miss Nellie Wagstaffe. She was a year older than Lanny, which wasn't so good, but she was an orphan and had a large fortune in her own right. She had pale blue eyes and lovely white skin, a quiet manner, a mild disposition—just the thing that a rather talkative and confident young man might prefer. She didn't carry her money with her and sit on top of it as her aunt did. Emily Chattersworth phoned over to Bienvenu and told Beauty that these old friends were to be at Sept Chênes for lunch, and that Lanny should come alone, since romance blossoms better in the absence of mothers. Lanny guessed what it was about—it had happened before.

Mr. Wagstaffe was a short, rotund gentleman in a white yachting costume, and had a white mustache decorating a fiery-red face; Lanny knew from his own experience that people dined well on yachts and that the sun of Africa was hot in April. Also he knew what it was to be inspected through a gold lorgnette, and it didn't cow him. He knew that when you sat next to a young lady who had several millions of dollars in traction and bank stocks in her own name, you were supposed to perk up and think of striking things to say. The trouble was with Mr. Wagstaffe's stories. He had a stock of them, and they weren't bad stories, but everything reminded him of one and the telling left little room for other conversation at a small luncheon table.

It happened that another guest had been previously invited for this day. Her name was Madame de Bruyne, and the hostess called her Marie. Lanny remembered having met her more than once at Mrs. Emily's country place, Les Forêts, near Paris; but that had been before the war, when Lanny was a youngster, and he couldn't recall that he had ever talked with her. She was a Frenchwoman, slender, with dark brown eyes and hair; she had delicate, pale features, and what Lanny thought the saddest face he had ever seen upon a woman; he had seen his mother in great grief, but this was a kind of permanent, settled sorrow. She smiled faintly at the stories, whether she understood them or. not. She said little—but then she had no chance, except when Mr. Wagstaffe had his mouth full of asparagus and mayonnaise. She was placed across the table from Lanny, and of course their eyes had to meet now and then. There was understanding in the woman's, as if she knew that he had lived most of his life in France, and would be thinking: *"Que les Américains sont drôles!"*

After the meal it was up to Lanny to invite the heiress to view the gardens and the scenery. He did so, and they chatted. She had been to the places which the *Bluebird* had visited; Lanny told about his trip and she proved a good listener. To try her out he described how the ancient ruins had made him feel melancholy; her comment was that there were so many troubles in the world nowadays, she didn't see the use of bothering about any that were so far off. Then they talked about the war; she had a brother who had been in the French ambulance service, and Lanny told her about Eddie Patterson, who had been killed in that service, and she said she would ask her brother if he had met him.

She was a pleasant enough girl, and Lanny could imagine himself pitching in and making himself agreeable and perhaps winning her; then he would be fixed for life, he wouldn't ever have to work. But it didn't seem to him like much fun, and the girl was entitled to better luck, though she would probably not have it. How many men were there who could come that close to several million dollars in one lump and not think it was cheap at the price? Such things subjected human nature to too great a strain!

The pair strolled in, and the aunt said they must be going, they had other friends to call on. Emily, who didn't know how the conspiracy had progressed, asked Nellie if she wouldn't like to stay a while; Emily would be glad to deliver her to the yacht. It was a bid; but the heiress said that she had better go with her aunt. This was the moment for Lanny to ask: "May I have the pleasure of seeing you again before you sail?" But he just wasn't interested enough to face that gold lorgnette swinging upon him. What he did was to bid the travelers a polite *bon voyage*, and thank Mrs. Emily for a pleasant occasion.

Madame de Bruyne said that she was sorry to have to bother her friend to send her home. So of course it was Lanny's duty to offer to drive her. "Oh, but I live far to the west of Cannes," said the French lady with the sad brown eyes.

"I like to drive," Lanny replied. It was kind of him, and Mrs. Emily knew that he was always kind—it explained why she was taking the trouble to find him a rich wife.

IV

On the way Lanny chuckled over the bouncing old gentleman who had left no time for conversation, also the heiress who had looked at the ruins of the Parthenon without feeling sad. Madame de Bruyne said that she was very young, and would learn more about sorrow as she went on. One needed suffering in order to appreciate any form of art. "But not too much," she added; "that dulls the sensibilities."

They were speaking French, and Lanny translated the words of Goethe about eating one's bread with tears. "Yes," said the woman, "and Heine gives the same testimony about his verses."

"So she reads!" thought Lanny, and added, out of his own reading: "The people who are sensitive to beauty expect too much of life, and it doesn't fulfill their hopes."

"I wonder about that problem with my own children. If I tell them what lies ahead, I may fill them with fears and spoil their childhood. On the other hand, would I let them walk into a burning house without warning them?"

"I think it depends on the children," said Lanny. "I had plenty of warnings of all sorts, but I don't know that they worried me. Generally they weren't real to me. We have to feel the heat before we know what fire is."

They continued exchanging ideas about life, and when they came to the little villa where Madame de Bruyne lived, she asked: "Wouldn't you like to come in for a while?"

Lanny thought he would, and sat in a modest drawing-room—it was the home of her aunt, she explained. She offered him something to drink, but he said he didn't take it, and she asked with a smile: "Did somebody warn you?" He explained that his father had done that; also he had watched people who drank. He didn't need stimulants, because he was happy anyhow.

"I've always remarked that about you," said the woman.

"I'm surprised to hear you ever noticed me," he replied.

"Oh, women notice personal details. I thought I'd like my two boys to have natures as sunny as yours. How have you managed to stay so, all through six dreadful years?"

He told her various things about his life. He mentioned the two friends he had met learning to dance "Dalcroze," one an English boy and the other a Swiss. "You are fortunate to have kept your friends," she said. "My brother was killed, and two cousins, my childhood playmates."

He spoke of Marcel. She knew that story; she knew Beauty and had seen the painting, *Sister of Mercy*, in the Paris *salon*. It was as if she had been sitting up on a cloud somewhere watching Lanny's life. He told her about his strange experience in his father's home in Connecticut, when a ghost or something of Rick had appeared in his bedroom at dawn, just as Rick crashed and lay near death in Picardy. The story affected her greatly; her lips trembled and she said: "I had the same sort of experience with my brother; but he died. I have never told about it, because it was so frightening, and I didn't know what to make of it."

Said Lanny: "My great-great-uncle in Connecticut, a Unitarian minister, believed that there is a universal consciousness, and that we are part of it, in some way that we do not understand yet."

They were talking about the deepest problems of the soul. Did Lanny believe that the dead still live? He told her that he didn't know what he believed; he had never been taught anything about religion, and hadn't been able to work it out for himself.

"I was brought up a Catholic," said Madame de Bruyne. "I was devout when I was a girl, but for several years the conviction has been coming over me that I don't really believe the things I have been taught. At first I was frightened by this realization: it seemed wicked, and I thought that God would punish me—but now I seem to have grown hardened to the idea. I cannot believe what seems to me unreasonable, even if I am damned for it."

"Whatever it is that gave us our reason doubtless intended us to use it," said Lanny.

"I've never had anybody say that to me," declared the woman. It sounded naïve, and Lanny was flattered to be taken as a spiritual adviser to so mature a person. He told her about Emerson, who had helped to give him the concept of spiritual freedom. She answered that Emerson was a mere name to her, and this pleased Lanny. He had met society ladies who would pretend to have read any book you mentioned; but when this one didn't know something she asked about it and listened to what you said.

Lanny saw that there was a piano in the room, and asked if she played. He had told her how hard he worked at it, and she invited him to play for her. He played several things, and she knew what they were; her comments pleased him. It seemed that he had never met anyone with whom he shared such quick understandings; their ideas fitted together like mortised joints in a well-built house. When he played happy music she forgot her grief, and their spirits danced together over flower-strewn meadows. When he played Mac-Dowell's *An Old Trysting Place*, her eyes were misty, and she did not have to talk. Lanny thought: "I have found a friend!"

V

They forgot all about time, and he was still playing when her aunt came in. Lanny was introduced to a wizened but agreeable old lady, who insisted upon serving tea for them. Over the ceremony Madame de Bruyne told about the capitalist from Philadelphia and his stories. "What was so funny about the horse-race?" she asked, and Lanny tried to explain American humor. He didn't mention that he had been expected to marry the pale-eyed heiress, but doubtless Madame de Bruyne guessed that. Before he left, he asked: "May I come again?" She replied: "We two old women are often lonely."

When Lanny got home, there was another "old woman" waiting eagerly to know what had happened, and sure that he must have made a conquest, having stayed so long. Beauty in her fancy had been dwelling in marble halls across the sea, and she clamored for the full story. Men are frequently unsatisfactory under such circumstances: they neglect to tell the things that women want to know, and they have to be plied with questions that bore them— "What was she like?" and "What did she say?" and "Was that all you could find to talk about? What have you been doing all afternoon?"

"I talked with Mrs. Emily for a while," he said, and, strictly speaking, this was true, though the "while" had been short.

"Was anybody else there?" persisted Beauty.

"A Madame de Bruyne."

"Marie de Bruyne? What on earth did Emily want her for?"

"I think she had been invited previously."

"And what did she have to say?"

"She doesn't talk much. She's one of the saddest-looking women I ever saw. She's grieving over a brother that she lost in the war."

"She has more than that to worry about," remarked Beauty.

"What else?"

"Emily says her husband is one of those elderly men who have to have virgins."

"Oh!" exclaimed Lanny, shocked.

"And she isn't a virgin," added Beauty, with unnecessary emphasis.

"She told me she has two boys in school."

"You had a talk with her?"

"I drove her home, and played the piano for her. I met her aunt, Madame Scelles."

"She's the widow of a professor at the Sorbonne."

"I knew they were cultivated people," said Lanny. "They have very refined manners."

"For heaven's sake be careful!" exclaimed the mother. "There's nothing more dangerous than an unhappily married woman. Remember, she's as old as your mother."

Lanny chuckled. "As old as my mother admits!"

VI

Lanny had said that young people don't take advice; and right away he set out to prove it. He inquired in the bookstores and found a copy of his much-loved Emerson and sent it to Madame de Bruyne by messenger. A couple of days later he called at teatime, and found his new friend at home; also he found that she had read the book. There are doubtless many women of the world who, when you make them a present of a book, sit down and read it straight through; but this was the first time Lanny had had that experience, and it seemed extraordinary to him. They discussed the Concord philosopher's abstruse and elevated ideas; they reason'd high of providence, foreknowledge, will, and fate, fix'd fate, free-will, fore-knowledge absolute; and found no end, in wand'ring mazes lost.

Lanny played music, and the widow of the Sorbonne professor came in and listened, and her comments indicated that she also had a cultivated taste. They invited him to supper, a frugal and unfash-ionable meal which the old lady herself put on the table; they had a maid only in the morning, it appeared. Gradually Lanny began to discover the situation in this household; Madame de Bruyne had left the rich husband who had to have virgins, and was staying with the sister of her mother long since deceased. They were interested in a school where the orphans of French soldiers were cared for, and went there sometimes to help. Madame de Bruyne was avoiding social life, and spent most of her time at home; but she would always be glad to see Lanny, and very soon he came to feel at home in this household, and would stay for lunch or supper, as they called their informal meals.

A worrisome situation for Beauty Budd! Her darling, her super-eligible offspring, was missing at odd hours, and contented himself with saying: "I was over at Madame de Bruyne's." If she asked: "What were you doing?" he would say: "Playing Debussy"; or maybe it would be Chabrier, or César Franck, or de Falla—they were all a blur to Beauty. Or perhaps he would say: "We were reading Racine"—or it might be Rolland or Maeterlinck. She was sure that this couldn't go on—sooner or later there would be an ex-plosion, dreadful to think of. But what could she say—she who kept a young lover on the place, and in a house which Lanny had con-structed for the purpose! Was this a most ingenious form of pun-ishment, devised by some angry god or devil who spied upon the sex-life of the social élite? How different our own actions appear when we see them committed by others—and especially by one for whom we have been planning the great wedding of the season, with half a dozen bridesmaids in pink duchesse satin and white hats, and carrying armfuls of roses to match the satin!

VII

She couldn't refrain from speaking. She came to his room, and shut the door portentously, and sat by him and gazed into his eyes. "Lanny, tell me honestly!"

"What, dear?"

"Are you falling in love with Marie de Bruyne?"

"Oh, for heaven's sake!" he exclaimed. "She's a good sport, and a most intelligent woman. I like to talk to her."

"But, Lanny—it's playing with fire! A man and a woman can't——"

"Forget it," he said. "She's a second mother to me."

"But isn't one enough?"

"You're the dearest that ever was in the world; but you haven't read the books that I'm reading, and you don't play the music I play——"

"I could, Lanny, if you really wanted me to."

"Bless your heart! It would be hard work, and it would make you nervous and maybe spoil your complexion. Let me have an auxiliary mother, and don't be jealous."

"It's not jealousy, Lanny! I'm thinking about your whole future."

"I assure you there's nothing to worry about," he insisted. "She's a really honest woman—and they're scarce, as you know."

"But, Lanny, it's not natural. You'll find you're getting involved with her."

"I hadn't thought about it, old girl; but if you insist, I'll ask her about it." There was a grin on his face.

But Beauty couldn't see any fun. "For God's sake, no!" she exclaimed.

She dropped the subject; but, oh, how she hated that creature, that shrewd, designing bundle of tricks! "Honest," indeed! The devil had made all women! This one knew that Lanny was naïve and sympathetic, so she pretended to be full of "sorrow"! "Hell!" thought Beauty. "As if I haven't had sorrow enough! But I smile, I make myself agreeable; I don't go around mooning and sighing, reading poetry books and quoting them while I make my eyelids tremble! My God, what fools men are!"

VIII

The anxious mother, meaning so well, had struck a spark in a tinder-box. Lanny went off and thought it over. Could it really be true that he was falling in love with Marie de Bruyne? What would it be like to love her? Right away, of course, nature began to tell him: a warm feeling stole over him, a delicious feeling, of which she was part and parcel—her goodness and kindness, as well as her beauty, which he hadn't noticed at first, but which had grown on him. He decided that if he didn't love her, he could easily learn to; and why not?

It was such an intriguing idea that he couldn't resist talking it over with her. Her reaction to it would be fascinating; he would know her better for it. He waited until the hour when the old lady usually was at the school; Marie didn't go so often—perhaps because she preferred the company of Lanny to that of orphan children.

They sat alone in the small drawing-room; Lanny in a large soft chair, leaning forward on his elbows. "See here, Marie," he said. "I've an interesting idea. I am wondering if you and I mightn't be falling in love."

"Oh, Lanny!" she cried; he saw that she was shocked.

"Hadn't you thought of it?"

Her eyes dropped. "Yes," she whispered. "I thought of it, but I hoped you wouldn't."

"Why?"

"We have such a pleasant friendship."

"Of course. But mightn't we be friends and lovers too? That might be twice as pleasant."

"It wouldn't, Lanny—it would ruin it all."

"For heaven's sake, why?"

"You can't understand——"

"I'd like to try. Will you answer me a few questions, fairly and squarely?"

"All right." Her voice was faint, as if she knew the questions would be painful.

"Are you the least bit in love with your husband?"

"No."

"Have you been living with him as his wife?"

"Not for a long time."

"Do you feel that you owe him any moral obligation?"

"It's not that, Lanny."

"Then what can it be?"

"It's hard to explain."

"Do the best you can."

"I gave my trust to a man, and I bore him two sons; then gradually I discovered that he was horrible in his habits."

"So you decided that all love is horrible?"

"No, not that. I decided I wouldn't stoop to his level. I would do my duty, even though he might fail in his."

"Of course you want to do your duty; you're that sort of person. The question is, what *is* your duty? Because one man isn't what he ought to be doesn't mean that all men are. Are my habits horrible?"

"No, Lanny, of course not."

"Because one love fails, does that mean that all love must be stifled? Are you a Hindu woman, who has to give herself to the flames with her husband's corpse?"

She said "No" again, but her voice was faint. His analogy was a rather violent one.

"What else?" he persisted; and as she hesitated, he went on: "You were brought up a Catholic, and you've been realizing that you don't believe all that. What about their ideas on the subject of the sex-life? Have you some of those superstitions still in your mind? They separate the love of the body from the love of the soul, and so they degrade both. The love of the body alone is a shame, and the love of the soul alone is a neurosis. Do you get what I mean?"

"I suppose so, Lanny." She generally did.

He had thought very carefully what he wished to say to her. He didn't wish to rush her off her feet, but to appeal to her judgment. Now he spoke slowly and precisely, as if it were a speech that he had learned. "If I should love you, I would love you all the ways there are. It would be a clean love, and an honest one, that you wouldn't have to be ashamed of. I would be kind and gentle; you wouldn't have to make any painful discoveries. I've had opportunities with women, but it's been a year and a half since I've taken one in my arms. That's not such a bad record for this part of the world—and for these post-war days. I have learned to control myself, and to know what I am doing; so I have a right to ask a woman to trust me. Doesn't that seem reasonable?"

"Yes, Lanny." Her voice had grown fainter still.

IX

For one of his age, Lanny Budd had acquired a considerable store of knowledge as to the structure and functioning of the feminine heart. At the age of thirteen he had discovered that his mother was the *amie* of a French painter, and had talked this situation out with her. As a result of the discretion thus acquired, he had become eligible for the pleasure cruise of the *Bluebird*, and had heard the conversation and observed the conduct of a group of ladies and gentlemen who might have come out of the *Decameron* of Boccaccio. Immediately afterward he had had the responsibility of helping his mother decide whether she was going to stick by her poor painter or be respectably married to a plate-glass millionaire from Pittsburgh. The war having come, Lanny and Beauty had read the romances of Stendhal and Anatole France together and discussed the opinions of these two authorities on love. After Marcel had been brought home with his face burned off, Lanny had helped his mother to nurse him back to life, and there wasn't much he didn't find out about those two in the process.

His own experiences, both on the Côte d'Azur and on the shore of Long Island, had taught him much, and in between his labors at the Peace Conference he had learned about his mother and his boyhood friend. He had built a love-nest, and watched two turtles pair who never meant to part. Furthermore, his head was full of phrases from the love-poets of England, France, and Germany, plus translations from the ancient Greeks. All that lore he was now putting at the service of Marie de Bruyne, who had told herself that her heart was a desert where no flowers could bloom or bird-songs be heard.

She said something obvious but painful: "Lanny, I am much too old a woman for you!"

He answered: "There are a few things you can leave to me, and that's one. I've met no end of young girls, and they're fun to dance with, and even to get thrills from; but when they try to make intellectual conversation it just doesn't come off. All my life I've spent time with older people, my mother and father and their friends; maybe that was a mistake, but, anyhow, it's made me so that I like to talk to you. When I say something about a book, you know what I mean, and if you answer, I learn something new, and that makes conversation a pleasure. Don't you think that's a part of love worth considering?"

"Yes, dear; but it mightn't be like that always."

"Always is a word too big for everyday use. None of us knows what he's going to be ten years from now; but if we have sense we can know what we are now, and what we need. I'm pretty sure you could make me happy, and I'd stand a chance to make you happy. The more I think about it the better I know that it would be lovely to take you in my arms. I could take you out of those dreadful memories that torment you; I could make love something different, so that you wouldn't go around looking like a mask of grief."

"Is that the way I appear?" she asked, as if shocked.

"That's the phrase I used to myself the day I saw you at Mrs. Emily's. But already the magic of love has been at work. You do love me a little, don't you?"

"Yes, Lanny," she whispered.

"Well, then, you have to choose—a great happiness or a great torment. Prudery, or monkery, or whatever you call it, says renunciation and loneliness; common sense says companionship and peace. Which do you want?"

"If it were only as simple as that, dear! But we live in the world!"

"Oh, yes; we have laws and conventions, and relatives and friends, and gossip and scandal, and superstitions that poison life and strangle happiness. What else?"

"You really think we have a right to do what we please?"

"I think that what you and I do in the privacy of our life would concern us very deeply, and concern no one else on this earth."

"I have two children."

"I don't begrudge you your children, and I don't want to take your love from them. There's plenty and to spare in your heart, I am sure."

"But they would find out about us, Lanny!"

"When I was thirteen and discovered that my mother was in love with Marcel Detaze, I told her that I wouldn't stand in the way of her happiness. Marcel became an extra father to me, and we never had one moment's difference in our lives."

"But that's extraordinary, Lanny."

"It may seem so to one who has been brought up to believe that love is sin; but I was brought up to believe in my reason. I take it as a matter of course that I should love you, and be kind to you, and do everything I could to make you happy—provided only you didn't let some black-robed priest tell you that I've lured you into mortal sin."

"No, Lanny, it's not that. But your mother would hate me dreadfully!"

"My mother has a dream for me to marry some divinely beautiful and fabulously rich daughter of the aristocracy, preferably English. When I was sixteen I had my first love affair with the granddaughter of an earl, but she turned me down for the grandson of another earl, and since then I have been more modest in my aspirations. You would suit me perfectly, and when my mother realizes that the matter is settled, she will adjust herself to it and perhaps bore you with her excess of kindness."

"But you ought to marry and have children!"

"I haven't any money to marry, and I don't seem to have any desire to reproduce myself. I have a delightful little half-sister at home, and Beauty insists upon spoiling her, so I have to take Marcel's place many a time. I know what he would say and I say it, and so my paternal impulses get satisfied. What I need right now is not a child, but friendship and happiness, and those are a part of love's gifts worth having and cherishing."

Her eyelids had dropped and he saw that her lips were trembling. He moved over to the sofa beside her and said: "I would like to kiss you." When she did not say no, he put his arms about her and gently touched his lips to her cheek. After a while he drew back his head and looked at her. "What do you say?"

"Lanny," she whispered, "I ought not decide such a thing in a hurry. I ought to think about it."

"That is fair," he answered; he released her and took one of her hands instead. "If you are going to be happy, you mustn't do anything that your reason and conscience don't approve."

"Oh, thank you!" she exclaimed. "That's the way to be kind!"

"How long do you want?"

"I don't know. I'll send for you. It's all so startling to me, so different from what I've been taught to feel. Play me something gentle and tender—like yourself." He played the Brahms *Cradle Song*, slowly and softly, and while he played he imagined that she was in his arms.

X

The young prodigal went home, and there was his mother, waiting in great anxiety. It would have been hard for him to conceal the shine in his eyes; he had never lied to her about matters of love, or indeed about anything except world diplomacy when that had been his job. Now he said: "Well, old girl, I followed your suggestion and had a talk with Marie about being in love with her."

"Oh, my God!" cried the mother. As he smiled teasingly, she clamored: "Well? What happened?"

"She wanted time to think it over, and I gave it to her. But I'm not sure that was wise. What do you think?"

Beauty thought a lot, and said it. He let her pour out her feelings, and ruin several handkerchiefs.

"See here," he said, at last. "You know what I did for you and Marcel, and what I'm doing now for you and Kurt. You owe me a debt, and you have to repay it. That's all there is to it, and you might as well pay up like a good sport."

"Oh, Lanny!" she sobbed. "I tried so hard to find you the right woman!"

"I know, dear; but you remember what Dr. Bauer-Siemans told me when I was a kid, that I couldn't expect to know what sort of man my mother needed. Now it's the other way around. You presented me to various young ladies who ought to have made me happy, but they didn't. I went out and found one for myself, and, believe me, I haven't any idea of letting her get away from me."

"A woman old enough to be your mother. Lanny!"

He had expected that from Marie, but not from Beauty. "Old goose!" he laughed. "Don't talk too loud or Kurt may hear you!"

"Yes, Lanny, but——"

"But that was you, while this is some other woman! What is sauce for one goose is sauce for any other."

Argument was so hopeless that she had to share his laughter, even while she went on sobbing. He went to the drawer of her dressing-table and brought her a handful of the tiny, delicate *mouchoirs* that ladies use; he dropped them into her lap, and said: "Cheer up, old dear. It isn't as if I'd gone out and picked up a tart on the boulevard. I've got one of the sweetest women you ever knew, and when you make up your mind to appreciate her you'll have a sister. It'll make our household hopelessly queer, I know——"

"Oh, Lanny!" she gasped. "Are you expecting to bring her here?"

"I couldn't on account of her husband; we mustn't take any chances of attracting attention to Kurt. Marie and I will work matters out by ourselves."

"Oh, dear, oh, dear!" lamented Beauty. "I was hoping to make our lives more respectable!"

Poor soul, he knew that this was the deepest longing of her heart; but there was nothing he could do except to go on laughing. "You began it!" he said.

"I know! I never really blame anybody else."

"Your chickens have come home to roost!" Lanny was young, and it seemed to him best to enjoy life as he went along. "They are roosting all over this baby-blue boudoir, and you and Kurt can hear them chirping on the headboard of your bed!"

5

Weep for the World's Wrong

I

ERIC VIVIAN POMEROY-NIELSON was sticking with his British tenacity at the job of learning to write. He had got several editors interested in his efforts, and every now and then would get a new idea and work furiously at it. When it was done, Lanny would find it "swell," but Rick would frequently declare it "putrid" and want to tear it up. Between the litter of manuscripts and the litter of a baby it was hard to keep the little villa in order, but Nina worked cheerfully, declaring that after what they had been through, it was happiness just to be alive. From time to time Beauty would decide that they were lonely, and would get up a picnic or sailing party, which really they didn't care about very much; but Beauty did.

One morning near the end of April Rick telephoned to Lanny and read a telegram from the editor of a liberal weekly in London. There was a conference of the Allied premiers opening at San Remo, a town on the Italian Riviera, and the editor suggested that Rick might like to try his luck with an article about it. The editor couldn't promise to take what he wrote, but he said there was a story in this conference, and it was up to a youngster to get the facts and present them acceptably. Rick considered this a great chance, and he was proposing to take a train that afternoon. Would Lanny like to go along?

Lanny didn't hesitate. "I'll drive you," he said. "Maybe I can help you get in on the inside."

Less than a year had passed since Lanny had registered a vow that he was through with international politics and the pompous bigwigs and solemn stuffed shirts who made the headlines at conferences. But time heals all wounds, and the war-horse resting in the pasture smelleth the battle afar off, the thunder of the captains and the shouting. Lanny wouldn't have admitted to himself that he wanted to gaze once more upon the cherubic countenance of David Lloyd George, or to see what the Frenchman Millerand or the Italian Nitti looked like; but when it was a question of helping Rick to get a story and perhaps make a reputation for himself, the devoted friend went into his dressing-room and started chucking his things into a couple of bags.

Meanwhile, of course, he was thinking about Marie. If only she would be sensible, what a delightful holiday they might make of it! Really an education for her! He'd not fail to give her the chance. He put his bags into the car, and gave Beauty a couple of hugs, and promised to drive carefully—there had been a dreadful accident to one of her friends the previous week. "All right—yes—I'll keep my eyes open." He shook hands with Kurt and told him to get that *fiesta* part of the Spanish suite into shape. Lanny couldn't say how long he'd be gone—one could never tell about those talk-fests of politicians—he'd stick by Rick and help him get about—good-by and good luck——

"Lanny, tell me!" exclaimed Beauty. "Are you going to take that woman?"

"Ask me no questions and I'll tell you no lies!" he chuckled.

II

Marie was alone in the house, except for the servant. He led her into the garden, where there couldn't be any eavesdropping. Three days had passed since he had left her, and he hoped that was time enough for thinking. He looked into her eyes to find an answer, but instead there seemed to be anxiety.

"Something exciting has happened," he said.

"What, Lanny?"

"There's an old town about ten miles inside Italy called San Remo. It looks out over our sea but it's older, and has a grand old Romanesque cathedral." (Lanny was grinning, for he didn't really think she'd want to see cathedrals.) "There are good hotels, and I've no doubt nice respectable *pensioni* where you get ravioli when you don't get spaghetti."

"I have been to San Remo, Lanny."

"A charming place for a holiday, don't you agree? Rick and I are leaving as soon as you can get your things packed. There's to be an international conference—a whopping big one—all the diplomatic world. Rick has an assignment to write it up and it may be the making of him."

"What an idea, Lanny—to take me to a conspicuous place like that! I couldn't fail to meet people who know me."

"Make it a brother-and-sister party. Stay at the most respectable place in the town. Arrive by train if you like, and meet me by accident."

"But nobody would believe that."

"Surely you have a right to be interested in international affairs! Aren't you curious to see the master minds who are making the world safe for democracy? You can stay in some near-by town if you prefer, and if you and I should disappear now and then—*cosi fan tutti!*"

"Lanny, it is sweet of you; but I've just had a letter with troubling news. My little Charlot is down with that dreadful flu, and I may have to take him out of school."

"Oh, I'm sorry!" he exclaimed.

"You see, dear, I just don't belong to myself. You can't think of me as you would of a debutante."

"I wouldn't think of a debutante. Where will you take the boy?"

"To our country place in Seine-et-Oise."

"Does that mean going back to your husband?"

"Not as his wife—never, Lanny. We can live in the same house and be polite to each other, as we have done in the past. He has a right to see the children, and I don't want to divorce him and make a scandal that would hurt them. These matters are different with us from what they are with you Americans."

"What is going to be your husband's attitude to our affair? Will he be jealous, or will he be glad to be let alone?"

"I don't know, Lanny. I've tried hard to think what to do. There are many painful possibilities. I am afraid of marring my children's life, and yours, too."

"Listen, darling," he said. "It's all right to worry about your children, but please don't take me on. There's no harm that you can do me, I assure you. I know what I want, and I mean to get it—the cost is no obstacle. I'll gladly tell the world that I love you. I'll put an advertisement in the papers for all the scandal-mongers to read. I'll put a sign on my back and parade up and down in front of your house: '*J'aime Marie de Bruyne!*'"

She couldn't keep from laughing. "Please, dear," she pleaded, "give me time. Take Rick and let him do his story. I'm waiting for a telegram about my son, and I'll write you later."

"That's all very well," replied Lanny. "But you overlook the fact that I'm in love. A man doesn't enjoy going off and leaving his woman without knowing how he stands."

"You can be sure there's nobody in my heart but you, Lanny."

"I wish I could accept your word, but I know there are a lot of other bodies in your heart. There's a large body called 'the world,' which you are afraid to expel. Why it should be malicious and hateful is something I've never been able to figure out, but it is. It likes to destroy other people's happiness. Look at what it did in the war—it has made a wreck of half Europe, just because some people couldn't bear to see other people free and happy! And now it wants to take charge of your life and mine; to say: '*Verboten!* Taboo! Keep off the grass! *Défense d'aimer!*' It has words in every language."

"I have given it hostages, Lanny. It will punish my two sons."

"Think about those sons, and how you mean to bring them up. Do you want to make them into time-servers and conformists? Are they going to have their loves in slum bedrooms and behind haystacks? If not, you'd better tell them the truth about love, and begin early, before the other boys have debauched them. One way to begin is to say: 'I have a lover, and you can see that he is honest and decent and kind, and nothing for you or me to be ashamed of.' "

They went into the house, and he closed the door of the drawing-room and took her in his arms, a long, long embrace. She clung to him, so that he knew she wasn't going to hold out forever.

"Marie, I love you," he declared, "and I'm not going to give you up—not for the Pope and all the hierarchy, the saints in heaven and the devils in hell. I'm coming for you, and I want to know I'll have you."

"All right, Lanny," she answered. "I'll work out a way."

III

The little town of San Remo lies in a sheltered bay, with a crescent breakwater forming its harbor and range upon range of mountains sheltering it from the northern blasts. The narrow streets of the Old Town climb the hills wherever they can, and the houses have triple buttresses against earthquakes; on the main streets they have arched loggias running together, not one daring to stand apart. When Rick saw this he said it was a lesson for the peoples of Europe—let them learn to build their states as they had built their homes!

High up on one of the slopes, with a walled road approaching it, stood a pretentious two-story villa having in front a semi-circular portico with tall narrow columns; Villa Devachan was its name. It had been the "Second Paradise" of the Theosophists, and now it was the council place of the Allied premiers and their advisers. Lanny Budd had seen so much of European splendor that he knew what he would find inside, even before he had an opportunity to enter. Large rooms with huge chandeliers dangling from the ceiling—how he would hate to be under one of them when the next earthquake hit! Heavy plush curtains protecting the inmates from the deadly possibility of a change of air. Gilt chairs with silk or satin upholstery, of colors which would quickly reveal the stains of human contact. Tables with inlaid tops and hand-carved legs, their curves as standardized as the beards of Egyptian pharaohs. Lanny had guessed that

Theosophical interior decoration would be no different from pseudo-Christian, and he found that he was right.

Each premier brought his elaborate staff, which had its own hotel or palace. From each nation came also a swarm of journalists, fending for themselves and grumbling bitterly over the sparsity of official "hand-outs." Also came delegations from the little nations and oppressed minorities; Estonians, Letts, and Lithuanians; Ukrainians, Hungarians, and Caucasians; Armenians, Arabs, and Assyro-Chaldeans. They had been told that this was "the New Freedom," this was "self-determination for all peoples," and they believed it, or said they did as a matter of policy. Some brought credentials, and others only moral powers; they put up in pensions or poor lodgings, and labored earnestly but for the most part vainly to get somebody to listen to them. When their funds ran out they borrowed from one another, or from anyone who looked as if he might believe in the brotherhood of man.

It was all so familiar to Lanny Budd, it was as if he had had an elaborate nightmare and now was starting it all over again. When he made this remark to a journalist from America, the man advised him to get used to this nightmare, because he would be riding it several times every year for how long nobody could say. The nations would be wrangling and arguing over the Versailles treaty until they were at war again. Newspaper men are notoriously cynical.

The Senate of the United States having refused to ratify the treaty or to join the League of Nations, Lanny's country had no representative at San Remo, not even an unofficial observer. But of course the American press had a large delegation, and among these were men whom Lanny had come to know in Paris, where he had served as a sort of secret pipeline through which news was permitted to leak. These men were under obligations to him, and greeted him cordially and took him and his aviator friend into their confidence. Lanny had advised Rick to say nothing about his proposed article, but to make his way with Americans on his war record, and with his compatriots on the basis of being the son of Sir Alfred Pomeroy-Nielson, Bart. Rick wouldn't be violating any confidences, because these correspondents were cabling "spot news" for various deadlines, and by the time a magazine article could appear they would be off on some other assignment.

IV

The Englishman, endeavoring to save his money, wanted to live *en pension*, but Lanny was used to living *en prince* and insisted that Rick should be his guest; it would be fatal to stop anywhere but at the most expensive hotel, for only there would you meet the people who were on the inside of affairs. On account of the crowds the pair had to bunk in one small room and bathe in a hand-basin; but they put on their "smokings" and went down into the dining-room, and the first person the American laid eyes on was the tall, sandy-haired young Fessenden who had been a member of the British secretariat in Paris. The last time they had met, this chap had been decidedly cool, because Lanny had resigned in protest against the concessions made by the American Commission, and Fessenden, a "career man," had been afraid for his future. But that had been nearly a year ago, and the world had changed greatly.

Now the secretary jumped up and greeted Lanny. He was introduced to Rick, and when he heard his accent and saw that he was "right," he invited the pair to his table, where two other young members of the staff were sitting. All three had been in war service, and they and Rick appeared to have secret passwords or insignia, for they fell to talking about one another's families and friends, old school ties, boat-races, cricket-matches, and other esoteric matters. Lanny, being an American, was not expected to produce credentials or to understand this conversation.

Before long they began talking about the task on which they were engaged, and it was better than listening to journalists who were being deliberately kept in the dark. These chaps had handled confidential memoranda, and one had just had a session with a department head in his portable bathtub. Rick remarked what a pleasant place the statesmen had picked out for themselves; whereupon Fessenden chimed in: "Did you hear what Lloyd George said to the premiers? A red-hot one! 'Well, gentlemen, we are in the Garden of Eden, and I wonder who will play the snake!'"

The San Remo conference had assembled amid direful forebodings. Many bitter disputes had arisen among the former Allies: over the remains of the Turkish Empire—Constantinople and Armenia, Syria and Palestine, the Hejaz, and especially Mesopotamia with its treasure of oil, vital alike to British, French, and Italian navies; over Russia and its Bolshevik government, and the war against it which had collapsed; over the *cordon sanitaire*, and Poland invading Russia and most of her neighbors at the same time; over German reparations and how they were to be shared; above all, over the new French invasion of the Rhineland, and the risk that France was taking of dragging Europe into another war.

There had recently been an attempted revolt of German reactionaries, known as the "Kapp Putsch." It had been put down by a general strike of the German workers, and there had followed a Communist revolt in the Ruhr, and the Socialist government of Germany had sent in troops to put that down. The move was a technical violation of the treaty of Versailles, and the French army had promptly seized a couple of German towns on the far side of the Rhine. Were they going to conquer their ancient enemy all over again, and were they expecting to get British sanction? This was the question these budding diplomats discussed with solemn faces. They told of the firm resolve of their chiefs that the French must be made to back down, and allow trade to be resumed and the German people to be saved from starvation and chaos.

To Lanny it seemed an odd thing to hear these official persons saying the very things for which the liberals on the American staff had been called "Pinkos" and troublemakers. So rapidly had opinion changed under the pressure of events! The British were now giving all their efforts to trying to get blockades lifted and trade started. But the French still lived under the shadow of a dreadful fear. Was German militarism to be allowed to come back? And if it did, would France again have Britain's help? With the French it was dominate or be dominated—and the moment they took to dominating, the British would begin giving help to the Germans, raising them up as a counter-force to France. As Robbie Budd had told his son repeatedly, it was dog eat dog all over Europe; and when Lanny had watched it for a while, he wanted to go back to Bienvenu and play the piano!

V

Fessenden said: "You must meet Mrs. Plumer; that's where everybody goes." This was a member of the English colony who had a beautiful villa up on the Berigo Road. Wherever the English live they have places like that, to which you can go if you have a proper introduction. Also there is always an English club, where the men drink whiskies and soda, and play billiards, and talk about the stock market, trade, and politics, in a language that you have to be brought up on to understand. Lanny and Rick were invited to tea by Mrs. Plumer, and received guest-cards at the club, and so they heard what had been said that day in the council chamber at the Villa Devachan. Rick exclaimed to his friend: "If it hadn't been for you, Lanny, I'd have been a fish tossed up on dry land!"

"I'm getting my share of fun," replied Lanny. "Only don't try to do too much in one day." There was a ceaseless round of activities, all day and most of the night, and it was hard for a man with a steel leg to get in and out of cars and up flights of stairs. Lanny would persuade him to come back to the hotel in the afternoon for a siesta. Even at the end of April it was hot in this sun-bowl of San Remo.

While Rick lay propped up on the bed making notes of what he had heard, Lanny would go out and wander through the narrow streets where old pirates from Africa had charged up the hills, slaughtering the inhabitants or dragging them off in chains. He strolled on paths shaded by palm trees, or by pepper trees loaded with white blossoms. He climbed to the heights where the wild flowers spread sheets of purple, gold, and pink. He gazed down onto red-roofed houses, and the blue and green sea which each and every Mediterranean people claims as its own. *Mare nostrum*—how many had made the boast through the ages, and their blood had been drained into the sea and their dust blown over the hills, and the very names of their tribes were lost to history!

Lanny always had the fancy to know what the plain people were thinking and saying, as well as the great and important ones who made the headlines. He and Rick would attend a session of the journalists in which the new Italian Premier would expatiate on the dire need of his people for coal and wheat, and the necessity of reopening trade with the Russians through their Black Sea ports. From there Lanny would drive his friend to a *trattoria* on an obscure street where most of the conversation was in the Ligurian dialect. Lanny knew some of it, just as he knew Provençal, because in his childhood he had played with the fisherfolk, many of whom had dwelt on the Côte d'Azur since it had been a part of Italy. For a couple of lire you could have a good meal in this *trattoria*—though served on a plain board table set on a floor strewn with sawdust. Lanny would start jabbering away, half in French, half in Italian, with a dark-skinned workingman in a sweaty shirt, and would report to Rick how the declarations of the liberal Francesco Nitti sounded to the dwellers in musty old tenements with cracked walls and the darkness of caves inside.

What they learned was that the workers of Italy were in a dangerous ferment. They despised and distrusted their political leaders, calling them cheats and liars, hired agents of the capitalist class. These *cattivi* had dragged their country into a war to no purpose, and now they left the people to starve while they stuffed themselves with rich foods and fine wines. Here in San Remo the workers had elected a Socialist mayor, and what was he? A banker! And what did he do? The gesture of the angry dock-laborer imperiled the glassware on the table.

It might have been difficult for a stiff young Englishman, brought up in the public school tradition, to get into the confidence of such a person; but Lanny made it easy for him. He bought an extra bottle, and when others perceived that free wine and free conversation were available, they moved over to listen and take part. Horny dark fists were clenched and raucous voices proclaimed that a change was coming in Italy, and soon; what the workers had done in Russia was not so bad as *le gazzette capitaliste* had made it seem. Already many of the factories in Milan and Turin and other cities were in the hands of the workers, who would be running them for themselves and not for the *padroni*.

VI

When this piece of research had been completed and Lanny and Rick were on their way to the hotel, Rick said: "I've an idea there's another story in Italy: the spread of Socialism."

"Let's go after it," said his friend.

"It's wonderful the way you can understand these people, Lanny."

"When I was a kid I used to haul the seine with fisherboys who talked this dialect, and one would take me to his cabin where his mother would feed us on dandelion salad and shrimp fried in oil. They always thought it was funny if anybody didn't know their words."

"It would be difficult to do anything like that in Berkshire," commented Rick. "But if I'm going to be a journalist I'll have to learn. After I get the San Remo article off I want to do one on the state of mind of Italian labor. Let's eat in places like that from now on."

"The food agrees with me," said Lanny.

They dined in a somewhat better place, frequented by intellectuals as well as workers. They watched the various types and Lanny speculated: this one might be a teacher at the *accademia*, and that one a musician in the orchestra of the Teatro Principe Umberto; a third might be the editor of the local labor paper. Rick asked: Could that large gentleman with the black beard and pince-nez be the Socialist mayor? "No," said Lanny, "he'd have come here when he was campaigning, but he'd be too important now. Which one would you like to talk to?"

"Can you just go up and talk to anybody in the place?"

"Italians are always ready for conversation. They will take us for tourists."

"But they're angry with Americans right now." Rick had been informed that on the previous day the city council of San Remo had voted to change the name of the Corso Wilson to the Corso Fiume —which was certainly a pointed gesture.

"They will tell us their grievances, of course," replied Lanny; "but they will talk."

Their attention was attracted to the table across the aisle, where several men were lingering over their coffee. Evidently it was a political discussion, and now and then a voice would be raised; they heard the word *Americani* more than once, and fell silent, listening.

At the head of the table, facing them, sat a dark-eyed Italian with a little black mustache; a smallish man with a pale, almost pasty face and melancholy expression when it was in repose. But now he was becoming excited, and waving his hands as he orated in a shrill, tense voice. "*Porca Madonna!*" Rick heard, and whispered to his friend: "What is *Porca Madonna?*"

"It is an oath," Lanny explained. "It is meant to be very offensive. It means that the Holy Virgin is a sow." He listened again and added: "They are talking about Italy, and the way it has been robbed by the Allies. That dark fellow is telling the filthy English bastards that the Italians are going to stay in Fiume, and if Nitti dares to yield it, they will cut his throat on the steps of the Villa Devachan."

"There's nothing for us in that lot," said Rick, hastily.

VII

The door of the *trattoria* opened and two persons came in, a man and a woman. It happened that Lanny was facing the door, and as the woman came up the aisle between the tables he had a good look at her. She was frail and gray-haired, with fine, ascetic features, and it struck him instantly that he had seen the face before. He tried to think where.

The pair were close to him when the woman's escort noticed the orator seated at the table. He stopped, turned toward the man, raised his clenched hand, and cried in a fury: "*Eh via, puh! Furfante! Traditore dei lavoratori!*"

Instantly the place was in an uproar. The insulted one leaped to his feet—whether it was to fight or to run Lanny couldn't know, for others on each side sprang up to restrain him. He began to yell curses at the invader, and the latter shouted back. The woman, greatly troubled, seized her escort's arm and began pleading with him: "*No, no, compagno!* Restrain yourself. The wretch is not worth it!"

"I will not eat with that *porco!*" exclaimed the man.

"*Su! Via!*" cried the woman. "Let us go." Amid jeers from those at the table the disturber let himself be persuaded to the door and outside.

The excitement was slow in subsiding. The diners talked volubly about what had been said and by whom. The dark-eyed man with the little black mustache considered that he had played the hero; he shook his fist and became inspired, telling what he would have done to the accursed one, the enemy of *la patria*. Working himself into a warlike mood, he challenged the enemies of Italy to come from all quarters of the earth and he would deal with them single-handed. It is the nature of Italians to say a lot about what they intend to do, and it is the nature of Englishmen to look upon them with an aloof expression which seems to say: "What unpleasant insects!" Lanny was amused by both types.

He explained to his friend that it was a political dispute; the new arrival had called the orator a traitor and betrayer of the working class. Probably this orator had belonged to the extreme left, but had become patriotic during the war; it was a common happening.

"I've been trying to remember where I've seen that woman," Lanny remarked; "and now it comes to me. You remember I told you I had an uncle who is a Red; and once when I was young he took me on a slumming trip—we called on a friend of his in a tenement in Cannes, and it was this woman. Her name is Barbara—I have forgotten the second name. My father was angry and made a fuss, and I had to promise that I would have nothing more to do with my Uncle Jesse."

"Would your father feel that way now?" asked Rick.

"Indeed he would; the day the treaty was signed my father and my uncle had a frightful row. Robbie has a regular phobia on the subject of the Reds and what they might do to me. You know they have a lot of facts on their side, and they are damned clever at making use of them."

"Listen, Lanny; I don't want you to do anything you shouldn't, but it might be a rare good thing for me to have a talk with that woman. She could tell me everything I need; and there's what you call local color, human interest—I'd get the feel of the people from her."

Lanny was taken aback. "I suppose—if it's a professional matter—" He stopped, and a grin came on his face. "That's exactly the way it happened at the Peace Conference. I had to go and see my uncle, because Colonel House wanted to get in touch with the Bolshevik agents!"

Rick laughed in turn. "But after all, Lanny, you're going to live in a different world from your father. You'll have to believe what you believe and not what he tells you."

Lanny saw that his friend was in earnest about the woman, so he said: "I wonder if we could find her."

"They'll be looking for a place to get a meal. They probably won't go far."

"All right. You sit here and finish your dinner, and I'll scout around and see if I can spot them."

VIII

It proved an easy assignment. In the third place Lanny looked he saw the pair seated at a table. As they were eating, he did not disturb them, but went back and fetched Rick, and the two of them approached the table together. "I wonder if you remember me, Signora," said Lanny, in French, which he knew the woman spoke. "You are, I believe, a friend of my uncle, Jesse Blackless."

"Oh, of course!" she exclaimed. She rose up and looked at Lanny's smiling features, and remembered. "You are that little boy who came to see me in Cannes!"

"No longer so little," he replied. "I have never forgotten you. Your name is Barbara—" He had expected to stop, but at exactly the right instant the other name popped into his mind. "Pugliese," he said—pronouncing it in the Italian manner, "Pool-yay-say."

"You have a remarkable memory!" she testified.

"You were sick when I saw you. I am glad that you appear to be better."

"We poor are hard to kill. We have to be."

"You made a great impression upon me, Signora. I thought you had the most saintly face I had ever seen. But perhaps you would not like to be described in that way."

The woman was amused, and translated the remark to her friend, whose French was apparently not so good.

"My name is Lanny Budd, and this is my friend, an English flier who was wounded in the war. He has a long English name which is hard to spell or to remember, so pretend that he is another little boy and call him Rick."

"I will do that if you will call me Barbara. Your uncle is a man for whom I have a high regard. He stands by his convictions. Where is he now?"

"I believe at his home, near Saint-Tropez. You know that he paints pictures when he is not rebelling."

Barbara smiled. Her face was sad and could be very stern, but it was lighted by intelligence and kindness, and Lanny the young man confirmed what Lanny the lad had judged, that she was a rare and good person in spite of her evil reputation.

She introduced her companion by the name of Giulio, and all four seated themselves. Rick ordered coffee, and Lanny ordered the tail end of a dinner. Now and then the two would exchange a glance, and Lanny knew that a member of the English ruling classes was getting a thrill out of addressing two dangerous Italian Reds by their first names. Now indeed he was a journalist, getting local color in great splashes!

Lanny mentioned that they had been witnesses of the recent fracas, and Barbara's face lost all its gentleness. "That is the most abominable little wretch that I have met upon this earth!" she told them. "When I first knew him in Milan, where I was an official of the party, he was a poor waif who came to meetings, a sick beggar who haunted our headquarters to sponge upon the kindness of members. Now and then someone would give him food—just because it

is impossible to eat with any satisfaction while a starving dog is
cringing by the table. You cannot imagine the misery of this ragged
and homeless one, lamenting the hopelessness of his fate, the worth-
lessness of himself, the pains he suffered from syphilis—this, I imagine, would not be considered quite good taste in England?"

"Rather not," said Rick, to whom the question was addressed.

"We of the party of course have to allow for the degradation of
the workers. It is our duty to lift them up and teach them, and so
we aided this poor Benito—the name is Spanish and means 'Blessed
One' and is freely bestowed by pious mothers. So we taught the
favorite of heaven the philosophy of brotherhood and solidarity,
and he proved to be quick at learning phrases and using them in
speeches. It was not long before he was addressing the workers,
denouncing all capitalists and clamoring that their throats should be
cut. There was only one person in the world to whom he could not
give courage, and that was his mournful self. There is a pun I used
to make upon his name, which is Mussolini. I would leave out one
of the *s*'s. The Italian word *muso* means—I cannot recall the French
word, but it is when a child has his feelings hurt, and he will not
play, but makes a face very ugly——"

"*Boudant*," supplied Lanny, and added for Rick's benefit:
"Pouting."

"That is it," said Barbara. "And so Benito Musolini means Blessed
Little Pouter. In that way I would try to tease him out of his self-
pity—and you see how in the end I succeeded. His poor thin cheeks
have filled out, he wears well-tailored clothes and orates in the
trattorie."

"How does he manage this?" inquired Rick, thinking of his
"human interest."

"He became the editor of the Socialist paper in Milan; and when
the British agents or French came to him he took their gold. The
paper changed its tone overnight; and when the party kicked him
out, he got more gold to start a paper of his own and to denounce
his former comrades as traitors to *la patria*. Now he is here getting
material for articles about the conference. He is all for the *sacro
egoismo;* he preaches to the starving workers the glory of holding

Fiume and seizing the Dalmatian coast, and that it is their sublime destiny to help fill a sea of blood upon which the Italian navy may sail to world empire. Never has there been such a transformation in a man—you should see him on the platform, how he has learned to thrust out his chin and swell up his chest—our Blessed Little Pouter."

"You are making a better pun than you know," put in Lanny. "There is a kind of pigeon which swells up its chest in such a way, and by a strange chance is called a pouter."

The woman was delighted, and told her friend about it—*uno colombo!* He laughed with glee, and learned to say it in English— Benito Musolini—Blessed Little Pouter Pigeon!

IX

Rick questioned his new acquaintance about the state of mind of the Italian workers, and she described the tragic years of slaughter and semi-famine. For her the war had been a struggle of rival imperialisms, and as always the people had paid for it with their blood and tears. But now they had learned their lesson, and soon were going to take affairs into their own hands.

"You don't think the war-mongers can mislead them?" asked Rick, by way of drawing her out.

"*Mai più!*" exclaimed Barbara. "Our people are disciplined; they have their labor unions, their great co-operatives, their presses, their schools for the children. They are class-conscious and mentally armed."

"Yes, but are they armed with weapons?"

"The soldiers are of the people; would they turn their guns upon their own? You see that already the workers have seized many factories and are holding them."

"But can they run them?"

"Our great weakness in Italy is that we have no coal; we are dependent upon your British capitalists, who will not give credit to revolutionary workers. But the Russian workers are digging coal, and soon it will be coming to us. That is why trade through the Black Sea is so vital to us."

"I see that Nitti has come out for the lifting of the blockade."

"Nitti is a politician, a twin brother to your Lloyd George. He makes bold speeches, but what he is doing behind the locked doors of the council chamber is another matter."

"You don't think he means it, then?"

"The Socialists have just shown him that they have the votes. If he does not wish to retire to private life, he must force the French to let us trade with our Russian comrades."

"You really believe," persisted the interviewer, "that labor unions can manage to run factories and produce goods?"

"Why can they not? Who is it that does the work today?"

"They do the manual work; but the directing——"

"Is done by technicians, hired by the capitalists. Why can they not be hired by the workers?"

They discussed the theories of syndicalism, or labor-union control of industry. Barbara hated every form of government; she would trust no politicians, whatever label they gave themselves. Rick pointed out that in Russia the workers had a strong government; syndicalism appeared to have merged with Bolshevism, which put everything into the hands of the state. Barbara attributed this to the civil war, which was really an invasion of Russia by the capitalist nations. Government control of industry might be a temporary necessity, but she didn't like it. Rick ventured the guess that if she were to go to Russia she mightn't find what she expected.

The woman rebel had one argument to which she would return. Could the workers make a worse mess of the world than their masters had done? Look at what they had made of Europe! One more such holocaust and the Continent would be a wilderness inhabited by savages wearing skins and hiding in caves. "Capitalism is war," declared Barbara Pugliese; "its peace is nothing but a truce. If once the workers own the tools of production, they do not produce for profit, but for their own use, and trade becomes free exchange and not a war for markets."

"I have to admit," said the interviewer, "that our British labor movement seems to have the sanest program at present." Lanny found that a startling opinion to come from a baronet's son. Was

Eric Vivian Pomeroy-Nielson turning into a Pink? And if he did, what would Robbie make of it?

<h1 style="text-align:center">X</h1>

The San Remo conference broke up at the end of ten days, and Rick had his article ready by that time. He had shut himself up in the stuffy hotel room while Lanny was out playing tennis with Fessenden and his friends, or inspecting a sixteenth-century palace and a votive chapel having wax images of portions of the human body which had been healed—including some not customarily exposed to public gaze. When Rick worked, he worked like one possessed, and Lanny read the manuscript page by page and kept his friend cheered by extravagant praises.

Really it was a first-class article, written by a man who had been behind the scenes and hadn't been fooled by official propaganda. Rick described the loveliness of the background of the conference; was it the region referred to by the hymn-writer, where "every prospect pleases, and only man is vile"? Here were flower-covered hills, roads lined with palm trees, hedges of roses and oleanders, cactus gardens and towering aloes; and here were elderly politicians whose minds were labyrinths full of snares for the feet of even their friends and allies. Rick cited official statements which had gone all over the earth and which were at a variance with facts. He showed how the old men used words to take the place of realities, until for their peace of mind they had to force themselves to believe their own propaganda.

The French wanted to weaken Germany, while the British wanted to raise Germany so that they could trade with her: that in one sentence was what all the conferring was about. They had effected a compromise by which they were going to do both at the same time. Privately they admitted that the Versailles treaty was unenforceable, but they solemnly told the world that it was not to be revised; they would "interpret" it—which was another word. They would bluff, and overlook the fact that no one heeded their bluffs. They had announced that they would not discuss the question of Russia, and the next day they proceeded to discuss it. They denounced Germany for not having delivered coal to France, but at the same time they pledged France to take no action about it. The French were helping to drive the Turks from Constantinople, but at the same time they were arming the Turks against the British; gun-running and smuggling were going on all along the Arabian coasts, and wherever else any traders saw a chance for profit.

The world had been told that it had a League of Nations, which was going to deal with all these problems. But what power had this League, asked Rick, and who cared to give it power? Instead of taking these issues before the League, the three premiers met in a locked chamber and settled them according to the interests of their three political parties. Such, it appeared, was to be the new government of Europe. They were to meet again at Spa, in Belgium, and the Germans were to be summoned to attend; the "Big Three" would again become the "Big Four." "*Absit omen!*" wrote Rick—for readers who had been educated in English public schools and therefore carried various tags of Latin in their heads.

Lanny couldn't find enough praise for this outspoken article, but it was hard indeed for him to believe that any editor would publish it. Rick said that was a chance he had to take; he would tell the truth, and if the editors couldn't face it, that was their readers' hard luck. "I suppose some leftist sheet would print it," he added; "but they probably can't pay."

The precious document was entrusted to the post, and after saying good-by to the friends they had made, Lanny and Rick motored back to Juan. A couple of days later they read in their newspaper that Lloyd George had returned to England and made a speech in Parliament reporting the outcome of the conference. Rick read it aloud, punctuating it with such words as "tommyrot," "bilge," and "hot air." Everything was lovely, harmony ruled in the hearts of all the Allies, and the British public might rest assured that nothing could weaken the solidarity of the victors in the late conflict. Germany was being disarmed and, in spite of all her subterfuges, this necessary work would be continued. "Airplanes we will get," declared the rosy-faced cherub with the snow-white mop of hair. "We cannot allow these terrific weapons of war to be left lying about in Germany, with nobody in authority to see to them."

"I can tell him he had jolly well better not!" commented the young Englishman, who had been up in the air so many times and had looked down upon the puny works of man from a height of ten thousand feet.

BOOK TWO

Someone Whom I Could Court

6

A Sweet Unrest

I

LANNY came home somewhat bored with statesmen, and resolved to devote his attention to a strictly private matter. He found
a letter which he opened with great eagerness. It said:

> DEAR LANNY:
> I have to be with my little son. I hope that you and Rick have
> been having a pleasant holiday, and that his effort will succeed.
> I have given a good deal of thought to your project of market-
> ing the pictures. I approve of it, and hope that later on I may be
> able to give you assistance. In the meantime, believe me, with all
> good wishes,
> MARIE.

Lanny didn't have to puzzle over that. He had told her that some
day he had planned to have Marcel's paintings put on the market; he
hadn't asked for her help, of course, but she had thought of this as a
camouflage which he would not fail to understand. Her fears were
very real to her; he wondered if they would ever permit her to be
happy.

She had given her address, and he wrote a note like her own, carefully guarded. The project for marketing the pictures was in his
thoughts continually, he said. He looked forward to having her advice, for he trusted her judgment about art more than that of any
other person. He hoped that her patient was improving. He posted
this, and tried to put his mind on piano practice, but found it far
from easy. All music now turned into Marie; when it danced he was
dancing with her, when it was sad he was sad about her, and when
it ceased, he was alone, and restless and discontented.

He took to wandering about at night, brooding over the problem of their love and what they were going to do with it. Beauty, watching her darling anxiously, sought to break into his confidence, and he could not very well exclude her. As usual, it was a relief to share his troubles, and he told what little his friend had imparted about herself and her husband. Under Beauty's relentless questioning he repeated talks with Marie, and from these his mother was able to comprehend the basis of this unfortunate entanglement. Lanny had always been a precocious child; he had always had ideas beyond his age—and so now he was bored by young girls and wanted a mature woman. Love to him didn't mean moonlight and roses, it meant what he called "conversation."

It was hard to gain understanding of a woman through the mind of a youth who didn't understand her very well himself. But Beauty kept on trying, for love was her field, and her curiosity was inexhaustible. It was hard for her to accept the simple explanation that Marie de Bruyne was virtuous; it was easier for Beauty to believe that every woman had some carefully concealed purpose. Did it please her vanity to keep a handsome and attractive youth dancing attendance? Or was she perhaps trying to control her husband by giving him cause for jealousy? Or could it be that she was an intriguer, and already had another lover? Such surmises the mother kept to herself, but she tried tactfully to convey the fact that women of the world are rarely simple and straightforward; even the best of them have more than one purpose, more than one facet to their characters.

Meanwhile Beauty took her friend Emily Chattersworth into the secret. Emily carried a share of the responsibility, she being the one who had introduced a susceptible youth to this *femme fatale*. Emily knew Monsieur de Bruyne, having once been the object of his attentions, so she could throw light upon the problem; she described him as a man of sixty or more, sturdily built, decidedly good-looking, and strongly attractive to women. He had, she reported, "a roving eye": he picked out the best-looking woman in a company and you felt that he was undressing her in his fancy. It was a form of mental disease, and ought to have treatment by a psychiatrist; but it was difficult to suggest that to a gray-haired man of good family and standing. The marriage, Emily said, had been one of those French affairs, arranged by the family; sometimes they turned out well and sometimes badly—but of what marriage system could one say more?

II

There was a day of excitement in the Pomeroy-Nielson family when a letter came from the editor in London saying that he was publishing Rick's article in his next issue. "It is convincing and informative," he wrote, "and I believe will make an impression. If you can continue to write on international affairs with such insight, you should be able to make a reputation."

Rick insisted upon giving Lanny more than half the credit for this happy issue. He did the same for the second article, which he now had ready to post to the editor; that was made out of Compagna Barbara, and the dock-laborer, and others whose minds Lanny had pumped for his friend. Rick had made skillful use of his data, so that you would have thought he had been living for a long time among the laboring masses of Italy, sharing their political secrets. The writer didn't reveal his own convictions, but left his readers with the idea that statesmen and others in authority had better get food into the country without delay, unless they wished to see what they had already seen in Russia, Hungary, and Bavaria. In due course the editor wrote that he liked this article also. He paid ten pounds for each, and Rick was as proud of these checks as Lanny had been of his first earnings.

This happy outcome gave the American a fresh understanding of the English people and their peculiar ways. It just hadn't seemed possible to him that an English magazine would publish such an indictment of English policy and procedure. That they paid for it, and held out the promise of a career to the man who wrote it, was something to be graven in one's memory. You might paint the crimes of the British Empire as black as you pleased, but you would never say anything worse than Britons themselves would be printing and proclaiming in public meetings; and little by little the opinions of that "saving remnant," the agitation which they maintained, would penetrate the case-hardened minds of elder statesmen, and British policy would be brought into line with the conscience of humanity. Watching Rick's budding career and helping him in various ways, Lanny once more began to take an interest in world affairs, and to descend more frequently from his ivory tower.

Hot weather came, and Rick and his little family were planning to return to their home. Rick wrote to his editor suggesting that on the way he might take in the conference at Spa, in Belgium, near the German border. The gathering would be of importance, because it represented the beginning of consultation between the Allies and their former foes. The editor agreed to reserve this topic for Rick, and again Lanny volunteered to act as chauffeur and cicerone. It fitted in very well with certain purposes of his own, he said. They got out their maps and planned a motor-tour, in the course of which Nina and the baby would be delivered to the Channel ferry at Calais, and then Rick would be set down in Spa and introduced to diplomats and journalists. After that Lanny would take the wings of a dove and fly away to be at rest in Seine-et-Oise, a district immediately west of Paris which happily had escaped the ravages of war. He wrote to his lady-love to say that he was going to be in her neighborhood, and would bring in his car some of the art-works concerning which he hoped to have her sage counsel.

III

The little town of Spa is in the Belgian Ardennes, and has mineral springs from which seven centuries of invalids have believed that they derived mysterious benefits. It is a forest and hill resort which has horse-racing and pigeon-shooting, and a casino with plenty of gambling; also a number of hotels suitable for three elderly gentlemen who had constituted themselves the government of Europe. Comfort is important to persons of advancing years, so in the winter season their assemblies would be scheduled for the Riviera, and in the summer's heat at some agreeable retreat in the north. Hopeful crowds would cheer their progress from one land to another, and a

swarm of newspaper men would follow and gather up such crumbs
of news as fell from their council tables.

A new stage of world reconstruction was beginning at this ancient
center of healing, for here came representatives of the new Socialist
government of Germany. It must be admitted that they looked much
like the old-time Prussians, and from their buccal cavities emerged
the same guttural sounds; but they were speaking for a republic,
and declaring their desire to serve the whole German people, not
just a military caste. They expected no cordiality, and their expectations were fulfilled; but at least they were not penned up behind
barbed wire as the German peace delegation in Paris had been.
Liberal-minded persons hoped that by tactful conduct they might
succeed in appeasing their former foes and so gradually bring back
the days of the "good Europeans." The meetings of the conference
took place in the large white villa which had been the Kaiser's headquarters during the war.

Lanny and Rick found most of the American reporters whom
they had met in San Remo. Several had read Rick's articles, so he
was now a personality, a member of the fraternity. They talked to
him freely, because his deadline came so long after theirs. Fessenden
and his friends were here, and also there was an English colony and
an English club; so Rick's way was made smooth. He and his friend
discovered that the healing springs which bubbled forth from those
Belgian hills found no counterpart in the hearts of the conferring
diplomats; from them came poisonous fumes of greed and hate and
fear. Lanny made this remark, and straightway his friend reached
for the wad of copy paper which he kept in his pocket. Lanny in
turn made note of the psychology of the professional writer, a man
with a split personality; one half of his mind thinks clearly and feels
keenly, while the other half keeps watch for "copy."

The most urgent question which troubled the gathering was the
delayed deliveries of coal from the Ruhr. The Germans having wantonly destroyed the French mines, somebody had to go without
coal; and was it going to be the innocent French or the guilty Germans? In vain the delegates from the new republic pleaded that if
they could not get their factories going they could not meet the

reparations demands. The French wanted to start their own industries, so that they could regain their share of world trade, and they
were embarrassed by the idea of having German goods coming into
France, even though it might be to pay war-debts. There was a
peculiar quirk in this situation, which was explained to Rick by an
English economist on his country's staff. Germany couldn't pay
with gold because there wasn't enough in the world, and she couldn't
pay with goods without ruining French industry and throwing
French workers onto the scrap-heap. Yet the political lives of both
French and British statesmen rested upon their willingness to go on
repeating day and night: "The Germans shall pay to the last sou!"—
or "to the last farthing!" as the case might be.

Rick, in his capacity of "liberal," wanted to hear what the Germans had to say; and this was not difficult, as there was a large
delegation on hand, all eager to talk to journalists. A large and
florid member of the Berlin city council talked vehemently to the
two young men about the effects of the starvation blockade, but unfortunately he was not a convincing illustration of his own argument.
The main grievance was that the Allies could not be persuaded to
fix the amount of the indemnities, and thus the Germans could not
know where they stood in any business affairs. Rick was prepared
to concede that, but the official answerer of questions went on to
contend that the treaty of Versailles was so bad that it justified the
Germans in refusing to comply with any of the terms that did not
seem fair to them. The young Englishman's patience gave out, and
he asked: "What do you want the Allies to do—fight the war over
again?" It seemed to Lanny that the method of "conference" didn't
always work as the liberals expected!

IV

Another subject which was causing embittered controversy was
the failure of the Germans to surrender war materials to the Allies
as the treaty had provided. Concerning this there could be no argument—at least from the Allies' point of view. Unless the war was to
be fought over again, for what did Germany need heavy guns and

bombing planes? In vain would suave confidential agents whisper into the ears of Allied staff members that German armies might be needed to put down the subhuman Bolshevist conspiracy that was establishing itself in eastern Europe. The French wanted this done, but by their own allies, the Poles and other border peoples; they wouldn't let any Russian territories be occupied by Germans—their *cordon sanitaire* was double-fronted, to keep Germans from going east as well as to keep Russians from coming west.

Lanny and Rick got an inside view of this special problem of German disarmament when they ran into a British officer, that Captain Finchley who had been Rick's superior in training-camp, and whom Lanny had met at the War Planes Review on Salisbury Plain a few days before the outbreak of war. He was glad to see them both, and interested to talk about the strange duty which had been his for the past year and a half—going into a hostile land to supervise the exportation of surrendered implements of slaughter. Captain Finchley was here to report to the Allied staffs concerning the progress of his labors; to tell them, among other things, that he had counted four hundred and seventy-three million cartridges and thirty-eight million seven hundred and fifty thousand shrapnel shells!

Such astronomical figures gave Lanny a depressing sense of the hopelessness of his father's future as a salesman of arms in Europe. How long would it take to shoot off that much ammunition? he asked, and the captain, who had had dealings with Robbie Budd and knew him well, replied cheerfully: "Don't worry! They'll be used in the end. They're for sale cheap, and some poor blighters will kill some other poor blighters with them."

"Who, for example?" inquired the youth.

"Chinese war lords are buying them to fight their rivals. South American revolutionists are using them against their governments. Traders are smuggling them in to the Bolsheviks, while the French are supplying them to the Poles to fight the Bolsheviks. The French are selling them to the Turks to fight us with, and I suppose our traders are selling them to the Arabs to fight the French with."

It all sounded rather shocking, but you couldn't blame a British army officer. He had his hands full unearthing secret hiding-places of the wily Germans and forcing them to load their own weapons into freight-cars; it was no good expecting him to travel over the earth and follow those arms to their final destinations. The British Empire was run under an ancient and honorable system known as "free trade," and anybody who had money had the right to buy arms and load them onto a ship and disappear from the ken of governments.

V

After several days of research Rick said: "I'm all right now, Lanny; and I can see that you are 'r'arin' to go.'" One read American slang in the movie "subtitles," and one adopted it.

"But how will you manage to get about, Rick?"

"I'll take a *fiacre* if it's far. I'll work it out."

So Lanny put his bags into his car and set out for Paris. The route took him through the very heart of the war zone, about which he had been reading and hearing countless times; but nothing could equal the actual sight—and the smell, which now, twenty months after the Armistice, still hung over those regions of horror. Forests were represented by a few shattered treetrunks thrusting to the sky, often with a raven or a buzzard on top. Villages once populous were represented by a smoke-blackened wall with a gaping hole that had been a window. Trenches were slowly collapsing, and with them the empty tins and the rags and bones that had once been soldiers wearing uniforms and eating meals. Shell craters still made one think of a land that had had smallpox; also, it seemed now to have vermin in the shape of parties of tourists parked by the roadside and poking among the ruins.

One crossed the vast series of trenches and entanglements which had been the Hindenburg line, and from there on the signs of damage grew fewer, the work of repair less hopeless. So he came to the Château Les Forêts, the summer home of Emily Chattersworth, where the "Huns" had had only a few days, and American money had put great numbers of men to work removing the evidence of their ravages. The dead bodies of a German division had been buried in the beech forests which Lanny had explored as a lad, and patient care was restoring the beautiful green lawns on which he had listened to Anatole France relating the sins of old-time kings and queens.

He spent the night here, and, sitting in the spacious drawing-room from which the valuable paintings and tapestries had been stolen, his good friend revealed to him that she was a sharer in the secret of this motor-tour. She was a wise woman, and in the course of more than twenty years had learned a lot about the ways of Europe; she told Lanny about Frenchwomen, the intense passions which animate them and the rigid conventions which bind them. Do not expect them to depart too far from those conventions and retain any happiness, for we are what social forces have made us, and we are not able to shed our skins like snakes and lizards. *Garde à vous*, Lanny Budd!—for when you venture into a woman's heart you are taking a long journey, and if you think you can retrace your steps, you may find that thorny barricades have sprung up behind you.

However, the experienced Mrs. Emily did not try to dissuade him from his enterprise. She understood his liking for older women, and it was not to be supposed that he would lead a celibate life on the Riviera, or anywhere else on the continent of Europe, unless he was in a monastery with heavy stone walls and iron gates. She told him what she knew about the woman of his choice, and about the man who was to become his associate in *la vie à trois*. Denis de Bruyne, owner of a large fleet of taxicabs and other business enterprises, would probably accept the situation when he learned about it, but that was a matter concerning which you could never be sure. The male animal under the influence of sexual jealousy is dangerous and unpredictable, whether he be the laboring brute in the slums or the master of money accustomed to commanding what he wants. Emily Chattersworth, who had lived among the masters in Newport and New York as well as in Paris and on the Coast of Pleasure, could tell strange tales of things she had seen and heard; she told them to her young friend, not sparing him, because he was stepping out on an uncharted path, and treasons, stratagems, and spoils might be his portion from the next day on.

VI

Lanny Budd was motoring on one of the smooth straight highways of France, in the pleasant mildness of a July morning, with a light haze tempering the glare of the sun and lending the landscape shades of pastel. Making a circle to the north of Paris to avoid the traffic, he was presently in the Seine-et-Oise country, a kind of rarefied suburb of a great city, with small fruit and vegetable farms mixed with villas and country residences of the well-to-do and medium classes. A gentle, pleasant land, which had known peace for generations; a land in which the old and the new are oddly mixed— an old church with dwellings huddled against it, as if seeking protection from a modern motor-road which has cut off one corner; a land of comfort and leisure, where even the rivers have time to meander, to make playful eddies and ripples as they slide past gardens with willow trees bending down to the water, and villas and summer cottages with tiny landing-piers for rowboats, and here and there a man or a boy sitting with a fishing-pole. A tantalizing dream haunts the souls of men and boys in rural France, and apparently they never lose it, but will sit for hours in a gentle glow of expectancy; if once the dream should happen to come true, they would rush home in excitement and mark a red circle around the date on a calendar: *Un poisson!*

Lanny had a different kind of hope, no less important to him. His heart was high, and each feature of the ever-varying landscape would suggest lines out of the poetry books he had learned pretty nearly by heart. Each stream might flow past her door, each villa might resemble hers, each walled garden—surely she would have a walled garden, with old pear and apricot trees trained against it, their fruits in the hot sunshine performing their quiet miracle. Now she would be walking in the garden, waiting for his call; his thoughts reached out to her in happy songs. There had fallen a splendid tear from the passion-flower at the gate; she was coming, his dove, his dear; she was coming, his life, his fate!

He arrived at the village which she had given as her postoffice address. Not wishing to attract attention he did not stop, but drove about slowly, observing the landscape, the direction of the roads, the names of inns and other landmarks. He couldn't expect to have the good fortune to meet her on the highway, nor could he recognize her home by some telepathic sense; but he had a plan, and it seemed romantic to him. *L'Enlèvement au Sérail*—he thought of Mozart's opera by its French title, and the gay music came tripping through his head. He would sing her some of it—he would be Belmonte, the dare-devil rescuer.

When he had the map of the region in mind he drove to a neighboring village and found a telephone. He called her number, and when a servant answered he asked for "Madame"—no name for any listening ears! When he heard her voice he spoke in a businesslike tone: "Madame, I have come to show you those pictures of which I wrote you."

She was not one to make any blunder. In a tone as matter-of-fact as his own she replied: "I shall be interested to see them. Where can we arrange it?"

"I am at your service, Madame. I have them in my car."

"I was about to go for a walk," she said—a very quick mind! "You might pick me up and take me to the village."

"Be so kind as to indicate the place, Madame."

"You know where the Quatre Chats is?" It was a little inn with a gay sign in the modern fashion; he had marked it, and she said: "A road runs west from there. I shall be on it shortly."

VII

He saw her coming, wearing a dark blue summer dress, and a sun-hat, as if she had been working in the garden. Blue dresses would have magic from that day on! Every motion of her slender figure pleased him; her whole personality radiated those qualities which he most esteemed. When she was nearer, he saw that excitement—or was it the walk?—had brought a glow to her cheeks; her step had a spring—the magic was working in her also. *Glücklich allein ist die Seele die liebt!*

He started his engine and turned the car about, and when she came to him, in she stepped and away they went. *L'Enlèvement au Sérail!*

He made no move to embrace her, or even to touch her hand. He whispered: "Darling!" It was enough.

"Where are you going, Lanny?" she asked.

"Whichever way there will be least chance of your being noticed."

"The first turn to the right," she said. He took it and found himself on a country road, following the bank of a small stream. Trees shaded it, and houses were few.

"Now, dear," he said, "listen to me. I have waited three months, and it seems as many years. I· have had time to think it over, and to know that I love you. I love you with body, mind, and soul. I have no doubt about it, and no fears of anybody or anything. I have come to tell you that, and to claim you. It all depends on one answer to one question. Do you love *me?*"

"Yes, Lanny."

"Do you love as I have just told you I love you?"

"Yes, Lanny; but——"

"Answer me some more questions. Are the boys reasonably well?"

"Yes."

"Who is in charge of them?"

"A governess."

"Where are they now?"

"They have gone fishing with her."

"Delightful!" he said. "Perhaps I saw them. Where is your husband?"

"In Paris."

"When do you expect him home?"

"He has no regular times."

"Then you need have none. This is what I propose: we drive over the roads of *la belle France.* When the time comes so that mademoiselle the governess will have returned to the house, you telephone her and inform her that you have received word of a woman friend who is ill, and that you have gone to her; you will write or telephone later. Then we continue to drive over the long roads of *la belle France* and see the country of which it is never possible to see too much. We will avoid all resorts and places where you might meet anyone you know; we will stay in country inns. We will have a week of happiness, and at the end there will be no possible way for anyone to find out where you have been."

"But, Lanny, that is mad!"

"I am mad, love is mad, and very soon you will be mad. But it will be a calculated madness, supervised by your wise mind and your honorable conscience. You have had time to think it over. You have a right to the joy I can give you, and I have a right to the joy you can give me."

"But, Lanny, I have no things!" Her phrase was the French one, *articles de voyage.*

"*Articles?*" he repeated, laughing. "*Articles* are for sale in *boutiques* and *boutiques* are to be found in *villes*, large or small. I have taken the precaution to bring a little money with me, and some time before long we will prove that there exist in France a *robe de nuit*, and a *peigne* and a *brosse* and some *mouchoirs*, and a *portemanteau* to carry them in, and possibly even a small bottle of *rouge vinaigre*—though I think from the present appearance of your cheeks that you will not need it!"

VIII

She began a long expostulation, and he let her go through with it. He had a formula of ancient and well-established power: "*Je vous aime.*" He had learned that it is not wise to let an hour pass without saying it to a woman, and in times of stress such as this its spell is more effective if it is repeated every two minutes. He drove very slowly, following the curves of the road with one hand, while he laid the other upon hers and poured out his heart.

"Chérie, sooner or later we have to take the first step." He was speaking in French—*c'est le premier pas qui coûte.* "I do not believe that you have ever known what it is to be happy in love. I really believe that you have borne two children without knowing what love is. That happens to many women, and they have to be taught. Then everything becomes simple, all problems become solvable, because you are determined to solve them, whereas now you are not sure."

She brought up one problem after another, but he persisted in laying them aside. "All that will be simple, when you know what love is. This is our honeymoon, and it is our time for happiness; let yourself be happy, I entreat you. Tell me that you love me, and tell me nothing else."

"You are trying to sweep me off my feet, Lanny!" Her voice had grown faint.

"Of course, dear! That is exactly what I am doing. If I were trying to teach you to swim, I would have to get you into the water. You surely know that I am no seducer; I do not find my pleasure in deflowering virgins, or in breaking marital vows. I am offering you my faith; I am pledging everything that I have. I am carrying you away because I know there is no other way to do it, and because I know that before this night is over you will thank me. You will no longer have any doubts, but will set to work with me in a firm and sensible way to face our problem and remove the barriers from the path of our love."

"Oh, Lanny! Lanny darling!" She began to sob softly to herself, and he knew that that was all right, for love is frequently born amid tears.

The car rolled on, mile after mile, past the summer landscapes of France, and she did not demand that it turn back. Late in the afternoon she telephoned to her home and told mademoiselle what Lanny had suggested, adding many injunctions which he had not thought of. Another drive, and they stopped in a small town, where they found it possible to purchase all the *articles de voyage.* She wouldn't let him come into the shop with her, because she feared she couldn't hide her tumult of emotion, and was ashamed to appear as the lover of one who was young enough to be her son.

"Almost, but not quite!" smiled Lanny. "Perhaps in the South Seas, or some of those warm places where they begin unusually early!"

IX

They continued westward, into a land of flat plains and ditches lined with poplars, and under the shelter of darkness halted at a little tavern. A waiter in a red-and-white-striped coat escorted them with candles to two connecting chambers provided with a superfluity of curtains, and ancient carved oak beds in which at least ten generations of sturdy Normans had been begotten. The man brought them a well-cooked supper, and manifested no curiosity as to their affairs; tourists of all kinds motored through this land in summer, and his concern was to get the largest possible tip from each.

In this safe retreat Lanny carried out his promise to make Marie happy, and she left him no doubt that he had done so; she accepted him as her fate, and there would be no further need of persuasion. In the morning the waiter appeared as a *valet de chambre* to open the shutters and let in the morning sun and tell them the weather prospects; he brought their *déjeuner* while they were still in bed, and this carried a comforting reassurance of domesticity. God was in His heaven and all was right with the world. Perpetual blushes suffused the cheeks of Lanny's *amie,* and laughter bubbled forth from her so that he was reminded of the healing springs which he had recently left.

They headed west into Brittany; a land of granite rocks of all sizes, of which walls and pavements and houses are built; a land of oak forests which the people carve into balustrades, and huge *armoires,* and *sabots* which clatter on the pavements; a land of wind and fog and gray skies, pleasant enough in July. The peasant women wear stiff white caps and bulging skirts with white aprons; from their apple orchards they derive a bitter and deadly cider; and over the door of every home they put a little niche for their saint. Since the sea winds do not respect sanctity, the people cover the niches with a pane of glass, from which they have frequently to rub the salt. It is a sternly royalist land and has a lady patron in heaven.

The fugitives from the seraglio drove to Saint-Malo, which neither had ever visited before. They climbed streets like long stairways, so narrow that you could almost touch the house-walls on

both sides; they walked on a broad city wall, and gazed down on
crowded tall buildings and a harbor enclosed by craggy rocks and
speckled white by little boats having the oddest mainsails divided
horizontally into several sections. They were followed everywhere by
urchins begging ceaselessly for a "paynee," and if you gave them one
you did not get rid of them. Lanny said this was a feature of all Catholic
countries. Marie said: "Of others also!"

They spent the night, or rather part of it, in an old inn, built lop-
sided in the ancient fashion, and having beds in enclosed shelves.
They cut short their stay because of the painful discovery that a
tiny round flat insect is the world's most aggressive enemy of romance. Lanny said this too was to be expected in Catholic lands.
Evidently Sainte Anne did not approve of what they were doing, so
they left her domain in the small hours of the morning, brushed off
their troubles with laughter, and saw the dawn come up like thunder
on the broad estuary of the river Rance.

X

They headed south toward the region of the lower Loire; and
while they watched the landscapes they talked about each other.
Their minds were opened as well as their hearts, and they had all
things in common. She told him about her girlhood, which had been
a happy one. Her father had been an *avocat* in the city of Reims;
the Germans had swept over the place, and the mother had died during the war; the father was now living with an older daughter in
Paris. Marie had been educated in a convent; it had not been altogether successful, she remarked ruefully. Lanny expatiated upon the
evils of superstition, which he thought of as a black cloud shutting
off the sunlight of knowledge from the mind and the sunlight of
joy from the heart.

She plied him with questions about his own life. She could never
hear enough about this youth who had come, clad in shining armor,
to lead her out of her state of resignation. How did it happen that
·one who had not yet attained his majority should think and speak

so like a mature man? He explained the unusual opportunities he had enjoyed; his father had brought important people to their home, his mother had cultivated them, and an only child had listened and learned how the *grand monde* was run. Before him fashionable ladies had talked freely—never dreaming that he was understanding the dreadful things they said. Also there had been books; he had begun learning about the world from pictures before he could read. There had been travel all over Europe; he had visited country homes —he had been on a yacht cruise——

"Yes, Lanny," she said, "but other children of the rich are dragged about Europe, and it doesn't mean much to them. You learn everything, forget nothing, and yet contrive not to become conceited about your mind!"

"I've enjoyed thrills when older people marveled over some precocious remark of mine—something which I had heard one of them say a short time previously. But I have always found it more interesting to be learning new things; about you, for example, and about love, and whether I am going to be able to keep you happy, and not let you slide back into that slough of resignation."

"Darling!" she exclaimed. "I have moved on a thousand years— out of the old night of the race, the Dark Ages!"

"You won't go home and start remembering some of the prayers you learned, and worrying about your immortal soul on its way to hell?"

"If I say any prayers, Lanny, they will be to you. I think about our love and a warm glow spreads over my being; little bells start ringing, little shivers pass over me like moonlight on water. I'm afraid to go home, because I look so happy; I don't see how it will be possible to hide my secret."

"You will have to watch your diet like my mother," he told her. "One consequence of this happiness is that your metabolic rate will be increased."

"Now that is what I mean about your mind!" she exclaimed. "Where on earth did you obtain that item of information?"

"That is too easy!" he laughed. "Rick writes for an English weekly, and in the last issue I read an article by an English surgeon on the subject of the female organism. He says that woman is 'an appendage to the uterus.' "

"*Mon dieu!*" exclaimed Marie. "So that is what is the matter with me!"

X I

They were in the "château country." They rambled at will, and between embraces they inspected tremendous castles from three to ten centuries old. They were escorted through vaulted halls where mighty lords had feasted, and into underground dungeons where luckless wretches had been tortured with diabolical contrivances. They shuddered at the realization of what cruelty had been and might still be in the hearts of men. The woman exclaimed: "Oh, Lanny! Do you suppose there will ever be a time when love will prevail in the world? When shall we be able to trust one another?"

"I'm afraid it's still a long way off," he said. "The best we can do is to make for ourselves a little island of safety." He recited some lines from Matthew Arnold which had struck deep into his soul during the dreadful years of the war:

> Ah, love, let us be true
> To one another! for the world, which seems
> To lie before us like a land of dreams,
> So various, so beautiful, so new,
> Hath really neither joy, nor love, nor light,
> Nor certitude, nor peace, nor help for pain;
> And we are here as on a darkling plain
> Swept with confus'd alarms of struggle and flight,
> Where ignorant armies clash by night.

X I I

In between these grave reflections they discussed the problem of Denis de Bruyne, involuntary participant in their intimacy. Marie said that as soon as she returned to her home she would tell him, as an alternative to a divorce, she must have an understanding that she was free to live her own life. He would, of course, know this meant a lover; but she would refuse to discuss the matter, taking the position that her affairs were her own.

"Suppose he declines to agree?" asked Lanny.

"He won't, dear!"

"While we are by ourselves, and have time to talk frankly, we dare not fail to consider all possibilities. When we part, will you be writing me about the marketing of pictures?"

"No, Lanny; I am going to be free!"

"All right; but suppose your husband says a flat no?" Lanny had already discussed this practical question with Mrs. Emily. "He may have you watched, and get evidence against you, and so be in position to divorce you and take your children from you. What will your answer be?"

"I cannot face such a thought, Lanny!"

"I am trying to protect your happiness. My father has a competent lawyer in Paris. If I go to him, tell him the situation, and put up the necessary costs, we can get our evidence first and you will have something definite to reply to your husband."

"Oh, no, Lanny! That would not be according to my code. Denis is the father of my children, and I cannot believe that he would be capable of baseness! He has his weaknesses, but he has virtues too. I could not make the first move in such a conflict."

He made certain that her scruples were deeply based. She would have to be attacked before she would think of fighting back. "It will become a contest in continence," he said. "If he opposes you, you will have to prove that you can live a celibate life longer than he can."

"I believe that with your help I should win."

They left the matter there. He would go back to Juan at once, and she would write as soon as she had news. In September the boys would be going to school, and then she would come to stay with her aunt in Cannes.

"Will that proper old lady sanction our love?" he inquired.

"I believe she will when I explain it to her. Anyhow, I will come to you in September. Will you be able to wait that long?"

"I can wait as long as I have to; but that doesn't mean that I shall enjoy it."

"You will have to take what I can give, dear. I believe that everything will be easier when my husband has adjusted himself to the idea that women too have their needs. You know that I myself required some time to adjust myself to the idea."

"I have not forgotten that waiting," he smiled. "Tell me again—have I kept my promises?"

"You have filled the cup of my happiness brim-full. You have given me a new life, and the courage to live it."

More landscapes and old châteaux, as they worked their way eastward in the direction of her home. She wouldn't let him take her near it, but had him set her down on the outskirts of a town from which a public conveyance ran to her neighborhood. When the time had come for parting, she said:

"One thing I want you to have in mind, darling—and never forget it. The time will come when you will want to marry, and it would be wicked for you not to marry—some woman who can give you children, and be in your life to its end. I want you to know that when the time comes, I will step out of your way."

"Forget it, dear!" he commanded. "My bump of philoprogenitiveness seems to be poorly developed." He didn't know the French for this long word, but said it in English, and added: "You may be astonished once more by the extent of my learning, so let me explain. In that wonderful library accumulated by my great-great-uncle I stumbled upon a work on the science of phrenology, containing a chart of all the bumps on the human skull. I examined my own with great interest, and was pained to discover that I have flat surfaces and even hollows at those places where the most desirable qualities are to be found."

"I shall never give any credence to that so-called science," declared Marie de Bruyne, with emphasis.

7

Sweet, Sweet, O Pan!

I

SAFE at home in his ivory tower, Lanny waited, and in due course the promised letter arrived:

CHÉRI:

I have had the talk with my friend as planned, and I am happy to report that all is well. It is a strange story, which I shall have the pleasure of telling you some day. As you know, I have been bitter, and have kept my feelings locked in my heart. This, it seems, has not been without effect upon my friend. He has been remorseful, and was deeply affected by the news I brought him. It was a strange and touching scene. There are worlds within worlds inside the human heart, and one could spend a lifetime studying a single one. May I live to have that pleasure! Suffice it to say now that the future gives us no occasion for anxiety. My friend concedes my right to be happy. I concede his, but doubt if that will help him. This is a story of only indirect interest to you, so I will not go into details. Everything is as you would wish it to be, and the schedule agreed upon will be followed.

Your devoted Marie.

Lanny read this letter many times and studied its phrases. It told him what he needed to know, but with much reserve, and he saw that caution was deeply rooted in her nature. Was she afraid that her letters might be opened by some other person? He had told her of his frank talks with his mother; but all the same Marie would keep their love as something for the privacy of their chamber, and would never spread it on paper. Leave that for the poets and writers of romance!

123

He told Beauty the events of their honeymoon, and answered her long string of questions. She had something to do with their future happiness, and Lanny was determined to have a clear understanding with her. Marie de Bruyne was his choice, and was worthy of all honor; she was going to be received precisely as if there had been that fashionable wedding with flower-laden bridesmaids. What he said was: "I ask you to treat her as I treated Marcel." A difficult stroke to parry! The mother could only answer, feebly: "If she is as good to you as Marcel was to me, Lanny."

"I let you be the judge in the case of Marcel, and now it is my turn to be the judge. So long as she makes me happy, my mother has to be grateful to her and receive her as a daughter."

"Or as a sister, Lanny?" Beauty couldn't resist the temptation. Claws have been given to cats for use, and they retract them only with reluctance. Lanny decided right then that the main headquarters of his romance had best be located in the home of the Sorbonne professor's widow.

With Marie's permission he went over to call on the old lady, who occupied her cottage the year round, as persons in modest circumstances have to do. Lanny sat down with her and told the story of his heart; he made love to Marie *in absentia*, by proxy, and the desert sprang into bloom, the birds sang in the garden of an elderly widow's heart. Madame Scelles was a most respectable old lady, but she was a French old lady and knew the customs of her country; she agreed that she would chaperon this romance and adopt Lanny as her son.

Also the dutiful youth wrote to his father in Connecticut. He named no names, but revealed that he had fallen in love with an unhappily married French lady, and had just had a delightful motortrip with her. Knowing his father, Lanny added that his *innamorata* enjoyed his piano playing, and that they read classic French literature together; she wore few jewels, and those few were family heirlooms; her idea of an acceptable gift was one of Great-Great-Uncle Eli's books. A cautious father might rest secure in the knowledge that his son had found for the gravest of a young man's problems a solution which would not involve him in any scandals, extravagances, or dissipations. "But tear up this letter and don't tell anybody in Newcastle!"

II

Strange as it might have seemed to an outsider, Kurt Meissner also appeared to have found a solution of his sex-problem. He stayed right there inside the walls of Bienvenu, rarely going out except for a long walk. Whatever discontent he may have felt he sublimated and poured into his compositions. The world outside might be a madhouse, beyond any man's power to control, but a piece of un-frozen architecture could be reshaped until one had got it right; that was art, and it was also science. If the world didn't like it, so much the worse for the world.

Beauty was not a little in awe of this tall erect young soldier with the smooth straw-colored hair and the pale blue eyes that could so easily turn to steel. Lanny watched their relationship and was amused by the developments. Beauty would take things from Kurt that she had never taken from any other man. The gay daughter of pleasure who had been willing to stake her whole future upon a whim had quarreled often with Marcel over his efforts to keep her from play-ing poker all night; but no one ever heard anything like that now. Kurt would make it plain that he expected Beauty's company at night, and he had it. Kurt would look at her across the breakfast table and say, quietly: "I thought you said you weren't going to have any more cream with your fruit." And Beauty would eat plain fruit. Kurt would say: "Do you really need to keep up with the fashions while half the children in Europe are crying with hunger?" So Beauty would wear a last season's costume, and send a check to the American relief, which now was helping to feed the children of Germany.

The pair had been living together for more than a year, and the first year is the hardest for the ill-assorted, who have much adjusting to do. Lanny, always curious about love, learned many things that might be useful to him in his own *affaire*. His mother was much enamored, and also had been cowed by grief and fear. She was almost forty, which is known as "the dangerous age." It is supposed to be a woman's last chance; if she doesn't get a man then and manage to hold him, she will have a lonely old age. Beauty was trying her best to hold Kurt; she would hide her weaknesses, she would starve her vanities in the effort to keep his respect. Both the men of her household were leagued against the poor soul; for Lanny told her that Kurt was a great man and had more brains than she would ever be able to share.

The result was to cut her off more and more from what is called "social life." If she could have worn Kurt as a decoration, a shining jewel in a tiara, she would have had a grand time in Cannes and Nice and Paris; she would have intrigued to have her protégé invited into the most elegant homes, and would have lured the musical élite to hear him perform his compositions. But Kurt had to be hidden; he had to be Lanny's music-teacher—and how could one confer distinction upon a hired person? So Beauty stayed at home, wore the dresses that Kurt considered becoming, and instead of repeating the chatter of the fashionable she listened while Kurt and Lanny discussed the Brahms *Variations on a Theme by Haydn.*

Kurt had become devoted to Baby Marceline, who no longer stumbled and groped, but danced to music with spontaneous grace; she no longer stammered a few childish words, but prattled all day, and was a little fairy in the household. Her mother's one idea of bringing up a child was to give it everything it asked for; and here again she ran head on into German ideas of *Zucht.* Beauty would say no, and the little one would start to wheedle, and Beauty would be on the point of giving way, when Kurt would remark: "You said no," and Beauty would decide that she had meant no. Nor did she dare to cheat and give way in secret, for when Kurt found that out, he became very angry. There could, he said, be nothing worse for a child than to discover a division in a household; to be able to play one of its elders against another, and to get its way by intrigue. Kurt called Lanny into conference, and of course Lanny agreed with him, as he always did. So Beauty had to give up the pleasure of spoiling her darling, and these two aggressive young males assumed still further command of the ménage.

III

A good part of Lanny's allowance was going for music scores new and old. He always pretended that he wanted them for himself; he and Kurt would practice them, Kurt using any one of his various instruments. Lanny had read somewhere that Liszt had performed the prodigious feat of taking a new opera score and rendering it so far as possible on the piano at first sight; to a star such as that Lanny had hitched his wagon. But just as in his father's business there was a race between the makers of armorplate and the makers of guns, so in the music world there appeared to be a race between performers and composers; as fast as the former have achieved some prodigy of technique, the latter proceed to set a new standard of digital agility.

Lanny didn't have to buy books, for there was that library, and Kurt stuck to the conviction that old books are the best. Kurt discovered America in an odd way, through the literature of New England transcendentalism. It was, he said, a pale copy of German philosophical idealism, but it was interesting to see a provincial people groping their way in a field of speculative thought and coloring it with their peculiar pioneer qualities. Kurt said that Americans pursued metaphysical activities in the same way that they hunted wild Indians in their forests, each man picking out his own tree or rock and aiming his own gun. Said Lanny: "I suppose the German philosophers march in well-ordered ranks, thinking in unison and armed with government subsidies." Kurt laughed, but all the same he thought that was the way to set about any undertaking, military or metaphysical.

Kurt read Herndon's life of Abraham Lincoln, and was greatly impressed by the spectacle of a railsplitter out of a pioneer cabin rising to become the leader of a nation in a crisis. But he was repelled by the details of democratic political manipulation, the things a man had to do in order to become "the people's choice" in a land which had no traditions and no discipline as Kurt understood them. "Such a career would be inconceivable anywhere in Europe," he declared.

"Are you sure?" Lanny asked. "Aren't you forgetting that you have a saddlemaker running your own country now?"

It had never occurred to the fastidious German aesthete to think of Fritz Ebert in that way; he had seen only the seamy side of German Social-Democracy and his prejudices against it were intense. But he had to admit that the movement had saved Germany from Bolshevism in the course of the past few months, and from his point of view that was a most important service. Also Kurt had been impressed by Rick's statement that the program of British labor was the most constructive now before the country. In these desperate times one had to be prepared to revise one's thinking, and Kurt was reading English magazines which were full of strange and disturbing ideas.

He received letters from his family that would leave him in a state of depression for days. The situation in Germany was appalling; there appeared to be an almost complete absence of necessities, and no way to get industry or trade started. The government could exist only by printing paper money, and as a result retail prices were six or eight times what they had been before the war. In Stubendorf it wasn't so bad, because this was an agricultural district, and crops were in the ground, and some harvested; so the Meissners had food. But the workers in the towns were starving, and there was chaos in most of Upper Silesia, which didn't know whether it was Polish or German, so people who should have been at work were arguing and fighting over the forthcoming plebiscite. There were "polling police," half German and half Polish, supposed to be keeping order, but much of the time they were fighting among themselves. There was that terrible Korfanty, half patriot and half gangster, who was inciting the Poles; in August he tried to seize the whole of Upper Silesia by force, and there was a state of disorder for several weeks. To Herr Meissner, comptroller-general of Schloss Stubendorf, order was the breath of life, and to Herr Meissner's son it was gall in the mouth to read of indignities which his father and family were suffering at the hands of a people whom they regarded as sub-human.

IV

One morning Lanny was called from his music practice to the telephone, and heard a man's voice, speaking English with a foreign accent. "Do you know me this time?" This time Lanny did, and cried: "Mr. Robin! Where are you?"

"At the station in Cannes. I have been to Milan on business and am on my way to Paris. I promised the boys I would not pass by without seeing you, if you would permit."

"Of course I will! Shall I drive over for you?"

"I will be taking a taxi."

"Be prepared to stay for lunch and tell me all the news."

Lanny went to his mother; she had never met Johannes Robin, but understood that he was in various business deals with Robbie Budd, and she took it as a law of nature that Robbie's friends had to be entertained. Lanny had told Kurt about the Jewish salesman of electrical gadgets who had served all through the war as a channel for Lanny's letters to Kurt, receiving them in Holland and remailing them into Germany. Kurt knew how the small Lanny Budd had picked up Robin on a train, and how the man had since become very rich by selling magnetos and other war materials to Germany. Kurt said he had no prejudice against Jews when they were great moral philosophers like Spinoza or joyous musicians like Mendelssohn, but he didn't care for those who coined money out of the needs of his people. However, it was necessary to take the visitor into the secret of Kurt's identity, for of course he would remember the name, and could hardly fail to penetrate the disguise of a Swiss music-teacher.

When the taxi arrived at the gate, Lanny was waiting to greet his guest. The dark-eyed and handsome Jewish gentleman became more expansive and self-assured with every year, but he would never fail to be humble with the Budd family, eager for their approval and grateful when he got it. Lanny explained how he was giving shelter to his old German friend, whose home had been turned over to the enemy and whose family had been all but ruined. Mr. Robin replied that both as a businessman and as a Jew he was without national prejudices; many of his best friends were Germans. Also he was a lover of the arts, and would be proud to meet a composer who, he felt certain, was destined to a great future. "Tell him that!" said Lanny, with a smile.

They sat down to a lunch upon which Leese had expended her talents, and the guest started in right away to say what happiness his elder son had derived from a short violin composition of Kurt's which Lanny had taken the trouble to copy out and send to Rotterdam. Hansi had played it at a recital at the conservatory, where many had inquired concerning its author. Then Kurt knew that he was dealing with no ordinary money-grubber, and he listened while Mr. Robin told about his wonderful first-born, who was now sixteen, and possessed such fire and temperament that he was able to draw out of pieces of dead wood and strips of pig's intestines the intensest expressions of the soul of man.

That darling Hansi, about whom Lanny had been hearing for seven years, had grown tall but very thin, because he worked so hard that it was difficult to bring him to meals; he had large soulful eyes and wavy black hair, in short, the very picture of an inspired young musician. "Oh, M. Dalcroze"—so Kurt was addressed in the household—"I wish that you might hear him and play with him! And you, Lanny—he talks about nothing so often as when shall he meet Lanny Budd, and do I think that Lanny Budd will like him, even though he is Jewish and so many people have prejudices against his race."

"Listen, Mr. Robin," the long-talked-of Lanny Budd remarked, on the impulse of the moment, "why don't you let those two boys come to see us?"

"Oh, but I would be delighted!" replied the father.

"What are they doing now?"

"Now they are in the country, where we have a lovely place. But Hansi will practice every day. In September they go back to school."

"In September I have an engagement too," said Lanny. "But why not let them come now and spend a week or two with us?"

"Would you really like to have them?" The Jewish gentleman

looked from Lanny to Lanny's mother, and each could see the gratification in his dark eyes.

"I am sure it would give us all great pleasure," said Beauty, to
whom "company" was as a summer shower to a thirsty garden.

"We have a lot of violin music that we should like to know better," put in Kurt. "I make a stab at it, but it is not like really
hearing it."

"If I would telegraph to them, they would be starting tomorrow."

"The sooner the better," said Lanny. "Tell them to fly."

The father turned pale at the thought. "Never would I take such
a chance with the two most precious of beings to me! I cannot tell
you, Madame Budd, what those two lads mean to me and my wife.
For whatever I do in this world I make the excuse that Hansi and
Freddi will make it worth while that I have lived." Beauty smiled
gently and told him that she knew the feeling well. He was a very
nice man, she decided, in spite of that one trouble for which he
couldn't be blamed.

V

Kurt went back to his work, and Lanny took the visitor to his
studio for a quiet talk. Now and then Robbie had mentioned in
his letters how well Johannes was doing, and Lanny was always
proud of this, because the Jewish partner was his discovery. The
firm of Robbie and Robin was engaged in a series of complicated
transactions, for which the New England aristocrat put up the
money and the refugee from a ghetto in Russian Poland furnished
the judgment and hard work. They were an active pair of traders,
and nothing gave Johannes more pleasure than to talk about their
successes.

He told the outcome of their first venture, the hundreds of thousands of hand grenades which had been turned into children's
savings-banks for the Christmas trade; those which had not been
sold last year were now in the hands of dealers, awaiting that season
of joy and brotherhood which comes but once a year and unfortunately does not last until the next one. They had bought an amazing

assortment of products which the American Expeditionary Force had brought to France and had to get rid of at any price: canned tuna-fish, wooden legs, and alarm clocks; thirty-seven thousand padlocks with two keys each, fourteen thousand gross of lead-pencils with erasers attached——

"You cannot imagine how many unlikely things are required by an army," explained Johannes Robin. "Can you suggest to me any patriotic organization which might be wishing to purchase an edition of twenty-five thousand lives of the one-time President, William McKinley?"

"I regret that I cannot think of one at the moment," replied Lanny, gravely.

"He was the most handsome statesman that could be imagined, but confidentially I admit that my efforts to read his speeches have been failures. I fear it will prove the least profitable of all my speculations, even though I bid only a quarter of a cent per copy for the books. It will be necessary to take off the covers, or 'cases,' as they are called, and turn the paper to pulp, and I must find out if it will be possible to restamp the cases and put some other books inside them, perhaps a life of Pope Benedict XV or else of Tovarish Lenin."

Mr. Robin went on to explain that he had been planning to move into Germany, but was waiting until matters settled down so that it would be easier to come and go. He was buying up properties of all sorts in the Fatherland. "Do not think that I am being vainglorious if I say that I am going to become an extremely rich man, for I have information as to coming events, and it would be foolish not to make use of my opportunities. If one is in business, one buys what one believes will increase in value and sells what one believes will lose in value."

Lanny agreed that this was according to his understanding of the game.

"Tell your father to trust me a little more, Lanny," urged the other. "I failed to see him the last time he came over, and I am sorry, because one cannot judge events from far away. Your father is troubled that I persist in selling German marks; in America he gets the propaganda which the Germans are putting out—you understand the situation?"

"I haven't been watching the money-market, Mr. Robin."

"You would not, being an art lover, and for that I honor you. But I explain that all over the world are people of German race who have money, and love the Fatherland, and the Fatherland needs help, but how can the help be given? If these Germans can be persuaded to invest in the Fatherland's paper money, life may continue at home. So the government gives out news to the effect that prosperity is beginning, that Germany is coming back with a rush, that there will be no more paper marks, that the mark has reached its lowest point—and so they sell plenty more marks. But they do not sell them to Johannes Robin—on the contrary, I sell millions and millions to Germans for delivery in three months, and when the time comes I buy them for half what I am due to receive. This troubles your father, because he considers it a risk. Tell him to trust me and I will make him a really rich man. not just one of the medium fellows!"   .

"I'll tell him what you say, Mr. Robin," said Lanny; "but I know that my father always prefers to invest in real things."

"He is wise in that he keeps his money in dollars, and when the mark is really down we will go into Germany and buy great manufacturing concerns for a few thousands each. I will take you, Lanny, and we will buy old masterpieces of painting for the price of a good dinner."

"I wouldn't know what to do with them," said Lanny. "I have a storeroom full of the paintings of Marcel Detaze which we ought to sell."

"Oh, take my advice and do nothing yet!" exclaimed the shrewd man of business. "Now everything is in a slump, but in a short time things will get started again, and there will be such a boom as no man has ever dreamed of. Then your father and I will be riding on top of the wave."

VI

Lanny went to the train to meet the young travelers from Rotterdam. He would have known them anywhere, having had so many snapshots of two dark-eyed, dream-smitten children of ancient Judea, whose shoulders some prophet had covered with his mantle, whose heads he had anointed with holy oil. Lanny Budd, in the Sunday school class of the stern old Puritan manufacturer, his grandfather, had learned about a shepherd boy named David, who had played the harp, listened to the voice of Jehovah, and entered into communion with the Almighty One, the Lord God of Hosts. If you counted up the number of man's descendants in a hundred generations, you could be sure that every Jew in the world shared the blood of that minstrel and future king; and here were two of them, stepping from the Blue Express, one carrying a suitcase and a violin case, the other a suitcase and a clarinet case.

Both of them eager, both with dark eyes shining and red lips smiling; a dream of seven years coming true for them—they were meeting the wonderful Lanny Budd! It is a pleasure to be able to make anybody so happy, and Lanny would do his best by kindness and gaiety to come up to their expectations. He understood the situation, because long ago Mr. Robin had revealed how Lanny Budd was the model of all things excellent to those boys; he was cultured, he had traveled, and he belonged to the ruling caste of the modern world, for whom the arts were created and before whom the artists performed.

Lanny remembered how thrilled he had been, how the whole earth had taken on hues of enchantment, when he had traveled to Kurt Meissner's home and seen a great castle with its snow-covered turrets gleaming in the early morning sun. Now came little Freddi Robin, at that same age of fourteen. He and his brother were seeing the Côte d'Azur for the first time, and semi-tropical landscapes were as magical to them as snow had been to Lanny. Trees laden with oranges and lemons, bowers of roses and cascades of purple bougainvillaea, rocky shores with blue water turning green in the shallows— all these sights brought cries of wonder, and then anxiety as to whether one was being too demonstrative in the presence of Anglo-Saxon reticence. Everybody at Bienvenu liked them at once; impossible not to, they were so gentle, so sweet-tempered and anxious to please. They spoke acceptable English, French, and German, as well as their native Dutch. Their eager conscientiousness was evident, and persons who knew the harsh world were touched by the thought of what these boys might be made to suffer.

VII

For so long Hansi Robin had been looking forward to the day when he would play a duet with Lanny Budd; and now in the generously proportioned drawing-room of the villa he got out his fiddle and tuned it to Lanny's piano. From his portfolio he took the score of the César Franck *Sonata in A Major*, made popular by Ysaye. He laid the piano part on the rack in front of his friend, and waited to give him time to note the key and the tempo, and to bend up the corner of the first page so that he could turn it quickly. He put his fiddle in position and raised his bow; then he put it down again, and said, in a low voice: "I am sorry to be so nervous. I have wanted so much to do this. Now I am afraid I may stumble."

"You are less likely to stumble than I," said Lanny, comfortingly. "I have heard this sonata, but I have never seen the score. Let us agree to pardon each other."

Little Freddi had his hands clenched tightly and also his lips, and could give no comfort to anybody. But Kurt and Beauty, who were sitting by, said reassuring things, and presently Hansi got himself together; he raised his bow and nodded, and Lanny began. When the violin came in, a tender and questioning melody floated onto the air, and Kurt, the real musician of the family, started inwardly, for he knew tone when he heard it, he knew feeling and *élan*. This music was restless and swiftly changing, it pleased and then became vehement; its fleeting forms were the perpetual miracle of life, something new unfolding itself, discoveries being made, vistas of experience being opened. The frail lad forgot his anxieties and played as if he and his violin were one being. When the sonata came to its climax in a long and well-executed trill, Kurt exclaimed: "Oh, good!" which meant a tremendous lot, coming from him. Lanny, who had been raised in France, jumped up and grabbed Hansi and gave him a hug. The lad had tears in his eyes; it was such a moment as doesn't come often, even to the emotional tribe of the music-makers.

Kurt asked for something else, and Hansi brought out a violin and piano arrangement of Wieniawski's *Second Concerto*. Lanny knew that Kurt disliked the Poles above all the other tribes of men; but the artist is above prejudice, and Hansi executed these fireworks with great éclat. The *Romance* wept and wailed, and when they came to the *allegro con fuoco* and the *molto appassionato*, then indeed Lanny had to get a hump on him, as the saying is. He missed some of the notes, but never failed to get the first in every bar, and he was there at the finish. An exhilarating race, and they wound up with a grand flourish, red in the face and proud of themselves.

Politeness required that they should hear Freddi also. He insisted that he wasn't anything compared to his brother, but they wanted him to play his clarinet, and Hansi produced the score of Haydn's *Gypsy Rondo*, part of a trio. Kurt took the piano this time, and Lanny listened to gaily tripping music out of the eighteenth century, when it seemed easier to be contented with one's lot in life. Lanny was proud of these two charming lads, and certain that they would be loved by all good people. He saw that his mother was pleased with them. Some day she would be taking them to play for Mrs. Emily, and they would be invited to give a recital at Sept Chênes, where all the rich and famous persons on the Riviera would hear them. Such is the pathway to fame.

VIII

From then on what a tootling and a tinkling, a blaring and a banging, in the studio behind the high garden wall! Lanny thumping valiantly the new grand piano, afraid of nothing; Hansi with his fiddle and a head full of millions of notes; little Freddi with his sweetly wailing clarinet; Kurt sometimes with a cello, sometimes a flute, sometimes a French horn—he could have played the kettle-drums if he had had a couple of them. Food was forgotten, sleep forgotten—time was so short and art so long! Now indeed would the passers-by on the highway stop and sit in the shade of the wall for a free concert. Sweet, sweet, O Pan! The sun on the hills forgot to die, the lilies revived, and the dragon-fly—there was no river for him to dream on, but the fishpond in the patio served the purpose, and everything in Bienvenu was happy, and wished that the two minstrels out of ancient Judea might stay with them and help to banish sorrow.

Beauty would send the maid and summon them to meals. Also she would insist that growing lads had to have exercise. "Exercise, my eye!" exclaimed Lanny, dripping with perspiration from the ferocious labor of trying to play orchestral accompaniments on the piano. However, she would make them go sailing and swimming; and surely Lanny ought to take them torch-fishing, and let them have at least one motor-ride along this world-famous coast!

One afternoon, while they were in the midst of their musical riots, the maid come over to report that there was somebody at the telephone, asking for "Monsieur Rick." A lady who said that her name was "Barbara." Lanny went to the phone, for he owed a debt of courtesy to this woman who had given his friend such great assistance. Rick had taken her address and sent her a copy of his published article, and had received a friendly letter, congratulating him upon the intelligence it displayed.

Now Lanny explained over the phone that Rick had gone back to England. Barbara told him that she was visiting in Cannes, and he didn't like to say an abrupt good-by and hang up; he always had the impulse to be friendly to people, and he told her that he and some musician friends were enjoying themselves, and wouldn't she like to come over for tea and hear them? Only after she had accepted the invitation did the thought occur to him that maybe an Italian syndicalist agitator might not seem so acceptable an acquaintance to his mother as she had to an English journalist on the hunt for copy!

He decided to exercise discretion, and tell Beauty no more than

he had to. It was an Italian lady he had met in San Remo, unusually
well informed as to the international situation; she had given Rick
a lot of data, so Lanny had thought he ought to be polite. "You
don't have to bother with her," he added. "Send the tea over to the
studio and we'll take care of her." It was a blazing hot afternoon, and
company meant dressing up; Beauty voted to have her siesta, and
Lanny was relieved.

IX

It was the assumption that persons coming to Bienvenu would
step into a conveyance; Lanny just forgot that some people were
poor—it is so easy to forget that when you live in an ivory tower!
Barbara Pugliese walked from the village, and arrived dust-stained
and sweaty, in which condition she did not look attractive. Lanny
was inclined to be embarrassed before his friends; but she sat quietly
and listened to the music, and expressed her appreciation in well-
chosen words. He decided that he was being a snob, and that two
Jewish boys whose father had been born in a hut with a mud floor
had no call to look down upon a woman of culture who had given
up her social position to help the downtrodden.

As it turned out, nothing could have been further from the
thoughts of the two musical Robins; they were glad to chirp for
anyone who cared to listen; and when the tea was brought, they
fixed their solemn dark eyes upon the strange Italian woman with
the sad thin face, and kept them there for the rest of the afternoon.
Lanny told them how his uncle had once taken him on a visit to
the "cabbage patch" of Cannes, and how he had there met a sick
lady who was living not for herself, but for the poor and oppressed
whom she had taken as her friends.

This was an invitation to Barbara to explain how she had come
to adopt this unusual way of life. She told about her girlhood in a
small Italian village, where her father had been a physician, and thus
she had grown up in daily contact with the bitter poverty of the
peasants. Her father had been one of the soldiers of Garibaldi, a
Free Mason and a rebel, so that early in life Barbara had been made

aware of the power of landlords and monopolists over the people. She told dreadful stories of suffering and oppression, and how, when she had tried to enlighten the victims, the priests had denounced her and stirred up mobs against her. But she had persisted, and her fame had spread among the peasants, until when she traveled to their villages the black-shawled women would come with torches to lead her to the place where she was to speak.

She told also about the crowded cities of Italy to which the tourists flocked, and about which the poets imagined romantic things. Rarely did it occur to these persons to visit the moldering slums, where the lace-makers sat on the balconies, not to enjoy the sunsets, but to catch the last gleams of light and toil for the last moment possible in order to earn a crust of bread for the children. Lanny thought it was just as well that his mother was not present, for she was fond of lace, and wouldn't like to have these distressing thoughts about it. Also she smoked cigarettes and favored an Italian brand, and would not have enjoyed knowing that they were made by tiny children, who contracted nicotine poisoning and crawled home to die. But Barbara Pugliese hadn't run away from such things—she had made these people her friends and helped them to form co-operatives, workers' schools and libraries, people's houses, all the means of their education and organization.

Perhaps it was not tactful of her to talk so long. After tea she should have said: "You will wish to go on with the music." But before her sat two heirs of the ancient Hebrew exaltation, drinking in her words as the thirsty multitudes on the desert had drunk the water that gushed forth when Moses smote the rock. "As the hart panteth after the water-brooks, so panteth my soul after Thee, O God!" Barbara was a propagandist, and here were two empty vessels to be filled, two dry sponges ready to absorb her doctrine.

Lanny could understand what was going on, for he himself had had the same experience nearly seven years ago. Now he was disillusioned and world-weary, or so it pleased him to think; he had been behind the scenes and learned the futility of efforts to save mankind from the consequences of its own follies and greeds. But to these naïve children with the blood of the prophets in their veins, this was the very voice of the Almighty One speaking from Mount Sinai; the woman who delivered it was holy, her aspect noble, her face beautiful—even though the wind had made her hair straggly, and dried perspiration gave her a shiny nose!

"Then you don't think the Bolsheviks are wicked?" exclaimed Hansi Robin.

"The Bolsheviks are trying to end poverty and war, the two greatest curses of mankind. Can that be wicked?"

"But they kill so many people!"

"Always through history you find slaves revolting, and they are put down with dreadful slaughter. You find that any killing done by the slaves is small compared with what the masters do. The capitalist system, which is the cause of modern war, has destroyed thirty million people by battle, starvation, and disease; what moral claims can it have after that?"

"But can't people be persuaded to be kind to one another?" This from the gentle Freddi.

"No one can say that we of the working people haven't tried. We have pleaded and explained, we have tried to educate the whole people; we have built a great system of co-operatives and workers' schools, paid for with our very lifeblood. But the masters, who fear us and hate us, are doing their best to destroy all these things."

So it went, until Lanny thought: "Mr. Robin wouldn't like this any better than my father!" He saw that he ought to break it up, so he said: "Hansi, won't you play something for Compagna Barbara before she leaves?"

Hansi started as it were from a dream. "Surely!" he responded; and to the woman: "We Jews have been an oppressed race for a long time. I will play you something from our modern music." He took his fiddle, and his brother, who also played the piano, accompanied him. Two shepherd boys took their stand by the Wailing Wall of their Holy City, and played music new to their friends, Ravel's *Kaddisch:* music of sorrow, music of tumultuous grief, anger, despair; music of a people once chosen by their Lord but forgotten through long centuries, and who cried out to Him in torment of body and bewilderment of soul. Barbara Pugliese was deeply moved, and exclaimed: "Oh, you must come and play music like that for our workers' groups!"

"Indeed we will," declared the pair.

X

As she was leaving, the revolutionist remarked to Lanny: "We have been having a sort of conference in Cannes. Your Uncle Jesse is there."

"Indeed?" said Lanny, politely. "How is he?"

"He looks run down, I think."

"I thought Uncle Jesse was made of leather," he smiled.

"You were much mistaken," was the reply. "He has suffered agonies of mind over the war on Russia."

"I will tell my mother," said Lanny. He didn't care to add that he himself was not permitted to see this painter-revolutionist. Of course it was possible that Uncle Jesse had told this to Barbara— he not being the sort to keep family secrets.

Lanny mentioned the matter to Beauty, who said: "Yes, I had a note from him. I suppose I ought to look him up." She had some shopping to do, and Lanny wanted to pick up some music which his friends had talked about, so he offered to drive her to town next morning.

As fate would have it, Jesse Blackless chose the same time to call upon his sister. He walked, because he liked to walk; he came by a short cut, so he missed them driving. When he rang the bell at the gate, the maid told him that the family had gone to Cannes, so he said: "I'll wait." As he walked up the drive he heard loud music from a newly erected building, and asked: "Who is that?" The maid told him: "Monsieur Kurt" and two young gentlemen who were visiting the family.

"Monsieur Kurt?" asked Jesse. "Who is he?"

"A Swiss gentleman, M. Kurt Armand-Dalcroze, who is M. Lanny's music-teacher."

"Oh," said Jesse. "I'll go over and hear them." He strolled over and sat on the steps of the studio, while Kurt and Hansi were playing the Mendelssohn violin concerto, an impassioned work receiving what Jesse judged to be a fine performance.

The relationship between Jesse Blackless and Kurt Meissner was of the strangest. Each had heard much about the other from Lanny, but the only times they had met had been in the darkness outside Jesse's tenement room, on two occasions when Kurt had appeared and put into the painter's hands a very large sum of money to be used in promoting working-class uprisings in Paris during the Peace Conference. On those two occasions Kurt had known to whom he was giving the money, but Jesse had not known from whom he was receiving it. Subsequently Jesse had been told who it was, but Kurt had never been told that Jesse had been told; a tangle of complications.

The painter had known that his sister was having a long sojourn in Spain and had taken it for granted that it meant a man; but he hadn't been concerned to know what man. Now he sat on the steps of the new studio, watching a tall and handsome blond Nordic playing an expensive new piano, and it didn't take him more than a minute to penetrate the camouflage of a false name and nationality. Of course this was Lanny's boyhood friend from Silesia; he must have met Beauty in Paris and become her lover, and now was being hidden in Bienvenu! The pieces fitted together.

XI

Jesse Blackless had been attending a secret gathering of a dozen or so left-wing labor leaders of Italy and France. He had been hearing stories of mass starvation and repression, of the arrest and jailing of workers, the organizing and arming of forces of reaction intended to stamp out the people's movements of both countries. It was a life-and-death struggle, most of it underground. The left-wing press was full of it, but the general public didn't read the left-wing press and the regular papers never mentioned it, so the events might as well have been happening in Mars.

So far as the leaders were concerned, their most desperate need was for money. Unemployed and half-starved workingmen couldn't even pay their union dues, to say nothing of supporting newspapers. And here in front of Jesse Blackless was a man who had played the role of Aladdin with his wonderful lamp, rubbing it and producing thick packages of fresh new banknotes! Jesse Blackless had not yet got over the shock of this experience, and never could get over the hope that it might happen again. So when the movement of the concerto was completed, he strolled in, introduced himself, and was introduced to the two guests.

He had never heard of the Robin family of Rotterdam, and took but the briefest glance at the lads. Not being a romantic or sentimental person, he saw them not as shepherd boys out of ancient Judea, but merely as youngsters who were in the way of an important conversation. At first he tried to figure out how to get rid of them, but then he decided to make use of them; instead of making a direct approach to the German agent, he would tell these children what was happening in Europe and let Kurt hear it by accident.

The pair seemed to have some idea of it already, and wanted to ask questions. All right, let them ask, and Jesse would answer. Thus for two solid hours the embittered revolutionist poured out his soul to the two sensitive lads. Nobody knew more about intrigue and villainy in the ruling-class world, and nobody saw with clearer insight the wellspring from which all these evils flowed, the greed of high finance and big business, their determination to crush the movement of the class-conscious workers, to tie it, cripple it, break its neck. Hansi and Freddi sat gazing in open-eyed wonder at this strange-looking gentleman, bald, lean, and with wrinkled leathery skin, saying dreadful things in a somewhat harsh voice, with a twisted smile that left you uncertain how much he really meant and how much was a cruel kind of jesting.

Jesse wasn't sure what Kurt's political views were, but to look at him he was a German aristocrat. So the painter explained that Germany was now listed among the down-and-outs; the British and French empires had her there and meant to keep her there. For a long time to come, the international workers would be the natural allies of the Fatherland; in left-wing labor throughout Europe lay the one hope of freedom for the German people. Jesse explained to the lads what the Versailles peace treaty meant to its victims, and why the Reparations Commission was still refusing to fix the amount of the indemnities. That must mean, and was meant to mean, bankruptcy for Germany, loss of her foreign trade, and slow, inevitable starvation for the masses.

At the outset of the talk Kurt had the belief that Jesse didn't know who had brought him the money. But everything the painter said was so directly to the point that finally Kurt decided he must have made a clever guess. Kurt had heard a lot about this Red sheep of his lady-love's family, and was glad to hear what he had to say. It wasn't even necessary to ask questions to help the conversation along; the two eager lads provided all the cues. They drank in the speaker's every word, and what he was doing to them was a matter he had no time to consider. Jesse set forth the grim facts which were making revolutions in many parts of Europe, and he explained them according to the system of thought which he called "dialectical materialism."

XII

The session continued until Lanny got back from town and came over to the studio. He was polite to his uncle, as always; but, keeping his promise to his father, he said no more than a how-dy-do. Kurt informed Jesse that he was now entirely out of politics, and devoting his time to music; whereupon Jesse, somewhat crestfallen, went over to the villa to meet his sister.

At once the two lads fell upon their host. "Oh, Lanny, what a time we had listening to your uncle! What a marvelous man!"

They poured out a chorus of excited praise; and Lanny, of course, had to make some response. "He is very well informed."

"I have never met anybody like him!" Hansi declared. "He explains everything that is going on in Europe. He makes it all so clear—it is like seeing a map for the first time."

"He has his very definite point of view," replied Lanny. He didn't want to throw cold water on their fervors, but at the same time he ought to provide some antidote for the double dose of Red medicine they had swallowed. "You must realize that there are other points of view, Hansi. The truth is never all on one side."

The retired artillery officer came to his friend's support. Two blasé, world-weary dwellers in the ivory tower, trying to keep two neophytes from venturing down onto that darkling plain where the ignorant armies clashed by night! Said Kurt: "Never let anybody make you forget that you are artists. It is your function to provide spiritual illumination for mankind and not to waste your faculties in the clamor and strife of politics. If you are good artists, that is all the world has any right to expect of you."

"But," argued Hansi, "how can our music have any real vitality if we harden our hearts to the cries of suffering people?"

"Poor Mr. Robin!" thought Lanny. What anguish in the home of a war profiteer and his wife, if those darlings returned to Rotterdam spouting the formulas of the Reds! And the worst of it was, there was so much truth in what these fanatics had to say; you could never answer them completely, and so your conscience was always being kept in a ferment. You wished the pests in Hades; and then right away you were ashamed of the wish!

8

With No Great Change of Manner

I

IN THAT summer of 1920 a fresh calamity fell upon an afflicted world. It started in the United States of America, that most fortunate of all lands; a severe spell of "hard times," a mysterious phenomenon which came every few years, and for which nobody seemed to have a clear explanation. Robbie wrote his own view, that the farmers, under pressure of war needs, had plowed up millions of acres of new land and greatly increased the crop yields of the country. Now there was no longer a market for so much food; the fact that people were starving made no difference, so long as they didn't have the price. The farmers, who had gone heavily into debt to buy high-priced lands, were now stuck, and half of them would lose their farms to the banks.

And of course when the farmers couldn't buy, the manufacturers couldn't sell. Budd's, which was so busy turning its swords into plowshares, now discovered that nobody had the price of a shovel. And over in Arabia, where Robbie's new company had struck a pool of oil, the wells had to be capped and shut down, because factory wheels were still and farmers were staying at home instead of driving motor-cars. A time of suffering and strain for everybody, and Robbie wouldn't be taking any trips to Europe, but would "stick around" and help his father and brothers to stand the financial siege. Lanny became anxious, and wrote offering to get along without his allowance for a while; but Robbie said that that was just chicken-feed—anyhow, it came out of the earnings of "R and R." That smart trader in Rotterdam was the only one who was making real money, because he kept betting on calamity and getting it.

However, Robbie was sure that everything would be "hunkydory" very soon, because he had had his way in the political affairs of his country. The Republican convention had met and nominated just the right sort of fellow: a certain Senator Harding of Ohio, who was known to all the businessmen and could be trusted. They were going to put him over with a bang, and from then on America would mind its own business and prosperity would come back and stay. So Lanny needn't worry his head about finances or any other problems; just go on with his piano practice and leave the rest of the world to his old man! Lanny didn't mention how two Red serpents had recently crept into his Eden and persuaded him once more to take a nibble at the forbidden fruit of the tree of knowledge.

It was something Lanny didn't mention even to Kurt Meissner, that all three times in his life when he had listened to Barbara Pugliese his mind had become confused and his conscience troubled.

Could it really be true that poverty was caused by the profit system? By the fact that owners of land and capital held their products for a profit, and that no more goods could be produced until the owners had got their price? Of course Lanny knew what his father would reply to such an argument. "Look at the producers now—bankrupt, and having to sell below cost! If they take their present losses, aren't they entitled to their future gains?" It was very complicated, and whenever Lanny tried to think about it he found himself stuck in a maze and not knowing which way to turn. Earlier in his life he had been content to say: "My father wishes me to believe such and so." But now he realized that this didn't satisfy anybody, and he was ashamed to say it. Did he have the moral right to believe what his father wished him to believe, rather than what seemed to be true?

II

Gather ye rosebuds while ye may, Old time is still a-flying! Marie de Bruyne had set a date, and the thought of her drove all others out of his mind. He visioned her by day and dreamed of her by night; he counted the days and then the hours. His music danced with her—or it came walking down a country road, clad in a sun-hat and a blue summer dress. He wrote to her: "Wear that dress!"

On the fateful morning he went and got the old lady and drove her to meet the train; sure enough, when Marie stepped from it she was wearing the honeymoon dress! In the interest of propriety he gave her a friendly handshake, and when her bags were safely stowed he drove Mme. Scelles to the establishment where she took care of her orphans; she said they would need a lot of care, so she wouldn't be coming home for lunch. She had tactfully seen to it that there was no servant in the house; and Lanny had told his mother to expect him when she saw him.

So there were at least two happy people in war-wrecked France that day. It wasn't so much that they asked of the world, just to be left alone in a room together. There was between them that perfect understanding which is the warrant and seal of love. His was gentle and kind, and hers was a blissful acquiescence. They shared, and would continue to share, everything they had. They could lie in each other's arms for hours in bliss, and it was hardly any less happiness just to hold each other's hands. That extended to all their activities; if an idea occurred to him, his greatest pleasure was to share it with her; if an adventure befell him, his first thought was to tell her about it. They could be silent for long periods; just to be together was enough. They did not have to make any apologies for wasted time, or feel any qualms or doubts concerning excess of passion. She was for him the reality of the poet's dream of

> Some one whom I could court
>   With no great change of manner,
> Still holding reason's fort
>   Though waving fancy's banner.

When their first transports had passed, Marie told him the strange story of what had been happening to her during the past few weeks. After sixteen years of married life, she had imagined that she knew her husband, but had discovered that she knew only the surface, and that deep below were caverns inhabited by strange creatures. The man had been shocked by her revelations; as a result of it they had talked frankly for the first time in their lives, and she had got a new understanding of the complexity of the human personality. Denis de Bruyne, vigorous and active businessman, was a victim of cravings which he did not understand and which since youth he had been unable to control. He was one of those sex-tormented beings which the Catholic religion produces in great number. He had been taught that sex was something forbidden and repulsive, and so he made it that; he wanted from it what he dared not permit himself to get, and thus what might have been the basis of ecstasy became a cause of shame and fear.

Now had come this sudden and to him distressing revelation that his wife, whom he had imagined aloof and "pure," had fallen into the same cesspool as himself. "He has several reactions all tangled together," she explained. "He has a certain amount of relief, because a weight of condemnation is lifted from his soul. My one transgression excuses his many, and he feels that we are partners in sin. On that basis we can talk plainly—while before it was almost as if I were a virgin."

"I suppose it's all right," commented Lanny, "provided he doesn't try to get you to repent!"

"But that's just what he did! I think he would have been glad to come back into the paths of virtue with me."

"Oh, my God!" exclaimed the youth.

"I tried to get him to understand that I am really in love, but that is difficult for him. One does not easily get over these attitudes that are stamped into one's soul in childhood. Denis can forgive me for sinning; he knows that I can go to confession and have the slate wiped clean; but that I should believe in my sin, and call it virtue, that is an act of defiance, a rebellion against the very throne of God."

"Did you tell him about me?"

"He asked me to, but I told him I had no right to do so without your consent. I promised to try to get it."

"What good will that do him?"

"He is genuinely concerned about my happiness. His basic idea is that it is the woman who is seduced and betrayed. He cannot believe that any man means well by a woman—I mean when he wants her sexually."

"Does he expect to reform me, too?"

"Don't laugh, dear! This is a Catholic land, and I am telling you what goes on in the souls of men and women here."

"Bless your heart," he said; "one has to laugh so that one need not weep. Nature has made life simple, and happiness easy. What devil is it that creeps into our hearts and creates taboos and superstitions? My mother told me that when she was a girl her mother put off a long-planned excursion because it was suddenly discovered that the date was Friday, the thirteenth of the month."

"Yes, dear; but this is different, this is his religion."

"What does it matter what name you give it, if it is crazy? The Catholic won't eat beefsteak on Friday, the Hindu won't eat it any day, the Jew won't eat it from the same plate with butter; and each one says: 'That is my religion; that is what God told me.'

But I say it's a notion that got stuck in the addled brain of some poor savage sitting in a cave gnawing the bone of an aurochs, or maybe the bone of an enemy he had just killed in battle."

They smiled together, and she said: "Don't let it worry you, dear. It will never make any difference in our love."

"Tell your husband that your lover is a faun; that he has no morals."

"What I have told him," she answered, gravely, "is that you have the best morals of any man I have ever known. I have told him that you believe in love, and that you grant me all my rights in love, and think about my happiness equally with your own." He took her in his arms again and kissed her many times, to prove to her that this was true, and that love is lovely and not mortal sin.

III

So began for these two a long period of untarnished happiness. A warm glow diffused itself through all the activities of their lives; love became music, it became poetry and art, dancing and swimming, walking and driving, eating and sleeping, and, above all, that "conversation" which Lanny, as a denizen of France, had learned to esteem so highly. Everything they did was touched with the hues of romance, doubly delightful because they could find more pleasure in each other's pleasure than in their own.

Seeing her son thus walking in the clouds, Beauty had to give up. After all, Marie was a lady, and she wasn't exploiting Lanny or getting his money for jewels and furs and expensive entertainments. He brought her to Bienvenu, and Beauty looked her over and couldn't deny that she was beautiful, with the golden light of the honeymoon upon her. The two women declared a truce; if they couldn't be mother and daughter, or sisters, they could at least be co-operators in the difficult task of keeping men satisfied at home. The cat's claws would be retracted, the serpent's fangs laid flat, the wasp's sting drawn out of sight; they would make no hurtful allusions to each other's weaknesses or defects, but would help each other by giving hints as to the whims and eccentricities of the dangerous male creature. More could not be expected of women in a highly competitive world.

They did not make the mistake of letting each other see the signs of their infatuation, for these are rarely pleasing to any but the infatuated ones. Lanny would take Marie to his studio; there was a library there, providing decorous excuse for long absences; also there were Marcel's paintings, and a story about each which Lanny knew and which Marie was interested to hear. She was impressed by these works, and that was one way to win the friendship of Beauty; for to praise them was not merely to endorse her taste in art and in husbands, it was also to promote the worldly aspects of her widowhood. Beauty was certain, and all her friends agreed, that some day she would make a lot of money out of that inheritance.

Another factor in the situation was Baby Marceline. As a boy Lanny had always observed that he could win the heart of any peasant woman by showing interest in her children, and Marie didn't need to have this ancient technique pointed out to her. Marceline was an easy child to love; affectionate and eager, she came at once to Marie as to an old friend. Also Marie appreciated Kurt, who was dignified and reserved in his attitude toward her; so all was well in the household. There was no end of joking among Beauty's fashionable friends when they came to realize the odd situation. But love outweighs gossip, and those two "cradle-snatchers," as they were called, told themselves that not one of the witty worldlings but would have snatched their happiness if she could.

IV

The elections in the United States were held in November, and resulted in a landslide for Robbie's candidate. This was such an important event that he wrote a special letter to his son, a sort of war-dance over the body of the stricken idealist in the White House. Never had there been a more complete repudiation of a personality and a set of ideas; the invalid Woodrow Wilson was still President, but no one paid the least attention to him—except that the Senate took delight in rejecting everything that he had done, and every request coming from the "nursery junta," as someone called it. On March 4 next the businessmen of the United States would take charge and show how a modern and up-to-date nation should be run. "Watch our smoke!" said Robbie Budd.

The man of business didn't ask what his son thought about these matters; he told him, and took it for granted that the son would agree—and for the most part Lanny did, for he didn't keep very well informed as to affairs in the land where his fathers had died. Robbie sent him the *Literary Digest*, a dull weekly which gave various points of view of what was going on, but as a rule Lanny found it more agreeable to play a new musical work with Kurt. Most of his ideas about world events came from the English weeklies in which Rick had contributions and which he never failed to send.

Rick wasn't coming to the Riviera that winter, for a number of reasons. For one, Lanny didn't feel free to invite him, on account of the hard times; for another, Nina had her second baby, according to plan, and she needed the care which she received in the home of Rick's family; for a third, Rick's health was growing better. Perhaps it was because he was happier; his work was succeeding, and his courage was triumphing over his pain. He still raged over his discovery as to the little intelligence with which the world was governed, but now he was able to get more pleasure out of the raging. Again Lanny observed the peculiar duality of the artistic temperament, which is bowed down with grief, horror, or other tragic emotion, then finds a phrase to express it, and slaps its knee, exclaiming: "By God, a masterstroke!"

Rick's eyes were still upon the theater. He would go up to London, attend a play, and then go home to write an article about it and offer it to the various weeklies. It was a difficult field to break into, but Rick had advantages in that his father was one of those amateurs who haunt the green-rooms and know everybody, and so was a mine of the sort of information a journalist requires. Sir Alfred could introduce his son to important persons, and everybody would be kind to Rick because of his having been a flier for king and country. Rick claimed no credit, but wrote to Lanny: "There are hundreds of fellows with as much talent as I have who are now peddling matches in Regent Street." Such remarks gave the letters of the baronet's son a decidedly pinkish tinge. All Lanny's friends appeared to be moving toward the "left." Was the whole world doing that? If so, it was going to be a lonesome place for the son of a munitions salesman!

There came a letter from Hansi and Freddi Robin, telling about their studies. The older brother said: "One of my teachers gave me an article from a Socialist paper telling about the progress of the labor movement in Italy, and it mentions Barbara Pugliese as one of the leaders. My teacher also gave me a book about co-operatives, and it is a wonderful movement that I am happy to know about. I shall never cease to be grateful to you for having put me in touch with it."

So, the Red plague had spread to Rotterdam! Lanny wondered: Was Mr. Robin going to be distressed and make a fuss like Robbie? And how was the devoted Hansi going to react when in some of those Red publications he came upon denunciations of war profiteers and speculators? Lanny would never forget what ferocious things they had said in the *affiches* announcing the meeting for which Kurt had put up the money and at which Jesse Blackless had delivered a fiery address.

V

Marie went home to her family for Christmas, and left Lanny in a sort of polar night. His mother sought to brighten it by a tree covered with tinsel and illuminated with a string of tiny colored electric lights. This was a present from Robbie Budd, who was a great fellow for discovering new gadgets and singing their praises. He said the lights would make a fireproof Christmas, which was important in Juan, whose fire-department fell short of Robbie's standard of competence. The lights gave pleasure to Baby Marceline, and to Leese and the maid, and to various children, relatives of the servants and of peasants and fisherfolk, their neighbors, who came in to receive candy and toys. They all noticed how deeply these scenes touched Kurt Meissner, and Lanny sympathized, because all his memories of Schloss Stubendorf had to do with Christmas. He knew that Kurt was still getting sad and painful letters from his family. It was the third Christmas since the Armistice—but how far the world was from the spirit of peace on earth, good will toward men!

Marie returned to Cannes, and the intimacy was resumed. She reported that her children were well, and that her relations with her husband were becoming stabilized. With Lanny's consent she had described the exemplary young man to whom her future was committed: a musician, a student, a person of experience and discretion far beyond his years. Denis had been relieved at the tidings, and had expressed the hope that he might have the pleasure of meeting this worthy one and assuring him of his esteem. Good form required that Lanny should express his appreciation of this considerate attitude.

It was all a matter of custom. If Lanny and Marie had lived in the sweet land of liberty, she would have proceeded to Reno, Nevada, and sworn to some more or less false charges against her polite husband; then she would have married Lanny Budd, and their friends would have thought it a queer match but moral. Marie, however, was a Frenchwoman, and a mother, and if she had taken such a course she would have been considered cruel and irresponsible; she would have broken up a home and shamed two old and respectable families, her husband's and her father's. She would never have been forgiven by either family, and her children would have been handicapped in their opportunities of marriage according to the custom prevailing.

The French way suited the French; it was discreet and kept the affairs of important persons a secret, save for those who had the right to know about them. Lanny had been a guest in more than one such household, both in France and in England. He knew, for example, that the greatest of living French writers had as his *amie* a highly respected lady, Mme. de Caillavet, and spent much of his time in the home of that lady and her husband, a wealthy banker. Lanny had met both Anatole France and his friend at Emily Chattersworth's, and knew that everybody considered Mme. de Caillavet the force which had driven a lazy writer to his best work and had made his fame in the world of letters. Incidentally, they considered that the now aged gentleman wasn't treating her very well. Lanny meant to treat the wife of Denis de Bruyne in a way which no one would criticize.

VI

The "crisis" had spread over the whole world, and statesmen were at their wit's end. Those of the victorious nations had told their peoples that times would soon be all right, because the Germans were going to pay for everything; so now, when times were all wrong, the obvious explanation was that the Germans were refusing to pay. A cheap and easy way out; politically easy, emotionally easy, because everybody was used to blaming the Germans for troubles.

In Paris there was another conference between the heads of the various governments, for whom life had now become a perpetual quarrel over reparations. Ever since Spa their experts had been meeting the German experts and discussing what Germany could pay; they had arrived at an agreement, but the Allied governments were not satisfied with the amounts and insisted upon more. The Germans said they couldn't pay the increases; the Allies insisted they could but didn't want to.

The perpetual conference was transferred to London, where Rick had the inside "dope" and passed it on to his friend. Rick sent newspapers and magazine articles which Lanny read with care. He had lived with these problems for the six most exciting months of his life; he had worried over them and argued about them. Now there was a melancholy satisfaction in finding that he had been right, and that the world was going to the devil exactly as he had foretold.

There just wasn't enough intelligence on the poor tormented planet; not enough statesmanship, not enough ordinary decency. The people weren't able to control the forces which modern industrialism had created; they didn't even have the means of getting the facts. There were a few honest papers, but they reached only a small public; the big press was in the hands of the big interests, and told the people whatever suited the purposes of the masters of steel and munitions and oil.

For example, that question of Turkey and Greece, one of the problems about which the statesmen were wrangling in London at the outset of the year 1921. Robbie Budd knew about it—he had to, for his own business was at stake, and in his sudden way he stepped onto a steamer and arrived in London, wiring Lanny to join him if he cared to. Lanny didn't go, because he was so happy with Marie, and there was nothing he could do in the oil business. Robbie wrote him a few sentences typed on his little portable machine—the sort of thing one wouldn't trust to a stenographer. "Z is here, keeping out of sight as usual, but pulling all the strings." Lanny knew who "Z" was, and he knew who "LG" was. "LG is in pawn to him, and he is directing policy. You would be amused to hear Z telling me about his sentimental interest in his homeland, when I know about the concessions he has been promised; he has already formed the companies. Don't say anything about this, of course."

Lanny felt embarrassed, because he had told Rick some time back about the relationship between the munitions king of Europe and the British Prime Minister, and right now Rick was on the trail of a story about the intrigues over Greece and her seizure of Turkish territory. Lanny told his father what Rick was doing, so that he could stop him if he thought it necessary; but Robbie answered that Rick couldn't get the real facts, and if he did they were so startling that nobody would dare to publish them.

And that was the way it worked out. Rick got what he thought was a story, and his magazine editors said their printers would refuse to put it on the presses. The libel laws were strict in England, and it was no defense to prove that what you said was true. "Yet they say they have free speech!" wrote Robbie. "They put on a show in Hyde Park every Sunday—anybody can get up on a stand and say anything he pleases—curse the King and the royal family in the presence of a few hundred poor devils and one or two American visitors—and that serves to convince the world that it's a free country!" Robbie Budd wasn't ever going to like the British ruling class—not even while he was shipping out Arabian oil under the protection of one of their warships!

VII

Easter holidays are important in France. The boys would be home from school, and it was their mother's duty to be with them. Would not Lanny take this occasion to make their acquaintance? Lanny perceived that, just as he himself wanted to share all his experiences and ideas with Marie, so she desired to have him love her darling boys, and at least to understand the gratitude and sympathy which she felt for her husband. A year had passed since she and Lanny had declared their love, and it might now be considered as established.

Lanny said all right, fine; they would motor up and back again. The best makes of French cars were famous over the world, and Robbie's generosity enabled Lanny to have one. Any time the whim seized him, he could command the great scenes of history to roll past him while he sat in comfort and security. He could stop in whatever inn he judged suitable, and servants would hasten to provide for his wants; he could stand by with clean hands and watch mechanics with greasy hands attend to the wants of his car.

Enjoying these privileges, he would never find it difficult to persuade some woman to travel with him and entertain him with gay conversation. Lanny had quoted to his father the verse of the poet Clough: "How pleasant it is to have money, heigh-ho!" What was the defect in Lanny's mind or temperament which caused him to be always a little uneasy about his pleasures, a little hesitant and apologetic? It puzzled his mother and father and some of his friends. Was it because he had read too many books, and got his mind full of images of skeletons at ancient feasts, of handwritings on the walls of palaces? Thus conscience doth make cowards of us all!

But Lanny had no troubles of conscience concerning Marie de Bruyne, and motoring with her would be a repetition of their happy first week. They followed the varied Riviera coast, past Toulon, where the French fleet kept guard over the Mediterranean, and the great harbor of Marseille, where Lanny had traveled since childhood to meet his father or friends who came by the southern route. Past the wide delta of the great river Rhône the pair came to Arles, and Lanny told the strange story of the half-crazed painter who had cut off his ear and sent it to a prostitute. Farther north was Avignon, seat of the popes in their days of exile; the travelers stopped to inspect the great palace which these potentates had been thirty years a-building. Then came the industrial city of Lyon, and then Chalon-sur-Saône, where their guidebook told them they might see the tomb of Abelard, but they didn't; it sufficed to talk about that old story of unhappy love, and thank whatever gods might be that they had been born in a day when love was free for the taking.

They crossed a ridge, and following the Burgundy canal and the valley of the river Yonne they came to Paris. Delightful for Lanny to drive about those splendid boulevards in the warm sunshine of early spring and tell his sweetheart about his adventures in the stirring war days. Some of them were still under seal—he couldn't say that Kurt had been a German agent, and that he and his mother had lived in terror of their friend's being caught and shot; but Lanny could tell how the police had seized him for the offense of possessing some of his Red uncle's incendiary literature. Lanny had never read Cicero, and didn't know that elder statesman's remark that we find pleasure in recalling past troubles; but sitting at a table in a sidewalk café, partaking of a delicious luncheon, he knew that he enjoyed telling the sweetest woman in the world how it felt to hear the clang of a cell-door upon you, and to wonder when it was opened if you were going to be led out and shot!

VIII

The Château de Bruyne bore that imposing title because for a couple of centuries it had belonged to the gentle family of the neighborhood; but really it was no more than a modest villa. Just as Lanny had imagined, it had a lovely garden, including a wall with a southern front and pear and apricot trees trained like vines against it. They were in bloom now, and so were the tulips and the fleurs-de-lis, the hyacinths and crocuses and narcissi. Everything was dressed up for the lovers, and they had the place to themselves for two or three blessed hours, the master of the house being in the city and the boys not expected until the morrow.

The old house was built of a reddish stone, and had some modern improvements. Marie explained that her husband's family had been ruined in the days of the Panama Canal fiasco, and the family had lost this home. Denis had made his own fortune and bought it back and had it fixed up for his bride. Better not think too much about that; better go upstairs and see the chamber assigned to Lanny, which had a door connecting with Marie's. A table would be kept in front of the door when it was not in use. This was supposed to fool the servants, but of course it wouldn't; they would tell the other servants of the neighborhood, and these would tell their mistresses in the regular way. But that did no harm, for an *affaire* remained a secret so long as you pretended it was; it didn't become a scandal unless you let it get into the courts or the newspapers.

All this suited Lanny; but he had to admit to some trepidation when the car of Denis de Bruyne rolled up to the door. It is one thing to read about *la vie à trois* in romances, but it is something else to be formally inducted into it. M. de Bruyne was in his early sixties—so Lanny could comfort himself with the reflection that if he was twenty years too young for Marie, her husband was twenty years too old for her. He was a solidly built, good-looking man, gray-haired, with dark, melancholy eyes and rather pale, aristocratic features. He was scrupulously polite to Lanny, treating him as an honored guest and not as a punishment for Denis's sins.

The pair practiced the French art of conversation, which meant that neither tried to force his ideas, but each brought forward such wit or wisdom as he possessed, and the other listened and in return received an equal share of attention. They talked about the state of the world, and the position of France in relation to her friends and her foes. They talked about the precarious condition of business, and also about the new *salon*, the opera, and the current drama—the fact that Denis de Bruyne was managing a large fleet of taxicabs did not keep him from being informed about these matters. If Lanny knew anything to the point he said it, and if he didn't he listened, and so the host was able to satisfy himself that the lady who bore his name had chosen a youth of discretion and taste.

Also, Lanny had the further task of winning the regard of two lads with whom he was to stand *in loco parentis*. This proved to be in no way difficult, for they were friendly and well brought up. Denis *fils* was fifteen and Charlot a year younger; they were dark-eyed and handsome like their father, and had their mother's sweet disposition. After the fashion of French boys they wore stockings which stopped far below their knees, and pants which stopped far above them, so there was a long bare stretch upon which the mosquitoes fed voraciously.

Most young Americans whom Lanny had met in Europe had seemed to him undisciplined and vacant-minded. These two French lads were serious, and accepted hard work as their destiny. Even during their holidays each practiced the piano for an hour a day, and gave another hour to reading some worthwhile book. So they had something to talk about; and when Lanny showed them Dalcroze dancing they found him a delightful companion. They played tennis with him, and on one occasion took him fishing, and his ideas concerning one aspect of French life were completely revolutionized—they caught no less than five small fishes.

Marie had repudiated Lanny's horrid idea of telling these children the truth about her lover; they took him as a family friend, and on that basis he passed a week of agreeable domesticity. Then Marie told him that her husband had received word that a widowed sister was arriving in Paris next day, and it would be necessary to invite her to the home. Denis was not yet prepared to share their secret with this lady, who was "devout" and at the same time observant; so Lanny was asked to spend a few days in Paris, after which the boys would be going back to school and Marie would be returning to Cannes. Of course one could always have a pleasant time in La Ville Lumière, especially in the delightful month of April; there was the *salon* to be visited, and plays about which Lanny could tell Rick. The world of art was reviving, and the art lovers of Europe were resuming their cosmopolitan attitude, flocking from one great capital to another to see what new wonders were on display.

9

Consider the Lilies

I

IMAGINE that one could walk freely into the Hotel Crillon, no longer sacred territory, guarded by American naval yeomen in white caps! Lanny strolled in, just for the fun of it, but he didn't put up there, because he told himself that one must economize in these hard times. He went to the smaller hotel where his mother had stopped, and where they knew him and were glad to see him. Again he didn't need any Cicero to tell him that it was pleasant to sit in the *foyer* and not shiver at the thought of the Sûreté Générale lurking behind the pillars.

Paris hadn't been able to afford a new coat of paint, but the ladies on the boulevards had. The tourists were returning, and everybody was trying to look cheerful and receptive. It was only if you went out into the suburbs that you would find war wreckage which had not yet been cleared away; only there would you be apt to notice the great numbers of young women in black, and the undue proportion of elderly men and cripples. Everybody agreed that victory was glorious, that fashions were daring, and the *salons* more brilliant than ever; the cafés and theaters were crowded every night, and if the ladies on the stage were not more naked, it was only because it is the nature of nakedness to be neither more nor less.

Fortunately intellectual entertainment had not been entirely overlooked. All the smart people were talking about the *Chauve Souris*, a refugee group of the Moscow Art Theater; a kind of "highbrow" vaudeville, clever and well acted. You sat in a hall of green-painted wood decorated with bunches of pink-painted roses, and having yellow-painted columns with white-painted teapots around them. A waiter in white overdress brought you iced drinks and preserves, while a droll little man by the name of Balieff introduced the scenes on the stage. First you saw a Russian episode with dancing, and then you saw Voltaire, and then the German Kaiser.

Between the acts Lanny looked about, and recognized a young attaché of the French Foreign Office whom he had come to know during the conference. Lanny joined him and they talked about times old and new. Lanny's attention was directed to the fashions, which were *très snob*—a word of praise in French. Some ladies were wearing a sort of elaborately embroidered apron—only they wore it behind instead of in front! They wore red hats of the most glaring shades—or else they wore black ones made of monkey-fur. Extraordinary the ravenous craving for monkey-fur which had seized upon women in the season of 1921; capes, collars, muffs, sleeves, handbags —the monkey tribes of all tropic lands were near to extermination, and still there wasn't enough, so the goat tribes were being sacrificed. Lanny said that some of the furs looked as if they were the trimmings from beards in the Quartier Latin; but his companion denied that any beards had been trimmed there.

Lanny was invited to spend the night in a place where they would find *très chic* ladies; but he explained that he had an engagement with a particular one, and returned to his hotel. Next day he went to the Grand Palais to inspect the newly opened Salon des Indépendants, and spent many hours remarking the hard, bright colors in which French painters were seeing the world. Oddities of many sorts provided topics for conversation. A nude woman being carried between the horns of a large brown bull against a green background was called *The Abduction of Europa*. A pink triangle set against an orange background and covered with spots of green and red—that was *An Expression of Simple Happiness*.

II

After Lanny had enjoyed his fill of such happiness he wanted to tell someone about it, so he telephoned to his friend Emily Chattersworth, who had just returned to Les Forêts. When he explained why he was in town, this hospitable soul replied: "Why don't you come out and stay with me? Isadora will be here tomorrow."

"Oh, gosh!" he exclaimed. "Are you sure I wouldn't be in the way?"

"Not in the least. You can play for her and she'll be delighted."

"You won't have to say it twice!"

Next morning when he arrived at the château, there was the divine one already installed, and saying very kindly that she remembered him from the days before the war. Possibly she did, but she had had a swarm of children on her hands, and he had been one more. Isadora Duncan at this time was forty-three, and her loveliness had become maternal; her gentle features showed the ravages of grief and pain. "The poor soul is terribly *distraite*," said Emily Chattersworth. "Try to keep her from drinking."

"I surely won't lead her into temptation," replied Lanny, and his friend said: "That's one reason I wanted you."

Isadora had just come back from a sojourn in Greece, and wore the costume of that land in its days of glory. Her art was based on the Greek spirit, and so was her life; in a long white stola, caught up and draped at the waist, she looked like a noble and gentle caryatid. She had regular and sweet features, with lovely brown eyes, and brown hair coiled into a loose knot at the nape of her neck.

She told about her adventures under the government of Venizelos, which had made her into a national institution. She had brought with her a few of the children whom Lanny had watched her training just a few days before the outbreak of war; she had taken this troupe to the United States, and then back to France, and so to Greece. They had danced among the splendid ruins which Lanny would never forget; he told how he and Marcel Detaze had stood among them and watched the dying of the sun and speculated about the dying of worlds. Isadora perceived that here was a kindred soul, and she talked glowingly about her life and labors.

She was the frankest-spoken person Lanny had ever met; she hid nothing from anybody, and said what she thought about everything. She had never really got over the tragic death of her two lovely children, followed by the loss of a newly born baby on the day the

French troops were called to war; all this heaping up of calamities had come near to unhinging the reason of a sensitive *artiste*. The world was a dreadful and cruel place! The hotel at Bellevue which she had planned to make the temple of a new art had served as a hospital for broken bodies and was now being made into a factory for poison gases. Greece, to which she had hoped to restore its ancient glories, had fallen prey to the pro-German King Constantine, who had driven Isadora's patron into exile and turned her and her school adrift. Now she had come to Paris and about ruined herself with all patrons by hailing Soviet Russia as the last remaining hope of mankind. She had waved a flaming red scarf during some of her dances, and so wasn't invited to dance very often.

III

She desired that this agreeable young man should play for her. He did so, and she was pleased. She took off her Greek sandals and put on one of her light dancing tunics. A servant set the furniture of the drawing-room back against the walls, so that the hostess could enjoy a treat—but not a free one, no, for Isadora was the most impecunious person who ever lived; all her life she had spent all her earnings on her school, and now somebody, man or woman, had to put up the funds for her and her art and her pupils, wherever on earth they might be. Consider the lilies of the field, how they grow; they toil not, neither do they spin!

The dancer was no sylph, and seemed better equipped to represent *Les Feuilles d'Automne* than the *Spring Song* of Mendelssohn or of Grieg. But life which had battered and bruised her cruelly had not tamed her ardor; she danced everything, and when the spirit possessed her she rose above the limitations of the flesh. Lanny had never seen her dance, and didn't see much of it now, for he had to sit at the piano and work hard. She was an exacting taskmistress; the best wasn't good enough for her, and she never stooped to flattery. Over his shoulder he got glimpses of the most graceful motions he had ever seen made by a human body; and when the dance was over and the dream had fled, there was a well-fleshed middle-aged woman, puffing audibly, lying down and covering herself with a robe, but still trying to communicate her vision, telling Lanny what the music meant and what the motions meant, and how the two were blended into something entirely new in the world. Isadora Duncan wasn't modest about her genius, and didn't need to be, for she had proved it in every great capital of the world. Starting as an unknown girl from San Francisco, she had created her art, and enormous audiences had accepted it with acclaim rarely seen in the theater.

Freedom was her watchword; freedom in her thinking, in her personal life, in her representations. She hated all chains upon the human mind and spirit; she hated injustice and stupidity, and when these things were brought to her attention she raged at them. She despised the conventional ballet; toe-dancing was to her simpering idiocy, and such forms as the minuet were expressions of conventionality based upon class dominance. The Anglo-Saxon peoples were long-limbed and free, and she gave them a long-limbed and free art form.

Lanny was startled to meet another defender of the revolutionary upheaval in Russia. He questioned her about this, and found that she didn't really know much about what was going on there—not as much as he himself had learned from Lincoln Steffens and Bill Bullitt and his uncle Jesse. Isadora took it on faith, because she had to have something to believe in, and because the so-called "capitalist world" had horrified her by its blind and bloody slaughters. She described to Lanny one of the great moments of her life, her first visit to St. Petersburg in the year 1905. Her train had been late and she had arrived alone in arctic cold and darkness, and while being driven to a hotel had seen a long procession of dark figures staggering under heavy burdens—it was the funeral of the workers who had been slaughtered by the Tsar's troops on the previous day. Against that age-old oppression her heart had registered a vow of hatred, and that same heart had leaped with joy when the peasants and workers had thrown off their shackles. "Peace, Land, and Bread"—how could any free spirit fail to acclaim that slogan? Surely not Isadora, who, before the revolution, had put on a scarlet tunic and danced the *Marseillaise* in the Metropolitan Opera House, to the great dismay of the wealthy patrons of that great New York institution.

IV

"Oh, Lanny," she said, "do stay for a while! You understand my work so well; and I must practice to keep my condition."

"I'll stay as long as I can," he promised. He played everything he knew and everything Mrs Emily had, and Isadora became possessed of her daimons, or muses, or both. She gave him glimpses of her Omar Khayyám dances, the first creation of her youth. To his infinite delight she showed him the dance she had made on her first visit to Greece, the chorus of the *Suppliants of Aeschylus*. She danced a Chopin prelude and a polonaise, and Schubert's *Marche Militaire*. She danced snatches of Beethoven's *Seventh*, and of Tschaikowsky's *Pathétique*. Both of them toiled and sweated—it was no unusual thing for her to lose four or five pounds in one morning's practice. Lanny had been working for years to acquire speed in reading, and now he knew what he had done it for.

The hostess had to go to the city, and they gave her a list of music scores which she promised to bring back. They were alone in the wide-spaced drawing-room, Lanny playing the *Second Hungarian Rhapsody* of Liszt. Here was a great musician and a great soul, Isadora said; the world didn't rate him highly enough. She rated him a tumultuous dance, ending in a wild climax; when she finished, she fled to Lanny and fell upon her knees, clasped her arms about him and clung to him, breathing as if all the air in the large drawing-room were not enough for her needs. She was a genius, and physically a colossal engine, the most thrilling that Lanny had ever encountered. He knew that artists and theatrical people were demonstrative in their manners, so he rested his hands upon her shoulders and waited for her to recover from her tremendous exertions.

Gradually he realized that she was going to stay right there. After her breathing had become normal, she still held him tightly, and her head lay against him. "Lanny," she whispered, "wouldn't you like to take me driving?"

"Why, surely, if you wish," he said.

"I am crazy about motoring. Nothing gives me such a thrill as to drive fast—very fast—ninety miles an hour!"

When this youth had received a present of a car, he had made promises to his father on the subject of speed. But he didn't think it necessary to go into details now. If Isadora wanted a ride he would provide it, and fast enough would be enough. "Where do you want to go?"

"Anywhere; I don't care, so long as it is far. Let us drive and drive, and not come back for a while, perhaps not ever. It has been a long time since I have met a man who might mean as much to me as you."

Lanny was startled, and not a little disturbed. He was made of flesh and blood, and here was a woman who had been one of the loveliest in the world, and still was one of its greatest artists. He knew that she proclaimed "free love" as a part of her religion; but he had had the idea that Emily would have told her about Marie, and so he would be able to play the piano and treat her as the Muse Terpsichore.

His hands trembled as they rested upon her; but that wasn't enough. "What's the matter, Lanny?" she whispered. "Don't you want to love me?"

"Listen, dear," he said—one must be as kind as possible—"I must tell you——"

He felt her recoil. "Oh, you are going to refuse me!"

"Please——"

But she didn't please in the least. She didn't want to hear arguments. "Oh, Lanny!" she exclaimed. "We could be so happy! Really, we are made for each other!"

"But I am already in love!" he blurted out.

"Oh, I know, but it can't be like this. I am Isadora!" She said it in a tone of awe, as he ought to have said it; as if it had been: "I am the goddess Diana!"—or possibly Venus, *pro tem.*

"I know, dear——"

"Lanny, it would be so wonderful! I had given up hope that I could ever be so happy with a man as I have been with you. You have thrilled me to my deepest recesses!"

"I am honored, of course; but I am really very much in love, and I'm bound in honor."

"Who is this woman?"

"I am afraid I oughtn't to tell."

"A married woman?"

"Yes."

"Oh, dear, oh, dear, how very annoying! Is she the type that would be jealous?"

"I have never tried her; and I mustn't."

"Oh, but this is humiliating! No man has ever turned me down—excepting only Stanislavsky!" There was a story there, he guessed, but she didn't stop to tell it. "Think what you are doing, Lanny! I have so much to offer you!"

"I know, Isadora; don't think I am ungrateful——"

"Am I not attractive to you?"

"You are one of the loveliest beings I have ever known."

"Oh, I am losing my charm!" There was a look of woe in the lovely brown eyes. "I am becoming an old woman!"

"You are an angel—and they are ageless and deathless, I believe."

"You are trying to make it easy for me—but you are refusing to love me!"

Tears were coming into her eyes, and he knew that pity moves the soul to love. "Listen, dear," he said, quickly. "You have known real love, I am sure. Haven't you been in love so that you just couldn't think of anybody else—not even a greater and perhaps more desirable person? Love isn't altogether rational, you know." He was doing his very best in a ticklish situation.

"I know, I know," she said. Perhaps he had stirred some memory in her soul. "Love is blind, love is crazy, often."

"Yes, that is it! That is the way with me."

"But, oh, Lanny, it is such a pity! I thought we were going to have a delightful time together! You understand me marvelously—and while your playing is far from perfect, it serves for practice."

"Thank you," he said, humbly. "Let me go on and play for you now."

"Oh, it isn't the same thing, it can't be! When you play and I dance, our souls flow together, they become one; yours gives me inspiration, and mine does the same for you. But when I have to think: 'He does not love me; he will not love me; he loves somebody else,' then all the fire goes out of me, and I think: 'I am an old and tired and discouraged woman, and the time has come that I have dreaded—when no man will be interested in me, and I am alone for the rest of my days.' "

V

Carrying the burden of that heavy sorrow, Isadora Duncan put her embroidered Chinese robe about her shoulders and led him out to the loggia from which you looked over the gardens and park in the rear of the gray stone château. There was an artificial lake, and steps leading down an embankment which resembled a dock for ships and had two towers like lighthouses from which the lake could be illumined at night. On both sides were gardens, and behind them a background of beech trees, the extensive forests for which the place was named. It was melancholy to think of all the unknown soldiers who were buried among those trees; and Isadora was in a melancholy mood.

She wanted this sympathetic youth to understand the soul need which had caused her to try to kidnap him—and was still causing it, for she couldn't believe that he wasn't going to change his mind and cry suddenly: "Let us go for that motor-ride!" She told him about the musician—"much better than you, Lanny!"—who had been her accompanist for many years. He was tall and slender, with a high forehead topped with hair like burnished copper; she had met him in Paris during the war, and amid the booming of the Big Berthas he had played Liszt's *Thoughts of God in the Wilderness*, St. Francis speaking to the birds. "I composed new dances, made all of prayer and sweetness and light. My spirit came back to life, and we became lovers, intense and passionate lovers—" She told Lanny about it, hoping to attract him by her vivid images, but only making him think about Marie.

Isadora always had to have romantic names for her lovers. The sewing-machine man who had financed her school for many years and had bought the Bellevue hotel for her—he had been "Lohengrin"; now this pianist became "the Archangel." They had moved to Cap Ferrat, not far from Lanny's home, and during the days when Lanny had been visiting the Budd family in Connecticut, Isadora had been dancing before the war-wounded or for their benefit.

After the war she had brought her pupils from their refuge in New York. "Perhaps I made a mistake," she said. "They had been children when I sent them there, and I forgot that they would come back young women. I took them with me to Athens, and the government gave us the Zeppeion for our school, and the Archangel played and I taught them new dances. All day we worked hard, and in the evening we would wreathe our brows with circlets of white jasmine flowers and stroll down to have supper by the sea."

But then had come the dreadful serpent crawling into that Eden. Isadora began to notice significant glances being exchanged between her Archangel and one of her lovely pupils. She had thought that intellect and soul had been dominant in his love for her, but now she learned that this was not so, and had the painful experience of watching the development of his intimacy with the young girl. A fury of jealousy seized her, and she wandered over the hills for a whole night.

"A frightful situation!" she exclaimed. "I could not turn this girl away from the school which had been her home. I had to go on teaching her, and pretend to be serene, devoted to the spirit of harmony, when it was as if I had some fierce creature gnawing at my vitals."

The episode was ended by a strange accident, the young King of Greece being bitten by a pet monkey and dying of infection; at least, that was the story, but everyone wondered, had he been poisoned? The country was thrown into political turmoil, Venizelos fell, and Isadora's school came to an end. She returned to Paris, and fell into a quarrel with her pupil, who took the Archangel away and blamed the teacher for having failed to live up to the doctrine she had taught.

"Maybe she was right," said Isadora, sadly. "We are not always strong enough to follow our own ideals. Anyhow, here I am, desolate, with an empty heart. Many women will say it is my folly to dream of holding a man's love at my age, but I cannot see it that way. There are spring flowers and there are autumnal flowers, and both have their beauties. I know that I have much to give—but, oh, Lanny, why is it that I have never been able to find a love that will last? What is the curse that rests upon me, that I can give happiness to millions of other people but cannot find it for myself?"

A profound question to put to one who had spent such a short time on earth—half Isadora's time. Lanny could only say what he had observed, that artists didn't seem a happy tribe; perhaps it was that they were meant to suffer so that they might turn it into beauty. Maybe the right thing to say was, not that artists suffered, but that people suffered, and thus became artists. Only desperate need of some sort would drive anyone to try as hard as they had to in order to excel. "That's what's the matter with me," said the young philosopher. "I've never really had to do anything, so I remain an amateur."

"Oh, don't let anybody change you!" exclaimed the daughter of the Muses. "Go on and be happy! Somebody has to, if we are not to forget the possibility!"

VI

Their hostess came back with a load of newly purchased music, and Lanny played and Isadora danced; but it was as she had said: the fire had gone out of her, and what had been play was now hard work. They all felt it, and Lanny was relieved when a cablegram came and changed the atmosphere at Les Forêts. The most marvelous cablegram that anyone had ever received, declared the *artiste* with the broken heart. It was from Moscow, signed by the name of Lunacharsky, Commissar of Education in the Soviet government. It said: "The Russian government alone can understand you. Come to us; we will make your school."

It took Isadora about two minutes to write a reply to that message: "Yes, I will come to Russia, and I will teach your children, on one condition, that you will give me a studio and the wherewithal to work." *

Lanny had never seen so quick a transformation in a human being. It was the rolling away of storm-clouds and the breaking of rainbows and bird-songs in the *Pastoral Symphony*. She began to dance; she danced all the spring songs that Lanny knew; all the bird music and the wind music and the fire music. She was sure what the answer would be, and she was going to Russia and make over the life of a hundred and forty million people—or whatever part of them were left after war and revolution.

She wanted Lanny to play revolutionary music, but he didn't know much of it, and there wasn't much in the Château les Forêts. Lanny didn't even know the *Internationale*—oh, shame, shame, not to know the *Internationale!* Isadora sang it, and he followed her, and learned it quickly; he played it with crashing chords, and their hostess, the formal and proper *salonnière*, watched, fascinated and perhaps a little horrified, while Isadora with her flaming red scarf rehearsed the tramping of the awakened and triumphant proletariat. She would produce it with ten thousand boys and girls wearing red tunics in the great square in front of the Kremlin; so she declared, while Lanny pounded out the prophecy that the international army would be the human race. "Oh, Lanny, don't you want to come to Russia with me?"

Fortunately the phone rang just then. It was Marie de Bruyne, telling him that she was leaving for Paris with her husband and would meet him at his hotel in a couple of hours. He said that he would be there, and hung up. Wishing to leave no uncertainty in the mind of his friend Emily, he remarked in the presence of both ladies: "That was a call from the woman I love, so I must go."

He kissed the warm perspiring hand of the new Terpsichore, and assured her that the memory of their revels would shine like a precious jewel in his heart forever. He told her that she was first among all women geniuses of this or any other time, and that he

---

* Details of these episodes have been taken from Isadora Duncan's *My Life*, and a few of her words have been quoted by permission of the publishers, Liveright Publishing Corporation.

was sure she would be happy in the workers' republic, building a new culture untarnished by the evils of capitalism. And so "*Au revoir.*"

VII

After that eagle flight, the lady of Lanny's heart seemed like a plain little domestic brown wren. But she was restful, and he was ready to rest! On the long drive south he told how it felt to be so high in the clouds, and moving so fast. He told the whole story—this was no disloyalty to Isadora, for she would tell Emily all about it, just as she had told Lanny about heartaches and ecstasies with her Archangel. She would find a romantic name for the son of an American munitions manufacturer: "Sir Galahad" or maybe "Young Joseph" or "my Anchorite." According to the laws of her being she would see it under some poetical aspect; it would become a sad little love that had died before it was born, and she would dance it to Ravel's *Pavane pour une Infante Défunte.*

The youth was surprised at Marie's reaction to the narrative. "Oh, Lanny, what a dreadful woman! If anything like that ever happens to you again, don't tell me, because it makes me ashamed for my sex!"

"But it isn't as bad as that, dear!"

"It seems to me as bad as it can be. A woman like that talks about love, but what does she know about it? What did she really know about you—your character, your soul, even your mind?"

He saw that he was treading on dangerous ground, and became cautious. "Mayn't she have intuitions? She's a genius, you know."

"She's a woman who changes her loves as she does her shoes; and no high-sounding names can make that any the less repugnant to me. Do you really think that great art can come out of such behavior?"

He wanted to say: "But it has!" Instead he asked: "Have you ever seen her dance?"

"Some years ago, and I thought she was lovely. But what I have heard about her wildness repelled me, and I haven't cared to see her again."

"It doesn't seem to have changed her art," argued Lanny; "at least so everyone agrees. She dances springtime and nature, grief and revolt, but no one ever saw her do a sex-dance of any sort."

It was plain that he wouldn't get anywhere with a defense of free-love *artistes*. It was the first tiny rift between Marie and himself, and he hastened to close it. He laid his hand upon hers and said: "Don't forget, darling, it is you I am driving, and not Isadora!"

She responded to his smile. "I thank you for that. But I don't thank *her!*"

They were silent for a long while, and when she began speaking again, her voice was trembling. "Lanny, that was a woman older than I; but some day there will be a woman younger!"

"That won't make any difference, dear."

"Some day I shall have to see what Isadora saw in Greece."

"Don't be silly, dear!"

"Let me say what I'm trying to say. I want you to know, whatever happens, all my life I am going to think about what is best for you, not for myself. No matter how much it may hurt, that is what I shall act on."

"All right, dear heart," he replied. "You think what is best for me, and I'll think what is best for you, and all will be well." Because it isn't safe to kiss while driving, he drew up by the side of the road for a few minutes.

VIII

When he got home he told both these stories to his mother; the story of the artist-soul whose cravings would never be satisfied, and the story of the mother-soul who thought about what she could give to a man instead of what she could get. Beauty said yes, there were those two kinds of women, and there was eternal deadly war between them. Beauty didn't give any fancy names to them; what she said was that a woman who really loves a man merges her life with his and tries to help him make something of himself; she chooses to express herself through him and through their children; she gives her youth and perhaps her health and her good looks, everything she has, to wifehood and motherhood; and then, when she has reached middle age and has nothing but that man and that family, and no chance of getting any other, then along comes some fresh little chit, thinking about nothing but the gratifying of her vanity, amusing herself by carrying a man off and breaking up a home——

Lanny couldn't keep from laughing. "Isadora isn't exactly a chit!"

"There are two periods when they do their raiding," answered the woman of the world; "when they're young fillies, first feeling their oats, and when their racing days are over and they're ready to be retired to the pasture. It's hard to say which is the more dangerous, but every wife hates them both and would like nothing better than to turn them over to the Apache Indians and have them roasted over a slow fire."

"You're mixing your metaphors," grinned the youth. "The Apaches didn't torture horses!"

"I'm not mixing my women!" declared Beauty, grimly. "Take my advice and don't let anybody fool you with toplofty words—soulmates and affinities, ecstasies and yearnings and romantic raptures. Burglary is burglary, and a woman suffers torment even to think about it; and when she tells you that she won't or don't, she's already doing it. The misery in her life is that she can never be sure what is going to happen to her man the next time he goes out of the house."

Beauty seemed unusually vehement on the subject of unmanageable men, and Lanny began to wonder about it. She explained herself very soon; her voice sank, and she said: "There doesn't seem to be any place for love in this world of ours—mine any more than the others'."

"What's the matter?" For a moment he thought she meant that Kurt was interested in some other woman, and he was shocked.

"It's the old, old story; I don't believe I'm going to be able to keep Kurt out of mischief. He gets letters from his family, and then he has fits of depression. He tries to hide them from me, but of course he can't."

"But what's wrong now? I thought he was so happy because Germany won the plebiscite."

"He doesn't think the Poles will obey; and he doesn't think the Allies will make them. You talk to him, Lanny. I can't, without making myself a scold and a shrew!"

IX

The elections in Upper Silesia had been held in the month of March, with the result that a majority of the districts had voted to remain with Germany. That didn't include Stubendorf, which had been given to Poland by the treaty; but it would save most of the industrial regions, and the coal and iron mines desperately needed by Germany if it was to resume as an industrial nation. Kurt had felt a great burden lifted from his spirit; but now had come that terrible Korfanty, organizing the young Polish patriots, arming them and drilling them all over Poland and even in Stubendorf. It was plain that they meant to seize the plebiscitary provinces.

Lanny went to Kurt, who showed him the letters he had received, and extracts from newspapers with accounts of the turmoil prevailing. It was undeniably terrible, with organized gangs raiding the homes of German patriots at night, carrying people away and beating them dreadfully. Poles and Germans just couldn't and wouldn't mix. Kurt drew harrowing pictures of the superstition and filth in which the Polish peasants lived; so of course they fell prey to demagogues and agitators—especially when these were secretly provided with arms and money by the Polish government. What was supposed to be an uprising of the Silesian peasants was clearly a raid by Warsaw, and a challenge to the fumbling and hesitant Allies.

Lanny couldn't say: "Kurt, you are under obligations to my mother, and you haven't the right to go off and leave her." No; but he could say: "Kurt, you always insisted that art comes before politics, the Idea before the Thing. In fact, it was you who taught me that, and I have shaped my life on it. I too have seen cruelty and wrong, and have impulses to leap in and stop it; but I've thought: No, Kurt is right; I am going to help to make beauty in the world, and prepare the minds of people for something wiser than fighting and robbing."

Kurt couldn't deny any of that. He remembered their talks in Hellerau, and on the height in front of the church of Notre-Dame-de-Bon-Port. Yes, he had said it, and he believed it still, at least with half his mind, the better half; but the other half hated the Polish usurpers and invaders, the preachers of militant nationalism—of the wrong nation. That half of Kurt was a trained artillery officer and wanted to go and serve a battery of field-guns to protect his homeland.

Lanny poured out his soul to his friend. "Perhaps you think I am just a playboy, and that it comes natural to me to be happy and to live in music. But let me tell you that I too am having moral struggles, I too wonder if I have a right to be happy while so many children are starving and half of Europe is in chaos. I don't know just what I could do about it, but I have crazy impulses to drop everything and try. I think maybe I'll do like Barbara Pugliese—go and live in the slums, and meet the poor, and help them to climb out of the pit. I know how dreadfully unhappy I'd make Robbie, but, after all, Robbie belongs to an earlier generation and he won't have to live in the world he's making. Then I think about you, Kurt; I say that you are wise and self-contained—at least that's the way you've appeared to me. Now I ask, if you can't survive as an artist, who in all Europe can?"

So they argued; and the disciple of Bach was convinced against his will. They renewed their pledges, and went back to their music— while Korfanty went on organizing the nationalist youth of Poland!

X

Happiness inside the safe retreat of Bienvenu, happiness for all the creatures which made it their home. The birds built nests in the vines and the high bushes, and raised and fed their young, and if these fell out they were replaced by friendly humans. The dogs barked at the birds, but it was merely an expression of the joy of living. Baby Marceline ran a little faster every day, chattered a little more freely, picked up some new ideas. Beauty, the loving mother, kept watch over all her pets and babies of various sorts and sizes; studied them, and within the limits of her understanding did what she could to fill their needs.

Lanny had brought from Paris the good tidings that the German ambassador had at last been formally received by the French government, so Germany was again a friendly nation and its citizens were free to come into France. They would sell the products of their country, or study at the Sorbonne or the Conservatoire, or sun their large fat backs on the beach at Juan—and while people might look askance at them, no one would call for the police. This meant that Kurt might emerge from his hiding-place and have himself fitted with a suit of clothes; also visit the music-store and make his own selection of compositions. Next winter it might be possible for Mrs. Emily to have him give a recital at Sept Chênes; something which Beauty looked forward to as a child toward Christmas.

The happy solution of Marie's marital problem made it possible for her to come and stay at Bienvenu. She took one of the guest-rooms, and combined forces with the mistress of the villa. It is hard enough for a mature woman to hold a young man, and if there are two such women, it is certainly the part of wisdom to make a co-operative enterprise of it. So Marie shared all the secrets that her man's mother knew about him, and Beauty had the advantage of the opinions that her man's best friend's sweetheart had formed about her man. This sounds complicated—but then Herbert Spencer taught that progress is a development from the simple to the complex.

So Lanny Budd enjoyed the most expert attention and service that the heart of youth could have desired. Marie de Bruyne laughed and sang with him, she danced and played with him, she climbed the hills and swam in the sea with him, she went sailing and fishing with him, she played his music and read his books, she adored him and praised everything he did, and at the same time spurred him to new efforts; she gave him sound ideas—in short, she was sweetheart, wife, mother, guide, and friend, and nowhere on the horizon of their life was there the tiniest trace of a cloud. Could you blame him for thinking that French arrangements for marriage and afterward are not so bad as they are represented in those Anglo-Saxon countries where pre-marital chastity and postmarital fidelity so generally prevail?

XI

Marie and Lanny in the goodness of their hearts had a guilty feeling as to Mme. Scelles, who had helped them so loyally and who now saw less of them. They decided to devote a day to her entertainment; so they loaded up the car and packed the old lady into the seat between them, and drove up one of the valleys where the cork trees grow, and had a delightful time. In the afternoon they called on friends of hers in a place called Cimiez, and played tennis and had tea; then, since the old lady was still game, they drove to "Monty" and had a sumptuous dinner at Ciro's, and gave their guest a twenty-franc note to lose in the Casino and feel devilish.

So it was after midnight when Lanny got home; and there he encountered a distressing scene—his mother, pacing the floor of her boudoir, her eyes red with long weeping, her face set in grim and bitter anger. "It's all over," she said. "Kurt is gone."

"*Gone?* Where?"

"To fight the Poles."

"Oh, my God! What happened?"

"There's a letter—he left it for you to read. From his father."

She indicated the escritoire and Lanny looked, but did not take the letter at once. "What is it about?"

"One of Kurt's friends has been killed in some of their rows. There's a long account of how Korfanty is overthrowing the plebiscite. He has declared himself dictator."

"And the Allies are allowing it?"

"So Kurt's father says; and the Germans are defending themselves. Kurt is wild about it, and I couldn't do anything with him. We spent hours wrangling."

"Couldn't you get him to wait until I came home?"

"I didn't try. If he doesn't care enough for me to stay on my account, I might as well know it now as later."

"Poor dear!" exclaimed Lanny. His mother's face was gray with anguish, and he saw that she had been through a siege. He put his arm around her and led her to the bed and sat beside her. "Don't take it too desperately. This Silesian question is bound to be settled before long, and he will come back."

"Never! I told him if he went it would be the end. It's the very same thing that I went through with Marcel, and I will not live such a life."

"Many women have to, Beauty."

"I am one who won't. If the men can find nothing to do but kill one another, I am through with them for the rest of my days."

"Let me stay, anyhow," said Lanny. "I don't want to kill anybody."

He judged it best not to argue with her. There was nothing very good he could say about the men, except that they loved their native land and their families, but didn't have enough collective intelligence to handle the new industrial forces they had created. Perhaps later on they might; but Beauty had chosen a bad time to be born on earth, and there was no way to save her from the consequences of that mistake. He said what he could to comfort her; they were as they had been before Kurt had come into their home—except that Beauty now had Baby Marceline, very good company and improving all the time. They would get along somehow.

XII

He got her into bed and gave her something to make her sleep. He himself had had practice in not worrying about what he couldn't help, so he didn't need drugs. In the morning he was awakened by the maid tapping on his door—M. Kurt on the telephone, she reported. Lanny threw on his dressing-gown and answered.

"*Allo*," said the voice of his friend. "I am at the railroad station in Nice. I want to tell you that I have changed my mind, and will come back."

"Oh, thank God, Kurt!"

"Do you want me?"

"What a question! Of course!"

"Does Beauty want me?"

"I gave her a sleeping-powder, so she doesn't want anything right now. But when she wakes up she will kill the fatted calf for you. Where have you been?"

"I spent hours walking up and down on the station platform at Cannes, waiting for the morning train. Here at Nice I saw a newspaper and read that the British government has sent six battalions to Silesia to enforce order. So I guess the torment of my people will end."

"I hope so, Kurt. But you ought to make up your mind to something and stick by it. You haven't the right to keep Beauty on tenterhooks all the time." Lanny, the young moralist, exhibiting firmness!

"You are right," said the other. "I have had it out with myself, and I will give you my word."

"Hurrah!" cried Lanny. "The death warrant of the fatted calf."

When Beauty awakened, she said that she herself was the calf, and she was dead, and had no interest in the news he gave her. He set to work to tempt her back to life—the first step being to ring for a pot of coffee. "You have won, old dear. He has tied himself down."

"I don't care, Lanny. I can't stand any more. I never want to see another man."

"There are a lot of us around, and you can't wear blinders; so cheer up and don't be a goose. It's no crime for Kurt to love his Fatherland, and if he finds it hard to choose between two duties, remember what a time you had making up your mind whether you were going to stick by Marcel or run off to be the plateglass queen of Pittsburgh!"

He began to cajole her, and reawaken her interest in making a career for a musical artist. After his recent encounter with Isadora, he was in position to explain these unstable creatures. Kurt had had a tremendous brain-storm, and as soon as he had got settled down he would proceed to see it *sub specie artis*, and make it the basis of a sublime tone poem or at least a piano sonata. A stormy first movement, *allegro molto*, in which the world breaks in upon the artist soul and a powerful war theme conflicts with and tramples down the lovely-woman theme! Second movement, *andante*, the woman mourns the departed man! Third movement, *scherzo*, the soul of the artist triumphs over the world! Finale, *alla marcia*, the themes of the first movement blend in a triumphant choral hymn, the victory of love over all the other forces of the world! "Can't you hear it, Beauty?"

He offered to go and play it for her, and so got her to laughing. Then he led her to her dressing-table and let her see what a perfect fright she looked. To start to improve herself was automatic; and he persuaded her that when Kurt appeared she would be her loveliest, she would kiss him and make him happy, and not say a word about the quarrel.

"I'll attend to the rest," said the determined youth, and he did; for when Kurt heard that outline of a piano sonata he said: "But, Lanny, that's very interesting! Would you mind if I took it up some day?"

"I'd brag about it for the rest of my life," said the faithful friend. "But I thought you didn't like program music."

"I wouldn't go into details," said the disciple of Bach, "but a hint doesn't hurt."

"So knocks fate upon the door!" said Lanny, smiling.

10

From Precedent to Precedent

I

IN THE middle of June the boys were to come home from school, and Denis de Bruyne very politely invited Lanny to spend the summer; the home didn't seem the same without Marie in it, he said, and Lanny was able to believe him. While the pair of lovers were discussing their plans there came a letter from Rick, saying that he had a commission from his editor to visit Geneva and report on the unfolding activities of the new League of Nations, upon which many liberals were now centering their hopes. "Big things may be happening soon," wrote the baronet's son. "I must get at the men who count. You know many of them, and I'm relying on you."

Lanny recalled that members of the American staff in Paris had transferred their services to the League. Also there was Dr. Herron, whose home was in Geneva and with whom Lanny had exchanged a couple of letters. It would be interesting to talk to him after two years. "Marie," he said, on the spur of the moment, "how would you like a trip to Switzerland?"

The idea took her breath away. She had missed the San Remo conference because she didn't dare risk a scandal; but now, being duly established as Lanny's *amie*, she could travel with him and be received with honors. "We could drive there in a couple of days," he said, "and spend a week or so, and get to your home in time to meet the boys. You'd enjoy knowing Rick, I'm sure."

"Oh, Lanny, I'd love it!"

"All right, chuck your things into your bags!"

That was how it was with the delightful leisure classes; a whim seized you, and you "chucked," and away you went. No need to bother about money, you bought a bunch of traveler's checks and cashed them one by one. No need to think about the car, for that was kept in order all the time. Just "hop in" and "step on the gas." These lively American phrases were coming into use all over Europe, largely because the movies had made that country so popular. You practiced *le sport* and *le flirt*, you offered *le handshake*, you drank *le coqtail*, you danced *le jazz*, and you aimed to be and were *très snob*.

Now Lanny "shot a wire" to Rick, and told Beauty and Kurt of their plans, and drove to Mme. Scelles's and told her; then, their last duty done, they drove once more up the wide valley of the Rhône. But this time they didn't turn off toward the west; they followed the upper reaches of the stream, winding through hills and climbing steadily into country where tall pine trees grew and the air was fresh and chilly in June. The stream became narrower and its course more rapid, until they were among high mountains with snow-capped peaks in the distance. In front of them was a great

dam over which the river flowed in torrents of green foam; and
when their car had got above the level of this dam, there was a long
blue lake, on the far side of it the mighty peak of Mont Blanc, and
along both shores the tall houses of a shining white city of watchmakers and money-changers and tourists.

The broad avenue along the lake front was lined with hotels
having green shutters, terraced lawns shaded by horse-chestnuts,
and dining-rooms with glass walls and roofs. In summertime the
cafés moved out to the sidewalks and the kursaal was crowded with
guests; the lake was gay with swans and ducks and gulls, two-decked
steamers painted white and gold, and tiny sailboats with red lateen
sails sliding over sun-sparkled water. But do not trust any Alpine lake,
for a sudden storm called the bise swoops down from the mountains and throws things into confusion—all music lovers know it from
the *William Tell* overture!

It was an aged city, and somewhat faded; a Protestant city, still
protesting the same things as four centuries ago. It had many me-
morials to John Calvin, and Lanny might stand and gaze at them
and learn where the religion of his stern old grandfather had come
from. There were a great many churches, and in most of them
Lanny might have listened to a pastor resembling the Rev. Mr.
Saddleback of the First Congregational Church of Newcastle, Connecticut—but Lanny didn't. He learned about the town from American newspapermen who were assigned here and who called it a
narrow and musty place, ruled by businessmen and bankers who
professed pious orthodoxy but permitted a normal amount of old-
world corruption for the benefit of the tourists. Geneva looked
askance at the League, considering that it brought undesirable
characters to town—including American journalists who put unorthodox ideas on the wires and padded their expense accounts for
the benefit of the *boîtes de nuit*.

II

Eric Vivian Pomeroy-Nielson was already on the job, and welcomed them with dignity. Marie had heard so much about him, and

here he was, a tall fellow with thin features and a keen expression, and wavy dark hair which resented efforts to control it. Marie's heart warmed to him at once, for she sensed a proud spirit struggling with physical handicaps; she wanted to help him, but Lanny had told her to do nothing, just talk about the job, in which the budding journalist was all wrapped up. He had met a couple of colleagues who had been at Spa, so he was already in touch with affairs. He was impressed by what he had found here; the League appeared to be really coming to life, and far too little attention had been given to it by the press.

Rick had put up at a modest-priced hotel, and Lanny and Marie decided to go where he was. The hotel gave them connecting rooms and asked no questions—in spite of the statues of very stern Calvinists all over the city. The first thing Lanny did was to make inquiries concerning a young member of the Crillon staff who had become a minor functionary of the League; Lanny's friends had been bitter against this chap Armstrong, being of the opinion that he had sold out his convictions for a soft berth; but he had taken the imputation mildly, saying there was work to be done and it interested him.

Sidney Armstrong had pale sandy hair and a round amiable face with horn-rimmed spectacles; he looked like a good "Y" secretary, and was doing much that sort of work, having to do with international problems of child welfare. He came to dinner, and was glad to tell about what was going on, and to meet an English journalist who had written an article dealing with the results of San Remo and Spa. There was a quiet tug-of-war going on between the officials of this infant League of Nations and those more important persons who attended the conferences of the Allied premiers and of the Supreme Economic Council. The League people thought they ought to replace these two bodies, and meant to do so in the end.

A number of different problems had been assigned to the League by the treaty of Versailles: the Saar district, Danzig, and all the "mandates"—a new name for a method of ruling the primitive races of the earth which it was hoped wouldn't be so bad as the old colonial method of missionaries with Bibles and traders with rum and syphilis. Other problems had been assigned by the Supreme Allied Council—those in which the Allies had no overwhelming interest, and which were found to be difficult and dangerous. There were Lithuania and Armenia to be protected; there were famines to be relieved, refugees to be fed, and all the prisoners in Russia, Turkey, and other countries to be repatriated; there were questions of health and transit, intellectual intercourse and child welfare, and traffic in drugs and in women.

Lanny brought up the subject of Upper Silesia, and Armstrong said this was an illustration of the mistake the Allied powers made in trying to settle problems which properly belonged to the League. People would believe in the disinterestedness of a world body, but who could believe in the disinterestedness of France with regard to Poland? The latter country had a bad, reactionary government, hard to handle; they had grabbed Vilna from Lithuania—another question the League was trying to settle. In Silesia the Poles were demanding all the wealthier districts, and it was a complicated situation, because, however you did the dividing, you gave a lot of Germans to Poles and Poles to Germans; also the economic interests —wherever you drew a boundary line you broke up industries and brought ruin to great numbers of people. Too bad they couldn't be moved across borders, like chessmen; all the Germans into Germany and all the Poles into Poland!

"What do you think will be the outcome?" asked Lanny.

"If the Allies can be induced to turn the question over to us, we'll appoint a commission, and it will work out the best settlement it can. We have, of course, no means of enforcing decisions, except as the great powers are willing to back us."

"Then," asked Rick, "one can say that the League will work only so long as it serves the purposes of Britain and France?"

The young functionary wouldn't answer that blunt question. "We'll just try to show what we can do, and the nations will support us if we make it worth while."

III

This serious and hard-working fellow introduced them to others of the same sort, and soon they were living *en famille*, as it were, with the League of Nations; an odd sort of colony of diplomats and secretaries gathered from a score of nations, inhabiting this ancient city with its stiff bourgeoisie for the most part devoted to money-making and the saving of their own souls by the method of doctrinal conformity. The League had purchased one of Geneva's biggest hotels, the National, with its quota of lawns and horse-chestnuts, and a statue of a Negro girl thrown in. The beds and dressing-tables had been moved out and the rooms filled with filing-cabinets, typewriters, and multigraphing-machines. The officials and secretaries dined in the city's restaurants and took their constitutionals on the avenues shaded with plane trees, but they were rarely invited to the homes of the citizens. Said Armstrong: "From what I hear we don't miss much."

The head nurse of this ugly duckling was a Scotch gentleman named Sir Eric Drummond, a caricaturist's dream of a British bureaucrat; tall, thin, with fair hair, a long neck and prominent Adam's apple; wearing, of course, a short black coat, a watch-chain, and dark-striped trousers, and carrying a black umbrella neatly rolled. He had had a dreadful time getting started, because nobody would send him any money; but he had gone patiently ahead, selecting with extraordinary discernment exactly the right sort of men to run what might some day become the biggest enterprise in the history of mankind.

Impossible not to sympathize with such efforts, and to respect the men who were making them. Lanny thought of that pitiful invalid, now a private citizen in Washington, from whose soul this League had sprung. Lanny had seen a picture of him, riding to the inaugural ceremony with his bland and well-fed successor; Wilson's face drawn and haggard, the mask of a man suffering, not his own martyrdom, but that of his hopes and dreams. Here in Geneva he had planted a little acorn which had become a vigorous sprout. Would it live to be a great oak? If it did, the name of

Woodrow Wilson would live on, while the names of his antagonists would be buried in the encyclopedias.

Such were the questions which Lanny and his friends debated in between their inquiries and interviews. Lanny had in mind the bitter scorn of his father and his uncle. Robbie Budd and Jesse Blackless were at one in their certainty that the League must collapse, and that it would be the struggle for markets and raw materials, the commercial rivalries of great states which would bring it down. Jesse hated that blind greed and the men who embodied it; Robbie, one of those men himself, took it as a basic law of nature, the condition upon which life was lived. Might it be that neither of them was entirely right, but that the greed of men might be gradually tamed and brought under the rule of law; that freedom might slowly broaden down from precedent to precedent?

Lanny had been reading a history of his own country, selected from several in the Eli Budd library. He had freshly in mind the loose Confederation which the thirteen colonies had formed while they were struggling for their freedom. It had served a temporary purpose, keeping them together until public opinion had time to form in favor of an enduring union. Might it not be that something of the same sort was happening here? Let the nations recover from their war psychosis and realize how much better it was to reason together than to fight, how much easier to produce goods with modern machinery than to take one another's goods by force—then you might see a real Federation of the World such as Tennyson and other poets had sung.

IV

Lanny called up George D. Herron and was invited to bring his friends to tea. The Socialist exile lived in a beautiful villa called Le Retour, but he was one of the unhappiest men alive, and a very sick one, as Lanny well knew. His face was like marble, and his black beard and mustache were turning gray; he seldom had an hour without pain, but what troubled him most was the agony of civilization. Herron was literally dying of grief over the mass tragedy which he had witnessed in Paris. He had poured his anguish into a book called *The Defeat in the Victory*, which was soon to appear through an English publishing-house. Impossible to get it published in his native land, where everybody was done with Europe, forever and ever, amen.

Herron was a gracious and charming host. He had conceived a sort of fatherly affection for Lanny, doubtless still thinking of him as a possible convert. Because he had lived in Geneva since the beginning of the war, he was a mine of information about the place and its doings. He had read the world's best literature in half a dozen languages, and so his conversation was that of a scholar as well as of a prophet.

Lanny told what his English friend had come for, so Herron talked about the League; it was a League of governments, not of peoples, and from none of the existing governments was any good thing to be expected. He said that the hope of the world now lay in its youth, which had the task of forging a new spiritual and intellectual sword for the overcoming of those greedy powers which ruled our society. While he said this the Socialist prophet looked into the eyes of two representatives of that youth, and seemed to be asking: "How well are you prepared for your task?"

Lanny mentioned the problem of Upper Silesia, and how it weighed upon him because of his German friend. That led Herron to talk about the experiences he had had with the Germans all through the war. It had been known that he was in touch with President Wilson, and was sending reports through the State Department, so the Germans assumed that he was authorized to negotiate with them—which wasn't so. First the Socialists and the pacifists, and later on, as Germany's situation became worse, the representatives of the government, came to Le Retour in an unceasing stream.

"They constituted," said Herron, "a veritable clinic for the observation of the German mind; and my conclusion was that there is something inherently amiss in its make-up. The German, in his present stage of development, cannot think directly and therefore morally. He still moves, he still has his psychic being, collectively speaking, in what seems like prehuman nature. The German commonly reasons that whatever accomplishes his ends as an agent or citizen of the State is both mystically and scientifically justifiable. No matter how reprehensible the means, there is no responsibility higher than these ends that can claim his confidence."

"Do you mean that this is the creed that every German has thought out?" It was Rick questioning.

"I mean it is the mental stuff of his motivation, whether conscious or unconscious. The sheer might that achieves the thing in view becomes his supreme good. You understand that I am speaking of a stream of visitors continuing over a period of three or four years. Each discussion, without regard to the messenger's intellectual repute, or his high or low official degree, began with his assumption that Germany was misunderstood and wronged, even to the extent of a piteous martyrdom. If ever there was any grudging admission that Germany might have been remiss, it was because of deception practiced by jealous neighbors upon this too trustful, too childlike people. And always Germany must be preserved from discovering that the responsibility was hers. As an instance, an eminent and official German of high intellectual quality—a German whom I had long held in affectionate admiration—continually sought to show me that the war must be so ended as to save Germany from the humiliation of a confession. The preservation of Germany's national pride, rather than the revelation of righteousness to her people, was basic in all this good man's quest for a better German future. Well aware as he was of the historical abnormality of his race, admitting it candidly enough in our discussions, yet so thoroughly German was he that he could conceive no peace except one that would save Germany from self-accusation."

V

All the time that Lanny Budd was listening to this pain-driven man, he had in the back of his mind a question which his father had asked after meeting him, at lunch in the Hotel Crillon: "For God's sake, who is that nut?" Now Lanny tried to make up his

own mind. "What is a 'nut'? And why is he?" Certainly Herron
had a mass of information, and had co-ordinated it into a definite
system of thought. He was an absolutist; he formed certain
standards of justice and truth-telling which he had derived from
the prophets and saints of old, especially Jesus, and he tried to apply
those standards to a world ruled by force and guile. Perhaps they
didn't apply to that world, and couldn't ever be made to apply;
Robbie avowed that they couldn't—and perhaps that was the way
to get along. But Herron refused to give up; he said, as Jesus had
said: "Be ye therefore perfect, even as your Father which is in
heaven is perfect." Nobody paid much attention to this modern
prophet, any more than to the old-time one. Manifestly, theirs was
not the way to get along and be happy in this world.

Nothing had been done or was going to be done according to this
prophet's standards of righteousness. He said it himself, in words
which had the ring of Isaiah and Jeremiah. When he learned that
Lanny and Rick had attended the San Remo conference, he read
from the proofs of his book about the doings there: "The Supreme
Council, gambling in last chances, tosses Armenia to the Kurdish
dogs and gaily stakes the destinies of three continents on the capture of new supplies of oil. The starving Poles, typhus-stricken and
at risk of national extinction, march to the blackmailer's music, stab-
bing Soviet Russia in the back while the British Prime Minister
negotiates with that same Russia for a trader's truce."

A terrible thing to hear such words and not be able to contradict
them! How pathetic seemed the labors of earnest and patient func-
tionaries, putting a patch of plaster here and a bandage there on the
body of the suffering world, when you listened to Herron's fateful
statement upon the four treaties which had ended the World War:
"These are not peace, they are rather a pitiless provision for a military and predatory government of the world. They are pregnant
with wars more destructive, both physically and spiritually, than
history has yet registered, with the resultant prospect of a generation if not a century of tartarean tortures for the whole family
of man."

VI

The three friends came out from that interview in a sober mood, and discussed the various points Herron had raised. Rick, with his practical English sense, said that it was easy enough to condemn what the Peace Conference had done, but that didn't get you very far; what you had to do was to have a shot at what could be done next and what forces you could make use of. Marie, with her logical French mind, detected what she said were inconsistencies in the prophet's fervors. No one had ever presented a clearer indictment of those German qualities which made the race a menace to the peace of Europe, and Herron himself had called for the military defeat of Germanism; but he overlooked the plain fact that to achieve such a defeat you had to generate anger and determination in other peoples, and such feelings just cannot be turned off by a stopcock the day an armistice is signed.

"For fifty years," said Marie, "we French have had the fear of German invasion, and who is going to rid us of it? How shall we be protected? Dr. Herron wants us to forgive, and let everything be as if there hadn't been any war; but how can we be sure how that will work? Suppose the Germans take it as a sign of weakness? Suppose they see it as credulity? There are things for which they went to war, and which they'd still like to have. Suppose they take them?"

Difficult questions indeed; not to be answered that day, or for many days to come! Lanny drove Rick to another appointment, and the two lovers went for a walk on the lake front. They looked across the darkling water to the peak of Mont Blanc, changing from snow-white to pale pink and then to purple. They went on talking about George D. Herron, and when Lanny expressed sympathy for him, his friend asked with some anxiety: "Are you going to let yourself be drawn into that sort of extremism?"

He smiled and reassured her. "Pretty soon I'll meet somebody who will argue the opposite, and I'll find myself agreeing with him— at least part of the way. I suppose that to be a man of action one has to be able to see only one side, and be absolutely certain that it's the whole truth."

Inside himself Lanny was amused to see his *amie* mounting guard over him, keeping him out of trouble, just as Beauty did with Kurt. Were all women always trying to keep their men for themselves? His mind went back over the histories which he had read. How many married heroes could he recall?

VII

The day came when they had to leave. Rick said he had got stuff for more than one article, so they put him on the evening train, and then by the light of a large golden moon they set out along the river Rhône. They spent the night at Bourg, and by steady driving they reached the Château de Bruyne the following evening. There Lanny resumed that agreeable life into which he had already been initiated. The boys returned the next day, and were pleased to find that they were to have the companionship of this friendly young man, who would make music come alive for them, teach them various kinds of dancing, and tell them entertaining stories about Germany and England and Greece, and also a family of Puritan munitions makers who had helped to deliver *la belle France*.

Lanny still urged that Marie should tell the boys the truth about their relationship, or let him tell it; but Denis had been shocked by the suggestion, and he had a right to say no. These must be good Catholic boys; that is, they had to be taught to look upon sex as something inherently shameful and unclean; but also it would be something irresistibly fascinating—nature would see to that—and so they would find out about it in secret ways. Sooner or later, from the gossip of servants or other boys, they would learn about Lanny and their mother, and would be forced to choose between thinking less of their mother and thinking less of the religion they had been taught. At that time Marie would have to fight for herself; but she couldn't do it now, and Lanny couldn't urge it without causing a rift in the lute which was producing such pleasant music for him.

They lived, externally, a most proper life. They made a rule that they would never so much as touch hands except when they were in their own rooms with the doors locked. Everywhere else Lanny

was a friend of the family, and when visitors came he met them
if he wished, or stayed in a corner of the garden and read his books.
He acquired a stack of music and played for hours, and Marie never
tired of listening. They went in to Paris for the various art shows,
for theaters and opera, and occasionally Denis would join them; he
was unobtrusive and they did their best to make him feel that he was
not *de trop*.

Robbie Budd went to London again, and Lanny offered to pay
him a visit, but Robbie wired that he would be in Paris in a couple
of days; Lanny was glad, for of course he wanted his father to meet
his *amie*. The *amie* looked forward to the occasion with feelings
in which curiosity and trepidation were about equally balanced.
Denis, most perfect of gentlemen, said that he had heard about M.
Budd, a very solid businessman, and would like nothing better than
to welcome him as a week-end guest at the château.

"By heck," exclaimed Robbie, when he heard the proposal, "that's
a new one on me!" But he was game. If he had been among the
Turkomans and had been invited to eat boiling-hot lamb and rice
with his fingers, he would have done so. Lanny was living in France,
and if he had found a French lady to make him happy, it was all
right with his father, who had given him an unorthodox start and
could hardly blame him for following his stars.

Lanny came in and met the morning train, and drove his
progenitor around while he attended to various business matters, and
then in the cool of the evening drove him out to the château. Robbie
had everything carefully explained to him in advance, and if he
felt the least bit queasy he certainly didn't let it show. He could
see at one glance that Lanny had found a woman of charm, and he
didn't have to talk with her long to see that she had both culture
and character. "I wouldn't mind having a woman like that myself!"
he said, and meant it as a compliment. As for Denis, he was the sort
of man that Robbie enjoyed being with; a sensible fellow who had
made his own way in the world, and knew what was going on and
could exchange ideas about it. In short, an agreeable family, and a
delightfully original way for a youth to spend a summer vacation.

"But don't say anything about it in Newcastle," advised Lanny. The father replied: "God Almighty!"

VIII

Listening to the conversation of two men of affairs, Lanny got an insight into the realities of French politics. Denis was a "Nationalist," which meant that he thought it was the business of the French government to look after the interests of France, and especially of French businessmen, the persons who would give employment to French workers if they were to get any. That was exactly the idea of Robbie's Republican party as to the United States, so these two understood each other perfectly; when Denis denounced the present French Premier, it might have been Robbie expressing his opinion of a certain scholar in politics who had departed from the White House five months previously.

The Premier of France was a man named Aristide Briand, and he was what the French call "a son of the people." His father had been an innkeeper in that Loire country where Lanny and Marie had spent their honeymoon—perhaps they had stayed in that very inn. Like most French politicians, Briand had begun as an extreme Socialist, but when he got power he smashed a strike of the railwaymen by the device of ordering them all on military duty. However, that wasn't enough to cause Denis de Bruyne to trust him, for he was called a "man of peace," which meant, in effect, that he was one more Frenchman succumbing to the blandishments of David Lloyd George, that master of the arts of political seduction.

Denis explained the situation. Britain had her vast overseas empire and her world trade; she would soon grow rich again, and that was what she was thinking about. But France lay with her most productive provinces in ruins, her people unemployed, and her hereditary enemy refusing to give up her arms, saying, in effect: "Come and get them!" Refusing to meet the reparations bill, deliberately destroying her financial system in order to ruin her rival, and repeating that offer which drove French businessmen frantic—to pay in goods, while French workers stayed idle and French businessmen got no profits!

Time after time, France would be invited to conferences, where the "Welsh wizard" would turn loose his oratorical blandishments; he would take the side of the Germans and persuade the French to give up this and give up that; to let history's greatest robber get away unscathed, with most of his loot safely stowed away in his fastnesses. "*Honteux!*" exclaimed Denis de Bruyne, and pounded his fist on the arm of his chair as he called the roll of these conferences of dishonor—San Remo, Hythe, Spa, Brussels, Paris, London. "*Il faut en finir!*" cried the "Nationalist."

While Robbie was there, early in August, another conference was called in Paris; an emergency one, as they were all coming to be. Imagine, if you could, the rosy little cherub with the lion's mane ensconced with all his staff in the Hotel Crillon, wining and dining the innkeeper's son, treating him as a social equal—and persuading him that the only way to settle the question of Upper Silesia was to refer it to the League of Nations! Playing upon those sentiments politely called "humanitarian," though to Denis de Bruyne they were the cheapest and most disgusting of a demagogue's stocks in trade. Talking about German "rights" to territory which every historian knew had been seized by the Prussian Frederick and which now was absolutely vital to Poland—and to France, if she was to have an ally on the eastern front to hold the ruthless Prussians in check. But of course England didn't want France to be strong on the Continent; she was setting Germany up as a rival—the "balance of power" policy!

Lanny listened to all this and kept his thoughts to himself. He had not told his host that he had a close friend from Upper Silesia, and how different these matters appeared from that friend's point of view. Lanny had come to the reluctant conclusion that his father's political beliefs were conditioned by his business interests, and he now decided that this French gentleman was in the same case. But Lanny wasn't there to educate him; all that Lanny cared about was a remark which his father reported—a remark which Denis had made *à propos de bottes,* as the French say, meaning *à propos* of nothing in particular:

"You know, M. Budd, the arrangement is excellent for all parties. When a woman is not satisfied she is liable to wander off, and I'd hate to have the mother of my children fall into the clutches of some adventurer."

To which Robbie replied with cordiality: "It seems to me, too, the arrangement is an excellent one for all parties, and I hope it may continue."

IX

Robbie Budd was in Paris because of another oil venture he was going in for; yes, in spite of the hard times, or rather because of them. Somebody else was in trouble, while Robbie, far-sighted fellow, had cash in several banks—and not those which had been closed! Robbie didn't tell much about it. Was he afraid that a youngster very much in love might talk too freely to a French lady? Or was it just that he had come to the realization that his son didn't like the smell of oil?

What he did tell about was Johannes Robin. It beat the Dutch the way that fellow was coining money! He had moved to Berlin, to be nearer his sources of information, and had just taken a trip to London to meet his associate. Six months ago he had dragged Robbie into selling the German mark short; he wasn't taking any commission, it was pure friendship, or gratitude—"and I suppose pride to be associated with us," added the father. "He wants you to play duets with Hansi!"

"He surely doesn't have to pay us for that," replied Lanny.

"Well, I agreed to go in with him, and every now and then I get a cablegram telling me that I have another deposit in a New York bank. We have a code, and he'll say: 'Methuselah seventieth birthday November'—that means that the mark will be seventy to the dollar in three months. You see, he predicted a long time ago that some day one dollar would buy as many marks as the years of Methuselah! Have you been watching the quotations?"

"I look now and then, because I know you're betting on it."

"It seems that Robin really has the inside dope. The mark was four to the dollar before the war, and today it's quoted at sixty-three. He insists it can't come back."

"I suppose there's nothing the Germans can do but go on printing money."

"What they are doing," said Robbie, "is reducing the public debt; an easy 'out' for a Socialist government."

"I had a letter from the boys," remarked Lanny. "They are happy about being in Berlin, it's such a wonderful city, and Hansi will have great teachers at the Conservatory."

"If things work out the way that doggone Jew says, he's going to own half the town before he's through."

"I'm afraid the Germans won't like him for it," remarked Lanny, dubiously. "They call such people *Schieber*."

"Well, if properties are for sale, he surely has a right to buy them. And of course if things get too hot, he can move back to Holland."

X

Lanny told about his visit to Geneva and what he had learned there. Robbie said he had no quarrel with the League as an attempt of Europe to solve its own problems; he didn't think it would last long, because, as soon as some major issue arose, the nations would fight it out; they would never surrender their right to do that. Robbie's concern was to keep the United States out of it; and on this point he was in a mood of extreme vexation, because the new President, upon whom he had based such high hopes, had already capitulated to the meddlers and the pacifists—he had just issued a call for an international conference for limitation of navies to meet in Washington on next Armistice Day.

To the head salesman of Budd's, who had put up campaign funds so generously, that was indeed a betrayal. Robbie Budd was too tactful a man to say to anybody, even his son: "This will knock out my chance for profits for many years." No, what he said was: "This will knock out America's chance to get an adequate armament industry. Britain and France will diddle us, they will fix up an agreement to leave us weak where we need to be strong; we will keep our part of the bargain, and then when it is too late find out that they have been wriggling out of their part."

"What do you suppose put Harding up to that?" asked the son.

"The proposal came from London. It's popular because so many people are sick of war, and insisting that something be tried. You hear it in the most unexpected places. The Reverend Saddleback preached what was almost a pacifist sermon. I didn't hear it, but that's what everybody said."

"That must have given Grandfather quite a jolt!"

"We have lived through so many earthquakes that we don't notice jolts any more. You can't imagine how things are at home. That nightmare in Russia has driven our agitators crazy; in New York you hear them shouting on every other street corner."

"And in Newcastle?"

"We don't let them get that far; but they're working underground, hundreds of them, Father says. Some day we may have a strike to deal with, but hardly while jobs are so scarce."

Lanny didn't say how he himself had been consorting with such enemies of the public welfare. He wondered: Had Johannes Robin noted his sons' interest in Red ideas, and perhaps mentioned to Robbie how the boys had met Beauty's Red brother? Apparently he hadn't, and Lanny didn't bring up the subject, for he knew exactly what his father would say, and when you have heard one line of discourse a certain number of times, you lose interest in hearing it again—especially when it has to do with your not doing something that you might want to do!

XI

Dropping the ticklish topic of politics, Lanny asked the news about that large and eccentric family at home. Old ones on the way out and new ones on the way in—but not so rapidly as in old days. Robbie's oldest brother, Lawford, continuing to be a "sorehead" and to quarrel with Robbie whenever possible. Grandfather Samuel showing his age, but still set in determination to run the business

and the family. Esther, Lanny's stepmother, helping to raise funds
for the needy, whom she no longer had to seek in Europe—there
was an abundance of them right in Newcastle. Robbie gave her a
large allowance to be spent on the former employees of Budd Gunmakers and their families. "You know," he explained, "people say
that when you give a hand-out to a tramp he makes a sign on your
gate to let the other tramps know that you're an easy mark. It's
about the same with your ex-employees, I find—they write to their
relatives and the whole gang comes hitch-hiking into town!"

Lanny asked about the children. The two boys were well, and
were going to be sturdy fellows. Bess, now thirteen, was a dynamo
of energy, and had commissioned her father to scold Lanny because
he didn't write often enough. "I ought to send her a present," said
the half-brother, and Robbie replied: "Send something to all of
them."

It was hard to think what to give to persons whose every want
was so carefully met. Lanny asked: "Do you think they might like
a painting?" He would have offered one of Marcel's, but he knew
that Esther would find it embarrassing to explain the stepfather of
her stepson—it sounded queer, and suggestive of a double im-
propriety. "I'll look in the shops and see if I can find something
French that will be different from what they are used to."

"Nothing sexy," warned Robbie.

"Oh, of course not. I mean something gay; something with a little
esprit."

XII

When he took his father into Paris to consult with oil tycoons,
Lanny went for a stroll on the Boulevard Montparnasse. You would
have thought that every other person in France aspired to be a
painter; not merely were there innumerable art dealers, but little
shops like grocers' and cobblers' would have paintings in the windows. Lanny's eyes were quick, and he didn't mind walking, so he
must have seen a thousand paintings that morning before he found
what he wanted, some very lively little wash drawings of Parisian
street scenes, full of character.

Having lived in France most of his life, he knew how to buy things. He knew that there was one price if you were French, a higher one if you were Spanish, a still higher one if you were German, and a triple or quadruple one if you bore the faintest sign of Americanism. It was a game, and the proper way to play it was to price other things first and say that all the prices were too high. You took only a casual glance at the thing you really wanted, and you asked its price indifferently, and then started out, remarking with a laugh that half that would be about right; as a rule your suggestion would be accepted before you got to the door.

Lanny offered a hundred francs for four of those drawings, with the right to make his choice. He picked out a jolly little Pierrot for Bess, and two street urchins for the boys, and for his stepmother a sturdy market-woman standing by her little handcart full of fruit, with her arms akimbo and an expression that told you how she would storm at you if you attempted to pinch one of her precious pears to see if it was ripe. The drawings were the work of an unknown artist, and when you made a purchase like that you were taking a chance in a lottery; the chance that your great-grandchildren might discover them in some dust-covered trunk, and recognize a famous signature, and sell them to a collector for several thousand dollars apiece.

To the Budd family the drawings would be a friendly reminder of one who had been a dangerous and disturbing guest, but was romantic while he dwelt overseas. Robbie promised to have them framed, and not to forget which one was for which. Then he made the suggestion that Lanny should take another walk, this time along the Rue de la Paix, and look into the windows of the jewelry shops and find a present for his *amie*. But Lanny thought it over and said no, he didn't think Marie would desire that; he was making her happy day by day, and that was enough.

Robbie thought it over in turn, and said: "Maybe you are right. If you start making presents you can't be sure where it will stop." The cautious man of business added: "Better not tell Beauty that I'm making so much money. Hard times are good for her!"

BOOK THREE

The Staircase of History

11

Woe to the Conquered

I

FOR a long time to come Lanny's life was destined to be governed by the calendar of a French boarding-school for boys. When the school closed, he would come to Seine-et-Oise, and when it opened again he was free to go to the Midi, or to any other parts of the world which appealed to him and his *amie*. In September the lovers returned to Bienvenu, and Lanny set to work upon a task which he had discussed with his father, the erection of another villa on the estate. The Riviera was becoming crowded, and in the "season" it was difficult to find anything to rent. Lanny hoped to invite Rick and Nina the coming winter, and, anyhow, it seemed sensible to have a guest-house. Robbie, who believed in buildings, was pleased to invest some of the money he was getting from Johannes Robin. He advised putting the house in one corner of the estate, so that it could be sold separately if ever they wanted to.

Lanny talked things over with his mother and engaged a contractor. Of course he wrote to Rick about it, and told him that the family's feelings would be hurt if he and Nina didn't make their plans to come for a housewarming during the winter.

In the midst of these operations who should show up but their old friend, the former Baroness de la Tourette, who had shed her title by means of an American divorce, and was now plain Sophie Timmons of Cincinnati, Ohio—and if you didn't like it you could lump it, said the daughter of a hardware manufacturer. Sophie was done both with the aristocracy and with men, she declared; she would be willing for the Bolshies to wipe out all the former, while the scientists rendered the latter superfluous by means of artificial parthenogenesis. Beauty had never heard that jawbreaker, but when Sophie explained the idea she approved it heartily. Men were mostly unreliable, and when you had two of them about the house all the time they were intolerable. Having said this, Beauty began running over in her mind all the eligible men she knew, to decide which was the best for Sophie Timmons.

Of course the retired baroness had heard about the queer extra-marital arrangements of this family, and was "dying with curiosity." Lanny had been her pet as a boy, and she had known Marie in society; it seemed to her the oddest prank that Cupid had ever played—and that was saying a lot. She had never met the fourth member of the family, and found herself a little in awe of a serious blue-eyed artillery officer, who, for all Sophie could ever know, might have fired the shell which killed her own *ami*, poor Eddie Patterson, driving an ambulance on the Marne front in the last days of the war.

Sophie settled down in her villa with a maid and a couple of servants, saying that she needed to recuperate from living with her family in Ohio. She liked to play bridge, so in the evenings she would drive to Bienvenu, picking up old M. Rochambeau and his niece; they would play for small stakes, because the elderly ex-diplomat couldn't afford to lose much. If this pair were not available, they would phone for Jerry Pendleton and press Marie into service. It was all right for Lanny to prefer to read, but it was considered "sniffy" if a woman took such a pose.

Lanny's ex-tutor was on call for any goings-on—a picnic, a sail, a swim. He had held a position in a tourist office during the winter, and Lanny now arranged for him to oversee the building job, as a pretext for helping him out. Jerry had two babies at home, and his little French wife was busy with these; if she had social aspirations, they could be satisfied by inviting her to a lawn party or something of a not too intimate nature. Women were a drug on the market in post-war France, but desirable men were scarce, and especially in this obscure village of Juan-les-Pins in the "off season."

II

In November Lanny had his twenty-second birthday, and his mother decided to give him a party. For two years and a half she had been hiding as it were in a cave on account of Kurt; now, under the guise of a celebration for Lanny, she was going to present his "music-teacher" to the world. It would be a tennis party and an *al fresco* supper, with music and dancing in the evening. Kurt Meissner would play, and he would be introduced under his own name. The few friends who had met him as M. Dalcroze would be told that that was his middle name, which he used for professional purposes.

One of the reasons for all this was that Kurt wished to go back and visit his people during the coming Christmas. Three years had passed since the Armistice, and that was surely enough for safety. As the treaty of Versailles had fixed matters, Kurt was a citizen of Poland, and that country being an ally of France, it would be easy for him to return. This was a way to get rid of the forged passport upon which he had been traveling as a German agent.

Affairs had settled down in Silesia, because the League of Nations had effected a compromise, dividing the industrial districts between Germany and Poland, but providing that for fifteen years there should be no customs barriers between the parts. A joint Polish-German commission was working out the details, so there would be no more fighting. Beauty was worried, but she couldn't deny the rightness of Kurt's desire to see his people after so long a time, and she was wise enough not to let him feel that she was putting chains upon him. Lanny was going along—to keep him in order, so he said with a smile. It would be eight years since Lanny had seen Schloss Stubendorf—and what an eight years in the history of mankind!

Lanny mentioned the proposed trip in a letter to the two young Robins, and right away came a telegram—oh, please, please, please—they paid for three extra words—come to Berlin and stay with them, and hear Hansi play the Bruch concerto! Kurt and Lanny talked it over. Kurt's oldest brother, an army officer, was stationed in Potsdam, and might not be able to get off for Christmas—most of them had to be on duty all the time, holding down the Reds. Kurt hadn't planned to see him, because he couldn't afford the extra journey; but Lanny said nonsense, he was going to pay for the whole trip. They would go to Berlin before Christmas, and Kurt would stay with his brother. He would never say anything to hurt the feelings of the Robins, he said, but he wouldn't bring himself to condone the doings of a *Schieber* by entering his home.

Lanny knew better than to argue about the matter. He hadn't told Kurt that Robbie was a *Schieber*, too, and that the money for the trip would come out of his ill-gotten gains! In the month of Lanny's birthday Methuselah had reached the age of two hundred; that is to say, with one American copper cent you could buy two marks' worth of anything in Germany—and you would be humbly thanked for doing it.

III

Lanny and Kurt descending from the *wagon-lit* in the Potsdamer Bahnhof, and being welcomed by Kurt's eldest brother, Emil, whom Lanny had never met before; an elegant tall fellow with yellow mustaches waxed to points, a monocle, and a long gray military cloak nearly to his ankles; clicking his heels, bowing from the waist, doing all the honors for Kurt's friend, who was also his employer—so the family had been told. A long thin face, this Prussian officer's, difficult to relax, and his pale steely eyes made Lanny think of an eagle's. Not that Lanny had ever seen an eagle's eyes, but he imagined what they would be like. The Prussian eagle had a double head, and Kurt was the other head of this one.

Emil did everything possible to maintain his pride, but Lanny noticed that his cloak was badly worn and faded, and had a telltale patch near the bottom—perhaps a bullet had carried some of it away. The truth was that Emil was lucky to have a job at all, for there were close to a million officers of all ranks who had been turned out of work by the Versailles treaty. The three walked along the platform, and Lanny noted many signs of poverty; a well-nourished face was rare, and the crowds looked as if they had got their clothes in second-hand shops. Germans would always be clean, even if they had to wash themselves with soda instead of soap; but they had no way to repair or paint their houses, or to mend things broken in civil war. Ragged beggars were everywhere, and women with pinched faces and pitiful finery—not even in Paris did you see so many prostitutes. Bodies of suicides were being found every day in the river and the canals of Berlin, and never did one of them have on underwear. Lanny and Kurt were ashamed to be dressed so well— and glad they had not let Beauty equip them with fresh outfits.

There was a military automobile with a uniformed chauffeur waiting for Kurt's brother. More heel-clicking and bowing, and Lanny saw them off, and took a taxi to the Robins' nest. The taxi looked as if it had been through several wars; it had a ragged seat and a bullet-hole through the window; but the apartment house where the *Schieber* lived was most elegant and had a functionary in a bright-colored uniform to open the door. The best of everything was yours if you had foreign money; keep it safe in the bank, and change it every day as you needed it, because it multiplied itself faster than rabbits.

One of the first things Lanny noted about the Robin apartment was that it had been specially provided with a steel door having heavy hinges and bolts. This had been put in by the previous tenants during the period of the Communist uprisings. A strange, precarious life in this world of runaway inflation! The owner of the fashionable apartment house had just called upon his tenants and informed them that he was no longer able to purchase coal, and that they would have to get together and work out some co-operative way of keeping themselves warm.

Never had Lanny received such a welcome as that Jewish family gave him. When the steel door swung open they all cried out with delight and came swarming around him. Freddi took his hat and bags and Hansi his overcoat. Mama Robin, whom Lanny met for the first time, was a hearty, active little woman whose German had a strong Yiddish accent; kindness exuded from every pore of her, and she was so eager to make her guest comfortable that she made him the opposite. He was used to the English form of hospitality, which

took it for granted that everything in the house was yours and let
you help yourself without comment. But when you sat down to
dinner with Mama Robin, she insisted that you eat this and enjoy
that and have more of the other thing; she would clamor until Hansi
would say, gently: "Mama, you are bothering Lanny." Then there
would be a discussion as to whether she was or not, and Lanny would
have to eat more than he wanted, in order to avoid hurting the feelings of this Jewish mother whose hospitality lacked a sense of
security.

But all the discomfort vanished when Lanny sat at the piano and
Hansi took up his violin. Then everybody fell silent, and mysterious
presences entered the garishly furnished room. Beauty came, not
Lanny's mother, but a goddess, white-robed, broad-browed, with
stardust in her hair; Joy came, the daughter of Elysium; Pity came,
with tear-dimmed eyes, and Grief with head bowed and dark robes
trailing. Life became transfigured, and human insects stirring in
primeval slime suddenly discovered themselves to be seers of visions,
members of a mystical brotherhood, allies of a godhead. Genius had
made its appearance upon earth, and its wonders were the heritage
of all worshipers in the temple of Art.

IV

But one couldn't play or listen to music all the time in this world.
Johannes Robin had to go out and make money for his family and
satisfy the ambitions which drove him. The mother had to attend to
her household duties, and three young fellows had to eat and sleep,
and see something of the great city of Berlin, it being Lanny's first
visit. Snow was on the ground, and bitter winds blew part of the
time, but there came one sunny day, and they hired a coach with a
bony nag, and inspected the Reichstag building, and drove down the
Siegesallee, which celebrated the war before the last with a double
row of enormous Teutonic heroes in white marble. It was not permitted to laugh at them, because these were dangerous times, and the
shivering old coachman might have been one of the Kaiser's own
guards. Berlin was orderly now, but street-fighting had been going

on for a couple of years and no one could say when it might break out again. Well-dressed people didn't dare go into the working-class districts, but they scolded because the workers were getting more of the depreciated marks than the people who had incomes. The hungry poor formed breadlines, while the speculators danced and drank in the night-clubs.

When Lanny got back from the drive he found "Mama"—so she told him to call her—in a great fuss because there had come a telephone call from the American Embassy, which of course sounded tremendous to her. Lanny didn't know anybody there and couldn't imagine what it might be, but he called and was put through to the chargé d'affaires—no ambassador had been named yet. The chargé, it appeared, was a fraternity brother of Robbie Budd, and had a cablegram telling him that Lanny was to be visiting the Robins.

The official wanted to show him the town, and would he come and have lunch at the Kaiserliche Automobil Klub the following day? Lanny accepted, and an embassy car called for him and brought him to a quite palatial building with lackeys in pink knee-breeches and white silk stockings and gloves. Lanny couldn't help thinking that he was in a movie—except that a modern American career man, his host, didn't fit therein. "Do you always do your guests as proud as this?" inquired the youth, and the chargé said: "They presented our staff with membership cards. We are the most important people in the world right now—we have all the wheat and the pork!"

Evidently Germany still had venison and grouse, and the velvet-footed servitors brought them enormous portions. Lanny wondered what thoughts would be in the heads of these lackeys. They might be Junkers or they might be Socialists, but in either case they wouldn't have any use for American bourgeois. Lanny told his father's old friend the news about Robbie and his business, and about the family in Connecticut. They talked about the European situation in guarded terms, for of course every waiter might be a spy, and a diplomatic official must neither betray secrets nor give offense.

V

The chargé said he had brought Lanny here thinking he might like to see some of the important men of Berlin. Into this stately dining-room came members of the ruling classes—not the politicians, the Socialist and popular party upstarts who might be kicked out any day, but the financial men and businessmen whose power would endure. They were large men with bull necks, red faces, and bristly mustaches or beards; the blockade had affected their bulk no more than that of the white marble statues on the Siegesallee. They wore the short black coats called "mornings," which had come to replace the longer frock-coats of old days. Those passing bowed to the American official, and several stopped and were introduced to his guest.

The chargé indicated a short but broad and bulky fellow, swarthy as a Mediterranean, with a thick black beard and dingy clothes that fitted him, so Lanny said, "like socks on a rooster." It was Hugo Stinnes, the coal magnate, and the youth mentioned: "I saw him at Spa. He laid down the law, I was told, and made the German delegation accept the coal agreement. The French are to pay the pithead cost and freight, plus five marks per ton to feed the miners."

"You can be sure Stinnes will get his share," commented the official. "He has bought up most of the newspapers in Germany, so the politicians have to dance to his piping."

There entered a handsome, elegantly dressed man with a small gray mustache and goatee and a nearly bald head. Passing their table, he stopped for a greeting. "Dr. Rathenau," said the chargé, introducing him. Lanny knew the name, for his father had praised him as a symbol of German organizing ability; he was the head of the country's great electrical trust, and during the war had been in charge of the supply of raw materials. It was owing to him that the Fatherland had been able to hold out so long, and now he was Minister of Reconstruction, with a still heavier task.

"A son of Robert Budd of Budd Gunmakers," said the chargé, and as the minister expressed his pleasure, the American added: "Won't you join us?"

Rathenau explained that he was waiting for a friend, but he sat down until this man should arrive. Lanny had a chance to study him, and decided that his face was both kind and thoughtful. His manner was suave, and his English flawless; he spoke long and polished sentences like a classical orator—but at the same time with the positiveness of one born to command.

Walther Rathenau had just come back from London, where he had been trying to persuade the British that it was impossible for Germany to meet the payment on reparations which was to fall due in a few days. With what could they meet it? They could sell only marks, and the results of that all the world's money-markets saw. The City men of London had already expressed their opinion on that subject by refusing to extend any credit to Germany, and giving as their reason the exorbitant reparations burden!

"They have decided to call another conference," said Rathenau. "It will be early next month, and I think at Cannes."

"Indeed?" said the chargé. "Then you will be right at Budd's back door. His home is Juan-les-Pins."

"I hope I may have the pleasure of seeing you there," added the youth, and the minister agreed courteously to renew the acquaintance.

"An extraordinary personality," said the American, after Rathenau had left the table. "He really understands the present situation, and it would be well if his advice were taken. The propertied classes of Germany are called upon to make sacrifices which hurt, and the fact that Rathenau is a Jew makes them even less willing to be ruled by him."

"He doesn't look like a Jew," commented Lanny.

"That happens with many of that race. But the Junkers know him, and will never forgive him because he is working with the Social-Democrats—even though it's in an effort to save them and their country."

VI

Lanny and Kurt took the night train for Upper Silesia, and in the morning were at the Polish border. A humiliating thing for Kurt to have to be examined by foreign customs officials and border police in order to get to his own home. The customs men were careless, but the passports were studied minutely; Lanny suspected that the officials didn't know how to read very well. They spoke a bad German when they were compelled to. Afterward Kurt quoted to his friend a saying that when you went east from Germany you were in half-Asia. The signs of it were rutted roads, dilapidated houses, vermin, and superstition.

Stubendorf was a predominantly German district, and the war hadn't reached here, so everything was in order, and the snow made the countryside look fresh and clean; only the worn and patched clothing told of extreme poverty. The little train which wound up the branch line had evidently been a troop train and was pretty much of a wreck, the seats cut to pieces and the broken windows boarded over. A farmer of the Schloss estate recognized Kurt and touched his hat and gave them a seat by a sound window, so they could look out upon the landscape which stirred them both deeply— Lanny because his previous visit to the "Christmas-card castle" shone in his memory like snow crystals in sunlight.

A sleigh met them and was pulled up the slopes by two rather feeble horses—for the war had left few good ones. On a high ridge the tiny town was clustered about the feet of the main building, the front part of which was modern, six stories high and built of gray stone. The Meissner home was one of the separate houses, and someone must have been watching at the window, for they all came trooping to the door before the two travelers had alighted from the sleigh. There were cries of delight, and the women had tears in their eyes.

Lanny had wondered what was going to be the attitude of Germans to an American, who had been an enemy only three years ago. Of course the members of this family knew that he personally had taken no part in the war, but still, his people had snatched victory out of the grasp of their people. Already in Berlin Lanny had discovered a peculiar fact, and here he found it confirmed—the Germans didn't seem to blame the Americans, they liked and admired them, and were sure that they had come into the war through a misunderstanding due to the subtlety of British propaganda. Now the Americans realized their mistake and were trying to atone for it, and the Germans would help them by explaining how right they had been.

But that would come later. It was Christmas eve, and every good German was sentimental about it, and if he hated anybody he stowed the feeling away on a back shelf for a week. Here was Herr Meissner, no longer stout and rosy, with partly bald head and pouches under chin and cheeks and eyes. And *die gute verständige Mutter*—Lanny always thought of Goethe's poem in connection with Frau Meissner; her brood had been reduced, for one son was in a hospital for incurables—nobody said what was wrong, but Lanny guessed it was a case of shell shock; another son buried in East Prussia, and in his place a young widow with three children. Also there was the Meissner daughter, whom Lanny remembered as singing Christmas carols and having a long golden plait hanging over each shoulder. Now she too was a widow with two children, and the little ones made the home gay, for they had no knowledge of war and no shadows over their lives. After they had been put to bed Kurt played for the elders the compositions upon which he had been working for so long. They listened enraptured, and could never get enough during his stay.

There were only a few lights on the Christmas tree, and the presents were simple, consisting either of food or of old things from pre-war days. The game in the forests had been greatly depleted, and now was being carefully guarded, but you had a little for Christmas; also you had an abundance of wheat and turnips from your fields, but sugar was among the precious metals and coffee a decoction from unnamed materials. You washed your remaining underwear with the care you would have given to the sheerest silk, for if you tore it you would have difficulty in getting a piece of thread with which to mend it. Lanny and Kurt had brought from France a priceless box of raisins, figs, and chocolates, and they helped to make a miraculous Christmas.

In this era of runaway inflation there were two kinds of rich people, the speculators and the peasants. The latter produced what

everybody had to have, and for which everybody paid a higher price
every day; so they hoarded their products, and now and then
brought home a large wad of paper money. The Polish mark had
taken its tumble in advance of the German, and there was a story
about a Polish peasant in a near-by district whose hut had burned
down during his absence, and he had torn his hair and cried that his
whole fortune had been destroyed. When they asked him what it
was, he answered: "Forty million marks!"

VII

The Graf Stubendorf whom Lanny had seen had died since the
war, and his oldest son ruled in his stead: a stiff Prussian general,
of whom everybody said that he had a very high sense of duty, but
nobody said he loved him. As his father had done, he greeted and
shook hands with all the tenants and retainers gathered in the great
hall of the Schloss; he was lacking in his father's geniality, but
perhaps that could be excused because the times were so dangerous
and the need of discipline so obvious. It was hard indeed for an
army officer whose home had been turned over to despised enemies
to talk about loving them for even one week.

As before, Herr Meissner spoke freely in the bosom of his family
about the affairs of Stubendorf and what the Graf had imparted to
him about political affairs. Lanny thought it could do no harm after
so many years, so he narrated how on his way home from his
previous visit he had been accosted in the railroad station by the
editor of a Social-Democratic newspaper, who had lured him into
talking indiscreetly about what he had heard at the Schloss. Lanny
said that he had often wondered whether the man had published
anything, and the Comptroller-General replied that he did remember
an article published in the *Arbeiterzeitung* which had puzzled them
all greatly, though it had never occurred to them to connect their
American visitor with it. Lanny assured his host that he had now
attained to years of discretion, so there was no possibility of such a
blunder being repeated.

Herr Meissner had somewhat altered his views. The Socialists were now comparatively respectable people with whom one was compelled, however reluctantly, to do business. Their place as public enemies had been taken by the Communists, who were plotting a revolution on the Russian model and therefore had to be regarded as wild beasts. The Socialists, no matter how unsound their ideas, at least believed in law and order and were willing to wait until they had converted a majority of the people to vote their way; meanwhile their help was urgently needed against the Bolshevik menace.

Eight years before, Lanny had sat and listened in silence to what the Comptroller-General told his family; but now he knew much that was of interest to all of them, and Herr Meissner asked him about the Peace Conference and the decisions it had taken concerning their homeland. Lanny outlined some of the discussions to which he had been an auditor. In return the host explained the attitude of the people here and made no effort to conceal the fact that no German had any idea of accepting the settlement as more than a breathing-space.

"The French won the war," said Meissner, "and we are willing to accept that, and to forgive and forget. It has happened before, and can happen again. But what has never happened is that a nation should be loaded down with a debt so out of all reason that every child knows it is not a real claim, but an effort to make it impossible for us to regain our trade and prosperity. To resist that is a fight for survival, and the people who do it to us choose to be our permanent enemies."

Lanny was there to learn and not to argue. He did not tell his host what he had heard Denis de Bruyne saying to his father, nor did he quote George D. Herron's analysis of the German mind. He listened to a detailed story of how the French had plotted to defeat the purposes of the Supreme Allied Council in Upper Silesia. Their army had not merely failed to play fair in the carrying out of the plebiscite decision; they had openly encouraged Korfanty and his *sokols*, the Polish patriot bands. They had allowed some four hundred Polish officers to come in and join these bands and they had permitted gun-running everywhere throughout the land. Here in Stubendorf Polish peasants had been freely recruited, and if information about this was turned over to the French army authorities they did nothing whatever. Said Meissner: "They had the same idea as in the Rhineland, that if a revolution could be accomplished, the Supreme Council would be compelled to recognize it."

The Comptroller-General went on to explain that since the British troops had come in things had been more tolerable. "We have the land, and the Poles can't do us much harm with their taxes, because their money goes down so fast that by the time the taxes are due they aren't so big as they were meant to be. They are still less when the government spends them!" The speaker smiled rather slyly, and added that the Berlin government had accepted the settlement because it had to, but no German in Stubendorf would rest until he and his property were back under the sheltering wings of the Fatherland. "Life means nothing to us otherwise," he said, and authorized Lanny to tell that to all the French and British people he met.

VIII

Kurt had a duty to perform, to visit his sick brother, who was in a private hospital. He said he wouldn't invite Lanny, because it would probably be a painful experience. The brother was in the care of a physician, an old friend of the family; when Lanny learned that the place was in Poland proper, he suggested going along and seeing a bit of the town while Kurt paid his visit. Kurt replied that there wouldn't be much to see, but he'd be glad to have company on a tiresome trip.

They rode on the branch line to the junction and then on another line, in another dilapidated day-coach. The town was in the war zone, and many of its ruins had not yet been touched. The hospital had one wing demolished, and rebuilding was going on. Lanny left his friend at the gate and set out to see Poland. Very few of the streets had any paving whatever; a few had board sidewalks, but many of the boards were missing. Though everything was covered by a blanket of fresh snow, deep ruts and hollows were visible, and one could imagine that travel would become difficult in springtime.

The center of the town was a market-square, with shops and drinking-places around it. Lanny looked in the windows and perceived that there was little merchandise on sale. Two sides of the square were lined with peasant carts. Country produce was set out, and ragged, hungry-looking people wandered by, stopping now and then to haggle. Many of these people were what are called "Water Poles"; of Slovak descent, they are accustomed to go into Germany as laborers, so they speak a mixture of German and Polish, and Lanny could understand a part of what they said. The peasants wore ragged sheepskin coats and heavy caps that could be pulled over the ears; they stamped their feet and beat their arms to keep warm. Lanny judged that in the matter of underwear they resembled the suicides of the Berlin canals. You could smell a single peasant several yards away in still air, and when you had a crowd of them the mucous membranes of your nose were assailed by a steady bombardment of the molecules of ammonia, so highly volatile.

Lanny wandered for a while, looking and listening, trying to imagine what it might be like to be a Polish peasant exchanging cabbages and turnips for greasy pieces of paper with Polish eagles and Arabic numerals on them. Everybody was polite to a magnificent *Fremder* in an elegant woolen overcoat, but few stared at him; they were too miserable and chilled for curiosity. Now and then a beggar followed, whining, but Lanny feared that if he gave to one he would be besieged. No doubt the peasants had the same fear, for they gave to nobody. Altogether Lanny's impressions of the new Polish republic were unfavorable, and it seemed to him that Paderewski would have done better to stick to the concert stage, and he himself to stay at the Meissner home and play accompaniments to old German *Lieder* for two gentle young blond Nordic widows.

IX

Two or three times Lanny passed the hotel where he was to be met by Kurt. It was an unpromising-looking place, so he made up his mind to suggest that they go hungry for a while. Kurt was staying longer than he planned, and Lanny sought in vain for something that could be called picturesque; there was nothing like that in sight, and he wished he had brought a book along.

He had started to walk around the square to keep warm when he saw three soldiers, wearing faded and worn uniforms and carrying bayoneted rifles, enter from one of the streets, leading before them a man with hands tied behind his back. Lanny stopped to watch, and saw one of the soldiers go into a shop, while the other two led their prisoner under a large bare-limbed tree which grew in the square. They stood there, waiting, and presently the third man came out of the shop carrying a long and quite heavy rope; he rejoined the others and proceeded to toss one end of the rope up over a limb of the tree. "My God!" thought Lanny. "They are going to hang him!"

The son of Budd Gunmakers had had many odd experiences during his twenty-two years in a bewildering world, but this was the first time he had ever attended an execution. He looked about him and observed that peasants and townspeople made note of what was going on, but made it quickly, and then turned back to their own affairs. Could it be that they had seen so many people hanged that it was less important than the sale of cabbages and turnips? Or were they for some reason afraid to show any interest or feeling?

It didn't occur to Lanny to be afraid. He was sure that Polish soldiers were not hanging anybody from the sweet land of liberty; and he had yet to meet any people in the world with whom he couldn't get along. Perceiving that the job was going to be a quick one, he started to walk in that direction. As he neared the group he noted that the prisoner was a mere youth, and that he was ragged, pale, and depressed-looking, just like hundreds of others whom Lanny had been watching and smelling. The soldiers also appeared to have missed bathing and shaving for many days.

By the time Lanny reached the scene there was a noose about the neck of the prisoner, and the three men had hold of the other end. "*Guten Tag*," said Lanny, with a pleasant smile, and added a magical word: "*Amerikaner.*" The Polish form happens to be "*Amerykanin,*" which was near enough.

The faces of the soldiers showed interest, and the leader, who might have been a corporal, said: "*Guten Tag, Herrschaft.*"

That was promising; he was a "Water Pole." Possibly he might have labored in America, so Lanny inquired: "*Sprechen Sie Englisch?*"

"*Nein, nein,*" was the reply.

Lanny had never learned to smoke, but he had discovered that the practice offered a passport to friendship all over this war-torn continent, so while traveling he kept a package of cigarettes in his pocket. Now he drew it forth, tore it open, and held it out. The three soldiers, who had laid their guns against the tree, now hung the rope over their arms and reached out dirty fingers for the lovely little white cylinders which the *Amerykanin* tendered. Grins of pleasure wreathed their faces, and when Lanny produced matches and proceeded to light each in turn, they were sure that he was a royal personage.

It seemed a reasonable guess that no military regulations would be violated if a prisoner lived long enough to watch his captors smoke a cigarette. But the *Herrschaft* had even more original ideas than that. "*Er, auch,*" he said, and pointed a cigarette toward the prisoner. Then he indicated the bonds. "*Los machen? Soll rauchen.*"

Delightful humanity of the noble lord from the land of unlimited possibilities! It was the sort of thing to be expected from people who sent over mountains of food and kind lovely ladies to distribute it among starving women and children. The American millionaire desired that the poor devil should smoke a cigarette in order to give him courage to be hanged! The soldiers grinned with amusement. Why not?

X

So far the youthful captive had manifested no interest in what was going on; he had stood staring sullenly before him. Lanny saw that he had dark eyes and hollow cheeks, and that he was shivering, whether from cold or fright could not be guessed. Certainly a most miserable human specimen, and perhaps to put an end to him would be the greatest kindness. But seeing the doglike eyes turned upon him, Lanny paid tribute to their common humanity by inquiring: *"Wollen Sie rauchen?"*

Apparently the man didn't know German; but what happened was plain in any language—the soldiers untied his hands, though keeping the rope on one wrist. Lanny extended a cigarette, and the prisoner took it and put it into his mouth. Lanny struck a match and lighted the cigarette. So there were four smokers, which meant four contented men for the time being. They smoked and inhaled deeply, giving every sign that it had been long since they had had such a chance.

The occasion called for conversation, and Lanny said: *"Was hat der Kerl getan?"* He pointed to the prisoner, and tried again: *"Was ist los?"*

"Kommunist," explained the corporal.

"Ach, so!" Lanny was duly shocked.

"Ja, Bolschewist," said the other.

"Aber," said Lanny, *"was hat er getan?"* He repeated this in several variations, but it was too much for the soldier's vocabulary, or possibly for his mind. Why ask what a Bolshevik had done? In order to be hanged, he didn't have to "do" anything, he just had to be. Surely any *Herrschaft* in the world would understand that!

"Aber!" persisted the stubborn American. He wanted to find out if the man had had a trial; but this too was hard to put across. Lanny tried all the German words he could think of: *Gericht, Richter, Untersuchung.* Again he couldn't be sure whether it was that Poles who went into Germany to labor for a few pfennigs a day never heard of such things, or whether the corporal couldn't conceive of applying them to a Communist. Apparently if you met one of these you simply tied his hands behind his back and borrowed or rented a rope and strung him up to the nearest tree for a lesson to the others. From the movies Lanny had learned that this was the practice with horse-thieves in the wild and woolly West, and it appeared that he was now in the wild and woolly East.

He hit upon one word which apparently was well known: *"Polizeiamt."* That seemed to worry the soldiers; their authority was being questioned, and by one who might himself have to do with the police. Lanny didn't want to worry them too much, so he distributed four more cigarettes, and the badly handicapped talk continued.

For the first time the prisoner took part. Maybe it was the smoke that waked him up, or maybe it was hope at work in his soul. He spoke rapidly in Polish, and Lanny listened closely, for in border lands foreign words creep in and often one word tells the subject of a conversation. Lanny was sure that he heard the word "America"; and then, more than once, a familiar but unexpected pair of syllables: "Brooklyn!"

The corporal turned to Lanny, and in his broken German made plain what was in question. "He says he knows the *Herrschaft*. In America. A city, Broukleen."

Lanny looked at the youth. Indubitably, there was the light of hope in his eyes; and for a moment it was obscured in one of them by the faintest trace of a wink. Lanny, who wasn't slow on the intake, turned to the corporal. "*Ja, gewiss. Ich kenn' ihn.*"

This threw the soldiers into obvious confusion. They began talking rapidly among themselves, and the prisoner joined them. The head man turned to Lanny again. "He says he is no Communist. He says the *Herrschaft* knows he is no Communist."

"*Ja, gewiss!*" repeated Lanny. "I knew him in Brooklyn, America. *Guter Kerl.* Good fellow. *Kein Kommunist. Kein Bolschewist.*"

Why did Lanny say all that? If he had been asked the question then, he couldn't have answered. Something welled up in him, quickly, unexplainably. Was it that he couldn't bear to see a poor devil hanged? Was it that he didn't believe in hanging anybody without a trial? Or was there some secret sympathy in his heart for the Communists? Had he come to the belief that, however they might be mistaken in their tactics, there was a share of justice in their cause? Since human motives are rarely simple, there may have been a bit of all these reasons in Lanny's mind.

Anyhow, he still had two cigarettes in his precious package, and he offered these, wrapper and all, to the corporal. "*Guter Kerl,*" he repeated. Still keeping his amiable smile upon his face, he reached into his pocket and produced some talismans of still more potent

magic; objects the existence of which had almost been forgotten in
"half-Asia"—four silver coins, German marks about the size of a
United States quarter, and having the double-headed Prussian eagle
upon one face. With these miraculous little disks one could buy most
anything in the land! Lanny handed one to each of the soldiers and
was about to give the fourth to the prisoner, but reflected that they
might hang him to get it, so he doubled the fee of the head man.
"*Guter Kerl! Mach' los!*" he said.

There could be no further argument. The rope was taken off the
other hand and the prisoner was free. The prince of the American
plutocracy shook the cold grimy hands of his three friends and said:
"*Danke schön,*" "*Leben Sie wohl,*" "*Adieu,*" and all the other
pleasant words he could think of.

"*Die Herrschaft nehm' mit?*" said the corporal, indicating the
prisoner; and Lanny said *Ja*, he would "take with," but where he
would take he had no idea—perhaps to Brooklyn, America!

That problem was quickly solved, however. Lanny strolled across
the square with his prisoner, followed by many curious eyes. When
they got into a side street, the still shivering youth exclaimed:
"*Dzieki tobie, panie,*" which is Polish for "Thank you, sir," and,
without waiting for a silver coin or even for a handshake, darted
behind a house and disappeared. Lanny wasn't surprised or dis-
pleased, for he understood that the Brooklyn alibi mightn't last very
long, and he had no more cigarettes.

XI

When Lanny told his friend about that adventure Kurt couldn't
help being amused, but at the same time he was shocked to the deeps
of his Prussian soul. "How could you have thought of such a thing?"
he exclaimed.

"But I didn't think of it," chuckled the American. "The prisoner
thought of it."

"You didn't know a thing about that fellow! He may have been a
criminal, a most dangerous one."

"It may be. On the other hand, he may be a poor devil who told some peasant that the landlords were robbers—which they doubtless are."

"You imagine they would sentence a man to be hanged for that?"

"I don't think anybody sentenced him. I think those soldiers just picked him up and started to hang him because they didn't like what he was saying."

"But that's absurd, Lanny! Governments aren't run on that basis!"

"I gathered that you didn't think so much of the Polish government."

No answering that argument; nothing to do but say that Americans were an irresponsible people, sometimes outright crazy. Kurt looked about him anxiously, thinking that a company of soldiers might arrive at any moment to apprehend them both. "We ought to get out of this town," he said; but it wasn't easy, for there was no train for a couple of hours. They found a sleigh which could be rented, and they had a cold and uncomfortable ride to the next town on the railroad. There again, Kurt was anxious; he even thought the Polish police or army might trace them to Stubendorf, whose Polish authorities would enjoy nothing more than having a serious offense to charge against the family of the Comptroller-General of the Schloss.

No, Kurt couldn't take the Red menace with the gay insouciance of an American playboy. To Germans of the upper classes *Bolschewismus* was real—the newest-born child of Satan. The Reds had seized Bavaria, and had come very near to getting Berlin; they had plundered and killed, and were still boring like termites inside the foundations and walls of the German state structure. Here in Upper Silesia, the moment the French and German troops were withdrawn, there would be an attempted uprising of the miners and factory workers. The German Reds hated the German government and the Polish Reds hated the Polish government, and at any time they were ready to combine against both governments; that was their idea of how to end war—but to Kurt it would be worse than all the wars that had ever been fought in the world.

In short, Lanny was made to realize that what he had done was no joke, but something very serious, that must under no circumstances

be mentioned to anyone in Stubendorf. Suppose there should come
a revolution in Poland, and he should pick up a newspaper and see a
picture of the Polish Trotsky or the Polish Bela Kun, and recognize
it as the man for whom he had lighted two cigarettes!

"It might be convenient for you," said the incorrigible American.
"It might enable me to save your life!"

1 2

The Best-Laid Schemes

I

LANNY had written to his mother an account of his meeting
with Walther Rathenau, and, as a result of this, when he and Kurt
returned to Juan they found Beauty in a state of delightful excitement. She had taken the letter to Emily Chattersworth, who had
pointed out the duty as well as opportunity which this circumstance
held out to them. The world is supposed to be run by majestic
statesmen who strut upon the stage and deliver resounding orations
amid the explosion of flashlight bulbs; but everybody knows it is
really run by clever women, who stay behind the wings and pull
wires. The statesmen-puppets do what is subtly suggested to them,
most of the time without knowing that they are being guided.

For three years now the rulers of Britain, France, and Germany
had been locked in a tug-of-war, in which all three countries were
exhausting themselves without any gains whatever. And now
through some prank of fate they were coming to Cannes, right on
Emily's front doorstep, just over Beauty's garden wall! The French
Foreign Minister had been an habitué of Emily's *salon* for many
years; Beauty knew Lloyd George's secretary, Philip Kerr—pro-

nounce it Carr—soon to be the Marquess of Lothian—pronounce it
as if you loathed him. And now Lanny had met Rathenau, who was
to head the German delegation! Surely the hand of Providence was
indicating to two American-French ladies that they should take
charge of the Cannes conference and bring the affairs of Europe
into some order!

The sessions were scheduled to be held in the Cercle Nautique,
a one-story clubhouse of stucco with a magnificent façade and very
elegant lofty rooms. There the resounding speeches would be made,
the men with black boxes would gather to snap pictures, the journalists would peer and pry and beg for crumbs of news. But if you
thought the real work would be done in that place, you would
indeed be ignorant of the *haut monde*. After the uproar had died
and the crowds had dispersed, the statesmen would slip away to some
quiet nook, where a gracious hostess would serve tea and minuscule
sandwiches, and by her presence would soothe their ruffled feelings.
Presently they would be talking amiably to one another about the
opposition at home and the impossibility of retaining office if they
made too many concessions—so be a good fellow, now, and let us
have this patch of desert, or that extra thousand million off the
reparations account!

Beauty and Emily had spent their lives equipping themselves for
this special service. They knew the vanities and foibles of each of
the elderly gentlemen. They had heard the problems endlessly discussed, and if they didn't understand them, at least they could talk
as if they did. Each was complementary to the other, for Emily
could handle the cultured ones, the highbrows, while Beauty understood the men of oil and guns and money. Kurt and Lanny had just
been to Germany, and could explain that rather terrifying race, and
help in the supreme achievement, which would be to induce the
British and the French—especially the latter—to enter into social relations with their former foes.

Marie de Bruyne rejoined the household and was offered a share
in the conspiracy. Marie wasn't nearly so keen about meeting Germans as the American ladies were, but she saw that they were
launched upon this adventure, and that the compliant Lanny was

going to be dragged into it; she was shrewd enough, and in love enough, not to throw cold water upon his mother's dreams. And then came Rick and Nina, according to the promise they had made some time earlier. A most fortunate circumstance for Rick, to be right in the center of a big story without any traveling expenses! Nina wasn't much on politics, but she had two babies that she surely didn't want to raise to be soldiers, and whatever prestige might belong to the wife of a future baronet she would use in helping persuade British diplomats to persuade French diplomats to attend tea parties with German diplomats.

II

The new villa, called "The Lodge," wasn't ready on time. What contractor ever did keep his word? When the Pomeroy-Nielsons arrived—crippled husband, lively little wife, two babies, and a maid— they had to be put up in a hotel for a couple of days, until the paint inside the house stopped smelling. Then the curtains had to be hung, and the furniture brought over from Cannes and put in place. Jolly fun fixing up a house—only two women never can agree where any piece of furniture ought to go, and there are some women who can't agree with themselves and are forever deciding that the center table ought to be against the wall or vice versa. If the husband is a writer, he doesn't care where you put the damn thing, if only it can be in the same place the next time he enters the room, and he wants the servants to understand that if they put his papers in order the only thing they have done is to make it impossible for him to find them.

Beauty left all those matters to Lanny, for she was at Sept Chênes most of the time, helping Emily to plan the pacification of Europe; sending the right letters and telegrams to key persons, calling in Sophie Timmons and other trusted friends and outlining to them the parts they were to play in the great world settlement. Lanny had to send a carefully worded telegram to the German Minister of Reconstruction, reminding him of their meeting and telling him that the home of Lanny's mother on the Cap d'Antibes would be at all times open to him as a quiet and safe retreat.

It really was a critical occasion; the fashionable ladies weren't exaggerating that. The German government was practically bankrupt, having no way to get foreign credit with which to meet the overdue reparations payments; and what action was France going to take? Poincaré and his Nationalists were clamoring for the occupation of Rhineland cities, while the British were making a supreme effort to persuade the French government that this course would bring ruin to them all. Britain had two million unemployed, and hardly any trade, and to risk another war might throw a large section of Europe into Bolshevism.

Such were the issues at stake when the great private trains came rolling into the Cannes station, discharging their loads of statesmen and experts. They came from cities of fog and snow turned black by discharges from millions of chimney-pots; they stepped out into dazzling sunshine and balmy air, and were driven along avenues lined with palm trees, past houses of white or pink stucco with shutters painted a bright blue; they gazed over rocky shores on which the blue and green Mediterranean broke in long white lines of foam. A delightful place to spend a holiday: elegant hotels and easy-going, carefree people; theaters, operas, and casinos in which music resounded and dancing and gambling went on all night. The half-starved, half-frozen populations of the northern cities read about it in the papers and took it none too amiably. Why couldn't these politicians do their conferencing at home, and save the cost of junkets to the playgrounds of the parasites?

A member of the British staff explained to Lanny that desire for a holiday had nothing to do with it; the statesmen got very little pleasure out of it. But their police and military authorities were afraid to have them gather in large cities in desperate times like these. Impossible to keep track of anarchists and troublemakers; to know at what moment a machine gun might be turned loose from a window, or a bomb be thrown from a housetop. But in small places like San Remo and Spa and Cannes the police could know who was in town, and stood some chance of protecting their important charges. France wanted no foreign statesmen to be assassinated within her borders. One could hardly say which would be the more awkward, for some Red fanatic to shoot a conservative statesman or for some misguided patriot to bomb a German.

III

Lanny got an inside view of this problem and the methods of handling it. He happened to walk into the village of Juan to make some trifling purchase, and who should be sitting on a bench by the edge of the strip of sand but his crimson Saint Barbara! He saw her first and stopped; she didn't fit the holiday crowd at a seaside resort, but sat staring out over the water as if she were quite alone. In the too bright sunlight her complexion had a jaundiced appearance, but nothing ever changed the sad dignity of her features; once more the romantic Lanny decided that he saw all the sorrows of mankind in that face, and wished that Marcel could come back to life and paint it.

Being now arrived at years of discretion, Lanny should have gone on about his business; but Barbara happened to turn and see him, and of course he had to greet her. It was natural for him to inquire: "What are you doing in this village?"

"I was staying in Cannes," she replied, "but the police have just put me out."

"What?" he exclaimed.

"They are afraid I will plant an infernal machine under their thieves' conference."

"You really mean they ordered you out of town?"

"They gave me just about ten minutes in which to pack my things. Worse than that, they drove out the working-class family with which I was staying; the man, who had a job, now has to go and look for one elsewhere."

"Well, I'll be damned!" said Lanny.

"You may, if you stay and talk to me," replied the woman, grimly.

It made Lanny a bit hot under his collar of gray Oxford cloth.

He would have liked to say: "Won't you come and stay for a while at Bienvenu?" but he knew of course that this would knock Beauty's plans higher than a kite. Instead he sat down by the woman, and said, a trifle embarrassed: "Look here, you may be a bit short of funds. Are you?"

The other flushed with embarrassment. "Oh, I couldn't let you do that!"

"Why not? You are working for your cause, are you not?"

"But you don't believe in my cause!"

"Don't be too sure about that. I believe in your honesty at least; and, as you know, I don't have to work very hard for my money."

A dangerous thing for Lanny to say, and a dangerous course for him to embark upon. If once you start subsidizing a saint, how can you know where you are going to stop? Saints rarely have means of support and, worse yet, they are apt to have friends in the same plight; their biographies are one series of hard-luck stories. The job of taking care of them should be left to the Lord, who has created locusts and wild honey for that purpose, and in extreme cases will send ravens, or manna, or miracles of loaves and fishes.

But Lanny was young, and in this respect would never grow up. He took out his purse and put three hundred-franc notes into Barbara Pugliese's hand. The franc had lost two-thirds of the purchasing-power it had had before the war, so this wasn't such a sumptuous gift as it seemed; but to the poor woman it was a fortune, and she stammered gratitude and embarrassment, which Lanny told her to forget.

"Have you any idea where to go?" he asked.

"I haven't made any plans, because, frankly, I was stranded. I want to go back to Italy and continue my work, but my friends beg me to delay, on account of the great danger."

"What danger?" he asked.

"Have you not heard what is going on in Italy? The employers are hiring gangs of ruffians to beat the friends of the people's cause, and often to murder them. Hundreds of our devoted workers have fallen victims to these *bravi*."

"How terrible!" exclaimed Lanny.

"It is a consequence of the tragic division in the ranks of the workers. When they were in possession of the steel foundries, and it was a question of holding and operating them, the Socialist leaders hesitated and refused their support."

"But how could they operate foundries without large capital?"

"The whole credit of the co-operative movement should have been put behind them, and they could have started to work at full capacity. But no, our Socialists are slaves to the idea of 'legality'; they hope to get possession of industry through the state, by electing politicians. Our workers have seen, time after time, that politicians lose all their working-class ardor as soon as they are elected, and begin putting the bribes of the bourgeois into their pockets. You see how much the masters care about 'legality'; they do not stop at organized assassination of those who dare to oppose their will. They have a new device now: their hirelings force the victims to swallow great quantities of castor oil mixed with benzine or iodine, which causes atrocious sufferings and leaves them physical wrecks for the rest of their lives. That is what is now going on all over Italy. I judge that your capitalist newspapers have not told you much about it."

"Very little," the young man admitted.

"These gangsters call themselves '*Fascisti*'; they have taken the ancient Roman lictors' symbol, of the rods and the ax. They are patriots, you must understand, and it is in the name of the *sacro egoismo* of Italy that they incite the youth to wage street-wars and wreck the offices of co-operatives and workers' newspapers. Do you remember that dark little wretch whom you watched in the *trattoria* in San Remo?"

"The Blessed Little Pouter Pigeon?" said Lanny, with a smile.

"The same. Well, he is now a member of the Chamber of Deputies, and one of these noble patriots that will restore the ancient glories of *la patria*. He calls his vile newspaper *Il Popolo d'Italia*, and every issue of it is smeared with the blood of martyrs. But that does not keep him from being *persona grata* to the police authorities of Cannes."

"You mean he is here?"

"He comes as a journalist, to observe and report the conference; but he brings with him a band of his ruffians, each with a revolver on his hip. That of course is to protect him against Italians. The French police know that he is their man, he serves the same capitalist *infamia* as themselves. You see, my friend, the class struggle grows more desperate every hour, and one is forced to take sides even against one's will. That is why you should ask yourself whether it is wise for you, a member of the privileged classes, to sit on a public bench in the company of a notorious agitator. If you decide that you have been making a mistake, rest assured that I will understand and not blame you."

IV

The conferees opened their sessions in the reception hall of the Cercle Nautique, and Walther Rathenau, master administrator, delivered an address full of figures, explaining the impossibilities under which the infant German republic was laboring. It was so convincing that the Allied representatives were annoyed, and in the middle of the address Lloyd George broke in: "If we listen to you much longer, we shall come to the conclusion that it is we who owe money!" That, of course, was for the record; it would be passed on to the newspapermen outside, and members of the Tory clubs in London would know that their Prime Minister was using the right sort of language to the recalcitrant foe.

The Allies were offering to accept 720,000,000 gold marks during the year, and 1,450,000,000 gold marks' worth of goods of one sort or another, mostly to the French. The British were whispering to the Germans, begging them to take this offer at once, because of the great danger in which the Briand government stood from its enemies; but the stubborn Rathenau was insisting upon making his speech, and trying to get the cash payments reduced to a round 500,000,000 gold marks. There was the usual deadlock of wills.

Meanwhile, behind the scenes, the appeasers were working busily. Mr. Kerr, pronounced Carr, had made a hurried trip to Sept Chênes with a couple of his staff to talk matters over with a widely famed

Riviera hostess. There was a large English colony in Cannes—in fact it was an English nobleman who had put his *cachet* upon the place and established it as the right one for the right people. There were many hostesses eager to serve their country, and ready to be vexed if preference was given an American; but this was an occasion when patriotic sacrifices would have to be made, and it seemed obvious that the French would come more freely to an American tea party, and meetings with Britons could thus be made to seem casual.

The arrangements amounted to a conspiracy against that son of the people, that orator with the silver tongue, the ragged black mustache, and the roomy paunch, Aristide Briand. They were going to surround him, flatter him, play upon his humanitarian sentiments, and persuade him to agree to a temporary moratorium, and not send his armies into the bankrupt German republic. The climax of their scheming was revealed by Emily Chattersworth with delighted chuckles; they were going to lure a French Premier into playing a game of golf with a British Prime Minister! That is the way they keep the political peace in the green and pleasant land across the Channel; the orators tear into one another across the long table which separates the rival front benches, and then they go off and play a foursome together, and afterward have a drink, and thus compromises are arranged and civil wars averted.

After his oratorical effort the German Minister of Reconstruction was in need of respite; and two of his aides put him into a car and drove him to a place where he might have his tired brow smoothed, metaphorically speaking, by an experienced smoother. He came to Bienvenu, where he met a charming hostess and her intelligent and sympathetic son, also a young German musician who had been twice wounded in the war, and was thus in position to put a seal of security upon these Americans and their *ménage*. Nobody else to bother a visitor, no stupid attempt to make a lion out of him and show him off to idle chatterers. If only all traveling diplomats, authors, lecturers, and other easily bored persons could find a place of refuge like that in every town!

The minister sipped his tea and nibbled his sandwiches, and then Kurt played the first movement of Beethoven's *Moonlight Sonata*, which has nothing to do with moonlight, but is an utterance of profound and poignant sorrow, suited to the mood of German cabinet members in these trying days. The weary man rested his nearly bald head in a soft chair and listened; when he asked for more, and said that he really meant it, Kurt played a couple of the tender little *Songs without Words* of Mendelssohn. Was he saying that the Jews had their place in German culture, and that their many kinds of services were appreciated by the Fatherland? Anyhow, it was a sign of understanding that an overburdened man of affairs was not asked to listen to noisy and disturbing music.

The minister and his friends were invited to come again, and said they would gladly do so. Their lovely hostess explained that she and her son did not like war, and had kept out of it, and had friends here who were supporting them in their efforts to bring the former foes together. If Dr. Rathenau or any of his staff would care to use Bienvenu as a place for inconspicuous meetings, the villa was at their service. Naturally this interested them, and Beauty told them about Mrs. Chattersworth and her other friends, and about the various British and French whom they knew and could invite to this place if requested. The German minister, who knew how the world was run, understood what all this meant. It was something beyond price in this crisis, and no price would be asked; but later, when the German republic had got on its feet, he might receive a note on perfumed stationery bearing the embossed initials or crest of this gracious lady, reminding him of their pleasant meetings at Cannes and inviting him to confer with her old friend and her son's father, the European salesman of Budd Gunmakers Corporation.

V

Lanny told Rick about his talk with Barbara, and everything that she had told him; whereupon Rick, the newshound, pricked up his ears and said: "If that movement in Italy is spreading as fast as she says, there ought to be a story in it."

"A horrible thing!" exclaimed Lanny.

"I know, but important. It's the employers' answer to Communism; and if one spreads, the other is bound to spread too. I ought to look into it."

"Want me to take you to Italy after the conference?"

"Why bother, if the movement has come to us? Do you suppose we could find that fellow Mussolini?"

"I should think the Italians in Cannes would know about him. A pretty ugly customer, Rick."

"We don't have to worry about that. If he's starting a movement, he'll welcome publicity, you may be sure."

Next morning Lanny drove his friend into the Old Town of Cannes, where there was a considerable Italian colony, and told the proprietor of a *trattoria* that he was trying to find a man named Benito Mussolini. The proprietor looked uneasy, and didn't know whether to talk or not; but Lanny explained that an English newspaperman wished to interview him, and the other loosened up sufficiently to say that he was staying at a certain Casa della Rosa not far away.

The place didn't deserve its name; it was dingy and decidedly third-class. When Lanny descended from his expensive car and went in, the neighborhood took note of it. When Lanny asked the woman in charge for Signor Mussolini, she looked him over carefully, went away, and came back with a sinister young fellow wearing a black shirt and having a bulge on his hip at exactly the spot where Lanny expected to find it. In his halting Italian Lanny explained that his friend wished to write an article about Signor Mussolini's movement for a leading English magazine.

"Where is your friend?" asked the other, suspiciously, and Lanny explained that an aviator crippled in the war had trouble getting in and out of cars, and was waiting to make sure that the signor would see him. The young fellow went to the door and took a good look at the car and its occupant; then he said: "I will see."

Presently the blackshirt returned and bade the two visitors follow him. They went down a hall and into a rear room which had only one window. The man they had come to meet had placed himself in an armchair in a corner at one side of the window; he had placed the chairs in which his visitors were to sit in the light of the window, so that they could be watched while he remained in shadow. An armed blackshirt stood near the window, and another by the wall in such a position that he was behind the two strangers. The one who escorted them remained on guard by the door. Evidently trust in one's fellow-men was no part of the creed of the new movement called *Fascismo!*

VI

Benito Mussolini was at this time just under forty. He was a medium-small man who did everything in his power to look large. He had a high-domed forehead, partly bald, and melancholy black pop-eyes, suggestive of goiter to a physician. When he wanted to look stern and impressive, he would sit very stiff and erect, and make his lower jaw stick out; but sometimes he would forget and relax, and then you would discover that he had a weak face. He did not rise to greet visitors, but kept his pose of being on a throne.

"*Eh b'en, mousseurs?*" he said. His French was bad, but he did not seem to know it, or perhaps held himself above such concerns.

The English journalist, speaking slow and careful French, explained that, like the editor of *Il Popolo d'Italia*, he was covering the Cannes conference. He named the papers for which he wrote, and produced his credentials; one of the guards carried them to the great man.

"Where have you heard about my movement?" he asked.

"It has been attracting a great deal of attention in my country," said Rick, tactfully. "Many people think it may offer a solution to the problem of the Reds."

"You will do well to study it from that point of view."

"I am here in the hope that you will make that possible, Signor Mussolini."

Lanny planned to take no part in the conversation, but to devote himself to studying the Italian as well as the shadows permitted. It appeared as if his ego had expanded at the idea that his fame had spread so far; but then he decided that this was beneath the dignity of a man of destiny. An upper-class Englishman was trying to flatter the founder of *Fascismo* in the effort to get an interview! He re-marked in a cold voice: "It is to be doubted if you English can learn the lessons of our movement, because your democratic capitalism represents a stage of social degeneration."

"That may be," said Rick, politely. "Of course if it were so, I should hardly know it."

"That is true," admitted the other. "But what can I do about that?"

To one who had nothing to do but listen and watch, it became clear that the man was playing a part which was difficult for him; a person with a strong sense of inferiority, he was lifting himself by the straps of his boots. His rudeness betrayed self-distrust; his violence was a product of fear. "He's a bounder!" thought Lanny.

Rick went on unruffled. "I hear contradictory statements about your movement, Signor. They tell me that it is anti-capitalist, and yet I find many of the capitalist class who support it ardently. Will you explain that to me?"

"They have perceived that the future is in our hands, because we represent the vital elements of the new, awakening Italy. We are the youth—or those among them who are not satisfied with stale words and formulas, but believe in action and in new fortunes to be won."

The founder of *Fascismo* was launched upon one of his orations. He had been delivering them once a week in his paper, ever since the war. He had been delivering them to his *squadristi*, the young men of Italy who had been trained in war and had been promised wealth and glory but had not got them, and were now organizing to help themselves. Their leader's ideas were a strange mixture of the revolutionary syndicalist anarchism whose formulas had been the mental pabulum of his youth, and the new nationalism which he had learned from the poet-aviator d'Annunzio and his Fiume raiders. If you could believe Barbara, the blacksmith's son had col-lected large sums of money for the support of the poet and had used them for his own movement. The ego of Benito Mussolini would bear no rival near the throne.

VII

The leader's French was inadequate to the explaining of these complex ideas, and he would use Italian words, and then forget and break into Italian. Lanny ventured to stop him, saying: "Pardon, Signor, my friend does not understand your language, and my own is unfortunately bad. However, if you will speak slowly, I will endeavor to translate."

The orator could not admit that his French was defective, and resumed speaking it. He explained his belief that violence is a sign of virility, and that any society in which it does not have its way is bound to degenerate. "I see that you have been reading Sorel," ventured Rick.

"I do not have to go to Sorel for knowledge," replied Mussolini, with a thrust of his jaw. "I was a pupil of Pareto, in Lausanne."

Rick asked him about the application of violence in the daily affairs of the Italian workers, and the leader made no bones about admitting that he and his *fasci di combattimento.* were using it in abundance. "Italy has been kept in chaos by the Reds for three years, and we are giving them doses of their own medicine."

"And when you have put them down, what then?"

"Ours is no mere movement of repression, but an awakening of those elements which alone are capable of reconstructing *la patria*."

"Just what is to be the nature of your construction?"

"A state in which all the various social groups have their proper places and perform their assigned functions under the direction of their leader."

"That being yourself?"

"Who else could it be?" This with another thrust of the jaw and a straightening of the shoulders. "You do not believe that I can do these things?"

Said Rick: "You would hardly be interested in the opinion of a representative of a degenerating society."

It was the sort of reply the editor had been wont to exchange in the days when he was a Socialist intellectual, sipping his red wine in the *trattorie*. For a few minutes he forgot that he was a man of destiny, being interviewed for posterity; he relaxed on his throne and crossed his legs, arguing with two bright young fellows who might be turned into disciples. "You will have to learn from us," he announced. "Our *Fascismo* is not for export; but you will have to devise some remedy of your own for the contradictions which bourgeois democracy is developing."

"*Si, Signor,*" said Rick. "But what if the ambitions of your Italian Fascism happen to clash with those of French imperialism, or German, for example?"

"There is enough and plenty to go round."

"Enough of what, exactly?" It was a trap question. Could it be that what this blacksmith's son from the Romagna had in mind was to divide the colonial possessions of the degenerating British Empire?

"The world is large," said the leader, smiling, "and the future is not easy to foresee. Tell me, are you going back to lie about me, as so many other journalists have done?"

This was meant for a diversion, and it served. "I am not that sort of journalist, Signor. I shall report exactly what I have seen and heard."

"Do you express no opinions of your own?"

"Sometimes—but always making plain that it is opinion and nothing else."

"And what will you say is your opinion of *Fascismo?*"

It was a condescension. The ego of the one-time proletarian starveling could not repress a desire for applause from a son of the effete British aristocracy! "May I speak frankly?" inquired Rick.

"What else would be of interest to me?"

"Well, I am struck by the resemblance of your technique to that of Bolshevism, which you so despise. In many ways you speak like a pupil of Lenin rather than Pareto."

"You are a shrewd young man. But why should I not learn from Lenin how to fight Lenin? If I capture a gun from a foe, shall I refrain from using it because it is the foe's invention?"

"I see," said Rick. "Would it be correct to say that your movement is one of middle-class youth, whereas Bolshevism is one of proletarian youth?"

"We bring all youth into our movement, and we guide them."

"To be sure," countered the other. "But that is what the Russians say also. You have different ends, but your means are the same. To us Englishmen it appears that your means will determine your ends in the long run."

"You watch us," said the founder of *Fascismo*. "We will show you something about a long run. My successor has not been born yet."

When the two went out to their car and drove away, Lanny said: "That fellow strikes me as a pretty cheap actor."

"Yes, but he has something, as you Americans say."

"Do you think he can make a go of it?"

"He might—in Italy. They are a turbulent people, and easy to fool. But of course some other upstart would unhorse him in a few months."

VIII

In the midst of these events Lanny received a letter from his father. Another international conference had been going on in Washington for two months, and to Robbie Budd it was like a perpetual toothache deliberately inflicted—and all the worse because it was being done by those whom he had helped to put in office. A "naval limitations conference," it was called, and the American Secretary of State had electrified the world, and almost electrocuted Robbie, by presenting an offer of the United States to stop its fleet-building program, which included sixteen capital ships and nearly as many old ones, in return for similar concessions by other nations and an agreement for each nation to keep a certain fixed ratio of naval strength.

To Robbie it was like the cutting off of parts of his own body. He really loved those beautiful ships—and especially he loved the deadly swift machine guns with which Budd's had been prepared to equip them and all their auxiliary vessels. It meant that contracts carefully and patiently negotiated would never be signed; it meant that workmen of Budd's would be idle, and their families would go without food, or at any rate without silk stockings and new cars. It meant that blundering fool politicians and pacifists with their heads in the clouds would lead the nation into a trap from which it might never escape. "The formula was supplied to Hughes by the British," wrote Robbie, "and the trap is of their making. Some day we shall need those ships, need them desperately and horribly, and then we shall mourn for them as a barren woman mourns for the children she didn't bear." It was the first time in Lanny's twenty-two years that he had known his father to become poetical.

The crime was going to be committed, and no stopping it. Robbie had gone to Washington and made sure. Nobody would listen to him, because he sold munitions and they took it for granted that he was thinking only about the money. As if a man didn't love his work; as if he didn't love the efficient things he made; as if he didn't think about the nation they were designed to protect! "We have the richest country in the world, and we should have the greatest fleet to protect us; we have earned that right and we should take it. But Britain is broke, and Japan is poor, and we let them lure us into a confidence game and persuade us to pare our fleet down to the level of what they can afford!"

It was a hard matter to satisfy patriots, Lanny observed. Here in Cannes, and even in his own home, he was hearing about the Washington conference from the point of view of the British and the French, and discovering that they were as ill-pleased as his father. To the French it was just one more diddling, one more combining of Britain and America against *la patrie*. The conference was proposing to restrict the submarine, the poor nation's weapon! If France gave it up, Britain would rule—and of course use her power, as she was using it now, **to** compel France to submit to being cheated by Germany! Briand had been to Washington, and had there heard criticisms of French "militarism"; they had actually suggested that France agree to the reducing of her army! What protection would they leave her? She had persuaded President Wilson to give her a guarantee against attack, but the United States Senate failed to ratify this agreement—and now they wanted to strip the nation of her last means of security!

So said a member of Briand's delegation in the drawing-room of Bienvenu; sitting in the same chair that Rathenau had occupied—though he didn't know it. He was talking to M. Rochambeau, the kindly and well-informed diplomat; and Marie was listening, deeply impressed by what her country's statesman was saying. For several days Lanny had been realizing that she was less and less pleased with what the other ladies were doing; that what they considered triumphs seemed like defeats to her. After this talk she came to him and said: "I think it would be better if I went and stayed a few days with my aunt. I am sure you will understand."

"Is it that bad, dear?"

"I just can't go on pretending that I agree with your mother and her friends; and when I keep silent, I wonder if I am shutting my lips too tightly and making myself look disagreeable. I'm not a skilled actress, and I can't be happy pretending what I don't feel. Let me say that Aunt Juliette is not well."

A little cloud, no bigger than a man's hand; and Lanny brushed it away quickly. Of course, it would be perfectly all right; the darned conference would be over and they could all forget politics and be happy again; they would live in art, which was the same to English and French and Germans and Americans, a garden of delight with none of its delicious fruits forbidden.

So Marie made her excuse—and of course didn't fool the mistress of Bienvenu for a single moment. "She's a French patriot," thought Beauty; "a Nationalist, like her husband."

When Lanny came back she said this to him, and he answered: "Oh, surely not that bad!"

"As bad as Poincaré!" insisted the mother. "They're all getting ready to invade Germany. You'll see!"

IX

The conspiracy was marching hour by hour. Rathenau's associates came to Bienvenu, and it happened that the majestic Lord Curzon,

that very superior purzon, dropped in, purely by accident. Also
came the American ambassador to London, Colonel Harvey; another "Kentucky" title, like that of Colonel House, but the new
ambassador took it seriously and could equal any British viscount
in self-importance. He had been a New York editor, and boasted
of having been the first to suggest the president of Princeton University for President of the United States; but when the campaign
had got under way, Wilson had become worried as to Harvey's
connections with the unpopular House of Morgan, and had asked
him to withdraw from the limelight. So now the Wall Street colonel
was a Republican, and Harding had given him the most highly
valued of all diplomatic prizes. He was supposed to be in Cannes
only as an "observer," but he was doing what he could to get trade
with Europe started up again.

Meanwhile the French statesmen were repairing to Sept Chênes,
and there too the British were dropping in, purely by accident, and
Lloyd George was explaining that he didn't really mean all the
harsh things he had said, but it was necessary to satisfy the *Times*.
It was while Emily Chattersworth was giving a luncheon for Briand
and Lloyd George that the latter sprang his invitation to a game of
golf, and it was hard for her to keep her face straight when the
French Premier accepted—yes, for that very afternoon! It actually
came off, and was the joke of the Riviera for several hours—that is,
until Paris was heard from! One can readily believe that the innkeeper's son cut no graceful figure with a golf club in his hands;
he had no idea how to hold it, and this showed plainly in the
pictures of which the papers were full.

But Briand enjoyed it; he was something of a gay dog, and liked
to be conspicuous, and his lack of subtlety kept him from being sure
whether people were laughing with him or at him. He was overworked, and glad to get out into the sunshine; he was followed by
a crowd of curious spectators, kept at a respectful distance by de-
tectives but making the scene pleasant with their bright costumes.

When he and the genial Prime Minister sat down to rest between
holes, Lloyd George said that he had just had a chat with Rathenau,
who was really a decent fellow and an author of some distinction—

why couldn't he and Briand have a private meeting and at least try to understand each other's point of view? Was it the sunshine, or the personal charm of the Welsh wizard, or perhaps the ineffable prestige of the British ruling class? Anyhow, in a burst of good nature Briand said all right, but where on the Riviera could they meet without a scandal? Lloyd George said he would undertake to arrange that, and a tentative date was made for five o'clock on the following afternoon.

Whereupon Bienvenu was thrown into the greatest turmoil of its twenty years' history. British emissaries arriving, French and German secretaries, police agents, secret-service men, all whispering together, and conferring with the hostess and her intelligent son—whom none of them had happened to observe in conference with an Italian syndicalist-anarchist on the beach at Juan-les-Pins! Lanny took them for a tour of the estate, and showed them the rear gate, which was on another road; it was his suggestion that the German minister and his aides should drive along this road and stop in front of the gate and slip in quietly while the car went on. They would have quite a walk to the house, but Dr. Rathenau was an active man, his secretary said. The French Premier would be driven in at the front gate and then it would be locked, and the walls patrolled from the inside, and neither anarchists nor newspapermen would get over.

Lanny had never seen his mother in such a flutter. Emily and Sophie Timmons had to come and advise her what to wear, and what kind of sandwiches to serve, and what color flowers for the drawing-room. She couldn't invite them to be present—the agreement was that nobody but herself and her son and her servants should be in the house. No, not even Kurt, there wouldn't be any opportunity for music this time; the destinies of Europe were going to be decided, and peace, real peace, would at last be worked out between France and Germany. Beauty had always wanted peace, even while she wanted also to sell guns! "Why, Lanny," she exclaimed, in the small hours of the morning, "Bienvenu will have a place in the history books!"

Yes, it was true! They would have a brass plaque made and set up

beside the front door: "In this house, January 11, 1922, the Premier
of France, Aristide Briand, met with Walther Rathenau, German
Minister of Reconstruction, and arranged the terms of reconciliation
between the two countries." "How's that?" asked Lanny; and his
excited mother kissed him and cried: "Oh, you darling!"

X

But alas for the best-laid schemes o' mice an' men! Just when the
last of the sandwiches had been made and wrapped in oil paper to
keep them fresh; when the wine had been packed in ice and the
flower arrangements in the various rooms completed; when the hairdresser had started on Beauty's coiffure, and the maid was laying the
proper dress on the bed—right at that instant came the most desolat-
ing of messages ever heard over a telephone wire: M. Briand's secretary, grief-stricken to announce that the Premier was compelled to
leave immediately for Paris, there being a Cabinet crisis which
required his presence without a moment's delay.

All on account of that wretched game of golf—or at any rate that
is what Beauty Budd would believe until her dying day. When the
pictures had reached Paris a howl of rage had arisen. Young and old,
rich and poor, male and female, all admitted with humiliation and
shame that the British were making a monkey out of their national
leader. Golf is not a French game; there was no French game at a
time like this, with widows mourning by the millions and tragedy
hanging over the land. Was that the way the destinies of *la patrie*
were being decided?—between two games of golf—or between a
game of golf and a cup of tea—the journalists didn't seem to agree
which way it had been.

The guilty statesman was summoned home—for the Riviera wasn't
really France, it was a playground rented or sold to the international idlers. The guilty statesman stood up in the Chamber and
defended himself in a long speech, which seemed to everybody a
defense of Germany rather than of France; it was full of unpleasant
figures, which meant that the people had been cheated ever since the
war, that their foes had got away with everything, and there was no

way *la patrie* could be recouped or saved. They had won the war but lost the peace, and now they had to decide whether to do it all over again!

Like a thunderbolt hitting one of the chimneys on top of Bienvenu came the news that Briand was out. Resigned, either in a fit of pique or because he saw that his foes had him! And all those intrigues and all those appeasements which had been arranged by Beauty and Emily and Sophie and Nina—all scattered like a house of cards in a hurricane!

The news reached the Cannes conference just as Walther Rathenau was in the midst of another of his elegantly polished speeches. It was hardly worth while finishing; everything was ended now, Poincaré was going to be the next Premier of France, and there would be no more conferences—so he had said, he wouldn't attend 'em! The Germans could go home and find some way to raise the money, or else there would be "sanctions," French troops marching into German cities, and we'll see who won the peace! And no brass plaque by the door of Bienvenu, and nobody to admire the flower arrangements, nobody to eat the sandwiches except the children of Mme. Scelles's school for French orphans—sandwiches don't keep, as everyone knows, and Beauty was sick at heart and done with hospitality forever, so she swore!

For the second time in his young life Lanny Budd had made an attempt to improve the nations, and they had stubbornly remained what they were. Once more he had to retire into his ivory tower, where he could have things as he wanted them; once more he reminded himself that the great masters of the arts were his servants always on call. His German friend had the same reaction; having had brief glimpses of the men who were running the world, he had decided that he preferred the three B's of music. Lanny's French *amie* was humble and apologetic; glad that the Cannes conspiracy had failed, but trying to hide the fact, and by sympathy and kindness to make up for her political intransigence.

Rick was the only one who got anything real out of Cannes. He wrote a coldly ironical article about the conference, and it was published. He wrote also an account of *Fascismo* and the interview with its founder, but this Rick's editor rejected; the article was well written, he reported, but that Italian bounder didn't seem of enough importance to justify the space.

13

The World's Mine Oyster

I

IN THE month of February the Washington Disarmament Conference concluded its labors. Robbie sent information about it, including a letter which he had written to one of the New York newspapers. Said the spokesman of Budd Gunmakers: "It is hard for a sane man to realize that there are people in the world who believe that a nation can keep out of war by being unprepared for war." He was so wrought up about the destruction of the American fleet—so it seemed to him—that he spent a week in Washington, pleading with senators against the ratification of the agreement, but all in vain. "The fools have the votes," he said; "they generally do."

This conference was the achievement of a Wall Street lawyer named Hughes, who had become a Supreme Court justice and was now Harding's Secretary of State. He was the stubborn Baptist type of mind—"Ask Beauty about them," wrote Robbie; "her father is one." Hughes was putting the job through to his own satisfaction, and even the powerful Budd family was helpless. He cut the major navies of the world about in half, and in his closing speech he did not hesitate to make the flat declaration: "This conference absolutely ends the race in competition in naval armament."

Robbie marked that in a newspaper clipping, and wrote on the margin the word: "Jackass." His letter accompanying it was a lamentation in the tone of the Old Testament prophets. "We make claims, such as the Monroe Doctrine, which require arms to back them up, and then we deprive ourselves of the arms. If that is not the way to invite challenge and calamity, put me down for a madman." Lanny read this, and returned to the study of Beethoven's pianoforte sonatas, which he did not find up to the great master's standard.

II

Baby Marceline was four, and the grandson and namesake of Sir Alfred was a month or two older; this is the age when they ask questions, and there was not much peace for the adults of either family, except at siesta time and in the evenings. It became the practice to lend them out, each to the other family, so that Alfy could answer Marceline's questions and vice versa. Lanny would play the piano for them, or put on phonograph records and dance with them, so by now he had a miniature Isadora school. He would listen to their prattle, and start life all over again, marveling at the strangeness of it; these little centers of expanding consciousness, like buds in spring sunshine, bursting with eagerness, with determination; so full of trust in life, so unaware of tragedies which might lie before them! A voyage in the dark, over an invisible sea, from one unknown port to another!

The young philosopher had observed that the children of the rich at this age appeared to be perfect. From their first hour they had expert guidance and the best of food and care; nature and art had combined to do all things possible for them. But from this age on there would begin a change; the needs of the mind were less easy to meet than those of the body. Being waited upon by servants didn't seem to be good for children; having their own way wasn't good; seeing their parents' self-indulgence wasn't good. By the age of fifteen many of them had become intolerable. Lanny looked back and decided that he himself hadn't done so well; he knew that his life had been too easy, and it still was—but how could he make it hard? He read stories of the Great Lord Buddha, and of St. Francis d'Assisi and others who had been born to riches and had cast them away; he decided that he might dare to do it, if only it wouldn't hurt his parents and his friends so deeply!

Marceline Detaze wasn't going to be spoiled so long as that stern German taskmaster lived in the house. Since the dreadful night when he had rushed away, Beauty had been more afraid of him than ever. She no longer had the idea that he would leave her for some other woman, but she was sure that he would go in a moment if his conscience so directed; if she failed to conform to his standards, to live what he considered a worthy life. That was one reason why she had worked so hard during the conference; if she could render a real service to Germany, Kurt would remember it all his days. He didn't blame her for the failure, but it was hard on her because he shut himself up in his music and was more than ever indifferent to the fashionable world.

Beauty could stand being a housekeeper and a mother for just so long, and then she had to be a butterfly and have a flutter over the social garden. She had to do something that would bring a crowd of people to Bienvenu and provide an excuse to buy a pretty new frock and call in a hairdresser and a caterer. She would invite people to listen to Kurt's playing, and some of them would prefer their own chatter, and Kurt's reaction would be the same as that of his idol Beethoven: *"Ich spiele nicht für solche Schweinen!"*

There was Emily Chattersworth with that beautful estate of Sept Chênes; willing to put it and all her social power at the disposal of a musician whom she admired. She would be going north before long, so it was now or never, and Beauty started agitating with Kurt to let them arrange a recital. Kurt said, what good would it do? The French weren't ever going to appreciate his music, nor would the sort of Americans who came to a casino town to gamble and play tennis and golf. What he was interested in was the fact that a publishing-house in Leipzig might bring out his *Spanish Suite;* that was a sign of hope reviving in Germany—but how in God's name could anybody know what price to print on a piece of sheet music, with the mark standing lower every afternoon than it had in the morning?

Beauty wouldn't give up. Suppose that just one person enjoyed

Kurt's playing? Suppose that one critic came and went out and wrote about him—wouldn't that be worth while? It was the same argument that she had had with Marcel, over and over, year after year. What was the matter with artists, that they wanted to paint pictures for storerooms and compose music for the bottom of an old trunk? Kurt said: "Why don't you start promoting Marcel?"—which was rather cruel of him, for her hesitations were caused in part by the fear that it might not be pleasing to Kurt himself. Marcel was France, and Kurt was Germany, and the war was still going on— even though it was called "reparations."

III

In the matter of the recital, Lanny took his mother's side, and finally Kurt said all right, he would come and play whenever he was asked to play, and give them the best he had. It meant that he had to go into Cannes and have himself fitted with heavy black evening clothes of the latest cut, with black silk braid down the trousers. That's the way they dressed a piano virtuoso, having not the remotest conception of the gymnastic feats he was going to perform, and the lather of perspiration into which he would be thrown. But never mind, he was young, and when he got home he could have a bath, and if the suit was damaged, Beauty would gladly pay the price for so much glory.

Mrs. Emily sent out her invitations—and never had she spent so much time upon the compiling of a list. There were all sorts of distinguished persons wintering on the Côte d'Azur that season. The lanky King of Sweden played tennis every afternoon, and Aga Khan, one of the richest men in India, rode polo ponies. There were several Russian grand dukes in exile, who would go wherever there were pretty women. There was the English Lord Derby, who looked like a caricature of John Bull, and King Alfonso of Spain, who looked like a caricature of his Habsburg ancestors. There were fabulously wealthy Argentinians and North Americans, Rumanian boyars and Turkish pashas, and even the King of Dahomey, whose black troops had helped to make the world safe for democracy.

Beauty knew a whole raft of such persons, having cultivated them for Robbie's business; but it was hard to be sure how they would behave at a musicale—they might come thinking it was a cocktail party and be bored and show it. What Kurt desired was a gathering of music lovers, and the problem was to find celebrities who could qualify in that field. Dear old Anatole France would come, of course, and sit and nod his long horse's head surmounted with one of his hundred brightly colored silk skullcaps. Maeterlinck was in Nice, but he was rather *passé*, wasn't he? Besides, a Belgian might not yet have forgiven the Germans. Blasco Ibáñez, the Spaniard, lived at Menton in exile, and his war novels were having amazing success in the United States, but Emily had sworn that she would never invite him again, because he had spat on one of her carpets.

Invitations to Sept Chênes were usually accepted, so there were a hundred or so of Europe's most eminent, and Kurt played his own compositions—not too long ones, his friends had cautioned him. It was music in the old tradition, yet its content was new; if there were any in position to understand what an ex-artillery officer was trying to say, they learned that life had given him chaos and grief, and that he had wrestled with them in agony of soul and tried to make some order and beauty out of them. What most of those present got was that he made a tremendous racket and gave them very few tunes that they could carry off and whistle. However, it was plain that a man had to work hard to bring all that out of a piano, to say nothing of composing it. It might be that he was really a genius, and it wouldn't do to guess wrong, so they applauded cordially and the evening was a success.

Beauty Budd—who was said to be his mistress—was never more lovely or more happy. After all the honors had been done she wrapped him in a warm overcoat and blanket and took him home in a closed car, and there he stripped off his cold clammy things and got into a hot bath, and while he lay there, she rattled away about all the famous persons who had been present, and what this one and that one had said to her, and to Emily and Nina and Marie and Sophie. It would take Kurt's *amoureuse* a full week to collect all the gossip and retail it to the family.

IV

Before the Cannes conference had broken up it had called another
to be held at Genoa early in April; and Rick said that he would have
to attend this. As it happened to be Easter time, Marie was planning
to go north to be with her boys. She had decided that she didn't
care for conferences, she didn't like the sort of people she met there
or the things they said about France. But she knew that Lanny enjoyed them, and felt that it was his duty to help his friend, so she
told him that he was not to miss it on her account. Lanny was in
something of a quandary; but the matter was settled by a cablegram
from Robbie, saying that he was on his way to Genoa and would be
in Juan in a few days. Dates with Robbie took precedence over
everything else because they ·were so scarce.

Robbie Budd was putting on weight. He had passed mid-forty,
and no longer played polo or any such violent game; he said that
during the winter he had got most of his exercise by letting a masseur
knead and punch him. When he arrived at Juan he was as eager as a
boy to get into the water, and Lanny saw once more that sturdy
hairy frame which had so delighted him all through his childhood
and youth. The post-war bathing-suits were getting scantier every
season, and you could see a lot of Beauty, who was proud of her
slimness; Lanny teased her by telling Robbie that all the credit for
it belonged to Kurt. A piano virtuoso also cut a good figure in a
bathing-suit, but Kurt would never leave off the upper part because
of the caved-in place in his side where the pieces of ribs had been
shot away.

Lanny was curious as to why his father was troubling to attend
one of these international diplomatic affairs. They went for a long
sail together and, thus protected from prying ears, Robbie revealed
a curious situation: he was going Bolshevik! Of course in a strictly
proper, business way, but even so it represented a tremendous condescension for him and his "syndicate," those friends who had put
money into oil with him and were now making a good thing of it
in spite of the depression. One feature which distinguished this
Genoa conference from the preceding ones was that the Germans

and Russians had been invited to attend on equal terms with the Allies. It was Lloyd George's dream of a general and complete pacification of Europe, a conference to end conferences; the Russians were going to be taken back into the family of business nations, and it would mean rich pickings for whoever was first on the ground and had the energy to break through the barriers.

"So," said the man of guns and oil, "your Red friends may be of some use to themselves, if they know which side their bread is buttered on. Do you know whether Lincoln Steffens will be at Genoa?"

"I had a note from him," admitted Lanny; "but he didn't say. He was in the States."

"I saw him at the Washington conference; a queer-looking duck. If he should come to Genoa I'd like to meet him."

Lanny was embarrassed. He was quite sure that "Stef" wouldn't want to be used in an oil game; but it would be difficult to explain this to Robbie, who would probably think it was just naïveté on his son's part. Lanny devoted himself to asking questions, and trying to get the inside of this startling development.

According to Robbie's information, the Russians were in a desperate plight; their industry had been destroyed in the civil war, and how were they ever to get it started again? Millions of people had died of outright starvation during the past winter, and how were peasants without plows or horses going to get grain planted this spring? There was that huge oil-field in the Caucasus, one of the richest in the world; it was pretty much a wreck, and obviously the Bolsheviks couldn't get drilling-tools and pipes and tank-cars except from those industrial nations which made them. There was some kind of big deal being planned—the field was to be turned over to an international consortium, the Russians getting a share of the oil. Robbie didn't know the details—it was Standard Oil which had the inside track and had got the State Department behind it—but he was going to get the whole story before he had been very long in Genoa, and he had the idea that he'd find some back door that he could jimmy open, or some hole big enough for a little fellow to crawl through.

These phrases were Robbie's own, and indicated to his son that they were going to the ancient Italian city on a burglary expedition, and that the son was to have an opportunity to serve as a "finger-man" or something of that sort. The United States was now under a regime of Prohibition, which meant that gentlemen like Robbie Budd had to buy their liquor from bootleggers, and these latter were becoming wealthy and powerful, and developing a culture and language of their own. Lanny had never met any of them, but there existed a machinery whereby their slang was spread throughout the civilized world with extraordinary speed. There was a cinema in Cannes which showed American movies, and any evening that Lanny felt the need of recreation he could enter for a couple of francs, and acquire from the "titles" the very latest up-to-the-minute phrases of Broadway and Forty-Second Street. So now he understood that his father was going to Genoa to get the "right dope" and to "muscle in" on the "racket" of the "big shot"—who in this particular melodrama went by the name of "Standard."

V

The expedition set out, Lanny driving his father in the front seat and Rick in the rear with the luggage. They were going to stop off in "Monty" for a conference with Zaharoff, and Lanny was seeking in his mind for a tactful way to convey to Rick the fact that Robbie couldn't invite him in. But the most punctilious of Englishmen volunteered: "I hope you don't mind if I don't go in, because some day I may want to write about Zaharoff, and if I met him through you my hands would be tied." So Rick sat in the car and read an English magazine; when he was tired of that he strolled to the edge of the embankment, and looked down upon the tiers of house-roofs and the bay, and listened to the sounds of the pigeon-shooting below.

In the previous year the old Greek trader had put on a white satin undercoat and trunk-hose, a plumed hat and white boots with red tops, and a crimson velvet robe lined with white, and had been formally inducted as a Knight Commander of the Bath; so now you addressed him as "Sir Basil." They were going to find a badly worried old bathing-master, Robbie said, for the Washington conference had knocked the props from under armament shares, and Vickers had suffered worst of all. They had turned to the making of elevators and freight-cars and oil-pipe and a thousand things, like Budd's; but where could you find anybody with money to buy them? The world's masters had come to such a desperate pass that they were even thinking of lending money to Bolsheviks—of course on their promise to forget their evil doctrines!

The ex-army officer secretary ushered them into Sir Basil's study, which had a window-box where some of the duquesa's tulips were performing their annual duty, each according to the laws of its being and heedless of all the others. Their master, of whose existence they knew nothing, was performing according to the laws of his being, which required him to plot and scheme day and night, spreading vast networks of intrigue in order to acquire pieces of engraved paper certifying to his ownership of properties in many parts of the world. A strange and mystifying thing called "power," which caused hundreds of thousands, perhaps millions, of men to obey his will, even though few of them had ever seen him and most had never heard his name.

Did it make him happy? Did it make a *bybloem* happy to select certain chemicals from rich garden soil and construct a blossom of pure white with great purple streaks? The young philosopher decided that there must be something in the tulip which brought satisfaction when it achieved exactly the right shade, and there must be something in an old Greek trader that stirred with pleasure when he put one more engraved certificate into a security box. But certainly this did not affect his features, which showed heavy strain, or his voice, which, though always gentle, was full of complaint about what was happening to his interests throughout the world. He was glad to see Robbie Budd and also his son, in whom he still saw the bright little boy who had stolen his letter and then apologized so gamely; but he had no sooner got them seated and served with drinks than he began lamenting the awful plight of the people of his homeland, who had got themselves launched upon a military adventure in the heart of the Anatolian hills, and no man alive could tell what the outcome was to be.

You could take whatever view you pleased of that Greco-Turkish war, which had now been going on for nearly two years. You could call the Turks semi-savages, and point to their hideous slaughters of Armenians and of Greeks wherever they got them in their power; thus you could think of the Greeks as emissaries of civilization—and if you happened to be one of them, and to be the richest man in Europe, with great arms plants in scores of different places, you could pour out tens of millions of dollars and keep their armies fed and supplied in the heart of Turkey, even after they had lost a great battle. But Robbie professed to know about the concessions which Zaharoff had been promised in return for all the Greek bonds he was buying, so to the American this was just one more business venture —and one that had gone sour. Hadn't the old devil begun his career as a salesman of armaments by going to his Greek government and persuading it to buy a Nordenfeldt submarine, and then going to the Turkish government and persuading it to acquire two submarines in order to be safe from the Greeks?

But of course Robbie didn't give any hint of all this in a business conference. He listened with sympathy while Zaharoff lamented the split between the British and the French over the Greco-Turkish issue. Zaharoff was a Grand Officer of the Légion d'Honneur as well as a Knight Commander of the Bath, and he desired amity between the two great Allies, the pillars of Christian civilization, as he called them; but the Poincaré government was persisting in arming the Turks, and in spite of Lloyd George's promises the British government took only a half-hearted interest—in short, they left the conquest of Turkey to their Knight Commander, who had spent a good half of his fortune on a private war and, if it weren't for his oil interests, would now actually be hard pressed for cash.

VI

All this, presumably, to explain why Zaharoff was intent on getting more oil as quickly as possible. Robbie had his own reasons for wanting some, and so the two men of affairs got down to business. Zaharoff didn't mention, as he had on previous occasions, that Rob-

bie's son must be careful and not talk about his father's affairs; that
went without saying, Lanny having now attained his full majority and being here presumably as his father's lieutenant. Zaharoff
talked about the various interests which would be represented at
Genoa—you'd have thought it was going to be an oil conference
instead of a political one. Deterding's men would be there, and
Zaharoff named them, and explained his relationship with Deterding,
who was Royal Dutch Shell and could be trusted a certain distance,
but no farther. Anglo-Persian would be there, and Deterding was
trying to get hold of its shares which the British government held,
but Zaharoff had a clear understanding with both Lloyd George
and Curzon, the British Foreign Minister, that the Dutchman wasn't
going to get them. Standard would be there, in the person of an
A. C. Bedford, and Robbie probably knew their crowd better than
Zaharoff did—but it turned out that Zaharoff was the one who knew
everybody better.

In short, the old Greek trader had all the data and had saved Robbie the need of taking notes by having the data typed out. He
showed papers which he couldn't possibly have come by honestly,
and this was taken for granted between the two as they talked; there
would be more acquiring of papers and bribing of servants and so
on at Genoa. Lanny learned something that his father had neglected
to mention, that among those present would be the ex-cowboy Bub
Smith, whom Robbie had used to demonstrate the Budd guns, and
who had been his secret man watching Zaharoff's companies during the war. Whether Zaharoff knew that wasn't mentioned, and
apparently it wouldn't have mattered—Bub was a dependable man,
and was going to watch some very tricky ones in Genoa.

Among them, Lanny gathered, was the American ambassador to
Italy; his name was Child, and he was a novelist—Lanny recalled
having read several of his short stories in magazines. Why had
President Harding appointed a flighty literary fellow to this high
diplomatic post? There must be some reason, and Robbie would
find it out, for he had letters to him. "But don't let him get any hint
about me," said Sir Basil, and Robbie said: "Of course not." The
ambassador, going officially as an "observer," would doubtless have

a staff, and Robbie would find a way to get next to some of them.

Lanny became somewhat uncomfortable as this long interview proceeded; he perceived that his father had become Zaharoff's "man," and that the latter was making no bones about giving him orders. Quite a difference from the time, eight or nine years ago, when the armaments king had suggested Vickers' buying out Budd's, and Robbie had graciously replied that Budd's might prefer to consider buying out Vickers! What had happened to make the difference? Was it the hard times, which had hit Budd's so hard and made profits scarcer? Had Zaharoff held out such rewards that Robbie and his associates couldn't refuse them? Had Robbie got in deeper than he intended, and was he now caught in the spider's web? He seemed quite at ease and satisfied with what he was doing, but Lanny knew that he was proud and wouldn't reveal his troubles if he had any. Whatever happened, Robbie must think that Lanny thought his father a great businessman and master of everything he touched!

Zaharoff was making plain the supreme importance of what was to be done at Genoa. Two years previously, at San Remo, Britain and France had agreed to the dividing of the Mosul oil, and Zaharoff had been in on both portions; but later on, after President Harding had come in, America, in the shape of Standard, had "muscled in" and grabbed a share. That must surely not be allowed to happen again! Zaharoff and Deterding and their associates—which included Robbie Budd's syndicate—were going to get whatever was obtainable of the oil of Baku and Batum, and Zaharoff was going to be sitting right here, pulling the strings and making sure that nothing was overlooked. He was going to have a courier coming every day to bring him news, and there was to be a code which Robbie was to keep on his person—apparently the old spider had sat and devised that code looking at the duquesa's flower-box, for Deterding the Dutchman was to be "Bybloem," and Lloyd George was to be "Bizarre," which is another variety of tulip. The old rascal had a sense of humor, too, for Viscount Curzon of Kedleston was to be "Ineffable," and Richard Washburn Child, United States Envoy Extraordinary and Minister Plenipotentiary to the Kingdom of Italy, was "Cradle!"

VII

The gossips told a story about how this conference had come to be called in a city of Italy. Someone had suggested it under the French name of Gênes, and Lloyd George had understood this to mean Geneva, and had consented accordingly: a neutral city, the home of the League of Nations. Only after arrangements had been made did he discover that Geneva is Genève, and that his conference was to be held under the auspices of a people which was far from international in its mind, and in a city crowded and far from comfortable for elder statesmen!

Genoa is a really old Mediterranean city. It has a fine harbor, which was used before the memory of mankind, but it has very little land, because the Ligurian Alps come crowding down to the sea, and the streets and alleys of the town have to go scrambling up them on steep stairways, and over bridges where there are ravines. So the buildings are tall, even the old ones, and crowded together, and there are many parts of the city where vehicles cannot go. Fortunately for Rick, the Palazzo di San Giorgio, where the conference met, was down near the harbor; a dark, melancholy Gothic building six or seven centuries old, which had long been the home of the Bankers' Guild of the city.

Twenty-nine nations of Europe had been invited to the gathering. The Italian government had taken charge of the occasion and commandeered all the hotels, but Robbie had brought a secretary and sent him on ahead to make arrangements, so everything was comfortable for the little party. There was Bub, the funny-looking fellow with the broken nose that he had never bothered to have fixed; he was full of important news, and went into a huddle with his boss while Lanny drove Rick to the Casa della Stampa, the club set apart for journalists. Rick had only to present his credentials, and he and his friend were admitted, and there were all the old gang and a lot of newcomers; greetings and introductions being exchanged, and gossip going at full blast.

International conferences had by now become an institution; this was number seven on Lanny's list, if you counted two in Paris and

one in Geneva. For him they were a delightful spectacle, a refined
sort of Roman holiday in which you were spared the sight and smell
of blood, though you knew it was being shed freely. For the journalist it was hard work, but also sport, a hunting expedition in which
each dreamed of bagging a creature with a priceless pelt known as
a "scoop." Each news-hunter tried to get as much as he could from
the others and give as little; but since the only way to get was to
give, there was a torrent of talk.

The fashion was to be "hard-boiled." The world could not be
worse than these men thought it, conferences couldn't be more futile, conferees more stupid or tricky. The newsmen always predicted
the worst—and so far their prophecies had been justified. Lanny and
Rick preferred the Americans, because their point of view was more
aloof, they were freer to say what they thought, both in conversation and in cabling. Now and then, however, Rick would decide
that it was too easy to be cynical about the problems of Europe,
and he would seek the company of some reserved and careful Englishman. The French and Italians one met less freely, because their
points of view were apt to be official.

Lloyd George and Poincaré had had a meeting at Boulogne prior
to this conference, and the former had been forced to agree that
the question of reparations was not to be raised. That, everybody
said, was like playing *Hamlet* without the ghost. The French Premier was refusing to attend, but had sent his Foreign Minister, and
was so afraid that this Barthou might fall under the spell of the
Welsh wizard that he was sending him a dozen telegrams of instructions every day—actually he sent more than a thousand during the
course of the affair!

When Lanny had had his fill of international intrigues he would
go out for a walk on the funny cobbled streets of this half-medieval
city. The principal ones were beflagged for the occasion, and the
cab-drivers wore ribbons dangling from their hats—Lanny didn't
know whether that was a general custom or a special honor. At
night everything was brilliantly illuminated, and the streets crowded
with a holiday throng; girls and soldiers and carabinieri everywhere.
There was opera every night, and dancing until morning in the

cafés and the *boîtes de nuit.* Lanny looked at sixteenth-century
churches with façades in stripes of black and white marble; he went
through palaces in which the gentlemen of Shakespeare's plays
might have lived their tangled plots. Now the stage was bigger and
the plots much harder to follow. How would a playwright manage
to put twenty-nine nations into a drama? All the world was a stage
in a sense that no sixteenth-century playwright could have dreamed!

VIII

Three years had passed since Lanny had seen Lincoln Steffens, but
he didn't look any older; his little gray mustache and goatee appeared to have been trimmed by the same barber, and his quiet business suit to have been cut by the same tailor. He was still the
quizzical-kind philosopher, amusing himself with other people's intellectual confusion. They ran into each other in the Casa della
Stampa, and Stef took him off to lunch, because he had been drawn
to this amiable playboy and wanted to find out what life had been
doing to him. "Have you made up your mind to anything yet?" he
asked, and Lanny, knowing the game, countered: "Have you?" The
other said: "I don't have to. I'm a philosopher." Lanny replied: "I've
decided that that's what I am."

In the inexhaustible library of his great-great-uncle, Lanny had
come upon the *Dialogues* of Plato, and it seemed to him that Stef
must have taken these as the model of his conversation. You'd have
thought it was Socrates asking you questions, always friendly but
searching your mind, leading you to the point where you realized
that you didn't know what you were talking about. But never would
he tell you that; you would see it. Never would he say: "Don't you
perceive that inconsistency?" The time would come when you
would begin to stammer and apologize for your own confusion of
mind.

Lanny was in a trying position here in Genoa, having to keep one
large part of his thoughts from Robbie and another large part from
Rick. He wanted very much to be honest, and suddenly he blurted
out: "See here, Stef, will you let me tell you something frankly?"

"Of course," said the other. Looking at this handsome youth with all the signs of wealth on him, he asked: "Are you in love?"

"Indeed I am," said Lanny, "but I don't make any problem of that. It's my father, and our business here in Genoa. Will you keep it to yourself, please?"

"Shoot!" said Stef.

"Well, you know about Budd's; and now my father has gone in for oil, and he's here on business."

"The town is full of them. What is it the Bible says: 'Wheresoever the carcase is, there will the eagles be gathered together'?"

"You know, Robbie has always taught me to hate the Reds. He raised merry hell with me in Paris because I met you and my Uncle Jesse. I got into a scrape with the Paris police that I never had a chance to tell you about. The result was that I had to swear off on meeting any more Bolsheviks."

"And you're breaking the rule now?"

"No, it's just the other way. The Bolsheviks have oil."

'Oh, I see!" exclaimed the muckraker, much amused.

'Now my father wants to meet them. He even wants to meet you."

"Well, why not, Lanny? I'd be glad to meet him."

"But you see, he won't be interested in your ideas the least bit."

"How can you be sure?"

"Because—I know Robbie. He's here on business."

"Listen," said the muckraker. "You never read any of my books, did you?"

"I'm ashamed to say I haven't."

"They're not easy to find any more. But see if you can get a copy of *The Shame of the Cities.* You'll see how, twenty years ago, I used to travel round and interview the toughest guys—the political bosses, and the businessmen who paid them and used them. There were some cases where they wouldn't let me quote them, but I can't recall a single case where they refused to talk to me frankly and tell me what they were doing—some of the very worst things. The System, I called it, and they had been following it all their lives, but they didn't know it, and when I pointed it out to them, they were thunder-struck and thought I was some sort of wizard."

"I don't think you'll find Robbie as naïve as that; he knows what he is doing and he believes in it."

"Maybe so; but this is what I've discovered—honest confession is one of the greatest luxuries the human soul can enjoy. There are few of even the richest men in the world who feel they can afford it."

"All I can say is," said Lanny, "if you can break through my father's coat of chain mail, I'll give you a certificate as a real wizard."

"You arrange for me to have lunch with him—just us two. You keep away; for of course it would be something different if you were there, he has to play a part before you."

"What he really wants, Stef, is for you to introduce him to some of the Soviet representatives."

"Well, why not? He won't shoot them, will he?"

"He wants to get oil concessions."

"They have oil to sell, perhaps. Why shouldn't they meet him?"

"It's all right, only I wanted you to know what we are up to."

The muckraker took this with good humor. "Bless your heart, I wasn't born yesterday, and neither were the Russians. All I need say is 'American oil man,' and wink one eye, and they'll buckle on their chain mail. They can take care of themselves, believe me!"

IX

The luncheon took place next day, in a private room of that particular "grand hotel" in which the Budds were staying; and just what happened was a secret which those two so different warriors would carry to their graves. What Robbie said was: "That's a remarkable mind."

"You bet!" said Lanny.

"Of course," the other hastened to qualify, "it's easy for a man who sits aloof and criticizes, and won't take any stand one way or the other. If he had to act, he'd find he had to make up his mind what he really believes."

"I don't know," said Lanny. "It seems to me he has some very firm convictions."

"What, for example?"

"He believes in facing facts and not being fooled, by yourself or anybody else. It seems to me that's fundamental."

"Well, it's like a gun, or a typewriter, or any other instrument; it depends on what use you make of it after you get it."

Robbie didn't say anything about having made any confessions. Instead, he remarked, with quiet satisfaction: "I got what I was after. He has given me a letter to one of those Soviet people, a man named Krassin, who he says is their expert on foreign trade. Do you know anything about him?"

"He's just a name to me; but I'll see if I can find out. A lot of the newspapermen have been meeting them, and they talk freely."

Lanny, of course, made haste to see Stef again to inquire what happened. It was rather disappointing, for the muckraker said: "He's just like all the others: a man who is unhappy about the way the world is going, but can't bring himself to face the idea that he has any responsibility for it."

"Are you free to tell me about it?"

"I'm afraid not all of it. Your father is a very proud man, I would almost say arrogant; and of course he can't have his own way, so he's going to suffer like the devil."

"I know that," agreed Lanny. "I've known it since the war began. He hated that mess, yet he couldn't help knowing in his heart that he had had a share in bringing it on."

"I told him about elephant-hunting in Siam. He made me think of a powerful bull elephant that has just discovered that he's inside a stockade, and he runs here and there and hurls himself against the barriers until he almost breaks his neck."

"And Robbie took that?"

"I suppose he took it because he never expects to see me again. He probably wouldn't take it from you."

"I guess not!"

"I'll tell you one thing that's important to you," said Stef. "I brought him to admit that he has no right to dominate your thinking. I pointed out to him that it wasn't respecting your personality. I backed him down on that."

"Oh, Stef, I can't tell you what that would mean to me! I've been living in a sort of jail. Do you think he really means it?"

"He meant it when he said it. Whether he'll be able to live up to it is another question, of course."

X

On one of the decorated streets of festive Genoa Lanny ran into three of those Caucasian gentry in high black boots and large black astrakhan bonnets who, at the Paris Peace Conference, had put their excited faces close to his and enveloped him in a fine salivary spray, while telling him in atrocious French the sufferings of their country under the heel of Bolshevism. Now they were here, no longer as official representatives, but as exiles and outcasts; they had been sold out, and whoever got the oil of their native land would pay no royalties to them. Again they surrounded the amiable Lanny Budd and poured out their woes, and he had a hard time making clear to them that he no longer had an official position, was no longer any sort of pipeline for either news or propaganda.

All the little nations were here; they had been officially invited and their coming had been trumpeted; but now who was to pay any attention to them? Their broken and bankrupt peoples needed steel rails and freight-cars, plows and seeds, oil for their lamps and needles to mend their breeches—in short, money, money, money, and who was going to give or lend it? They were besieging the hotels and villas of statesmen, and making life miserable for secretaries; they were sitting in the cafés, drinking themselves melancholy, and ready to weep on the shoulder of any stranger who would listen. Especially they wanted to get hold of Americans, because America had all the money there was left in the world. Lloyd George had a marvelous new scheme for an international loan of two billion dollars for the reconstruction of Europe. America was to put up half;

and a dozen times Lanny was asked: What did he know about it? When would it be available? How would it be divided? Where did you go to get your share?

Painful to an idealistic youth to have to confess that he wasn't trying to help the world out of all these troubles! Painful to have to hear his own voice, speaking inside him: "I am one of the wolves, roaming the edges of the pack, looking for a stray or a weakling, a young one or an old that I can pick up! I am the son of a wolf; and no use telling myself that I don't like what my father wolf is doing, because I live on what he kills."

In short, there was a moral crisis in the soul of Lanny Budd. The Genoa conference was for him no holiday, but a time of inner strife and deep-seated unhappiness. Except for his brief talk with Stef he never mentioned it; and certainly his father did nothing to make it easier for him—for Robbie's mind was on the kill, and he had no time for foolishness. If he was aware that his son was disturbed over helping him to get an oil concession, he must have brushed it aside as something fanciful that a youngster would have to get over quickly. Time enough by and by to sit around and listen to radical chatter called "ideas"; but right now there was big money to be won or lost, and if Robbie needed an introduction he asked for it, if he needed information he asked Lanny to go and get it, and he didn't stop to say: "If you wouldn't mind," or: "If it would be consistent with your notions of delicacy and good taste."

So Lanny roamed the streets of this ancient city with a smoky fire of discontent inside him. Did he need so much money? Did anybody need it? Even granting that you needed it, did you have a right to wreck the world to get it? And after you had wrecked the world, did you have the right to call yourself a "practical man" and everybody else a "dreamer"? These questions had been shaping themselves in Lanny's mind for a matter of eight years—ever since July 31, 1914, to be exact.

Yes, it was a crisis. Hitherto Lanny had been ordered to think what he didn't want to think, and that had been trying enough; now he was ordered to say what he didn't want to say and to do what he didn't want to do, and that was far worse. He suddenly found himself thinking that this wonderful father who had been the ideal of his childhood and youth was somewhat of a bull-headed and insensitive person. Lanny still loved him, of course; that was what made it so miserable, so destructive of peace; it was possible to love your father, and still think such treasonable thoughts about him!

The thoughts took the form of imaginary dialogues, in which Lanny would say: "Look, Robbie, have you forgotten what your father did to you? He wrecked your whole life—so you told me many times—he made it impossible for you to be happy. And now are you going to do it to me?"

14

Blood of the Martyrs

I

LLOYD GEORGE set off the Genoa conference with one of his eloquent and most persuasive speeches. Where everybody else was worried and frightened, he was witty and gay. In his verbal flights he manifested both determination and generosity; this was the greatest gathering in Europe's history, he said, and the Continent was going to be restored. It was such good news that the delegates from twenty-nine nations arose and cheered him to the echo. Then, the ceremony over, the British delegation retired to their Villa d'Albertis and began wrangling with the French and Belgians over the conditions upon which a loan might be made to Russia; they continued this procedure for a matter of six weeks, when the conference came to an end with nothing accomplished.

At the first meeting with the Russians Lloyd George put in the

British claim against the country for British property damaged or confiscated; the amount was two thousand six hundred million pounds—quite a tidy sum which the Russians would kindly acknowledge as a debt. Chicherin, the Soviet Foreign Commissar and head of their delegation, replied courteously that they would be pleased to balance the claims against the Russian claims on the British government for damage done to Russia by British armies at Archangel and Murmansk, and by British-financed armies of Wrangel, Kolchak, and Yudenich, the total of which amounted to five thousand million pounds. After this exchange of bills due, the British retired for tea and the subject was dropped.

The French, of course, had a huge claim against Russia, the money which their bankers had lent to the Tsar. The Soviet's argument was that this money had been used to arm Russia for the benefit of France, and the debt had been paid by ten million lives. Also they advanced against the French a claim similar to that against Britain: Denikin's White Russian armies had been munitioned by France and guided by French officers, and they had ravaged the Ukraine for three dreadful years. Thus Bolshevik Russia *versus* bourgeois France, and on what basis could they settle such a quarrel?

Lloyd George, the practical fellow, said: "Let's forget the old claims, which the Russians are obviously in no position to meet. Let's get something real. Oil, for example! The Russians have it, and we can drill and pump it. Let's lease the district for a matter of ninety years, and pay with a part of the oil." But the stubborn Poincaré sat in his Paris office, poring day and night over his documents—he was a pasty-faced, pragmatical lawyer, and words were sacred to him, ancient bargains must be kept and ancient precedents followed. He made it a point of honor that the Bolsheviks should acknowledge the debt. Said the sarcastic Robbie Budd: "They should do what the French are doing to us—acknowledge, and then **not** pay!"

II

The Russians had been segregated at a little place called Santa Margherita, some twenty miles down the coast; they were in a comfortable hotel, but to reach it you had to travel by a slow train or motor on a dusty road. Robbie sent his letters of introduction to delegate Krassin, an appointment was made, and Lanny drove his father; they were escorted into the Russian's office, and Robbie got a jolt, for he had expected to meet a proletarian roughneck, and instead here was a tall, old-world aristocrat with fine features, coldly polite and reserved, speaking better English than Robbie did French. Leonid Krassin was an engineer who had managed the great Putilov arms plant in St. Petersburg before the war; he knew all there was to know about the Baku oil-field, because in earlier days he had been in that city as manager for the A.E.G., the German electrical trust of which Walther Rathenau was head.

This Red foreign-trade expert conducted a sort of kindergarten class for the benefit of a businessman from far-off New England. He explained the viewpoint of his government as to the difference between Tsarist obligations and those which the Bolsheviks themselves might incur for the rebuilding of their country. The oil of the Caucasus they considered a heritage to be preserved and worked for the national benefit. If foreign concerns were willing to help in getting out this oil, concessions would be granted for reasonable periods, and all agreements would be strictly kept. Foreign engineers and skilled workers would be welcomed, but insofar as Russian labor was employed, the labor laws of the Soviet Union would have to be conformed to. The Soviets desperately needed oil, but they also needed the contentment and enlightenment of their long-oppressed people.

Robbie brought into play those arts which he had spent so many years in acquiring. He explained that he was an "independent," not controlled by any of the great oil trusts. He took it for granted that this would count in his favor; but the Russian suavely explained that this was a misconception of the Soviet attitude—they did not object to big organizations, but rather preferred dealing with them because they were generally more responsible. "What you Americans call independence, Mr. Budd, we Communists call anarchy; we think that the more quickly industry is integrated and rationalized, the more quickly will it be ready for social ownership."

So Robbie had to hustle and think up a new line of sales talk. He assured Mr. Krassin that he represented responsible people with large amounts of capital. The Russian asked how long a lease they would expect, and intimated that Lloyd George's idea of ninety years would hardly be pleasing to Moscow; twenty years would be better. When Robbie said that was hardly time enough to get the full benefit of development work, the Russian suggested that the government should pay the value of the investment, or part of it, at the end of the lease. They had a discussion as to whether they would pay the value of the field, or only of the money put in. Robbie said that, according to American ideas, one acquired the ownership of the oil that was in the ground; but the Russian idea was that this oil belonged to the people, and that lessors could expect payment only for the value of wells and machinery.

To Robbie Budd life hardly seemed worth living on terms such as those. As he and his son were driving home he said: "That gives me a pain in the neck—about the people owning the oil. The people will never touch it—a bunch of politicians have got control and mean to hold onto it."

Lanny had an impulse to say: "You believe in a government, Robbie; and what can any government be but politicians?" But that was the kind of remark the younger man had learned not to make; it would only mean a tiresome argument and do no good. Say some polite nothing, and let Robbie have it his way.

III

Through Steffens Lanny met a number of left-wing intellectuals. They too were here as "observers"; they wrote stories about international affairs for newspapers and magazines of the various warring Communist and Socialist and labor groups. They sat around in the cafés and argued till all hours, and exchanged ideas and information with sympathetic journalists of the various nations. Some had been to Russia, and regarded this experiment as the one really important thing in the world. The first whom Lanny met was a big, amiable ex-minister, Albert Rhys Williams, who had had adventures which do not often fall to the lot of a man of God. He had summed them up in the titles of two books, *In the Claws of the German Eagle* and *Through the Russian Revolution*. He was friendly with the Soviet delegates and their staff, gave them advice, and tried to explain them to those "bourgeois" journalists who would listen.

There was a tall, extremely handsome, fawnlike man with a soft, caressing voice and prematurely gray hair: Max Eastman, editor of a New York magazine, the *Liberator*. It had been the *Masses*, but the government had suppressed it during the war and indicted and tried its editors. Max had fallen very much in love with a gay young woman on the Russian staff, and was threatening to follow her back home. There was a liberal and pacifist editor named Villard, not able to find much encouragement in anything that was going on here. There was an English editor, Frank Harris—at least, Lanny thought he was English, but learned that he was a Central European who claimed to have been born in Ireland, and had worked as a cowboy in the Far West of America. A fiery-looking man with a heavy black mustache, he was the possessor of a golden tongue, and when he talked about Shakespeare or Jesus you would have thought you were listening to the great one in person; but then the talk would turn to someone against whom Harris had a grudge, and he would pour out such malignancy that you shrank in dismay.

Present also was an American-Jewish sculptor by the name of Jo Davidson; a short, broad fellow with a spreading black beard, quick dark eyes, and deft fingers. He journeyed where the great were to be found and made portrait busts of them. The Russians were preoccupied, much worried men, and Davidson had to get them at whatever they were doing, receiving visitors, eating their lunch, shaving themselves. They didn't know that he understood Russian, and talked intimately among themselves; Jo went ahead and modeled their features and kept their secrets.

Lanny made the discovery that "celebrities" had highly developed egos. They had fought their way up in the world, and hadn't done it by being polite; they had sharp and well-developed spines, claws, and stingers. They were convinced of their own importance, and expected and received deference from plain nobodies whom they met. There was no one of whose unimportance they were more certain than a rich man's son, and for the honor of their acquaintance they permitted him to pay for the food and drinks. Frank Harris even tried to borrow a large sum of money from him, which fortunately Lanny didn't have; he was asked if he couldn't get it from his father, and took refuge in the statement that his father disapproved of the company he was keeping.

There were few things these intellectual battlers agreed about, but one was everywhere taken for granted, and that was the evilness of oil as an influence in international affairs. Wherever you smelled it there were treachery, corruption, and violence. Nor in discussing this matter did any of the left-wingers consider it necessary to spare the feelings of the son of Robbie Budd. If he didn't agree with them, what was he doing in their crowd? If he couldn't bear the truth, let him stay with his own! Lanny tried to do so, but made the discovery that he preferred the harsh and ugly truth to the polite evasions he met with among the "respectable" people.

IV

Walther Rathenau had become the Foreign Minister of the German republic. He had a difficult problem in Genoa, for a huge reparations payment was falling due at the end of May, and no moratorium had been granted; on the contrary, Poincaré was declaring that "sanctions" were going to be applied without fail. The Germans were trying to induce the British to intercede, but couldn't even get at them, everybody being occupied with the squabble over Baku and Batum. The Russians couldn't accomplish anything either, so of course it was natural that the two outcasts of the conference should combine forces. On the sixth day a bombshell was exploded under all Genoa, and the report of it was heard wherever cables or wireless reached. The Germans and Russians had got together at the near-by town of Rapallo and signed a treaty of amity; they agreed to drop all reparations claims against each other, and to settle all future disputes by arbitration.

This treaty seemed harmless enough on its face, but then nobody at Genoa took anything as meaning what it was said to mean. The general belief was that there must be secret military clauses to the agreement, and this enraged the Allied diplomats. Russia had the natural resources and Germany the manufacturing power, and if these two were combined they could dominate Europe. It was the thing the German diplomats were always dropping hints about, and the German general staff was believed to be plotting it. Hadn't the German government brought Lenin and the rest of the Red agents into Russia in a sealed train, and turned them loose to wreck the Tsar's government and take Russia out of the war? By that maneuver the Kaiser had almost won, and here was another trick of the same sort!

The reactionaries hardened their hearts, and the liberals were unhappy, seeing the failure of all efforts at reconciliation. What a tragedy! lamented Villard. The German autocracy was dead, and here was a republic, an oppressed people trying to learn self-government, but nobody would help them, give them any chance to survive! To this the left-wingers replied by mockery. What did capitalism care about a republic? Capitalism was autocracy in industry; that was its essence; it didn't want to help anybody to survive, it wanted to make profits out of human need. The oil men were running this conference, and to them republic or kingdom was all the same—so long as they could get concessions and protect their monopolies throughout the world.

Cynical and cruel-sounding, but there was Lanny Budd's father coming to him to prove that the cynics had it right. "Between you and me," said Robbie, "I think there's a lot more to this Rapallo deal than anyone admits. It means that the Germans are going to get the oil."

"But, Robbie, the Germans haven't capital enough to run their own industry!"

"Don't you fool yourself, the big fellows have money. Do you imagine that Rathenau hasn't got it?"

Lanny couldn't say. He could only wonder, while his father went on to spill what was in his mind. He wanted Lanny to go to the German minister at once, and explain to him that his father was representing a big American syndicate, and might be able to make some useful suggestions to the German delegation.

Lanny didn't want to do it the least bit. He had been trying to be a young idealist, and now Rathenau would think he was just one more schemer. But Lanny couldn't say that—it would be making his father another schemer. He tried feebly to explain that Rathenau was a hard-pressed and exhausted man. Lanny had seen him and knew that it was so.

Said the father: "Don't be childish! One of the things he's exhausted by is trying to get oil for Germany. Now he has the inside track with these Russians, and nothing ought to please him more than to fix up a deal by which American capital would be made available to them both."

So Lanny phoned one of the secretaries whom he had come to know at Bienvenu, and an appointment was arranged. He met that much-harassed statesman again—and, oh, such a tragic face! It seemed that the Jews were born to suffer, and it became their features; at any rate it made them look more like Jews. This man whom the Prussian aristocrats scorned was carrying all their burdens for them, expiating their sins, pleading for mercy with the foes they had so wantonly affronted. He was the scapegoat for another people —the Jews not being allowed even that luxury for themselves!

But it appeared that Robbie was right. Rathenau was a businessman, used to talking to businessmen. He said that he would be very glad to hear what Mr. Budd had to say; he made an appointment for that very day, and he and Robbie spent an hour in conference. It must have been important, because Robbie didn't tell his son much about it, but had his secretary, who had hired another car, drive him at once to "Monty." Lanny was left behind, because he had a date to take Rick to a press conference at the Palazzo di San Giorgio, where Lloyd George was going to answer the questions of newsmen concerning Rapallo, and what it meant, and what would be the attitude of the British government to a *rapprochement* between German Socialists and Russian Communists.

V

It became Lanny's singular duty to drive his father several times
to the Soviet hotel at Santa Margherita. Elaborate negotiations were
under way, and before they were over, Lanny had met all the
heads of the delegation and many of the subordinates; he heard
stories of the revolution they had made, and had their hopes and
their fears explained to him. He watched with amusement his
father's growing surprise at the qualities he kept discovering in
Bolshevik leaders. Remarkable men, Robbie was forced to admit;
their wits had been sharpened in a school of bitter struggle and
suffering. The American hadn't expected to find genuine idealism
combined with worldly cunning—in fact he hadn't considered it
possible for such a combination to exist in human beings. Least of
all had he expected to meet scholarly persons, with whom he was
interested to engage in theoretical discussions.

Chicherin, Soviet Foreign Commissar, was a former aristocrat who
had been trained for diplomacy in the Tsar's school. He had many
of the characteristics which one found in Englishmen of that class;
he was tall and stoop-shouldered, sensitive and shy, careless in his
dress and absent-minded like some funny old college professor. He
lived in his work, hating to trouble anybody, and trying to do all
the work, even to the sharpening of his lead-pencils. He turned
night into day, and appointments with him were apt to be for two
or three o'clock in the morning; even so, he would be unavoidably
late and would apologize profusely.

In the meantime Robbie and his son would chat with Rakovsky,
Bulgarian-born revolutionist, and his wife, who had been a Russian
princess and was now a Communist who used a lorgnette! Both of
these were clever talkers, and Robbie said he didn't see how Russia
could ever be industrialized while she had so many of these. Rakovsky, discovering the fog of ignorance concerning the Soviet
Union which enshrouded Genoa, went to the university and obtained the use of a large lecture hall, and there every afternoon
he explained Bolshevik ideas of history to whoever might wish to
come. He spoke perfect French, being a graduate of a Paris medical

school and having written a book on French culture. The journalists of that country were annoyed to hear him discuss their history, and they would rise and heckle him, but quickly discovered that he knew things about the French Revolution which they hadn't heard before. It was one of those European halls in which the lecturer is down in a pit, and the seats for the audience are in tiers in front and on both sides of him; it wasn't long before the place was packed to the doors—the journalists of all nations were deserting the conference and coming to listen to Rakovsky.

All this was a liberal education for Lanny, and he hoped it might be for his father; but these hopes were not realized. Robbie's mind was on his expected concession, and on the long reports he was sending to Zaharoff, and his code messages to interested parties in Paris and London and New York. What Robbie wanted to know about these Bolsheviks was, would they keep their word and, no less important, would they keep power? That was what the businessmen had such a hell of a time making up their minds about. For four years and a half they had been betting that these fanatics, half idealists and half criminals, would be swept away; but somehow, unaccountably, they were managing to hang on. This imposed upon an American businessman an annoying task, that of understanding a new philosophy, a new economic system, a new code of ethics. In this Robbie's son was helpful to him, and might have been more so if only the son could have kept his head and drawn the line at the proper point; but the young idiot kept taking these fellows seriously, and this upset Robbie and made it hard for him to keep his mind on his work.

There was in the group a rolypoly Jew known as "Papa" Litvinov; round-faced, florid, fond of good living, a hearty, rough-and-ready sort of fellow who might have been boss of a construction camp in the Far West. Robbie employed men like that, and knew how to laugh and jolly them along; if he could have had Litvinov to run the Caucasus oil-field, he would have felt certain of getting out the stuff. It was this man's duty to explain to the would-be concessionaire the labor code of the Soviet Union; that was very important to Robbie, so he listened closely and asked many questions, all from the point of view of a businessman, thinking: "Shall I be able to get any work out of them on that basis?" But there was Lanny, thinking: "How fine for the workers! They can be self-respecting men under such a code!" He would say something like that to the Russian, and the latter would beam with pleasure and start off on a long discourse that had to do with labor psychology instead of production costs of crude oil at the pipeline terminus. Robbie would feel himself in the position of Alice through the Looking-Glass.

VI

Lanny was present at a luncheon which his father gave to the American ambassador, Mr. Child, whom between themselves they always called "Cradle." He was a smooth-faced, boyish-looking man, talkative, and greatly impressed with the service he was rendering his country by seeing that its businessmen got their share of whatever was being distributed at Genoa. The luncheon took place in a *cabinet particulier* of Robbie's hotel, and present also was an admiral of the navy who had been assigned to assist Mr. Child as "observer." This elderly gentleman was doubtless well trained to observe enemy ships upon the sea, but he knew nothing at all about the oil business, and was certainly not a competent observer of the machinations of Robbie Budd.

The father had warned Lanny under no circumstances to drop any hint as to Robbie's connections; he was an "independent," representing an American syndicate, and that was all. The author of popular fiction, to whom words came easily, told what he knew about the conference, what it was doing about oil, and what the Americans wanted it to do; this included a great deal which A. C. Bedford, the big Standard man, would certainly not have wished to have communicated to a Grand Officer of the Legion of Honor and Knight Commander of the Bath.

Again Lanny was being disillusioned. He had always had business put before him as a matter of patriotism; all his young life, when Robbie had talked about his activities, he had been increasing the wealth of America and providing jobs for American workingmen.

Budd's was an American munitions plant, and in building it Robbie was providing for American security. Now America must have oil for its ships abroad wherever they were traveling; and so on. But here was this "independent," in secret alliance with Deterding, the Dutch-Englishman, and with Zaharoff, the Greek citizen of all countries in which he owned munitions plants; and Robbie Budd was intriguing as hard as he could to thwart the efforts of the American ambassador and the companies he was backing! However much you might dislike Standard Oil, it was an American concern, no less so because it was privately owned. Neither the American people nor the government was going to own Robbie's concession; Robbie's associates and backers were going to own it, and Robbie himself was going to run it.

So really it appeared that patriotism was just a screen, behind which selfish interests were operating; old Dr. Samuel Johnson had been right in his bitter saying that patriotism is the last refuge of a scoundrel. Lanny didn't want to think such thoughts about his father, and tried with all his might to keep them from sneaking into his mind. He sat there with nothing to do but listen, and of course he couldn't help seeing how Robbie was deftly leading a man who was a good deal of a nincompoop into telling exactly what instructions he had received from the State Department regarding the support he was to give to Standard Oil and its agents in Genoa.

The ambassador was a bitter hater of the Bolsheviks, and spoke contemptuously of statesmen such as Lloyd George, who were willing to compromise with them; "shaking hands with murder," was the phrase. Of course Mr. Child didn't know what a lot of such handshaking Robbie had been doing, and Robbie didn't mention the matter. He listened, and learned how Mr. Child was working with Barthou, French Foreign Minister, against the British in their efforts for a compromise. The French wanted to suspend all the trade treaties with the Bolsheviks and go back to the policy of the blockade, the *cordon sanitaire;* that was Secretary Hughes's idea of statesmanship, and how should "Cradle," his agent, guess that Robbie Budd would be on the British side in a struggle for the rights of property against Red revolution?

VII

The ambassador told what he had seen in Italy during the year since his appointment. He considered that the country was in a deplorable plight, in imminent danger of a revolution on the Bolshevik model. The cost of living was ten times what it had been before the war, and everywhere you went were beggars asking for a soldo. The people were hungry, the factories idle, the steel mills working on half-time. Already there were regular soviets in the factories, and the police and army were utterly unreliable; the government was so benevolent that it took everybody on its payroll, and it was so liberal that it couldn't enforce order.

"You can't imagine how it is unless you live here," said Mr. Child. "You wish to ride on a street car, but there is a strike; you are told that a carabiniere has struck a street-car worker, so they are all insulted. Next day—*ecco!*—the carabiniere has apologized to the worker, and the cars are running again!"

The ambassador went on to tell a story which he thought would amuse Mr. Budd, who came from New England. A couple of Italian anarchists in Massachusetts had recently been convicted of a payroll hold-up and murder, and sentenced to death. Mr. Child searched his memory and recalled the names, Sacco and Vanzetti. Had Mr. Budd ever heard of them? Robbie said he hadn't. Well, it appeared that the anarchists in Rome had heard of them, and a deputation of five young fellows had come to the American Embassy to demand justice for their comrades and fellow-countrymen. Mr. Child had had an agreeable chat with them, and sent them away satisfied with his promise to have the matter investigated. Subsequently one of these young men had come back and asked for a job! So matters went in this nation which had had sixty-eight governments in the course of sixty years.

The ambassador had been able to find only one hopeful thing in Italy, and that was a new movement called *Fascismo*, about which he talked a great deal. Here was a spirit of unity and resolution. Perhaps that always happens in human societies, he said; when the need grows desperate enough, the organism evolves a remedy. The

Fascisti were organizing the young men of Italy and teaching them a program of action. Their leader was a former soldier named Mussolini; Mr. Child had never met him, but had heard a lot about him, had read some of his articles and admired him greatly.

Lanny spoke up, saying that he had met him. The other was interested to hear about the interview, and asked Lanny's impressions of the man. Mr. Child confirmed Mussolini's claims as to the character of the movement. "Everywhere I see these young blackshirts marching I get the feeling of clean-cut, vigorous youth, conscious of its reforming mission."

"Aren't they sometimes rather violent?" asked Lanny.

"Well, but you have to consider the provocation. It seems to me we're going to need a movement like that at home, if the Reds go on extending their activities as they are doing. Don't you think so, Mr. Budd?"

"I do indeed," said Robbie, cordially. So they were better friends than ever, and Mr. Child told delightful stories about his adventures in the strange role of ambassador. He was much taken with the King of Italy, an energetic little pint-sized man—really a liberal, and quite democratic in his tastes. He had been standing on the piazza, talking with Child, and it was a cold day; the King had bidden the ambassador put his hat on his head. Could anything have been more considerate? Robbie agreed again, but Lanny couldn't help his rebellious thoughts. If you were going to have your king democratic, why have one at all? And why should an ambassador from a republic be so very keen about kings?

VIII

Lanny told Rick about this conversation—the parts having to do with Mussolini—and Rick agreed that the American envoy was a poor judge of Italian character and social forces. They saw Benito Mussolini now and then in the Casa della Stampa, and thought less of him each time. Being now in his homeland, he was even more the braggart and *poseur*. He made a bid for Rick to write about the progress of his *Fascismo* during the past two years; he insisted that he now had four hundred thousand youth of Italy enrolled under his banner. Rick wanted to say: "In your eye!" but remembered that he was a gentleman, even if Mussolini wasn't.

Talking about the Blessed Little Pouter Pigeon and his movement made Lanny remember Barbara Pugliese. He had received a letter from her, thanking him for his kindness and giving him an address in Turin. Since her work of speaking and organizing caused her to do considerable traveling, it occurred to Lanny that she might be coming to the conference, so he wrote a note to the Turin address, giving the name of his hotel. Then he forgot about the matter, because at this moment another bombshell exploded under the conference—the publication of a report that the Soviet government had made a deal with Standard Oil, giving them an exclusive lease upon the Baku field.

An anti-Bolshevik delegate had handed to a New York newspaperman a typewritten sheet containing the substance of the alleged agreement. The newsman tried to verify it, and only got laughed at; for two or three days he went about with that possible great "scoop" burning a hole in his pocket. His newspaper, the *World*, was anti-Standard as well as anti-Bolshevik, so he took a chance and put the story on the wire; it was published, and in an hour or two was back in Genoa, where nobody but the Russians and the Standard people could know whether it was true or not, and nobody would believe anything that either of these groups might say. There was a great uproar, and Robbie had to jump into his car and hurry off to Monty to reassure the frantic Sir Basil. Robbie was quite sure it was a *canard*, because his man Bub was on intimate terms with the young lady secretary of one of the Standard agents.

The fuss died down in two or three days, but it had the disagreeable effect of concentrating the attention of the entire world upon the subject of oil at Genoa and causing the newspapermen to ask prying questions. The Bolsheviks referred to themselves as "proletarians," a fancy word that the American newspapers always put in quotes; now their reporters began writing about "petroletarians" at Genoa, and that wasn't so funny as it sounded. The plain people were sick of war and famine, and didn't care to risk any more of it to help private interests grab some Russian oil.

IX

One evening Lanny went to the opera and, finding a poor performance, came home early. Rick was at a reception in one of the English villas, and Robbie was in conference with some of Zaharoff's men. Lanny had just begun to undress and have a quiet read in his pajamas when a "buttons" tapped on his door and informed him that down in the lobby was *uno ragazzo* asking to see him. Lanny hadn't met any of these in Genoa, nor was he enlightened when the other kept insisting that the *ragazzo* was *molto stracciato;* Lanny had never had occasion to use or hear the word "ragged" in Italy, though he had seen the condition in abundance. He went down into the lobby, and met a street urchin with large dark eyes and peaked face, having in his hand an envelope which he held out to the well-dressed American. Lanny saw at a glance that it was the letter he had written to Barbara Pugliese in Turin.

"*La signora ammalata,*" said the boy, and Lanny knew what that meant; he had seen her ill before. The boy was clearly in a state of fright, and having once got started he talked with rapidity. Lanny didn't know all the words, but made out that *la signora* had been beaten, that she was badly injured, perhaps dying, they had found her in the street, she had had this letter with her. The name of the hotel was upon it, and Lanny's name as the sender, so the boy had come in haste to him.

Perhaps it wasn't altogether wise for Lanny to set out for an unknown destination with a stranger, especially since he had in his pocket a purse containing a considerable sum of money. But he thought of only one thing, that this woman who had so captured his admiration had fallen victim to the ruffians of the Blessed Little Pouter Pigeon; she was in need of help, and Lanny had no idea but to hurry to the garage where his car was stored, and set out to drive under the lad's direction. They came to one of those slum neighborhoods which constitute a horror in every Mediterranean city; wind-

ing streets through which a car could hardly be driven, the remains
of last week's garbage polluting the air. They got out in front of
a tall tenement, and Lanny locked the car and followed the lad
through a pitch-dark hall, into a room lighted by one smoky kerosene lamp. There must have been a dozen people crowded into it,
all chattering excitedly; but they fell silent when the stranger appeared, and moved back to give him access to a bed on which lay
a dark form.

Lanny couldn't see very well, so he took the lamp, and then had
a hard time not to drop it, for the sight was the most dreadful that
had come under his eyes since that day when he and his mother
and Jerry Pendleton had taken Marcel to Paris with his crushed body
and burned face. The face of Barbara Pugliese, about which Lanny
had imagined so many romantic things, had been beaten until it
looked like a piece of butcher's meat; one eye was closed and the
socket such a mass of blood that there was no way to know if there
was any eye left. The ragged coverlet of the bed was soaked in
blood, and so was Barbara's dress.

"Is she alive?" Lanny asked; and that started everybody to talking. They didn't seem to be sure, so Lanny put his hand over her
heart, and found that it was beating faintly.

He managed to make out that the people in this tenement didn't
know Barbara, hadn't ever heard of her. They had heard screams,
they had rushed out and seen a group of youths pounding a woman
with blackjacks. The reputation of the *Fascisti* was such that the
bystanders didn't dare make a move; they just stood and waited
until the assailants had finished their job, and marched off singing
their hymn of glory, *Giovinezza*. Then the people had carried her
inside. They hadn't dared to notify the police, for fear of being
implicated with what they knew must be a Red; this was by now a
familiar story in the slums of Italian cities. They had looked in the
woman's purse and found the letter; none of them had been able
to read the contents, which were in French, but one had been able
to read the name of the hotel on the envelope, and Lanny's name
above it.

Now they had but one idea, which was to get the *povera signora* off their hands, before the blackshirts came back to finish their job and perhaps to include her supposed friends in the lesson. The people were in a panic about it, and made plain their intention that if the *signor* wouldn't take charge of his friend, they would carry her out in the street and leave her in front of some other house. So Lanny said all right, but they must help him; he took the woman's feet, and two of the men took her by the shoulders, and they carried her to the car and laid her in the back seat. She was unconscious, and did not even groan. There was no time to think about protecting the car cushions; they just laid her down, blood and all. Lanny, afraid of getting lost in these tangled streets, promised the boy a lira to ride beside him and show him the way to one of the main thoroughfares.

As he drove, he tried to think what to do next. To appeal to the police would be futile, for had he not heard Mussolini boast how the police were in league with his blackshirts, or at any rate afraid to interfere with them? To take the victim to a hospital would be risky, for those in charge might themselves be Fascists; the same was true of any doctor to whom he might appeal. The Italians were making an omelet, and now Lanny had one of the eggs on his hands. He decided that he was going to get Barbara out of Italy; he would do it with only enough delay to let his father know what he was up to.

X

The good Samaritan parked his car and hurried into the hotel. Nothing else to do; he was no doctor, and knew very little about first aid to the injured. Robbie was still at his conference in the reception room of their suite, but Lanny interrupted, and took him into another room, where he told the distressing news.

"My God, son!" exclaimed the horrified man. "What is this woman to you?"

"It will be hard to explain, Robbie. You'll just have to take my word that she has impressed me as a noble personality, perhaps the greatest I have ever met. I'll tell you all about her some day, but not while she's lying there perhaps dying. I have to save her if I can, and I don't know anybody in Italy to trust."

"Can't you find any of her friends?"

"I can't go driving around with a half-dead woman in the car, asking for the headquarters of the Socialist party—which have probably been smashed up or burned long ago."

"Have you thought that these blackshirts may attack you yourself?"

"That's a chance I have to take. If I didn't take it, I'd never respect myself again as long as I live."

"What do you plan to do with her when you get her into France?"

"Put her in a *maison de santé* and get proper care for her. After that I'll wire Uncle Jesse. I've no doubt he'll come, or give me the address of some of her friends. She has them everywhere, because she's a speaker, a well-known person in her movement."

"Suppose the woman dies before you get her to a hospital?"

"That's another chance I have to take. All I can do is to tell the truth about what happened."

"But don't you see that you'll be branding yourself as a Red sympathizer? The newspapers will be full of it."

"I know, Robbie, and I'm sorry; but what can I do?"

"You can let me phone to a hospital here, and have them come and take the woman off your hands."

"Even so, won't the police want to know how I got hold of her? Won't I have to show the letter I wrote her? I'll be here in Genoa, in the hands of the gang—and what will Mr. Child's great hero Mussolini do about it?"

"It's hell!" exclaimed Robbie. "I've been warning you from the beginning about associating with these people, and writing them letters. God knows I tried hard enough to keep you out of the hands of Jesse Blackless and all his crew."

"You did, Robbie, and it's damned unfair that I may drag you into such a mess."

"Well, what do you propose to do about that?" The father was greatly provoked, and made no effort to conceal it.

"I've thought about it a lot, Robbie. I don't agree with your ideas, and I want to be free to think what I have to, so perhaps I ought to drop the name of Budd—I'm not really entitled to it, it's just a sham. I ought to carry my mother's name, and I'm perfectly willing to take it and set you free from this continual discomfort. I'm of age now, and ought to be responsible for myself, and not drag your family into scandals."

Lanny meant it, and his father saw that he meant it, so he changed his tone quickly. "I'm not asking you to do anything like that, Lanny. I'll excuse myself from my guests, and drive with you to France."

"That's not necessary, really. I'm not in any serious danger—no police are going to stop my car, once I get started. I'll drive carefully, and the woman can just lie there. When I get to the border and tell the French officials—well, it's no crime to have found a wounded person, and to be trying to help her."

Robbie said: "I'll send Bob Smith with you. He can return on the train. I don't think you ought to come back into Italy."

"All right," assented Lanny. "I've seen enough of this conference, God knows."

"And one thing more, son. If you feel this urge to try to change the world, can't you for Christ's sake manage to work out some peaceable and orderly program?"

"Indeed I want to, Robbie!" Lanny said it with deep feeling. "Come and help me. Nothing would please me so well!"

XI

The good Samaritan didn't stop for his things; they could be forwarded later. He grabbed the astonished Bub Smith, who was getting ready for bed. "Come on—right away. You're driving with me to France. Bring your passport and your gun. Don't stop for anything else—it's an emergency." When they were getting into the car: "There's a woman in the back seat. I'll tell you about her when we get started. She may be dead." The ex-cowboy had had his share of adventure, and was not too easily jolted. He hoped his employer's son hadn't committed any serious crime; but if he had, it was all in a day's work.

Lanny had known of persons being injured in automobile wrecks, and had learned that when one suffers from concussion of the brain and shock, the important thing is to keep him quiet. So he drove carefully, avoiding jolts and sudden turns; now and then Bub would look behind, to be sure that the body was safe on the seat. Just before they reached the border the ex-cowboy got into the rear seat and lifted the woman to a sitting position and held her in his arms. Not very pleasant, but part of the job.

To the border guard Lanny said: "I have a sick lady. I am taking her to a *maison de santé*. Where shall I find the nearest?"

He was an American, driving an expensive car; his papers were in order, and he had no luggage, so there was no reason for delay. They told him where to go, so in a short while Barbara was in a French private hospital with a doctor in attendance. This man had heard of the terrible blackshirts across the border, and fortunately was not a sympathizer of theirs. He examined the woman and made his report; evidently the *squadristi* had taken their time and made a thorough job of disciplining her; they had pounded the whole front of her body, and then rolled her over and worked on the back; hardly a square inch that was not bruised. There were several fractures of the skull, one of them basal, so there was no possibility of operating, nothing to do but leave it to nature. There was a little spark of life in her, and it might survive; they would give stimulants to keep the heart going.

Lanny phoned his father as soon as possible in the morning and sent a telegram to his Uncle Jesse at his home. Bub took the morning train back to Genoa, promising to send Lanny's clothes. The youth wrote to his mother and to Marie, telling what had happened, and then settled down to wait—there was nothing else to do. He slept, and then walked for a while, thinking about his life and what this new crisis meant to him. He had made certain that there were forces in the world which he hated with all his heart and wanted to fight; but just what they were, and how he could recognize them— that would take a bit of study.

He decided that he wanted to talk to Rick, and telephoned his friend, who said that he had had all he needed of Genoa, and came by train and joined Lanny that evening. Uncle Jesse arrived from the other direction, so there were three social philosophers, with nothing to do but argue—for the poor gray-haired old woman still lay unconscious, and it would do no good to her or them to sit and look at her smashed face.

Uncle Jesse had the whole problem laid out in his mind, as if it were a map. He said that Fascism was the answer of capitalism to the workers' attempt at freedom; Mussolini was right in saying that it would spread to other lands, for capitalism was the same in all lands, and would defend itself by the same methods—that is, by subsidizing gangsters, to operate under the label of patriotism, that being the cheapest and easiest of all labels.

Rick, on the other hand, insisted that Fascism was a reaction of the middle classes caught between the two millstones of capitalism and Communism; the white-collar workers suffered all the effects of social breakdown, unemployment, the high cost of living, loss of hope—and they turned for help to any demagogue who promised relief. These two arguers went at each other hammer and tongs, while Lanny sat and listened, and tried to figure out which he believed. He decided, in his usual uncomfortable way, that he believed both at the same time.

It was the best chance he had ever had to understand the ideas of his forbidden uncle. He made up his mind once more that he didn't like him, but also that that had nothing to do with the matter. Bald and wrinkled and harsh, Jesse Blackless was like some old bear of the forest that has fought his enemies until his hide is ragged, his ears missing, and his teeth broken—but still goes on fighting. Jesse Blackless had a cause that he believed in, and Lanny knew few such persons, and couldn't help admiring his grit. Also, once the uncle's bitter sarcasms had got into his mind, he found that it was hard to get them out. They stuck like burrs in wool.

Lanny mentioned his father's suggestion that he should find some peaceable and orderly way to change the world. Jesse said that was a pleasant phrase with which to evade an issue; Robbie had doubtless forgotten it already. When Lanny said he'd remind him, and try to convert him, the uncle said: "Then there'll be two disillusioned idealists instead of one!" When Lanny pointed out that several of the Bolsheviks in Genoa had been members of the capitalist class, Jesse said: "Oh, sure; some individuals go over to the workers, but does that abolish the class struggle? When one rich man turns traitor, the rest of the rich men don't follow him—they hate him."

XII

Two days passed, and they were in the midst of an argument in Lanny's hotel room when a message came from the hospital: Barbara Pugliese was dead. They had to arrange for a funeral; a conspicuous and public one, as a matter of propaganda, a demonstration of working-class protest. The news of Barbara's fate had been published in labor papers, and several journalists and labor leaders came; they took the body to Nice, and the coffin was placed on a truck draped with flowers, and thousands of workingmen and women marched behind it, carrying banners and signs denouncing the vicious *Fascismo*. Uncle Jesse had managed to keep his nephew's name out of the affair, and nobody paid any attention to a well-dressed young American and an English journalist, the latter limping painfully with the procession.

At the grave the throng stood with bared heads and listened to eloquent tributes. A bald-headed American painter told the story of a life consecrated to the cause of the humble and oppressed. Never had this heroic woman flinched from any duty or sacrifice; she had the courage of a lion with the sweetness of a child. Tears came into the orator's eyes as he told of their long friendship, and then rage shook his voice as he denounced the Italian blackshirts. His nephew listened, and agreed with every word he said—and at the same time was ill at ease to find himself in such a company and in such a mood. He looked at these dark, somber people, unfashionably dressed, their faces distorted by violent passions; they were not his kind of people, and he was afraid of them—yet something drew him to them!

"Labor has one more martyr to add to its roll, which is as long as human history." So the speaker declared, and quoted the saying about the early Christians: "The blood of the martyrs was the seed of the Church." It sounded strange from one who hated religion as Jesse Blackless did, but Lanny realized that these Reds were founding another kind. They disliked to hear that, but so it was, and the more you persecuted them, the more you spread their faith over the earth. It was a hard way for truth to be taught, but maybe Uncle Jesse was right in his belief that human beings were ready for no other. An uncomfortable and irrational world that Lanny Budd had been born into! Once again it had dragged a young artist out of his ivory tower, and was buffeting him about in a fashion that interfered greatly with his convenience and his sense of dignity.

15

Roman Holiday

I

LANNY and Rick came back to Juan, and Marie came to join her friend. She knew that he was troubled in spirit, and she was gentle and sweet to him; listened sympathetically to the story of Barbara Pugliese, never tried to argue with him, dropped no hint that he had done anything wrong. But among themselves the ladies consulted anxiously; Marie and Beauty and Nina, and Sophie and Emily when they happened to drop in. How was an impressionable youth to be kept from falling into the hands of agitators, fanatics, and enemies of the public welfare? They were at one in the conviction that they had had a narrow escape from disagreeable publicity. Beauty trembled when she heard what Lanny had said to his father about changing his name; she knew out of what intense emotion such words must have come. She had buried the name of Blackless deep in the past, and got no pleasure out of the thought of its resurrection.

Robbie, having failed to get what he wanted in Genoa, went back home to consult his associates. He stayed only a few days and then returned, for the conference had referred the problem of Russia and its oil to the Supreme Economic Council, summoned to The Hague in June. Rick, his reputation now established, had got an assignment from a daily newspaper to report this affair, and the natural thing would have been for Lanny to take him there, as he had to Geneva. But Marie said: "Oh, Lanny, no more conferences! I missed you so!"—and it was easy for her lover to give up the idea of going, because he was sick of the smell of oil. "Let's stay at home and read some good books," pleaded the woman, not realizing that there might be a difference between them as to what books were "good."

Before they went north for their summer, Lanny made a search of Eli Budd's library. The old gentleman hadn't gone in heavily for economics, and what he had was of the old school. But there were two books by a writer named Bellamy, of whom Lanny had never heard. He read *Looking Backward*, and it seemed surprising to him that this book wasn't more talked about. He tried to find any of his friends who had read it, but there wasn't one. He couldn't see how anybody could fail to want to live in a world like that, a world in which human beings helped one another instead of wasting their efforts trying to keep others from succeeding. Lanny read *Equality*, a still less-known work, which gave him a scientific statement of how a co-operative economy might be organized and run. It seemed to him that this was the best thing that had come out of America, the genius of a practical people applied to the most important problem which confronted mankind.

But, alas, how few Americans were heeding their great social prophet! There was another America, not so different from the Europe in which Lanny lived; a land of poverty and unemployment, of desperate strikes and labor revolts—all the phenomena of that "class struggle" about which Jesse Blackless talked incessantly, which he made the core of all of his social thinking. While Robbie was trying to get the oil of the Russians, other "petroletarians" at home were engaged in appropriating the reserves of their country's navy—with the help of purchased members of President Harding's Cabinet. That was Robbie's own administration, which he had helped to choose and elect. He defended it stubbornly, refusing to believe the story until it was forced into the newspapers by a Senate investigation. Then Robbie belittled it, talking about it sourly as the work of agitators, Red sympathizers, enemies of private business. Lanny didn't argue, but he saw clearly that the oil game was the same, whether it was played in Washington and California or in Italy and Holland.

II

Lanny motored his *amie* to Seine-et-Oise, and Rick took his family by train to Flushing, put them on a packet-boat, and then went to The Hague. Lanny subscribed to the paper for which Rick was writing, so it was the same as receiving long letters from his friend. Also he got news from Robbie, who came to Paris to consult with Zaharoff at his home on the Avenue Hoche. Robbie told about the swarms of oil men at The Hague, and the struggle going on among them, and with the Russians, and with the Supreme Economic Council. The building of the Tower of Babel was the only thing with which you could compare the effort to allot the world's petroleum supply.

The Russians wanted a loan for the reconstruction of their country, and they were using the oil as a bait, saying that without the loan they would prefer to struggle along and repair their own fields as best they could. The British wanted to make the loan, but the French and Belgians and many of the Americans insisted that Bolshevism must be starved out and made to fail. What would become of the intellectual defenses of private property if every street-corner orator could claim that the Communists were rebuilding their country? The oil men would get together and pledge themselves to negotiate as a whole and make no separate offers; then they would wait to see who would be first to break the agreement, and each would be afraid of being the last.

Johannes Robin was at The Hague. He had to know what was going to be decided, not only about oil, but about Germany. The mark's future depended upon the outcome of these negotiations; and of course a speculator had to be on the spot and keep his "pipe-lines" in repair. The statesmen who had the decision in their hands had secretaries and clerks who got inside information, and would pass out tips to a dependable person. The statesmen themselves had powerful friends who knew how to make use of their opportunities, and were generous and discreet in seeing to it that public servants were not left to suffer destitution in their old age.

So Lanny, reading imaginative tales of a perfect world, lived in contact with one which was tragically different. Settled in the comfortable ménage of the Château de Bruyne, reading, practicing the piano, playing tennis with two happy youths, enjoying the society of a lovely and devoted woman, Lanny knew that he was among the most fortunate of men. He tried to keep himself in a mood of gratitude, but on the twenty-fifth of June of that year 1922 he picked up a morning newspaper and read that Walther Rathenau, Foreign Minister of the German Republic, being driven to his office in a large open car, had been startled by a smaller car rushing up beside him, with two men in it wearing leather jackets and helmets; one of them had produced a repeating-gun and fired five bullets into the minister's body, and immediately afterward the other had thrown a hand-grenade into the car.

They had done that because he was a Jew, and was presuming to manage the affairs of Germany and to seek appeasement with both France and Russia. They had done it because it was a violent and cruel world, in which men would rather hate than understand one another, would rather do murder than fail to have their own way. To Lanny it seemed the most dreadful thing that had happened yet, and he bowed his face in his arms to hide his tears. He would never forget his memories of that kind and gentle man, the wisest he had found among the statesmen, the best heart and the best brain that Germany had had in this crisis. To Lanny it was as if he heard the tolling of a bell of doom; the best were going down and the worst were coming to the top in this corrupt and unhappy civilization.

III

Jesse Blackless had taken up his painting again, perhaps in despair concerning the human race. He had come to Paris and set up housekeeping with a young woman who worked on the Communist newspaper *L'Humanité*. He seemed happier that way, and it was pleasanter for his friends, for there were now chairs for them to sit on, and no longer a frying-pan decorating the center table. In fact, the painter and his *amie* set up a sort of *salon* for Reds, who would come at all hours and drink his wine and smoke his cigarettes and tell him the news of the underground movement in the various parts of Europe.

Lanny had declared his independence, and the form it took was to visit his Communist uncle and meet some of these dangerous and yet fascinating personalities. It was Lanny's form of a "spree"; vicious or not, according to your point of view—but he told himself that he wanted to understand the world he lived in, and to hear all opinions about it. Maybe he was fooling himself, and it was just a seeking of sensation, a playing with fire, with what the Japanese police authorities call "dangerous thoughts." Certainly it was a mistake if he wished to remain an ivory-tower dweller, for a bull in a china shop can do no greater damage than one idea inside a human psyche.

There were bookstores in Paris in which Red literature was sold; Lanny visited one of these and got several pamphlets, including an English translation of Lenin's *The State and Revolution*. He took these home and smuggled them into his room, keeping them out of sight and reading them surreptitiously, as if they had been pornography; he knew that both Marie and Denis would have been shocked by it, and that it would have been polluting the minds of two innocent lads to let them know that such printed material existed.

The Soviet leader was another victim of the practice, so widespread in Europe, of shooting bullets into the body of anyone

with whose political beliefs you disagreed; he had been an invalid
ever since the shooting, and was soon to die. But here was his
powerful mind, beyond the reach of any assassin's bullet; he gave
what seemed to Lanny a mathematical demonstration of the forces
which were destroying the capitalist system and making it necessary
for the organized workers to take control of society. The Russian
thesis was that there was no way this change could be brought
about except by the overthrow and destruction of that bourgeois
state which was the policeman of the exploiting classes. This thesis
apparently applied to a land like Russia, whose people had never
known free institutions; but did it apply equally to France and
Britain and America, which had enjoyed the use of the ballot for
long periods? This was an important question, because if you were
applying the Russian technique to countries where it didn't fit, you
might be making a costly blunder.

When Lanny suggested this to Uncle Jesse's friends, they laughed
at him and said he had a bourgeois mind; but he wanted to hear
all sides, and took to reading *Le Populaire,* the organ of the Socialists. These disagreed violently with the Communists, and each
called the other bad names, which seemed to Lanny the great
tragedy of the workers' movement; he thought they had enemies
enough among the capitalist class, without dividing among themselves. Yet he was forced to realize that if you believed revolutionary violence to be necessary, you were apt to be violent in advocat-
ing it; while if you believed in peaceable methods—well, apparently
the men of violence would force you to be violent against them!

IV

Robbie Budd didn't get the concessions upon which he had expended such efforts. All the oil men were vexed, and all the governments; the dream of the bourgeois world, to solve its problems
at the expense of Russia, wasn't working out. The Bolsheviks were
in danger of losing their temporary status of genial conversationalists
and resuming that of diabolical monsters. Robbie went back home
without seeing his son again, and without giving him any further

warning about his conduct. Could it be that the father had thought
it over, and was really going to try to let him have his freedom, as
Lincoln Steffens had suggested?

In the month of August the Greek army in the heart of the
Anatolian hills sustained a terrible defeat, and fled in rout to Smyrna
on the coast, where the Turkish cavalry followed them, driving
them into the sea and slaughtering tens of thousands. "Our friend on
the Avenue Hoche has lost his concessions," wrote Robbie, and
explained that Standard would probably get them from the Turks.
"Also the stock of his Banque de la Seine has fallen from 500 to
225." Rick, at home in England, reported an underground convul-
sion in politics. For the first time it was being asked publicly what
was the connection between the Prime Minister and the mysterious
Greek trader who had become Europe's armament king. Presently
it was asked in the House of Commons—which meant that the
newspapers could repeat it. This was like taking Sir Basil by the
scruff of his crimson velvet robe and dragging him into the glare
of a spotlight, something which Lanny knew would cause him
intense distress.

This Turkish victory was a grave blow to British prestige. The
weakest of the Central Powers, overwhelmingly defeated less than
four years earlier, was now publicly tearing up the treaty which had
been forced upon it. The triumphant Turkish armies, having captured great quantities of Vickers motorized artillery and tanks, all
made by Zaharoff, came to the gates of Constantinople and were
kept out only by fear of British naval guns—also made by Zaharoff.
It looked for a while as if Britain had another war on its hands, and
without any help from the French; it was poor consolation to see
France apparently headed for another war with Germany, without
any help from the British. The outcome was that in October Lloyd
George was forced to resign—the last of the Versailles statesmen, the
"Big Four" who had set out with so much authority to settle the
problems of the world!

Lanny and Marie were back in Bienvenu when that happened.
They were happy, because Lanny was "behaving," according to
the standards of the ladies of his family and their friends. He kept

the worst of his Red literature buried among the respectable books of a New England clergyman, who was not in position to protest against such treatment. He kept his Red ideas buried in his own head, and did nothing about them except to make cynical remarks concerning statesmen. That shocked nobody, it being the fashion in the smart world to accuse political persons of venality as well as stupidity. There was even a fringe of the well-to-do, those who went in for advanced ideas, who were beginning to find good things to say for the Reds. They had been able to survive for five years, in spite of civil wars and famines, and that seemed a miracle. Also, they had the support of popular writers such as Barbusse and Rolland and Anatole France. The last-named came to a hotel on the Cap, and Lanny went to call on him. The old man was showing his many years, but his brain was as clear as ever and his tongue as incisive; the things he said about the situation in Europe differed but little from what Lanny had heard in the establishment of his Red uncle.

Lanny was as happy as one could have expected a sensitive person to be in those troubled days. His *amie* was all that he needed, and he never looked a second time at any of the fashionable ladies, married or unmarried, who spread their charms before him. He dutifully put on the proper clothes and attended the social functions which his mother gave, and some of those of Emily and Sophie when they made a special point of inviting him. He was proud of the success of his two best friends. Rick was working that autumn on a play about the war, and the scenes which Lanny read interested him, and he made suggestions, and thought well of himself when some of them were accepted. Kurt had completed another suite, this time having to do with a soldier's life, and Lanny watched the parturition and birth of an art-work, having all the pleasures of the event and none of the pains. Also there was Marceline, five years old and growing fast; she was by now the liveliest little dancer you ever saw, and knew most everything that Lanny had to teach her along that line. She was a little duck in the water, and a little enchantress everywhere. Very amusing to watch her use her eyes, and practice her arts on every new person who came along. Kurt might be ever so stern a stepfather, but this was a fundamental instinct of the female organism, and he might as well have tried to stop the bougainvillaea in the patio from putting the purple color into its blossoms.

V

In this autumn there came an event whose importance in the history of Europe was realized only gradually. The workers of Italy called a general strike in protest against the permitted cruelties of the blackshirts; the strike failed because the workers had no arms and were powerless against unlimited violence. In this hour of confusion the *Fascisti* took their opportunity and began to assemble; their editor, that Blessed Little Pouter Pigeon at whom Lanny and Rick had laughed, sounded his slogans of glory and summoned his youth to the building of a new Roman Empire.

The American ambassador, "Cradle," played an important part in these events, and was so proud of it that he came home and boasted about it in print. Mussolini came to the embassy and had tea with him, and charmed him so greatly that he defended the dictator and everything he did from that time on. A new government, to have any success, has to have funds, and the editor was seeking support for a movement to restore law and order to his strike-ridden land. Surely an Italy without labor unions, without the co-operatives which deprived businessmen of their profits, ought to be a sound investment! The ambassador thought so, and persuaded the great House of Morgan to promise a loan of two hundred million dollars to the government which Mussolini was planning. Let no one say that America wasn't doing its part in building defenses against the Reds!

There were said to be a hundred and sixty thousand former army officers in Italy, most of them out of jobs and in need of funds. Many had joined the *Fascisti*, and they now led the "March on Rome" which skilled propaganda would make into a heroic episode. Their founder did not walk with them, but traveled more quickly and safely in a sleeping-car. Eight thousand dusty and bedraggled youths could, of course, have accomplished nothing without the acquiescence of police and army. The pint-sized king with the democratic sympathies was told that his cousin had joined the *Fascisti* and was ready to take his throne unless he obeyed orders; therefore he refused to sign the order declaring a state of siege, and the black-shirts entered the capital unopposed.

That "cheap actor" whom Lanny and Rick had interviewed in Cannes now made his appearance before his sovereign, wearing a black shirt, a Sam Browne belt, and a sash of the Fiume colors, and was invited to form a government; later he appeared before the Parlamento and told them that he was the master. No longer was it difficult for him to play the pouter pigeon, for he had had several years' practice in thrusting out his jaw and expanding his chest. The name of Benito Mussolini was flashed around the world, and that interview which Rick had peddled in vain among British editors now suddenly became "spot news." Rick dug it out and rewrote it with fresh trimmings, and his editor paid for it gladly.

VI

The founder of *Fascismo* had proved his thesis of the beneficence of violence. The Americans had a phrase, "climbing onto the band-wagon," and Lanny could imagine all the time-servers, the petty officials and bourgeois "intellectuals," who would hasten to pay homage to the new Roman emperor and make him drunk upon his own glory. A master actor by now, he had served first the left and then the right, and had carefully selected the best phrases of both. Every day he would produce new stunts to delight the Roman mob; he would jump over hurdles to show how lively he was, and be photographed in a cage with a toothless lion cub to show how brave he was.

But woe to those who had fought him, and taught him to hate them! There is no one who hates with such bitterness as a renegade, who has to keep the flame hot that its roaring may be louder than the voice of his conscience. The Socialists, the pacifists, and even the harmless co-operators were shot in their beds or hunted in the mountains; and meanwhile the new ruler in whose honor this Roman holiday was celebrated would stand before the Chamber of Deputies and solemnly ordain: "There shall be no reprisals." That was the pattern of this new society, as Lanny came to know it; boundless cruelty combined with bland and pious lying. The *Fascisti* would develop falsehood into a new science and a new art; they would teach it to one dictator after another, until half the human race would no longer have any means of telling truth from falsehood.

Lanny knew what was happening in Italy, because he was continually meeting victims of it. That was the heritage which his friend Barbara Pugliese had left him; she had told some of her friends about this generous-hearted American youth, and now they had his address. Lanny remembered what his father had said about the practice of hobos in the United States; he had got a mark on his gatepost, and there would be no way ever to get it rubbed out!

The first who came was that young Giulio who had been with Barbara in San Remo and had shouted his contempt at Mussolini in the *trattoria*. The *squadristi* wouldn't overlook a person like that; they gave him his dose of castor oil, and Lanny could hardly recognize the wreck of a human being who appeared at the gate of Bienvenu one morning. He was put into a hospital for a few weeks, but nothing could help him very much, for his digestive tract had been ruined; Giulio was a medical student, so he knew about his own case. He was the first of many who came, each with a more harrowing story; and of course this wasn't pleasant to the ladies of a villa on the Cap d'Antibes. They were sorry of these unfortunates, but also afraid of them, for who would have wanted to treat them that way unless they had done something very terrible? Anyhow, it kept the place in an uproar, and they couldn't see what Lanny had to do with it, or how he expected to set himself single-handed against the new Roman Empire.

Lanny had been able to hide his Red literature, but he tried in vain to hide his Red refugees. It got so that Beauty and Marie worried every time he went to Cannes, for fear that he was meeting some evil companions; it could hardly have been worse if he had been suspected of having another mistress! The people in the village were talking about it, and Beauty was afraid the police authorities might take cognizance. France was a free republic, and proud of its reputation as a home for the oppressed of other lands; all the same, no police like to have swarms of Reds pouring into a country over all the mountain passes and even in rowboats. Beauty could never forget that she herself was a suspected person, living with a German whose past would not bear investigation.

VII

There was another conference, this time at Lausanne, on the other side of the beautiful Lake Geneva. The British had to make a new treaty with the Turks; and of course the French had to be there to get their share. The new Italian Premier had to be there, because the day of glory had arrived, and never again would anybody decide any question about the Mediterranean without consulting him. The new emperor revived the phrase of the old ones—it was *Mare Nostrum*, "Our Sea." To make sure that the world didn't miss the point he kept a long-nosed British nobleman, the "ineffable" Earl Curzon, and with him a Premier of France, waiting like a couple of office boys for a chance to see him and find out what he wanted. A revolution in conferences!

The Turkish treasures were at stake, and that included Mosul, an even more magical name than Baku; so Robbie Budd came again, and all the other oil men. In order to punish the French for having aided the Turks, the British had recognized the Emir Feisal as ruler of Syria; at long last a promise was partly kept, and that dark brown replica of Christ whom Lanny had met and admired during the Peace Conference would come into a part of his own—but not the part with the oil! Tom Lawrence, the blue-eyed, sandy-haired young British agent, had changed his name and was Aircraftsman Shaw, blacking the boots of some minor officer at home. Would he now go back to the desert and resume his place as companion of one who scorned to be called king because he was a descendant of the Prophet? This world that Lanny Budd had been born into was full of strange stories, and travelers from the Mediterranean lands were listened to with interest in his home.

Lanny hadn't planned to go to Lausanne; but the conference ad-

journed for the Christmas holidays, and there were Robbie and
Rick available. The former had business in Berlin; also, Kurt was
planning to spend another Christmas at Stubendorf, and Marie was
going north to be with her boys. So Lanny, with the Fortunatus
purse of his father, laid out a journey for himself and his friends.
He and Kurt would escort Marie to Paris, and then go to Lausanne
and pick up Robbie and Rick and take them to Berlin, where Lanny
and Rick would visit the Robins, and Kurt his brother; then Kurt
and Lanny and Rick would go to Stubendorf—Rick's first visit to
that place. They would come back to Lausanne and leave Rick for
the second stage of the conference, while Lanny and Kurt proceeded
to Paris to pick up Marie again.

A jolly thing to plan journeys with the help of a self-renewing
purse! You and your friends would be transported from country to
country, would talk to the people, gather the news, visit operas and
theaters and art-shows; ride on fast and comfortable trains, stop at
de luxe hotels, eat food novelties in the most elegant restaurants,
have all your burdens carried for you, and by the magic of a pocket-
ful of paper money see everybody smiling, obsequious, and delighted. But pay no attention to the signs of bitter poverty on the
way; half-starved children begging for bread, women selling their
bodies for it—and now and then a Red being hanged or beaten into
insensibility!

VIII

Another of those great international gatherings, with diplomats
from a score of countries and publicists and journalists from twice
as many. Lanny knew so many of them that it was like a larger,
outside family, a fluid periphery of friendship. You didn't know who
was coming, but there they were; then presently they were gone and
others had come. Life consisted of talking and listening to talk;
there was a modern, perfected method whereby you hammered out
your talk on little typewriter keys, and "filed it," and next morning
it would be on a million breakfast tables, or maybe ten million.
Moving in that world you were close to the seats of power, and
something you said or did might help to "make history."

Mr. Child was there, with a large staff. America had come back into the affairs of Europe, after three years of vowing "Never again!" Mr. Child announced America's policy regarding the Near East; it was "the open door," and who could deny that this was a delicate and tactful way of asserting Standard's claim to twenty-five percent of Mosul oil? The Russians were there, still trying for their loan, and dangling an empty oilcan in front of the noses of Robbie Budd and others. Deterding and the rest of the big fellows had agreed upon a boycott; they had formed an organization called the Groupement, pledging themselves to buy no Russian oil, and now they were waiting to see who would break it first. Robbie predicted that it would be Deterding himself; and sure enough, within two or three months he had bought seventy thousand tons of kerosene and taken an option for another hundred thousand. He had thought, so naïvely, that the agreement applied only to crude!

Berlin would have a poor Christmas this year. The mark stood at nearly one thousand to the dollar, and all but the very rich were poor. Everybody was fear-stricken, for the quarrel with France had come to a crisis; the reparations payments were long since overdue, the coal deliveries in arrears, and there was that round, pasty-faced Poincaré with his jaws clenched, determined to move in and seize the Ruhr, industrial heart of the Reich, without which half the Germans would starve. Rick, eager journalist, wanted to interview people of all classes and write an article after he came out; he found them glad to talk to him, for the hymn of hate had been forgotten and they thought of Britons as friends and protectors against French avarice.

Lanny and Rick went to stay with the Robins. Comfort and safety in that warm nest, and Papa Robin a mine of information about everything that was going on, political and economic. Trust a *Schieber* to know! The hard-working man of affairs was troubled by the bad name which people gave him, and defended himself with vigor. It wasn't he who was going to invade the Ruhr and drive the mark still lower; all he did was to know it was going to happen. People who believed that it wouldn't happen were eager to buy marks for future delivery; if Johannes didn't sell them, others would, and what difference would it make?

But the Robins didn't spend all their time talking about money. Far from it; there were Hansi's fiddle and Freddi's clarinet, and a great stack of accompaniments which Lanny would play or make a stab at. Hansi had had a year of drill by the best teacher in Germany, and it was astonishing how he had grown; he played with authority, and Lanny was greatly delighted, and the others were delighted with his delight. Touching to see how they all praised one another, adored one another, forming a solid family phalanx. The father would conquer the world of finance and the son that of art, and there would be two ways to reduce the handicap under which the Jews labored in this part of the world.

IX

Lanny had written to the boys about Barbara, and now he told them details of that dreadful story, and saw horror in their faces and the tears in their eyes. Their abhorrence of the blackshirts was instinctive, and their sympathy with the rebel refugees complete; they had none of that inner conflict which Lanny perceived in himself. Was it because they were members of a persecuted race, with ancient memories of exile deeply buried in their souls? Or was it that they were more completely artists than Lanny? The artist is by nature, one might say by definition, an anarchist. He lives in the freedom of his own imagination, and represents the experimental element of life. If "authority" should intervene and tell him what to think or to feel, the experiment would not be tried, the brain-child would be born dead.

To the sons of Johannes Robin it seemed the most natural thing in the world to accept those ideas which so greatly troubled the son of Robbie Budd. Of course it was wrong that some should be born to privilege while others did not have enough to eat. Of course it was right that the disinherited should protest and try to change the ancient evils of the world. Who would not demand food when he was starving? Who would not fight for liberty when he was oppressed? Who could fail to hate cruelty and injustice, and cry out for it to be ended? So asked Hansi, and Freddi knew that his adored elder brother must be right.

They asked what Lanny thought, and he was ashamed to tell them of his hesitations and bewilderments. It seemed cowardly not to believe what was so obviously true; it seemed weakness to consider such questions as what would offend your father or imperil your mother's social position. Having met Lanny's Red uncle, the Jewish lads didn't think of him as a dangerous man, but as an amazingly understanding one, and they wanted to know where he was and what he was doing and what he had said about the present state of Germany and France and Russia. Lanny mentioned books that he had read, and Hansi declared that when the summer came and he had free time, he was going to learn the difference between Communists and Socialists, and try really to understand the tormented world in which he lived.

Lanny wondered, what was Papa Robin going to make of that? He asked the question tactfully, and learned that it had never been raised in the family. Both Hansi and Freddi took it for granted that their father would want them to believe what was right. Lanny didn't say it aloud, but he thought: "Suppose you take to associating with Reds, like me? Suppose you start rescuing them from the Fascists, and having refugees come to this home with the heavily barred steel door—how will it be then?"

X

Lanny hadn't had much talk with Kurt's older brother Emil on his previous visit, but this time Emil had leave for Christmas, and the four of them traveled to Stubendorf together. Lanny sat and listened, as he liked to do, while the serious Prussian officer discussed the state of his country, and the English journalist plied him with questions. Rather easy-going himself, Lanny liked to watch Rick work efficiently; he would jack himself up and resolve to do likewise, but he didn't always keep the pledge. However, when Rick had a few pages of the article done, Lanny would read them, and make comments and suggestions which Rick found useful. Perhaps that was work, even though others got the credit for it.

Emil might have been described as Kurt without those elements of sympathy and imagination which made Kurt an artist. The elder brother was wrapped up in his professional duties, and when he thought about politics and world events it was as part of the problem of the defense of Germany. He was disturbed, not to say tormented, over the present situation, because Germany was without defense, and the French armies were assembled at the border, ready to move at any moment. From the point of view of a military man that was the worst of all possible situations; Emil's fear of what the French would do was conditioned by what he himself had been taught to do under similar circumstances.

They talked about Italy, and the Prussian officer's viewpoint of events there provoked a lively argument. Emil spoke of the Fascist "revolution," and when Rick objected to that term he said: "Call it a 'counter-revolution' if you choose, but names don't alter the fact that it's a natural reaction against the futilities of so-called democracy. The people attempt a task which is beyond their powers, the governing of a modern state, and they are brought to a plight where they are glad to have a strong man get them out of it. The strong man studies the people, understands them better than they understand themselves, and promises them everything they want; he constructs a program with an appeal which they are powerless to resist. Say that he's 'fooling them,' if you wish, but even so, he gets control, and having once got it, he keeps it—because modern weapons are so efficient that those who have them are masters, provided they are not afraid to use them. The machine gun and the airplane bomb with poison gas promise mankind a long era of firm government."

Such was Emil Meissner's interpretation of Fascism; and he revealed the interesting fact that a movement not unlike it had been under way in Germany ever since the end of the war. It was a native product—never would you hear a Prussian staff officer admit that virile and scientific Germans might learn anything from degenerate and soft Italians! The movement called itself the National Socialist German Workingmen's Party, and its center was in Munich; one of its leaders was General Ludendorff, who next to Hindenburg was regarded as the nation's greatest war leader. This new party promised the German people deliverance from humiliation, and it was spreading with great rapidity. If it took the form of fresh opposition to France and Britain, these nations would have only the stupidity of their own statesmen to blame. So declared this stiff yet passionate Prussian officer.

X I

Christmas at Schloss Stubendorf was even more pinched and straitened than it had been the previous year. With the mark so low, it was impossible to import anything, so in a country district like this you lived as in primitive times, upon what you got from the soil or made with your hands. But you could still have courage and loyalty, *deutsche Treu und Werde;* also the tender sentiments of the *Weihnachtsfest* were unaffected by inflation of the currency. The Meissners played a great deal of music and sang all the old Christmas songs; everybody was gracious to the visiting strangers, and the two young war widows experienced hot and cold flushes in the presence of the eligible young American. He had no way to let them know that he had an *amie,* so he never offered to play accompaniments for one without also inviting the other.

Rick, of course, was deeply interested in everything he saw here, and in everyone he met. "Upper Silesia after the Settlement" was the form the data were taking in his professional mind. A joint Polish-German commission had worked out an elaborate protocol, having six hundred and six sections, and it seemed to be working pretty well; but if France invaded the Ruhr, would Korfanty the troublemaker get busy again? Herr Meissner and his sons discussed these questions at length; of course nothing pleased them more than the idea of having a sympathetic English journalist report their point of view to the outside world.

Among Kurt's friends in the village was a lad named Heinrich

Jung, son of that *Oberförster* who provided them with an escort whenever they wished to go hunting. Heinrich, it appeared, was studying forestry in Munich, and had joined the National Socialist German Workingmen's Party about which Emil had told. Since Rick was so interested, Kurt brought the lad up to the house and had him talk—something that was not difficult, for his movement was a prose-lytizing one, and he knew its formulas by heart. He was nineteen, and sturdily built; war and famine hadn't hurt him, for he had got both food and schooling in Stubendorf. He had extraordinarily bright blue eyes, rosy cheeks, and pale hair over which the barber ran the clippers once a month. Heinrich performed conscientiously all his duties to the Fatherland, which included explaining the new creed to two visitors of Aryan blood like himself. He and his parti-sans were known as "Nazis," because that was the German pro-nunciation of the first two syllables of the word "National."

Lanny had decided that Communism was a new religion; and here was another, this time German instead of Russian. It inspired its youth with the idea that they were destined to redeem the Father-land and make it over into something new and more wonderful. It filled them with a fervor of faith; it taught them to march and drill for the cause, to sing songs about it, to be ready to die for it. The program of these "Nazis" sounded so completely Red that at first it was hard to understand how any army officer could be sympa-thetic to it. It held out all imaginable promises to lure the poor and unhappy. All German citizens were to have equal rights; all were to work, and unearned incomes were to be abolished; the bonds of "in-terest slavery" were to be broken, war gains confiscated, trusts na-tionalized, department stores communalized, speculation in land pre-vented, and land for common purposes confiscated without compen-sation. Usurers and profiteers were to suffer the death penalty, a paid army was to be abolished, and lying newspapers suppressed; on the other hand, there was to be higher education for all good Ger-mans, and for youth every benefit and advantage they could imag-ine. The blue eyes of Heinrich Jung shone like those of a young archangel as he invited the two Aryan strangers to give their sup-port to this redemptive enterprise.

"This looks like the seed of a new revolution," said the impressionable Lanny to his English friend, when they were alone in their room.

"Maybe so," replied the more critical journalist, "but to me it sounds like the old Pan-Germanism dressed up in a new stage costume."

"But, Rick, can they get the young people wrought up as Heinrich is, and then not do any of the things they have promised?"

"Political slogans are like grain scattered to draw birds into a snare. Find out who's putting up the money for a political party, and then you know what it will do."

Lanny, enthusiastic himself, couldn't take a cynical view of the enthusiasms of other young persons. "They really have inspired that lad with a lot of high ideals, Rick; I mean loyalty, self-sacrifice, devotion to duty."

"But isn't that what every master wants of his servants? The Kaiser preached it long before the war. What you have to do, Lanny, is to look into Pan-Germanism. They talk about the superiority of the Aryan race, the making over of the world, and all that, but at bottom it's no more than the Berlin-to-Baghdad railroad, so that Germany can get the oil of Mosul; it means colonies in Africa, which aren't of any economic use to Germany, but have harbors which can be fortified and serve as hiding-places for submarines to cut the life-lines of Britain."

"Maybe you're right," admitted Lanny, "but don't say any of that before Kurt, for he wouldn't take it very well." Lanny, still working at his self-appointed task of keeping Britain and Germany reconciled!

XII

On their way to Switzerland the three friends had to pass through Munich, so Heinrich, returning to school, traveled with them. They talked with him further, and Rick probed his mind. Once you knew his formulas, he could do nothing but repeat, and that soon became monotonous. They discovered that the lad knew

little about the outside world, and didn't seem interested to learn;
he was going to make it so different that what it now was didn't
really matter. If you told him something about England or France
or America that didn't fit in with the National Socialist formula,
he was too polite to say that he doubted, but he let it slip off the
outside of his mind without penetrating.

Rick, the efficient journalist, was just the opposite of this. Much
as he was repelled by Pan-Germanism, whether in its new or old
stage costume, he considered it his business to know about it. He
remembered the bad guess he had made about Mussolini, and he
didn't want to repeat it with General Ludendorff, or whoever might
be the coming savior of the Fatherland. "Let's stop off for a day in
Munich, and let me get the smell of this movement." Lanny, who
had the curiosity of a deer concerning any new phenomenon of the
forest, said: "O.K." Heinrich, of course, was overjoyed, and offered
to take them to headquarters and see them properly introduced.

The place had been a *Kaffeehaus*, in the Korneliusstrasse, a
working-class district. There was a large room with a few tables
and chairs, and pamphlets in the windows. There was a counter
where the members paid their dues, and a couple of small private
rooms in back. The place was called the Braunhaus, for everything
of the Nazis had to be brown, as that of the Fascists was black; let
no one say the Germans were imitating anyone! Instead of the lictors' fasces, Nazis wore the Oriental swastika, or hooked cross,
on an armband, and carried it on their banners; but they didn't have
many, for cloth was scarce. Practically all the Nazis were young
ex-soldiers, and many wore their old uniforms turned inside out.

A young party official answered the questions of the visitors, and
told them about conditions throughout Bavaria, where fighting
among the Reds and the Catholics went on almost daily; the members of the new party were accumulating arms and drilling in the
near-by forests, for the purpose of putting an end to all that. It was
their declared purpose to seize the government, first of Bavaria and
then of the republic. They were a peculiar combination of con-
spirators and propagandists; they told you exactly what they were
going to do, and indeed everything but the date of the uprising.

"And that," said the young party official, "is because we don't know it ourselves."

The visitors were fortunate in having arrived in Munich on the day of a great meeting in the Bürgerbräukeller, and if they would attend they would learn all about the movement, and would hear a speech by "Adi." This was short for Adolf, the great orator of the party; his last name was Schicklgruber, but this was rarely mentioned; it not being considered a very dignified name.

Lanny took Rick and Kurt to the Aden Hotel and, after the fashion which Robbie had taught him, put them up in proper style. They spent the rest of the day looking at pictures in the Schack Gallery. After supper they took a taxi to the beer hall in the Rosenheimerstrasse. The term "beer hall" in Munich means something really big; this was one of the biggest, with tables and seats for a couple of thousand people. The Munichers sit in these seats and by slow sipping can make one stein last all evening. Of course if they can afford it they take much more, and the practice seems to agree with them, for the fortunate ones acquire large round bodies and great wads of fat on cheeks and necks.

The place was crowded; but a piece of paper money obtained front seats for three strangers, and they looked about the smoke-filled room and were sorry for the German people—for not even in Poland had Lanny seen more pitiful clothing. Evidently what in Rick's country were known as "the lower orders" had turned out to hear their favorite orator. At the table with Lanny and his friends sat a man who told them he was a party journalist; a little lame fellow with twisted features and a shrill voice. When he had become acquainted with the visitors he told them a lot about Adi, not all of it favorable, by any means.

There was a large band blaring loudly, and when it played *Deutschland über Alles*, everybody stood up and gave the Nazi salute, the right arm extended upward and in front; then they sat down again, and the shrill voice of the party journalist told them of the unhappy childhood of Adolf Hitler Schicklgruber, how he had left home, struggled in vain to be an artist, and had become a pitiful bum living in flophouses, earning a few pfennigs painting

postcards, or sometimes houses. In the war he had been a lance
corporal, and had been gassed. After the war his army superiors had
sent him to a secret meeting of Munich workingmen, to spy upon
them and report what they were doing and planning. Adi had found
out, and the next time he came it was not as a spy but as a convert
to the cause. Now he was one of the leaders of that movement which
was inspiring the German people and preparing to make over the
world.

The band struck up, and Charlie Chaplin came upon the stage.
At least Lanny and Rick thought it was an imitation of that little
comedian, whose pictures were the rage all over America and Europe at that time—even the highbrow critics raved over him and
called him a genius. The features by which you knew him were
baggy pants and big shoes, tousled hair and a tiny dark mustache, a
pasty face and a simper. The man who hurried onto the stage had
all of these, and also a very soiled old trench-coat. Lanny and Rick
really thought he was going to do a comic "turn" in imitation of the
little Hollywood comedian. But then they realized that this was the
man they had come to hear make a speech.

XIII

The music and the applause ceased, and the orator began. He
spoke the dialect of the district of Austria where he had been born,
and at first it was hard for Lanny to understand him. He spoke with
violent gesticulations, which caused his much too big clothing to
flap about him. He had a bellowing voice, and when he became excited it reminded Lanny of a turkey gobbler he had listened to in
Connecticut. Presently he worked himself into a frenzy, and then it
seemed that what he was saying no longer made sense; but the
crowd seemed to find something in it, for when the orator's voice
gave out and the sentence died in a gabble, they drowned it out
in thunders of applause.

The substance of the discourse was the wrongs which Germany
had suffered during the lifetime of Adolf Hitler Schicklgruber. Having heard the story of his frustrated life, one didn't have to be more

of a psychologist than Lanny Budd to understand how he had come to identify himself with his Fatherland and its woes. Germany's lack of resources before the war had caused Adolf Hitler Schicklgruber to have to sleep in flophouses; the Versailles peace was Adolf Hitler Schicklgruber's failure to reap glory and wealth from the war; the shouting of the excited audience in the Bürgerbräukeller was Adolf Hitler Schicklgruber's determination to rise in the world in spite of all the efforts of his enemies to hold him down.

These enemies were many, and the orator hated and cursed them in turn and in combination. They were Britain and France and Poland; they were the Reds inside and outside of Germany; they were the international bankers; they were the Jews, that accursed race which was poisoning the blood of all Aryan peoples, infecting the German soul with pessimism, cynicism, and unfaith in its own destiny. Adi seemed to have got his enemies all mixed up together, for the Reds were Jews and the international bankers were Jews, and it was the Jews who controlled Wall Street and the London City and the Paris bourse; apparently he thought that the same Jews had brought Bolshevism to Russia; they were in control of the world's finances and at the same time were starving the German people for the purpose of forcing them into the clutches of the Reds!

This tirade lasted for more than two hours, going back again and again over the same grievances and the same threats. Lanny thought he had never heard anything so fantastic in all his life. But there was something terrifying about it, especially the effect it had upon this packed throng. It was like seeing the war break out again, as Lanny had seen it in Paris in the dreadful summer of 1914; like hearing the trampling of the troops, the guns clattering on the roadways, the crowds roaring for blood.

When they came out, and were safe in their taxi, Lanny said: "Well, is that the German Mussolini?"

Rick replied: "No; I don't think I'll ever have to write about Herr Schicklgruber!"

He talked along that line, but when he finished, Kurt said, quietly:

"You are making a mistake. You could write a very important article about that man and that speech. He is confused, but so are the German people. Also he is desperate—and they are that, too. Believe me, he is not to be overlooked."

BOOK FOUR

Money Grows on Trees

16

Contend for Homer Dead

MORE than once Lanny had said to his mother: "I think we ought to do something about Marcel's paintings." He would say: "I don't want to live on Robbie the rest of my life, and I think he'd respect me more if I showed him I could make some money." It had been agreed between them that when any of the works were sold the proceeds would be divided into three parts, the third to be kept for Marceline's *dot*.

One day Emily Chattersworth phoned and invited Lanny over to lunch at Sept Chênes. "There's a man coming I think you'll like to meet. He's an art expert, and he's heard about Marcel's work. I won't invite anybody else, so you can have a chance to get acquainted."

Thus came Zoltan Kertezsi, a middle-aged Hungarian who had been taken to New York as a child and since then had lived all over the world. His father was an engraver and the family was musical, so Kertezsi had grown up with art; he was an excellent violinist, and when Lanny told him about Kurt and his work he was so much interested that he forgot about Marcel for a while. He was a man with a kind and gentle face, and fair hair and mustache; his graciousness was somewhat airy; he moved with a kind of lightness so that at first you might think he was affected, but you discovered that it was the expression of a personality. He loved delicate and refined things, and had spent his life seeking them, studying and savoring them.

The profession of art expert was a new one to Lanny, and he listened with interest while this rapid and eager talker explained it with humor and the opposite of pretense. He described himself as a sort of upper servant to the rich, new or old, a culture-tutor to grown-up children, a guide and bodyguard to amateur explorers of a field where more snares were laid for their feet than had ever existed in the defenses of the Meuse-Argonne. This was a new view of the art world to Lanny; he had thought of a painting as something to look at and enjoy, but Kertezsi said that was very naïve—a painting was something to be sold to a pork merchant or the dowager empress of a chain-store system, persons who had acquired huge sums of money in a short time and were seeking some way to distinguish themselves. The crimes committed in the course of selling art-works to them were more numerous than would ever be listed by the Sûreté Générale. Kertezsi didn't say that he was one of the few honest experts in Europe, but that was the impression his conversation gave. He was simple, swift, and precise in his judgments, and Lanny was delighted to follow wherever his conversation led.

It led to Guatemala, Tibet, and Central Africa, where Kertezsi had traveled seeking native works for museums. He had climbed to monasteries in high mountains, and discovered long-buried palaces in jungles and deserts. He had had strange adventures, and liked to tell about them. He loved every beautiful thing that he had ever bought or sold, and would describe each with ecstatic words and airily gesticulating hands. He would become so absorbed in telling how he had found a great David or Rossetti's *Blessed Damozel*, and by what extraordinary luck he had been able to purchase it, that he would forget all about his *mostele à l'anglaise*, and Mrs. Emily's considerate butler would leave his plate to the last moment, hoping he would remember what he was there for.

II

Lanny decided that this was a man he wanted to know; so after luncheon he took him over to Bienvenu and introduced him to Beauty and to Kurt, and took him down to the studio and opened the storeroom of paintings. This, too, was an adventure, for by the magic of art Marcel Detaze, burned up in the fires of battle, came back, sat with them, and told them the intimate secrets of his soul; he made a new friend, and to Lanny it was more exciting to see this happen than it was to make one for himself.

The introduction was carried on chronologically. First, those lovely paintings of the Cap, in which a son of the cold north had expressed his delight in sunshine and color; the blue and green sea lifting itself heavily, breaking into curves of white foam or showers of sapphire flame. "How he loves it!" exclaimed Kertezsi. "You see how passionately he paints; he is trying to say something that he cannot say; perhaps he will never be able to. But the man has talent, extraordinary talent. The whole Riviera is here. How could people fail to know this work?"

"He was a very shy man," replied Lanny; "he didn't know how to advertise his stuff, and was always more interested in trying to do something better."

"We must find a way to make him known," said the other. "You have a treasure here."

Lanny brought out the scenes of Norway. Now the painter had gone into a strange world, and was awed by it; these waters were cold, these rocks were dark, and these people lived hard; it was a feat just to be alive on a Norwegian fiord. "They are all summer scenes," said Kertezsi. "But you feel that he is thinking about winter."

"He painted many of them in the winter, after he had come back."

"His brushwork has become different. He is groping for a new technique. This isn't the same water that he watched from the Cap, or the same paint that represents it."

Then Greece and Africa. Lanny told about the cruise of the *Bluebird,* and how he and Marcel had felt, and what they had talked about. The other man knew all these places, and got the intense feeling that had been poured into the work: the melancholy of Greece and the hard, stern cruelty of the lands from which the corsairs had sailed, from which the slavers had raided across the deserts into the jungles since time more distant than the eye of history could reach. Marcel had lived alone in his little cottage on the Cap, painting these pictures while he waited for his beautiful blond mistress to come back to him, and perhaps the fear of a great sorrow had hung over him during this time.

Then the war, and the painter's dreadful mutilation; so there was a new man to know. The art buyer had heard something of the story —perhaps Emily Chattersworth had told him. Lanny brought out the sketches which he had managed to keep his stepfather from destroying; and then one by one he set on the easel those war works into which Marcel had poured his horror, grief, and love of *la patrie*. That *Soldier in Pain*, tormented by the little Hun devils, which the painter had insisted was only a cartoon, but which Kertezsi now said was worthy of Daumier. That *Fear*, which the critic said could have been done by no one but William Blake at his best; that portrait of Beauty called *Sister of Mercy*, which Lanny said she would never sell and which Kertezsi predicted would be borrowed for exhibition all over the world if they knew about it.

"Really, Mr. Budd," said the visitor, "it is a mistake not to let the public have this work. I don't suppose you need the money, but I point out that, from the purely business point of view, if you let part of these treasures go, they will work for the rest. If you sell all but a small part, what you have left will in course of years become worth more than the whole thing if you keep it hidden."

"We have often talked about putting some of them on the market," assented Lanny. "How would you suggest going about it?"

"Suppose you begin with a test. Take one of these Riviera sea-scapes, just an average one, and put it up at a London auction room, say Christie's, at one of their really good miscellaneous sales—a little later, when the foreigners are crowding into the hotels. I'll do a little boosting in a quiet way—I mean, I'll get some worthwhile people to look at it, and perhaps I can find some rich American friend to bid for it. You never can tell what may happen; the dealers get to whispering among themselves: 'Zoltan Kertezsi is interested in that Detaze, he says he's a coming man,' and so on—that's the way the game is played, and there's no harm in it, because I really will be interested. You can put a minimum price on the picture if you wish, and if it fails to bring that, I'll bid it in, and in that case you will only be out the commission of the auction room."

"What do you charge for such a service, Mr. Kertezsi?"

"A flat ten percent, whether I am acting for the buyer or the seller. Many dealers will charge both parties, but that I have never done. If you wish me to represent you and try to interest buyers, you may pay me; or if you prefer that I take a chance and try to find some one of my customers who will commission me to buy the picture at a certain price, I will do that."

Said Lanny: "It will seem strange to be making a lot of money out of Marcel's work, when he was able to make so little during his whole life."

To which the other answered by quoting the couplet on the disputed birthplace of an ancient poet:

"Seven wealthy towns contend for Homer dead,
Through which the living Homer begged his bread."

III

Rick hadn't brought his family to the Riviera that winter, because his play had been accepted by one of the stage societies and he had to be on hand to assist in the production. That was something exciting, and Lanny wanted to see it; now he had a double excuse, because of this offer of Zoltan Kertezsi, which Beauty decided to accept. They picked out what they considered a good specimen of Marcel's seascapes—*Sea and Rocks*, they named it—and the arrangement was made for it to be put up at auction just after Easter. That being the period when Marie went north, Lanny drove her, and then went on to London—the obliging ferry took your car across, so you spoke of motoring to London as if the Channel wasn't there.

Rick's play was just going into rehearsal, so he was in town and much occupied. Lanny went to the theater with him, and lived again those days in Connecticut when he had acted in one play and helped to stage another; memories swept over him—and they were intensified manifold when he chanced to looked over the list of plays showing in London and saw the announcement: "Phyllis Gracyn in the sensational New York success, *All Things for Love*."

"Well, well!" he thought. "She's made good!" Indeed, that was the heights for an American actress, to be starred in a London production!

Lanny decided that he wanted to see her act, and persuaded Rick to go with him. Of course he had told his friend about the old love affair, and Rick was curious to have a look at the lady; as for Lanny —well, if you are going to be jilted and have your heart broken, let it be by somebody who is somebody!

The play wasn't much, they agreed; a society drama, the conventional "triangle," with Gracyn playing the part of a young music student who becomes involved with a married man and gives him up when she realizes that he cares more about his family's reputation and social position than he does about love. The "star" herself was the life of the play; the same delicate boyish figure, seeming not a day older than when Lanny had held her in his arms nearly five years earlier. She had acquired poise and skill in putting her personality across; nothing could be more spontaneous than her gaiety, and her charm was controlled like water from a tap.

"I don't wonder you fell for that," said Rick. "Does she still cause you melancholy feelings?"

"I like what I have much better," declared Lanny. "What sort of life would I have chasing about in the entourage of a stage queen?"

"Count yourself well out of it," agreed the other. "I'm having troubles with a stage queen myself just now."

A few days later Lanny saw his old sweetheart having luncheon in the hotel where he was staying. She was with a fashionably dressed man and Lanny had no mind to interrupt, but she saw him and sent the waiter for him, so he went over to her table. The man to whom she introduced him was her producer, and Lanny wondered, was she playing the same old game? Not *All Things for Love*, but *A Part for Love!* She was showing her old friend off to her new, as Lanny had shown her off to Rick. She seemed delighted to see him— but he wondered, can you ever trust an actress? They learn to do these things on the stage, and can they keep from practicing offstage? It was a case of once bit, twice shy.

He paid the customary compliments to her performance, and was

prepared to go, but she wouldn't have it so; she made him sit down
—one didn't give up old friends so lightly. She wanted him to know
that success hadn't gone to her head; she told the other man how
Lanny had helped her in her struggling days, that bitter, lonely
time when she had been a high school student, pining to get onto
the stage but having no more idea how to set about it than if it
was the pearly gates of heaven she wished to crash.

"How are you, Lanny, and what are you doing in London?" He
told her that he had a friend with a new play; also a painting of
his stepfather's was to be sold at auction. "Oh, do they have auctions
of paintings? Could I come and see it? I might buy one, just to show
that I'm getting culture!"

"A lot of people buy them for that reason," smiled the young
man-about-town. "Naturally I'd be pleased to have you attend."
Zoltan Kertezsi had explained that it was important to have people
looking at the picture and asking questions about it, especially prominent persons—and who could serve better than the star of a current
stage hit?

IV

One thing Robbie Budd had always insisted upon in his travels:
you must stop at the most expensive hotel in town, because that
way you meet the people you need in your business. Now, being in
business, Lanny learned how wise this precept was. Walking through
the lobby, with its elaborate display of marble and brass and ormolu
and plush, who should be passing but Harry Murchison, that plateglass manufacturer who had come so close to kidnaping Beauty
Budd and her son and carrying them away to his valley of smoke
and steel! Nearly nine years had passed since that had happened,
or rather failed to happen, and the young businessman from Pittsburgh had grown stouter and more serious than ever; but Lanny
knew him at once, and the other had to stare for only a moment
or two. He greeted his almost-stepson cordially, and asked the polite
questions, how was his mother, and was she with him, and what was
he doing. When Lanny told him, he said, in much the same spirit
as Gracyn: "I'd be interested to see your stepfather's painting. Could

I come, and bring my wife?" Of course Lanny said he'd be delighted to meet Mrs. Murchison.

He wasn't clear in his mind just how much Harry knew about Marcel Detaze. He had known that Beauty had a lover down on the Cap, but did he realize that this was the man? Had he told his wife about his adventure, or misadventure, in the far-off days before the war? That was one of their family secrets, into which Lanny was not expected to pry.

Adella Murchison was a tall, good-looking, youngish brunette who had been her husband's secretary and still took that attitude, doing for him many of the things that secretaries do. They had three children at home, and Lanny knew that they had been married soon after Harry's return to the States; he made a story out of it in his imagination: the heir of a fortune had lost his great love, and was lonely, and a woman employee had "caught him on the rebound," as they say. Lanny liked her because she was straightforward and unpretentious; she said that she didn't know much about painting, but would like to learn, and he gave her such instruction as time permitted.

The rooms of Christie's are in a very old building on King Street, near St. James's Palace. They are extraordinarily shabby, which tells you that they are so aristocratic that they don't have to bother about looks; they are intended for persons so important that their clothes look as if they had been slept in, and who carry rolled umbrellas that have begun to turn green with age. There is a man at the door who is prepared to receive royalty. You go upstairs and find four or five rooms where the paintings are on exhibition, and a salesroom with backless benches on which you sit if you come early. (Proceedings begin at one o'clock, which keeps you from getting any lunch.) The most fashionable people crowd in, those who love expensive art, the critics who write about it, and the dealers who buy and resell it; also the inquisitive public that likes to observe celebrities in action.

The tone of the place is very English, that is to say, dignified, solemn, even pompous. You stroll through the rooms and inspect what is offered. If you are "anybody," you are known to "everybody," and they watch you, and try to guess what you are there for. The cash value of a work of art is one of the most highly speculative things in the world—Zoltan Kertezsi said, almost as much so as the cash value of a woman. It can be changed for better or for worse by a casual phrase, the lifting of an eyebrow, a depreciatory smile. There are some whose word is taken, and others whose money is taken, and of these two forces there can be an infinitude of subtle combinations and shadings.

Lanny had explained to his agent that he was bringing a multi-millionaire from Pittsburgh, a place that sounded like money. Both Harry and his wife looked like money—vulgar, American money that had to be manifested by new clothes. There also was the adorable Phyllis Gracyn, even more elaborately dressed, and it was soon known that the handsome young man who was showing her the Detaze—number 37 in the catalogue—was the scion of Budd's, the American munitions works; he was the owner of the painting and stepson of the painter. Such items cause polite murmurs among visitors at art-sales.

When the important Zoltan Kertezsi came along with a German chemicals man who was in the financial pages of the newspapers, that, too, was something to whisper about; the Germans were said to be putting their money into paintings and diamonds, because they couldn't trust the mark any more. The newspapers have reporters at these sales, to note who bids and what prices are paid, and that is one of the ways that reputations are made for artists both living and dead. The *Sunday Times* had singled out *Sea and Rocks* for praise, and the French dealers who were present had of course made note of that. Now they saw Zoltan Kertezsi leading his man in front of that picture and pointing out its merits. Everybody began suddenly talking Detaze. Oh, yes, that French painter who had had his face burned off in the war and had worn a mask for years. A work of art about which you can tell such a story to your friends is obviously much more interesting than one by a painter of whom you can say only that he was born on such a day and died on such another day.

V

The room was packed to the doors when the sale began. Those who expected to bid sat close under the auctioneer's pulpit; he knew most of them and their ways, and required only the faintest sign from them. An attendant would set a painting upon a high easel; the auctioneer would give its catalogue number and say a few words about it; reserved English words, no circus-poster adjectives, no motion-picture language. This is the right little, tight little island, where we know our own minds and tolerate no nonsense. Give us the facts, name of the artist, his nationality and date, and perhaps what collection the work has come from; we know the fellow, and if we want the thing, we nod our head one-quarter of an inch, enough for the auctioneer and not enough for the chap alongside, for it's none of his business whether we have bid or not.

But the dealers, of course, are different. Those fellows are out to make money; rather vulgar chaps, you know, full of gossip and gabble; they want to know whether Detaze is going to go, and they watch for the signs, and try to find out who is bidding, and whom he represents. They are all playing a game, each against the others, and they run here and there like a herd of stampeded animals—not physically, of course, but emotionally, in their judgments of art, and what will increase in value and what will not. They are playing a thousand little tricks upon one another; each having his favorite that he has stocked up on, or got options on, and is trying to promote. He can't do it alone, of course; he has to persuade some of the others that here is the coming man; has to get him into the newspapers, and lure rich clients into thinking that he is tops, not merely for the moment but for the future. Buying a painting is one of civilization's most fascinating lotteries.

Zoltan Kertezsi had done an excellent job with that Detaze. Somebody started off at twenty guineas, and then the bidding became picturesque: the American actress, the Pittsburgh plateglass man, the German chemicals man all mixing in. They bid it up to five hundred and seventy-five guineas, which was a terrific sum for a small work, the first of its creator's ever to come on public sale. The wind-up was striking too, for an entirely unknown person stepped in at the last moment and said five hundred and eighty, and all the others quit. He was a quietly determined old gentleman with a neatly trimmed white beard and gold pince-nez; he gave the name of John Smith, which must have been a pseudonym; he counted out a stack of fresh crisp banknotes, got his bill of sale, tucked the painting under his arm and walked out to a taxicab, and that was the end of that particular Detaze. It just disappeared off the face of the earth and nobody ever heard of it again.

There were other consequences of this sensational sale. The German chemicals man decided that he wanted a Detaze, and would pay the price he had bid at the sale, five hundred and sixty guineas, if Kertezsi could find him one as good as the *Sea and Rocks*. Then Harry Murchison called up Lanny and swore him to secrecy, and said he wanted to have such a seascape hanging in his home when his wife entered it again. He too would pay what he had bid, five hundred and fifty guineas, and would trust Lanny to pick him out a good one. Lanny was embarrassed to sell to a friend, but Harry said nonsense, the paintings were for sale, weren't they, and he wouldn't have a fit of shyness if Lanny were trying to buy some plateglass.

Lanny wrote his mother about this good outcome; but before the letter arrived she sent him a telegram, saying that a man unknown to her had come to Bienvenu and asked to see samples of Marcel's work; after seeing them, he had offered to buy everything they had, two hundred and seventeen paintings, for a flat price of two million francs, and he would have the money wired to Beauty's bank in Cannes within a couple of hours if she accepted the offer. Lanny was in a panic for fear Beauty might be tempted and he sent her back a red-hot telegram: "For heaven's sake no, we'll get several times that before we are through. Answer immediately assurance."

Lanny said that at Zoltan Kertezsi's direction, and Beauty wired that she would comply, but it was the awfullest temptation. A few hours later she wired that the mysterious visitor was now offering three hundred thousand francs for the privilege of selecting twelve land- and seascapes. Kertezsi said that was more like it, and he advised taking the offer. "Obviously some dealer thinks he can do business with them, and that means he'll be getting publicity for Detaze and building him up. He'll be working for us, and it's all right to pay him for it."

So Lanny wired: "Accept offer but specify in writing no wartime pictures included." At the same time he wired Jerry Pendleton to go at once to Bienvenu and see to the handling of the transaction. That redhead was a good fighting man, and wouldn't be too polite to inspect what the mysterious stranger was carrying off the premises.

VI

Things went on happening. Next morning Mrs. Murchison telephoned, saying that her husband was lunching with a business associate, and wouldn't Lanny come and lunch with her; she had something confidential to tell him. Lanny said: "Of course," and hoped it wasn't a flirtation; he had had that happen more than once, but he thought of the former secretary as a frank and sensible woman, and he himself was not available for an affair.

When they were settled in the hotel dining-room, she asked if she might tell him a little about life in Pittsburgh, and he was tempted to reply: "I once thought I was going to live there." Instead, he answered discreetly that he'd be interested to know all about it.

She talked for a while about a city that had worked very hard, and now had more money than it knew what to do with; especially the women who had both time and money on their hands. She talked about a social set whose members were selected on the basis of their having about the same financial means. Adella Murchison's dark eyes sparkled with mischief as she described "young matrons" who played golf and bridge, and gossiped about one another, and discussed their children and their servants and their ailments.

"It doesn't sound so different from home," said Lanny, and wondered what was coming out of this.

"I can't afford to be upstage with my husband's friends," continued the woman. "They had him when I was just an employee. So I said to him: 'We're getting into a rut, Harry. Let's break away for a while and see something of the world; let's get some fun out of our money.' So I got him over here, and I want to accomplish something before we go back—already I know he's getting restless."

"What is it you want?" asked the young man, trying to be businesslike.

"I want some culture! I listened to you and Mr. Kertezsi talking, and it was like moving into a different world. Of course I know he was talking partly for my benefit—I've been in business offices and I know a line of sales talk when I hear it—but at the same time he does love beautiful things."

"No doubt about that."

"Do you remember his telling about the big sausage man from Kansas City who bought a Greco and took it home with him, and right away he became famous, and all the people who had never come near him now wanted to see his Greco? It isn't that bad with us, but I thought, if we had something really first class of our own, interesting people might ask to see it, and they would talk about it, and that would be better than playing bridge, or dancing to jazz music over the radio—you know how 'smart' people pass their time."

"I live on the Riviera," said Lanny.

"I suppose that's where the bored people in Europe go. Anyhow, I've decided to take Mr. Kertezsi's suggestion and get a Greco. I'll tell you frankly, I didn't know what it was—if it hadn't been that an art expert was talking I'd have thought it was a kind of lizard."

"A gecko, I believe it is," ventured the other, and they laughed.

"I've acquired a book on art," continued the "young matron." "I looked in the index, and now I know enough about El Greco for conversation. In the book there's a painting of an old man, supposed to be El Greco himself."

"I'm afraid you can't get that. I saw it in the Metropolitan in New York."

"There are others, I suppose?"

"One might be found. But it would cost a lot."

"About what do you think?"

"One or two million francs, for a really fine one."

"I never can get this currency business straight."

"Fifty or a hundred thousand dollars—maybe less, with the franc dropping as it is."

"I think I could get Harry to spend that. He's been impressed by the idea that paintings are an investment."

"No doubt about that," Lanny assured her. "Tell him about Yussupoff, the young cousin of the Tsar, the one who killed Rasputin. He barely escaped from the Bolsheviks with his life, but he managed to bring out his two Rembrandts, rolled up. He can live in luxury for the rest of his life on the sum that Joseph Widener paid him for them. If you should have a revolution in Pittsburgh, now—!" They laughed, as the rich always do at revolutions—beforehand.

VII

Adella Murchison talked some more about her culture aspirations, and then came to a part of the matter that she said was a bit delicate. "What does Mr. Kertezsi charge to buy a painting, or to advise in the buying?"

"Ten percent."

"That's a lot of money for what may be very little work."

"What you pay for is his expert knowledge, which it took a long time to acquire. You have to be sure what you are buying."

"What is on my mind is that he might be persuaded to divide the commission with you; because we should want your advice also."

"Oh, but I'm not an expert, Mrs. Murchison!"

"I have listened to you two talking; and I said to myself: 'There's a young man who really loves art as I should like to love it.' I want the painting I get to be one that you think is worth while. I want to hear you tell me why. I want you to show me the fine points—in short, give me a sales talk about that picture, so I can take it back to a smoky city where I have to change my window curtains twice every week and my husband has to keep a supply of clean shirts at the office."

"You are paying me a compliment, Mrs. Murchison, and of course

I'll be glad to help you and Harry, and tell you everything I can. But you don't need to pay me for it."

"I knew you'd say that. But in Pittsburgh we think a young fellow ought to earn some money; indeed, we don't think well of him if he doesn't. I'm sure Harry feels that way. How is it with your father?"

She was smiling, and Lanny smiled at her. He understood that she was being extremely kind.

"Both Harry and I would feel badly if we had to pay Mr. Kertezsi five or ten thousand dollars while we knew that a friend of ours was doing half the work for nothing. I'd rather take a chance on your expertness, and employ you to find us a painting. There must be ways to find out if a Greco is really a Greco, without paying quite such a big fee."

"As a matter of fact," said Lanny, "I know where there's an undoubtedly genuine one on the Riviera; it belongs to the Duquesa de San Angelo, who is a relation of King Alfonso, and it's been in her family since it was painted."

"Well, that makes it easy; I mean, if you know that she really is what she claims to be."

"There's no question about that; the family is well known."

"Do you suppose she would sell it?"

"It wouldn't do any harm to ask."

"Have you seen it?"

"No, but I could see it, because our friend, Mrs. Emily Chattersworth, knows her."

"Well, there you are. What do we need of an expert?"

"For one thing, you'll pretty certainly get it cheaper if you call Kertezsi in. He knows how to buy, and I don't."

"Maybe so; but certainly he ought to divide the fee with you."

"I'll talk it over with him if you insist."

"The main thing with Harry will be that the picture is genuine beyond question. As for me, I hope it will look like something I can recognize."

"It will be a portrait, probably of one of the duquesa's ancestors."

"And I'll be able to know it's a human being? Some of the new art I've seen, it's hard to tell!"

Lanny laughed. "El Greco was a representational painter, though he was one of the strangest. Tell me, are you absolutely set on one of his?"

"I may change, after I've read some more in that book. But El Greco sounds romantic. If anybody said: 'The Greek,' I'd think it was a bootlegger, or maybe a fish-and-oyster stand across the way from our glass plant. But El Greco is a name one can imagine things about, and if I have an old master at the head of my staircase, I'll find out all about the man it portrays, and I'll read about his time, and the first thing you know, I'll be an authority, and professors at the university will be asking to bring their classes to look at it and hear me tell about it."

"If that's what you want," chuckled the other, "you can be sure a Greco would fetch them in swarms!"

VIII

Lanny Budd and Zoltan Kertezsi had become very friendly; they had played a lot of music together, and Lanny had listened for hours to Kertezsi's stories of "old masters," where they were, and how he had caused them to be in that place. Whatever Lanny knew about the art business he had got from his new friend, so he took the problem of Mrs. Murchison to him. Kertezsi listened, and said that the lady was right about the splitting of the commission; this was a common practice of dealers when somebody brought them a customer, or helped them to find or obtain a work which met some customer's demands.

"But in this case," added the Hungarian, "you have found both the customer and the work, so why do you need me at all?"

"But I'm not competent to handle it, Zoltan."

"Listen," said the other. "Don't you ever expect to earn any money in your life?"

"I want to very much, but I'm not an art expert."

"Why not consider becoming one? It's along the line of your interest, and there's plenty of easy money in it."

"But I don't know enough!"

"Why not learn? Adopt the modern educational method and learn by doing. I'll be delighted to help you."

"Well, that's awfully kind, but I couldn't let you do it without your having a share."

"Listen, my dear boy; I have made all the money I need if I live to be a hundred. I have made it by hard work, and close attention to the whims of the wealthy. Some time ago I said to myself that I could now afford to do what I please—which is in my opinion the greatest luxury a man can enjoy on this earth. I said to myself: 'From now on the art lover is first and the art dealer is second. From now on I will say only what I think.' To one of the richest men in America I recently said: 'Your taste in art is very bad, and if you are determined to buy a thing like that, you will have to get someone else to do it for you. I am interested in helping your collection only provided that you permit me to point out to you the difference between great art and rubbish.' It was a revolutionary uprising, akin to that of the Bolsheviks."

"Has it succeeded?"

"So far, yes; but of course one cannot tell when counter-revolution may arrive."

Lanny was amused, and thought it might be fun to deal in art on that basis. But Zoltan told him that he couldn't expect to take such an attitude until his reputation was established. Moreover, he would find that some of the rich had real taste, and were making extraordinary collections which they intended to bequeath to posterity. Each person was an individual problem, and you had to study your patron, as well as those from whom you expected to buy. Whatever you did would be hard work if you wished to do it well. Zoltan narrated anecdotes, illustrating the patient siege which must be laid to collectors and would-be collectors, first to meet them and then to meet their desires.

What the dealer wanted out of this proposed transaction, he said, was a friend; he liked to meet the sort of people who appreciated what you did for them, and would make a return because they were built that way. He wouldn't bother about the money, because that was so easy when you knew the right people. The important thing was to have access to them, and this was equally true whether you wished to sell a picture to the wife of a Pittsburgh millionaire or to find out whether a Spanish duchess living in exile was in need of funds and might be persuaded to part with one of her family treasures.

"Perhaps," said Zoltan, "you never stopped to figure out the effect of the war upon this business. Europe has had to turn over most of its gold to America, and still owes it God only knows how many billions. One way that debt is being paid is with old masters. American millionaires are coming over here in droves to buy art, and there are literally thousands of rascals and parasites working day and night to persuade them to accept trash. Don't you see that here is a useful career for a man who has instinctive taste, and also the tact, or social prestige, or whatever you wish to call it, so that he knows how to convince others that he is honest?"

So Lanny paid another secret visit to the lady from Pittsburgh and told her that he would make an attempt to find her a Greco, or something as good. Zoltan Kertezsi was going to advise and guide him, and the two would spend a lot of time, each trying to persuade the other to receive the commission. Mrs. Murchison referred to this as an "Alphonse and Gaston act," and then, discovering that Lanny had never read the American "funnies," she explained that there were two Frenchmen who were always getting into trouble because in emergencies they stopped to bow to each other and say: "After you, my dear Alphonse. . . . No, after you, my dear Gaston." Lanny promised that they would do their bowing alone, and not bother Mrs. Murchison with it.

IX

Rick's play had its opening performance; and Lanny, on the strength of all the money he was going to make in his new profession, invited his friends to a dinner party *de luxe* before the show. It was a painful play, not made for the entertainment of the idle rich; it had to do with the psychology of a British flight officer at an air base who had to send mere boys out to their death, knowing that they had received only scant training. He was an unhappy officer, and all of them drank a great deal, and war appeared a hideous and filthy business, which everybody in England was solemnly resolved never to touch again. This play of Rick's was the sort which stood no chance with the general public, but would have a critical success and be a very good start for so young a writer.

Lanny drove Rick back to The Reaches, as the Pomeroy-Nielson home was called, and saw that green and pleasant land once more, and met that friendly and agreeable family. Four years had passed since he had been there, but it was as if he were returning after four days in town. They made no fuss over you, but put the house at your disposal, and well-trained servants ministered to your wants. You punted and played tennis, and played music for those who cared to listen; then in the twilight you sat outside, or if the spring evening was chilly you sat before a fireplace, and heard talk about the problems of the world by persons who had a share in governing it.

A very disturbed and unhappy world just then, and if you had wisdom or knowledge to contribute it was welcomed. The French had moved into the Ruhr and a new war had begun, a strange and puzzling kind, never before tried; blockade and slow strangulation applied to one of the greatest industrial districts in the world. The Germans, helpless as regards military force, were trying a policy of non-co-operation. The workers simply laid down their tools and did nothing; and what could the enemy do? They couldn't bring in French labor and work the coal mines, because the machinery was complicated, and, moreover, the mines were among the most dangerous, the control of firedamp being a special technique which the Germans had been learning for centuries.

So everything just remained in a state of paralysis; the Germans shipped in food, barely enough to keep their workers alive, and printed mountains of paper money to pay for it. Robbie Budd had learned from his partner in Berlin that the government was permitting Stinnes and the other Ruhr magnates to print money to pay their own workers, an absolutely unprecedented action. Of course it could have only one effect: the mark was now tumbling in an avalanche; the firm of "R and R," which had foreseen this, was making money faster than if they owned the printing-presses themselves.

British statesmanship, the most conservative in the world, looked upon all this with horror. Downing Street had explicitly disapproved the French invasion, and the alliance seemed about at its last gasp. France was isolated on the Continent—unless you chose to count Poland, which Sir Alfred Pomeroy-Nielson and his friends mostly didn't. They thought that Poincaré was leading the country straight to ruin. France simply didn't have the numbers or the resources to dominate Europe; the old trouble against which Clemenceau had railed—the fact that there were twenty million too many Germans —was still unremedied, and the seizure of the Ruhr wasn't going to alter that. Not even the most rabid French patriot would propose to starve all those workers to death, and putting Krupp and his directors into jail, as the French had done, wasn't going to kill even one German.

X

A strange thing for Lanny to leave this realm, this England, where everything was so serene and rational, and arrive a few hours later in Seine-et-Oise and spend an evening listening to one of Poincaré's supporters, one of the pillars of the Nationalist party. Denis de Bruyne was quite exultant, because he believed that Germany was going to be brought to her knees at last; the peace which had been lost by the Allies was to be won by *la patrie* alone. The hereditary foe was to be disarmed, the indemnities to be paid, the treaty of Versailles to be enforced. Lanny found that this treaty was taken as a sort of holy writ by a French businessman; a text like the law of the Medes and Persians, which altereth not.

Knowing how futile it would be to argue, Lanny held his peace to the best of his ability. But Denis knew that his young visitor had recently been in Germany, and couldn't resist questioning him. Wasn't it true that the Germans had hidden great quantities of arms, and that they were insulting and sometimes even abusing the Allied commissioners who were supposed to find and destroy them? Yes, Lanny had to admit that this was true; he had heard about thousands of rifles walled up in vaults in the monasteries of Catholic Munich; but he was forced to add that he didn't see how the French could ever get these except by invading the country, and did forty million people have the military force to garrison and hold down sixty million? If they tried it, could they stand the expense, or would they bankrupt themselves? Was it possible to run modern industry by force, in the Ruhr or anywhere else?

These were questions to trouble any capitalist; and it is only human to be annoyed by a person who forces such unwelcome facts upon your attention. Lanny was glad that he was spending only one night in the Château de Bruyne; and perhaps his host had the same gladness. How did he feel about having this arrogant and self-confident young man carry away with him the chief treasure of the château? Denis was paying for his sins; but rarely does it happen that we love the rod which scourges us, however much we may have deserved it.

XI

Lanny, motoring his sweetheart to Juan, carried with him the uncomfortable certainty that she too was a Nationalist; she believed all those things which her husband had told her about France and the outside world. She considered Kurt Meissner one of the few good members of a cruel race which was bent upon the subjection of *la patrie;* she considered Eric Vivian Pomeroy-Nielson one of the few cultured members of a nation of shopkeepers which was willing to set the Prussian monster on its feet again as a counterforce to keep France from becoming prosperous and powerful. She believed these things because they had been taught to her from childhood, and because they were in all the newspapers she saw.

There was no use trying to change her mind about any such matters; Lanny had tried it and discovered that he caused her distress. She considered that her lover was credulous, because of his generous temperament, his impulse to believe that other people were as good as himself. She considered that he was being misled by German and British propaganda, and by his faith in his friends. Worse yet, his sympathy for the poor and afflicted led him into the trap of the

Reds, and that was something which filled Marie with terror. She tried not to voice it, but kept it locked in her heart; she would watch her lover, and note the little signs of what he was feeling and thinking, and often the image of him which she constructed in her mind was more alarming than the reality. Nothing could ever change that, for she was a cautious Frenchwoman of middle age, and he was an imaginative youth, descended from ancestors who had crossed a stormy ocean in order to have their own way in a land where no white man had ever lived before.

Lanny told her about his adventures in London; and here again his enthusiasm encountered her fears. What sort of woman was that who invited a handsome young man to meet her secretly, and pretended to wish to buy a picture at an unthinkable price? In vain Lanny assured his *amie* that Adella Murchison was a straightforward American type; Marie had never met such a type, and was not to be fooled. The woman was a subtle schemer, and the longer she delayed to reveal her true purpose, the more dangerous she was. Though Marie had declared her willingness to give up her lover when he was ready for marriage, here was a married woman, a mother of children as Marie was, and toward such a one she had no impulse of self-sacrifice, but on the contrary the feeling of a tigress on guard.

However, the desire for money is a powerful force in the French; and Lanny was firmly convinced that these Americans might actually send him a million francs to buy a picture, and pay him a hundred thousand additional for the service. Of course it is well known that rich Americans are fantastic, and the bare chance of such a thing was not to be thrown away. Marie didn't want the money for herself, but she wanted Lanny to want it—it would be a way to tone him down and make him into a careful conservative citizen. So she informed him that she had met the Duquesa de San Angelo, and thought she could arrange for Lanny to see the painting. In her secret soul Marie resolved to keep a day-and-night watch over that strange female from the valley of steel and smoke—and, oh, how the Frenchwoman was prepared to hate her if she ventured to move so much as an eyelash in the direction of Lanny Budd!

17

Merchants of Beauty

I

THE war of the Ruhr continued; a war of starvation, of slow decay; a war carried on within the countless cells of millions of human bodies. How long could they endure the steady weakening, the fading away of their powers? There comes a time when an underfed man can no longer labor, a time when he can no longer walk, no longer stand up, no longer move his arms, his tongue. The women bear their children dead, and those already born acquire distended stomachs and crooked bones; they cease to run and play, but sit listlessly staring ahead, or crawl away into some dark corner where their wailing will not be punished. Nature, more merciful than statesmen, usually steps in at one of these stages, and sends the victim some germs of pneumonia or of flu, and puts an end to his misery.

It was a war also of ideas, of propaganda; cries of anguish mixed with those of hate. To the fastidious Lanny Budd it seemed like a fight between two fishwives in the marketplace, screaming, cursing, tearing each other's hair. It was something hardly to be dignified by the name of politics; just a squabble over great sums of money and the means of making more. Lanny, by right of birth, was privileged to know about it, and his father explained that on the one side were Stinnes and Thyssen and Krupp, the great Ruhr magnates, and on the other side the de Wendels and other French steel men, who had got the iron ore of Lorraine and now wanted the coal and coke of the Ruhr so as to work it cheaply.

Robbie Budd was in Lausanne again; or back and forth between there and London and New York. The great conference was still going on—and that was another squabble over property, the oil and other natural resources hidden in the Turkish land. Robbie, with the help of Zaharoff and his new associates, was "horning in" on Mosul and getting a big concession; he was elated about it, also not a little harassed, and to his son rather pathetic. Why he wanted so much more money was something he couldn't answer, and it was better not to embarrass him by repeating the question.

The Turks were getting back Constantinople and much of what they had lost in the World War. The French were on top, and the British humiliated—but they were holding onto the oil and to Palestine, through which the pipeline was bringing the precious fluid to the sea. The Russians were attending the conference, for they had rights to defend in the Black Sea, and were still hoping for loans. One of their delegates was Vorovsky, with whom Lanny and his father had talked at Genoa, and whom Lanny remembered vividly: a thin, ascetic intellectual with wistful gray eyes, a soft brown beard, and the delicate, sensitive hands of a lover of art like Lanny himself. Now an assassin shot him dead in a café; and in due course a jury of moral businessmen would acquit the killer, thus informing the other Whites in Switzerland that it was open season for Bolshevik diplomats.

II

It was in the midst of such world events that Lanny Budd, having learned that there was money in art-works, set about the task of learning how to get it out. Marie phoned to the duquesa, who graciously agreed to permit a young American connoisseur to inspect her family treasures. She proved to be a little, wizened, dark old lady whose dental plates didn't seem to fit her very well; in appearance she was as far from aristocratic as you could have imagined, but Lanny had learned that that was frequently so, and he did not fail in any of the courtesies which a highborn lady would expect. The duquesa was dressed in black for a husband who had been killed in the Moroccan wars two decades or more ago.

She showed him the paintings herself, and told him their histories;

he listened attentively to everything she said, and remembered it, and praised the paintings—for it was no part of his technique to conceal his love of great art. The Greco proved to be a portrait of a clerical member of the duquesa's family: a strange figure of a man, distorted like so many of this painter's representations; abnormally tall and lean, and having fingers longer and thinner than nature has ever seen fit to lend to man. A dark picture, rather sinister, and Lanny couldn't imagine that Adella Murchison would want it in her house.

But there was a Goya; and, oh, what a Goya for a valley of steel and smoke! A figure of a soldier, splendid, yet decadent, and with a touch of the painter's satire; a costume with all the colors that a man of arms must have put on when he went to report a victory to King Charles IV. It was a grand piece of composition, with everything arranged to lead your eye to the tall figure with the face of a warrior and the eyes of a bird of prey. Yes, if a plateglass man's wife wanted something to stir her imagination, and that of the professors of her university, here it was!

Also there was a Velásquez, a double portrait. Lanny had read that many pictures attributed to Velásquez had really been painted by his son-in-law; but superficially they could hardly be distinguished from the real ones, and fetched very high prices on the chance that the master might have put his brush upon them. Being now in the process of learning, Lanny asked the duquesa about this, and saw right away that he had hurt her feelings. He was sorry—but he knew all the same that he had brought down the price, if price there was to be.

Only when he was ready to leave did he venture to ask timidly whether his hostess had ever considered the possibility of parting with any of these treasures. She answered proudly that she never had; and this was in accordance with what Zoltan Kertezsi had foretold. Obeying instructions, Lanny said tactfully that if it ever should happen that she was disposed to consider a sale, he hoped that she would not fail to let him know, as he had friends who might be interested. The little old lady hesitated, looked troubled for a minute or so, and then said that she might be willing to consider parting with one or two of them; but the price would have to be very, very high. So Lanny knew that the trading had begun.

Zoltan had said: "Never under any circumstances make an offer, but invite the owner to set a price." He did so, and the lady told him that the price of the Greco would be at least a million and a half francs, and that of the Velásquez at least two million—for the duquesa took no stock whatever in the del Mazo theory, she declared. No, no, it was a genuine Velásquez, one of the best, and was reproduced in various books of art. Then Lanny asked about the Goya, and was told that the old lady couldn't part with that for one franc less than a million. That too was famous. Lanny noted down the names of the books in which reproductions of these paintings were to be found; he was sure that these would be in the British Museum, so he wouldn't have to get photographs. He thanked his hostess over and over again and took his departure.

III

Lanny posted a letter to his client, telling her the details of his interview, the prices asked for the pictures, and where the reproductions could be seen. His advice was that she choose the Goya and authorize him to pay a million francs for it, but of course he would try to get it for less. According to the advice of Zoltan, the actual cash should be sent to Lanny's bank in Cannes, for a bank draft or express order would be of feeble effect compared with the physical presence of a large bundle of crisp new banknotes. Lanny sent this letter by the new airmail system, and waited in no little trepidation.

Marvelous people, these Pittsburghers! Two days later came a telegram: "Will take your advice forwarding money thanks good luck. Adella Murchison." Just as simple as that; she tossed him a million francs as if it had been the price of two theater tickets! Lanny had never seen so much cash in his life, but Zoltan had assured him that any bank could obtain it if you gave notice. Lanny called his old friend Jerry Pendleton and arranged to take him as a bodyguard, Beauty having insisted upon that precaution. She made Lanny load up one of the Budd automatics and made Jerry promise to keep it right on the seat of the car.

When the money was at the bank Lanny phoned the duquesa, asking permission to see her about a matter of business. He drove Jerry to the bank, where they were escorted into a private room, and no less than three officials came in to witness the sensational transaction. The highest denomination of note which the French government printed was a thousand francs, and the money was banded up in packages of fifty each; if Lanny had been a really careful business person he would have counted every one of the notes, but he was satisfied to count the packages and the contents of one. He signed the receipt in triplicate, and put the precious bundles into a satchel, and he and Jerry went out to their car, feeling decidedly self-conscious, and looking about for anyone bearing a resemblance to the gangsters of the American movies.

They drove to the heights above San Raphael, where the duquesa's château was situated. Lanny left five of those valuable packages in Jerry's care, and carried the remaining fifteen in the satchel into the presence of the little old lady. Seated in her drawing-room, he made a carefully studied speech: "Duquesa, I have interested a friend in the purchase of your Goya, and am authorized to offer you the sum of seven hundred and fifty thousand francs in cash for it. That is the very best that I can do. It is a large sum of money, and I believe that if you think it over you will realize that it would be wise to accept it." To assist the thinking process, Lanny opened the satchel, and proceeded to count the packages of virginal banknotes onto the table in front of his hostess. The last of the fifteen he placed in her hands, so that she might feel the weight of it, and make certain that it was actually composed of notes having the guarantee of the Banque de France.

It was not a pretty spectacle that Lanny watched during the next half-hour. The old woman's mouth had come open simultaneously with the satchel; her black eyes shone with an unholy light, and her fingers trembled as she clutched this extraordinary dynamic package. It appeared as if she tried to put it down, but couldn't manage to do so. She started to bargain for more; the painting was one of the most beautiful in the world—actually, she attempted to talk about beauty! It was a family heritage—she even tried to talk about whether she had a moral right to part with it! But all the time her eyes kept wandering to the other packages, and her hand could hardly be kept from stretching out to them.

Lanny felt sure from various signs that she was not going to let that money go out of the house. So he took a firm tone; he had tried his best to get more from his friend, but that was absolutely the maximum obtainable. He was intending to get up and prepare to take his departure, if necessary, but he didn't have to. "*Bien!*" exclaimed the Spanish lady, suddenly; and Lanny produced the receipts for her to sign—two copies, for he meant to have one as a souvenir of an adventure which might never happen to him again! He had left a blank space for the amount, and he now filled it in, and placed the documents and his fountain pen in front of the duquesa.

But it couldn't be settled so quickly as that. The elderly aristocrat wasn't going to be content with counting packages; she was going to count seven hundred and fifty notes, and make sure that each had one thousand francs printed on it. With her skinny old fingers shaking she broke the bands around one package, and with her quavering old voice she counted aloud from one to fifty, occasionally stopping to wet her fingers on her tongue. One package counted, she set it aside, and went to work on the next; Lanny sat and waited patiently while this performance was repeated fifteen times. Fortunately the bank had made no mistakes, and at last the job was completed. There being no other excuse for delay, the duquesa looked at the pile of packages, she looked at the two receipts, and from them to Lanny. Was she at the last moment trying to get up the nerve for a fight?

She was trembling, and Lanny was trembling—it is always hard upon the nerves, dealing in large sums of money. But at last she took up the fountain pen, and with slow uncertain fingers wrote her name on one piece of paper, then on the other, and permitted Lanny to pick them up and put them into his pocket, together with his pen. He thanked her and shook hands with her, and her final act was to summon a man-servant to carry the heavy picture down to the car. She might have claimed the frame, and Lanny was prepared to have her do so; but she had probably never seen the picture out of the frame, and may have thought they were one. It was so big that it would barely go into the car.

They drove to the bank, where Lanny put the rest of the money on deposit. They drove to a carpenter shop and had the precious object securely crated, and then saw a truck carry it to the express office, where it was shipped to Mrs. Murchison in London, insured for its full purchase price. Lanny sent the new owner a telegram, telling her what he had done, and sent her by registered mail her receipt and a bank draft for the rest of the money, less his commission and the various expenditures. Only as time passed did he realize the impression he had made upon the plateglass couple by the return of approximately a hundred and seventy-three thousand francs. The story would be told in Pittsburgh, and the fame of it would radiate in many directions; years later someone would introduce himself as a friend of the Murchisons, and say: "I understand that you buy paintings and return part of the money if you don't have to spend it all."

IV

So Lanny had made some real money, easy money; it grew on trees for him. He found that he had grown a foot in the estimation of his family and friends. He did the "Alphonse and Gaston act" with Zoltan, and the result was that the expert consented to take one-third the commission; also Lanny gave one of the smooth virginal notes to his bodyguard, surely the largest sum that that redhead from Kansas had ever earned in so short a time. This left the budding art dealer a net of forty-nine thousand francs, or, at the prevailing rate of exchange, somewhat less than twenty-five hundred dollars; but it wasn't going to be exchanged, it was going to be spent in France, and forty-nine has a much more exciting sound than two and a half.

Lanny looked back upon a time, only four years distant, when he had been so pleased at receiving two hundred dollars a month from the disbursing officer of the State Department of the United States government. By five months of assiduous day-and-night labor he had then earned one thousand dollars. But now he had worked only a few hours, not more than one good day altogether, and see what he had! From that time on it would be difficult for Lanny to contemplate the system known as "individualism" without a certain amount of indulgence; also he would be disposed to look upon all kinds of public officials, from postmen up to premiers, as ill-rewarded drudges, the most pathetic of wage-slaves.

And what he had got was only the beginning, he found. The Murchisons received their valuable shipment and had it uncrated in their hotel room and hung up on the wall, opposite a sofa where they could sit and study it. So they discovered for the first time what art was, and is, for it remains what it is, *semper eadem. Ars longa, vita brevis!* Adella saw that gorgeous if evil old warrior occupying the position of honor in her drawing-room, and she got books about the time and its court painter, and began to prepare and rehearse her "spiel." Before long it occurred to her that there was space at the top of the broad staircase of her home where something splendid seemed to be called for. She got a photograph of the dubious Velásquez, and learned from the books that this painter's works were almost unobtainable; she decided that nobody in Pittsburgh would ever have heard of del Mazo, surely none of her friends, at least. She went to work and persuaded her husband, and then sent a wire to Juan-les-Pins, asking what the double portrait could be had for.

Lanny answered that he thought Zoltan should come and look at the work, and give his expert opinion whether it was a Velásquez; if it wasn't, that would help to shatter the old duquesa's nerve. His guess was that a million francs would do the trick, but it might be well to send a million and a half. How easily Lanny now tossed off such figures!

The program was carried out according to schedule. The expert came, and gave his shattering opinion, and the elderly aristocrat flew into a rage and considered herself personally insulted. Zoltan said that was something he had learned to expect; these people were used to having their own way, and truth and reality were not vital concepts to them. But a million francs was; so let the old creature have a while to think about them. Lanny brought his friend to Bienvenu, where the ladies all treated him as if he were an archangel sent down from the skies to set a golden crown on Lanny's head. Zoltan had his fiddle, and for two days Lanny and Kurt played sonatas with him, and they had a grand holiday, no less enjoyable because of the thought of the duquesa in her château—which they had converted into a hot griddle for her to be toasted on!

V

The money arrived at the bank, and on the third morning Lanny and Jerry went and got it. Zoltan insisted that his pupil must handle the matter, while the teacher amused himself with a more humble role. Since the picture was too big to be got into Lanny's car, Zoltan would hire a small truck and park at an inn near the château, where Lanny could telephone in case of victory. Lanny left ten of the bundles of banknotes in Jerry's care, and took in twenty and laid them out on the table. He sat and listened to scolding, whining, almost weeping; he thought: How odd that a duchess should not be a "lady"; that *noblesse* should manifest so little desire to *oblige!* It was like pulling all the old woman's teeth all over again to make her take a million francs for that dubious Velásquez. Lanny had to pretend that his dignity was affronted, and put the money back into the satchel and start to take his leave; when he was almost at the front door the châtelaine called to him *"Eh bien! Revenez!"*

It was a game, and he had won. She composed her face, and went at the serious business of counting one thousand banknotes. Everything must wait until she had accepted the money and signed the receipts and Lanny had them in his pocket. Then he telephoned, and the duquesa rang for her servant; she was quite cheerful now—it wasn't so hard to make the best of being a millionaire. The great picture was so heavy that Lanny had to help the servant carry it down the steps; and here came Zoltan, the truck-driver, with a lot of blankets, one of them waterproof, for wrapping the precious treasure. Off they drove in triumph, Lanny following the truck, and Jerry with the automatic on the seat beside him.

This time they came to Bienvenu, for it had been decided that Jerry should drive that precious freight all the way to London, Lanny following with Marie in his car. It was June, and time for their trip to Seine-et-Oise; they would take a little excursion to London, where Marie would meet that ex-secretary who was scattering her husband's money like a drunken sailor—that straightforward American type in whom she still found it impossible to believe. But she had to admit that if Adella Murchison was setting a trap for Lanny, she was certainly baiting it generously!

An odd sort of holiday! The truck broke down and had to be repaired, and meanwhile the treasure was carried into a bedroom of an inn, where either Lanny or Jerry stayed with it every moment. On their overnight stop they saw to it that Jerry got a room with a good stout bolt, and he slept with the gun under his pillow. They took both truck and car across on the ferry and delivered their consignment to its owners—also a bank draft for half a million francs less expenses. Adella met Marie, and behaved like a woman of the world, giving no sign of being shocked to discover that this exemplary young lover of the arts was also the lover of another man's wife. She spent most of the time hearing Lanny's story of the purchases, and asking him questions about the paintings; she made no signs with her eyelashes or anything else, and so Lanny's *amie* had to give up and admit that there really was an "American type."

VI

The two dealers went fifty-fifty on this second transaction, so Lanny had almost a hundred thousand francs. That was news to take to the Château de Bruyne, to lend glamour to *la vie à trois*. Impossible for a businessman not to respect a youth who had performed such a feat! From that time on Lanny Budd would be no playboy but a serious man of affairs. When he entered a home of wealth, he wouldn't be thinking, as formerly: "Am I going to be bored here?" He would be thinking: "I wonder if they buy paintings, or if they have any they'd like to sell." When he saw a beautiful work, he would enjoy its beauty, but his mind would go on to the thought: "I wonder what that would bring," and then: "I wonder who would be interested in it." He would run over in his mind the different persons he knew, and the art collections he had seen or heard of—not those in museums and galleries, but paintings in private homes, where they had been for a long time, so that the owner had had a chance to get tired of them.

A similar transformation took place in the minds of the ladies who played a part in Lanny's life. To them art had been an expensive form of pleasure—conspicuous waste, to use Veblen's phrase; but now it became a source of income, it was game to be hunted. Beauty Budd began thinking of all the persons she knew in or near Paris; all the rich homes to which she might arrange for Lanny to have access, and work up schemes of plunder. It was the thing that Beauty had done for Robbie for some twenty years, and there wasn't a device that she hadn't put to use. Now, of course, it was a double pleasure, for Lanny was young, and her maternal impulses came into play. Sophie, the ex-baroness, a childless woman, shared these feelings; also Emily, the *salonnière*, who had taken Lanny as a sort of foster-son. She even began to think of certain of her own paintings which it might be fun to replace with others having somewhat more lively colors.

But the most eager and most active friend was Marie de Bruyne. Here was the way to make her lover into something substantial and useful! Marie didn't want his money, but she wanted him to have money; her mind, at once unselfish and materialistic, wanted him to take hold of life and make himself a place in it. Above all, here was the way to get him out of the clutches of those dangerous Reds! When he had to earn money, he would learn the value of it; he would become a man among men, competing with them, winning their respect, and bringing all his faculties into play. Marie loved art herself, and wanted Lanny to love it, and wouldn't have turned him into a manager of taxicab companies like Denis or an oil operator like his father. No, she understood his fine gifts and wanted to cultivate them, and it seemed to her a most happy development that he should be able to combine his love of art with the easy acquisition of the money he would need for the gratifying of all his tastes.

After consulting with Denis she invited Zoltan Kertezsi to their home, and for a week they played music and talked art, and it was wonderful for Marie's two boys as well as for her lover. The woman herself listened and learned, for she must know all the phrases, all the cues, so that she could guide a conversation into proper channels and help to start a deal or to put one through. Zoltan knew a thousand stories about painters and paintings, and there was hardly a subject you could mention that he couldn't connect with the buying or selling of art. And one thing leads to another, as we all know.

Yes, Zoltan was a wonderful fellow, and wouldn't have been different if he had really been that archangel sent down from the skies to tear Lanny Budd out of the hands of the dangerous and disreputable Reds, and make him into an art authority. Marie devoted a full week to cultivating this Hungarian gentleman, making him comfortable, praising him, drinking in his stories—always, of course, with Lanny present, Lanny kindling with delight, warming both hands before the fire of life. Also two lads budding into manhood, who had hardly been aware of art before, listened to stories about enormous sums paid for paintings by the richest and most famous persons; they too began to kindle, and wanted Lanny to take them to the Louvre and the Luxembourg and let them see such wonderful creations, and try to understand what it was about Jan van Eyck's little painting of a madonna and child which caused it to be worthy sixty-four thousand francs per square inch!

When Zoltan was gone, Marie began taking Lanny about to the rich homes in the neighborhood, to show him the treasures they contained and give him a chance to mention that he knew many Americans who were on the hunt for such things. Most of Marie's acquaintances would be sellers, not buyers, so when she told what her young magician had been able to do for a Spanish duquesa, she shaded the story in favor of the seller's side; the American millionaires were represented as infatuated persons scattering their money like Millet's *Sower* with his bag of seed. On the other hand, when

Denis brought out a great banker over the week-end, a man who might be a customer, the unnamed duquesa was transformed into a slightly ridiculous person whom Lanny by extraordinary cleverness had managed to hold down to very low prices. *Mutatis mutandis,* is the Latin phrase; and Zoltan said that Latin is a wonderful language, well suited to apothegms and inscriptions, since it says so much in a few words.

VII

This development came at a fortunate moment in the life of Lanny and Marie. Three years had passed since their intimacy had begun, and that is time enough for lovers to discover what is wrong with each other. Their physical happiness was as complete as ever, but intellectually there were large tracts where they would never meet. Marie wasn't a political-minded person, and would have been content to avoid the subject; but Lanny couldn't or wouldn't do so; he kept meeting persons who stirred him up, persons whom his *amie* hated and feared. He knew it, and refrained from mentioning those persons; but somehow it always came out where he had been, and even if he didn't say what he was thinking, Marie guessed it, and it made her unhappy and him impatient.

They might have let each other's ideas alone; but the world and its events wouldn't let either of them alone, it kept forcing itself upon their attention. That dreadful strangling process was going on in the Ruhr, and the cries of it penetrated the ears of every thinking person in Europe. Germany was down and France was at her throat, and either you sympathized with France, or else you were a friend of the Boches, and therefore a suspect. Denis de Bruyne would come home from conferences with members of his party and would tell what he had seen and heard, what Poincaré was doing and what his supporters expected to get out of it, and to Lanny it seemed repulsive, almost crazy; he would know that his beloved one agreed with these ideas, and Marie would know that Lanny hated them. The only way they could avoid quarreling was to wall off portions of their minds completely from each other.

Robbie came to Paris after the close of the Lausanne conference in midsummer, and spent a Sunday at the château. He listened to everything Denis said, and they talked as two businessmen who understand each other's point of view; but Lanny knew that his father wasn't saying all that he thought, and when they were alone Robbie remarked that France was in one hell of a mess, and that men like Denis were blinding themselves to her plight. He said that Poincaré was really a very timid and incompetent bureaucrat, a slave to routine and red tape; he had promised the French people things that he couldn't deliver, and now he was scared to death by what he had started and didn't know how to finish.

"France can starve Germany into bankruptcy," said Robbie, "but France will get nothing out of it, and will only cripple both countries. The plain truth is that France hasn't the economic resources to support the military role that her pride forces her to play. The part of wisdom would be to accept her position as a second-class power and tie her fortunes to those of the British Empire; but she may put off doing this until it's too late, and the British offer of an alliance may not be renewed."

If that was the situation, it was obvious that an ardent Nationalist and his wife were not going to be very happy people in the years to come. Their country would suffer, and they would look around for somebody to blame. They would blame the Germans for failing to pay indemnities. They would blame the British for encouraging the Germans. They would blame the Americans for not ratifying President Wilson's treaty of alliance and for trying to collect debts which France couldn't pay and pretty soon wouldn't want to pay. Altogether it was going to be a mess; and how was Lanny going to be happy in a home where people were bitter against the Americans, how was Marie going to be happy in a home where people out of the kindness of their hearts felt sorry for the French?

At this critical moment came the picture business; something new, something exciting to both lovers, something they could do in harmony. It provided excuses for traveling and seeing new places, for meeting important people; it provided abundance, even luxury, for both of them—and it is a sad fact about most humans that if we have abundance· and luxury for ourselves, it is easier to put off doing something about the troubles of other people. This new activity of Lanny's brought applause from nearly everybody he knew; even his Red uncle smiled indulgently and called it a harmless way for a playboy to pass his time. "It surely makes no difference which of two bloated parasites owns a painting, and if in the process of ex-changing you collect some of their cash—well and good!" Uncle Jesse didn't add that he and his friends would come around and try to get a share, to pay the perpetual deficits of their party press.

Robbie Budd, of course, was tickled to death by the develop-ment. It didn't make any difference to him how his first-born made money; any way would serve to establish sound habits and teach a youngster to take care of himself. Robbie promised to spread the word in Newcastle that Lanny had become one of the leading art experts of the Continent; he would talk up old masters as a form of investment second only to oil. He would be sending over a string of customers and orders—perhaps Lanny's stepmother would be the first! Could Lanny suggest any paintings that would relieve the austerity of Esther's walls?

Also there was Johannes Robin—had Lanny written the boys about his good fortune? Yes, Lanny had done so, and they had replied, begging him to come to Berlin and set up in business. Many of the aristocracy and other depressed classes were selling their art-works; many of the *Schieber* were buying. "Let me know if you have any-thing good," the Jewish trader had scrawled on the bottom of a letter.

"He'll buy anything you offer, just to please you," was Robbie's opinion. But Lanny didn't care to do business on that basis.

VIII

The budding expert decided to take his new profession seriously and make a success of it. He would study the books on art and make elaborate notes. He would drive into Paris and see what the dealers were offering, and familiarize himself with the prices current. He would keep a little notebook in his pocket and jot down the various items. Following the suggestion of his businesslike father, he started a cardfile on the various painters, where their works could be found, and the prices; also a cardfile of the persons he met who might become purchasers or sellers; their names and addresses, interests and tastes—anything about them that might be of use at some particular moment. In course of time these files would acquire a considerable size, and be worth their weight in diamonds to their owner.

Both dealers and painters were glad to meet Lanny Budd and to talk shop with him. He looked like money, and it was obvious that he knew moneyed people; word spread that he was the stepson of Marcel Detaze, a pre-war painter in whose work there appeared to be quite a boom. Critics were mentioning it, and dealers had inquiries and didn't know what to say. They would ask Lanny, and he would say that Detaze was being handled by Zoltan Kertezsi. Lanny and his mother had decided that this was the wise way to deal with their problem. Zoltan really understood Marcel's work, he had started the boom, and his steady pressure to keep it going would be worth more than the commission they would pay him. All would-be customers who wrote or came to Bienvenu were told that Zoltan Kertezsi was the sole authorized agent.

The Hungarian came often to the Château de Bruyne that summer, and the happy sounds of his fiddle were heard in its drawing-room. He adopted Lanny as his pupil, filled him up with information and wise counsel, and threw several opportunities his way. In one of the aristocratic French homes to which Marie took Lanny was a Drouais, a perfect gem of a Drouais, a portrait of a gaily dressed, exquisite little noble lady with a round face, and dimples in her rose-pink cheeks, and the funniest little twinkle in her bright brown eyes—a picture so full of life that you felt you were sitting in the room with her, and might kiss the tips of her little pink fingers. Zoltan had sold several works of the French master, and didn't even have to see this one; Lanny's delight was enough, and Zoltan wrote to a client in Boston who was making a great collection, and in due course came a cablegram saying that six hundred thousand francs were at his disposal at Morgan, Harjes et Cie.

So Lanny and Zoltan went together and bought the picture for five hundred and fifty thousand francs, and divided the commission.

Lanny had another small fortune, and the two pals came home and played the *Kreutzer Sonata* to tell the world how cheerful they felt. Lanny began to figure what he was going to do with all this money. Said he to Zoltan: "I'll come on an old master that's really a bargain, and I'll buy it for myself, with no commission!" Said Zoltan: "Find some new painter, a coming genius, and buy him up and put him in the storeroom along with Marcel, and you can live on him the rest of your days."

"And grow fat like M. Faure!" added Lanny—referring to an importer of wines and olive oil who came to look at a picture, and would sit in a chair and study the work for a long while, and gradually his eyelids would droop and he would have a little nap, and wake up with a start. You mustn't notice what had happened, for he would sometimes buy the picture to make it all right. He was a very kindly old gentleman and a pleasant customer to deal with; he liked drinking scenes and nude ladies, and that made it easy to please him.

Zoltan said he had several customers with peculiarities of one sort or another; one old Jewish lady, a friend of his mother, had raised half a dozen children and now had a dozen or more grandchildren, and would buy paintings of babies—nothing else. Zoltan had sold her a handsome Scotchman by Raeburn, thinking to seduce her imagination; but no, some other dealer had come along with a couple of Romney babies, and had persuaded her to trade a picture worth thousands of pounds for one worth half as many. Lanny had never heard so many funny stories as Zoltan told.

IX

That summer was the climax of the agony of Germany. In the effort to maintain the passive resistance of the Ruhr she printed and spent some three and a half trillions of marks; and it is a strange law of the process of inflation that the effect exceeds the cause many times over. By the end of May of that year one American cent would buy fifteen hundred marks, and by the end of July it would buy ten thousand. Abroad, this process was called "the mark swindle," and it was estimated that Germany had taken more than a billion dollars out of America alone; but the speculators had got a great part of it, and the firm of "R and R" was among the successful.

In September Germany gave up. Impossible to feed her population any longer. The miners and steelworkers of the Ruhr would go back to work under French supervision. It was a time of triumph for Poincaré and his supporters; they proclaimed it as a vindication of their policy and an assurance of peace at last. Lanny wasn't sure, but he was glad of any chance of reconcilement, and accepted politely the assurances of Marie's husband. When he drove her to the Riviera he believed that their happiness was again secure.

But right away in Bienvenu there began to appear one of those little clouds no bigger than a man's hand. Beauty had written to her son that Kurt was in a terrible state of agitation over what was happening in his Fatherland, and that she again was in dread about him. Lanny hoped that the surrender would settle this trouble, but he discovered that Kurt was one of those Germans who weren't going to surrender. Terrible letters had come from Kurt's home; he didn't want to show them to his friend, he didn't want to talk about the subject, but just to lock it up in his heart and brood over it; his music became more and more somber, and in Beauty's heart a worm of fear gnawed unceasingly. Some day her lover would decide that music wasn't enough, and would go back to fight for his country's liberation!

Five years and a half had passed since the forces of nature and the accidents of man had thrown Beauty and Kurt into each other's arms. Assuredly it was one of the oddest of couplings, yet it had worked out unexpectedly well. So long as Kurt wanted nothing but to go off by himself and invent new combinations of musical sounds, Bienvenu and its mistress offered a wellnigh perfect solution of life's problems. Beauty had her home to run, and her baby to bring up, and when her social impulses became overwhelming, she could dress herself and go to parties with no worse penalty than some playful teasing by her lover. It had become the accepted practice that once during each winter Emily Chattersworth would get up a recital and invite the most distinguished persons, who would be duly impressed, and thus the respectability of the *liaison* would be maintained:

Beauty Budd's lover was a great artist, a future celebrity mewing his mighty youth. Visitors who came to the home rarely saw him; he would be busy with his work, and they had to make the best of that. When they did see him he was clean, his hair was trimmed, and his manners were impeccable. Many a rich woman wished she might have such a handsome and serviceable male, who would stay at home and "behave himself"—that is, would have no eyes for any younger woman.

X

But time passes, and all things change, and apparently no happiness is without its enemies. After three years of living in the same house for months at a time, Beauty's lover and Lanny's *amie* had come to the point where they could manage it only by never opening their mouths in each other's presence. They respected each other, and didn't want to quarrel; but they were France and Germany, and one was at the other's throat. At the table it became the rule that no political subject was ever touched on, even remotely; nothing that anybody had read in the paper, nothing that Robbie or Rick had written. Several intimate friends understood this, and helped to keep the rule; then they would go away and speculate as to how long this strange tension could continue. Little by little they began to notice that when Marie was at table Kurt was apt to be absent, and vice versa. Marie was finding more excuses to be with her aunt, and Lanny would go there to visit her.

Then came another serpent creeping into this Eden. The thing that Beauty and Marie and all Lanny's friends were so happy about, the wonderful new easy-money profession that he had discovered— that failed to satisfy the ethical sense of his mother's beloved; it was the commercializing of art, which to the austere German artist was the profanation of a sanctuary. Very certainly Kurt wasn't commercializing *his* art; he couldn't, if he wanted to—for how could any music publisher continue to put a price on musical works and, when he had sold them, discover that the proceeds wouldn't buy food for his employees, to say nothing of buying more paper? The fact that Kurt, who was producing original work, stood no chance of getting any reward for it, while Lanny, who produced nothing, was having fantastic sums of money dumped into his lap—that situation mirrored the economic and moral decay of Europe at the end of the year 1923.

Nor was the trouble remedied by the fact that Lanny, out of the kindness of his heart, kept clamoring to be allowed to put up money for the publishing of his friend's work. That was charity, and Kurt was thinking about justice. To him the situation was a symbol of the oppression of the Fatherland, the crushing of the spiritual impulses of a great people by the three plutocratic empires which called themselves democracies and which had obtained the mastery of the modern world. Lanny and his mother and father represented one of these empires, Rick represented another, and Marie the third, and Kurt didn't want to live by the charity of any of them; he didn't want to talk about it with any of them, and did so only when Lanny questioned him, and tried to console him or to argue with him. Lanny insisted that this was only a temporary condition, and that time would remedy it; but Kurt didn't believe in time, he believed in human effort, and he said: "If the German soul is ever set free, it will be because Germans set it free."

Lanny had to go and explain all this to his mother, and they had to make new rules for keeping the peace in their safe warm nest. They mustn't talk too much about making money out of art; they mustn't exult about "deals," or about the price that a new Detaze had brought. Also, they must not force Zoltan Kertezsi upon Kurt, because Kurt said he didn't care for merchants of beauty. Only after he had said this did Kurt realize that it wouldn't sound very kind to his patron and friend, Lanny Budd.

18

Into This Wild Abyss

I

THE two Robin boys were always trying to devise ways to be of use to their Lanny Budd in his new profession. They didn't see him often, because during the time when he was at Bienvenu they were busy with their studies, and during the holidays he was at the Château de Bruyne, where he couldn't invite them, they being at that susceptible age where they were not supposed to know about sexual irregularities. But now had come this new development—Lanny was a businessman, and so was Papa Robin, and in the course of his activities as money-lender Papa acquired a great deal of information as to the affairs of important persons. He was glad to help such persons, because he was a good-hearted fellow; but he charged them ten percent interest, the prevailing rate in Germany, and of course he made them give adequate security.

As it happened, they sometimes owned valuable paintings, and offered these as security. And how was a businessman to be sure what they were really worth? Papa Robin needed expert advice, he said. Did he really need it, or did he just pretend to need it, in order to do a favor for the handsome and socially prominent son of Robbie Budd, who played accompaniments so delightfully for Papa's darling boys? Lanny would never be sure about that; it was more easy money that would be laid in his lap.

At first he said he was too busy to come to Berlin, which looked like a dignified way of saying that the offer was too small for his attention; Papa had made a cheap bid, and had been properly rebuked. So naturally he was called upon to do better; the two boys wrote again, saying that one of the deposed noblemen of Germany was in serious financial straits; he had a palace near Berlin and another in Munich, and both were filled with art treasures, of which many had to be sold; of course it had to be done in strict privacy, for such people don't let their troubles be advertised. Papa had lent this gentleman a lot of money, so Papa had something to say about the sales, and if Lanny and his friend Mr. Kertezsi would come and give their time to the matter, it would be a great favor to Papa, and there would be really large sums of money for all concerned.

Lanny forwarded this letter to Zoltan, who was then in London, and Zoltan wrote a business letter to Johannes Robin, laying down very stiff terms; he and Lanny would have to be put in exclusive charge of the selling, and would receive a ten-percent commission on all sales they might arrange. The offer was accepted, and an agreement was signed by Johannes Robin, and by Prince Hohenstauffen zu Zinzenburg, who couldn't help himself, for it was a polite and refined sort of foreclosure. Zoltan wired Lanny to meet him in Munich, to help pluck the fine feathers out of the German goose on its way down the staircase of history. He actually wired that, and wasn't arrested for *lèse-majesté!*

It was the beginning of November, a delightful time of the year in Bavaria; why not have a family holiday? If we're going to make so much money, let's get some fun out of it! Beauty hadn't had a trip for a long time, and Marie hadn't been anywhere except back and forth between the Riviera and Seine-et-Oise. If two pairs of lovers went, they couldn't get into each other's way; Kurt could attend the concerts and opera, and interview music publishers, while Beauty and Marie could have tea with the deposed Princess Hohenstauffen zu Zinzenburg. They would go on to Berlin and see the sights—doubtless it wasn't altogether pleasant in Germany just now, but it was surely educational, something that you could tell your children and your grandchildren about; it might never happen again that a great nation would have its currency entirely devalued, and you could exchange one French franc for the price of a diamond ring. Lanny said this for the benefit of Marie—and when Kurt wasn't in the room.

All during that year Kurt had been receiving literature of the

National Socialist German Workingmen's Party, sent by Heinrich Jung, son of the Oberförster of Schloss Stubendorf. This young enthusiast had the dream of making a convert out of one who was looked upon in his home community as a future musical genius. And right at this juncture Heinrich wrote a letter full of portentous hints: "Great events are due in a few days. I am not allowed to tell about it, but history will be made. You will learn from your newspapers that our labors have not been in vain."

Of course both Lanny and Kurt could guess what that meant— the Nazis were going to attempt their long-planned uprising. Could they succeed, as Mussolini had done, or would they fail, like Kapp? Kurt decided that he would like to be on hand; and Beauty decided at once that she would go along to keep him out of mischief. Marie came to the same decision. Was it just to watch Lanny, or was she making a genuine effort to be interested in his ideas? Could she endure the sight of Germans? Could she feel sorry for them in their dreadful plight? The human heart is a complex of motives, and Marie de Bruyne, torn between passionate love and passionate hatred, could perhaps not have sorted out the different forces which took her to the land of her hereditary foe.

II

Lanny sent an airmail letter to Rick, telling him of the program and inviting him to help spend some of the money that grew so abundantly on trees. Lanny quoted the words of Heinrich, and interpreted them; surely if a *coup d'état* was going to be attempted, it ought to be good for an article. The one which Rick had written, "Upper Silesia after the Settlement," had made a good impression, especially at Stubendorf, where it had been translated and published locally. Lanny wrote: "Come and help us to hold Kurt down. Those Nazis will be swarming about him, and Beauty will want to scalp every last one of them."

The family purchased tickets and made test of that slogan which was spreading the fame of Fascism throughout Europe and America: "In Italy the trains now run on time!" But this was equally true in the people's republic of Germany, at least so far as concerned the fast international expresses; these were for the rich, who must be served and made comfortable, for they brought foreign exchange, the most precious thing in the Fatherland. At this moment it was increasing in value at a rate which suggested Jack's beanstalk in the fairy-tale. If you owned so much as one round red copper cent with the head of an American Indian on it, you could lie down to sleep with the knowledge that you were a millionaire, and that you would wake up a multi-millionaire. The figures were fantastic, seeming to belong in the realm of nightmare. On the day that Lanny and his friend arrived in Munich one dollar would buy 625,000,000 marks, and the next day it would buy a billion and a half. On no day did it go backward, and when they left, a dollar was worth seven trillion marks.

Impossible not to pity the distracted people who had to live in the midst of such a cyclone. Employers paid their workers for a half-day at noon, so that they could rush out and buy some food before it was out of their reach. People bought whatever they could find in the shops, regardless of whether they had any use for it; so long as it had value it could be sold later on. In the midst of such confusion a foreigner moved like an enchanted being; his status was that upon which the fancy of all races and times has been exercised —he had the lamp of Aladdin, the purse of Fortunatus, the touch of Midas, the Tarnhelm which rendered him invisible so that he could walk into any shop and take whatever he wanted. Omnipotence places a heavy strain upon human character, and not all visitors to the Fatherland made wise use of their magic. To put it briefly, many proved themselves to be the vultures which the Germans called them behind their backs.

III

Zoltan Kertezsi arrived the same day as Lanny, and the two men of business proceeded at once to the palace of their aristocratic client. There wasn't going to be any social intercourse, they discovered; Seine Durchlaucht's steward received them, and escorted them to a large *salon* where all the paintings had been hung, and left them to make such examination as they wished. They would have the freedom of the *salon* at reasonable hours, and might bring clients to inspect the offerings. But this, as it happened, was no part of their program, for Robin had made the loan in pounds sterling, and it had to be repaid in the same currency, which meant that sales must of necessity be made to foreigners.

An odd and miscellaneous collection, with a great deal of commonplace German stuff which Zoltan said would have to be auctioned off in Germany later on. But it might be that the amount of the loan could be realized from the "good stuff" alone. There were some Holbein drawings, and one small portrait; there were two Hobbemas, and a very luxurious Rubens, besides large and less valuable canvases by his pupils. Modern France was represented by two bright lilyponds at Giverny by Monet, in that pointilliste style which he had developed, and which had caused Sargent to remark that the old man had become color blind—he could see nothing but color. Modern Germany was represented by a superlative Menzel, a romantic Feuerbach, a head of a peasant by Munkacsy, and a group of mythological subjects by Arnold Böcklin, whose patron Seine Durchlaucht's father had been, so the steward told them.

They made a list of the paintings which Zoltan thought could be sold without delay, and then he put his young assistant through what amounted an examination. Let each take a copy of the list, and set down what he considered a proper price for each item. This proposal made cold chills run up and down Lanny's spine, but he admitted that it would be educational, and when they compared lists, Zoltan was kind enough to say that Lanny hadn't done so badly. They discussed each painting, and gave their reasons, and Lanny thought the Böcklins ought to be higher because the painter was well known to Americans; they appreciated what Lanny called "philosophic content." But Zoltan said that that was something rarely recognized in sales; the pictures were *démodés*.

The proposed prices had to be approved by both creditor and debtor, so a schedule was prepared, and two copies placed in the hands of the steward. Seine Durchlaucht couldn't have done much more than glance over it, for a copy with his signed approval was returned within an hour, and Robin's O.K. came by telegraph next day. Zoltan sent off several cablegrams to clients in America; all he had to do was to describe one item in a few words, with the name of the painter and the price, and in the next three days he had sold the Holbein, one of the Hobbemas, and one of the Monets. It was all in the knowing how, he said, with a happy smile.

I V

Lanny decided to try the same method. He cabled his father about two Böcklins whose "philosophic content" he thought would appeal to Esther Budd; also he cabled the Murchisons about the Rubens, a female nude which he thought might give a jolt to Pittsburgh. He had had a couple of jolly letters from Adella, enclosing a bunch of newspaper clippings in which the Goya and the Velásquez were reproduced and the full story told. Said the plateglass lady: "My dreams of cultural prestige have been fully realized!" Lanny now told her that Zoltan expected the Rubens would be sold within a week, and Adella's reply came within twenty-four hours: they had put Lanny's message in the hands of a well-known steel man of advanced age who collected fair ladies in the name of art, and his money was in the Munich bank two days later.

Lanny's stepmother would be more cautious, naturally; she might travel to the New York or Boston public library to find out all she could about Böcklin. When her reply came, it was a request that the sale be held up until she could receive photographs of the paintings; but Lanny had to answer that it was first come first served, and Zoltan was pretty sure one of his British clients would cable acceptance on receipt of a letter. Lanny smiled, realizing the mental stress of his cautious Puritan stepmother, invited to pay eleven thousand dollars apiece for two paintings that she had never seen. Probably it was Robbie who decided the matter; anyhow, he cabled the cash, and included a commission for Lanny, even though Lanny had said he wouldn't accept one.

A list and description of all the paintings was prepared, with photographs of some of them, and sent with a letter to a number of persons, including names which Lanny had accumulated. Zoltan expected that most of the collection would be sold in that way, and he would take the remainder to London under bond. Wherever and however they were sold, Lanny would receive half the commission; he couldn't raise any question this time, for Johannes Robin was assuredly his client. So Lanny could afford to have a splurge in Germany; if he wanted any paintings he could buy them, and the same would apply to any of the girls he saw on the streets or in the cafés. Zoltan said this sadly, for he was a tender-hearted fellow, and was sorry for these pathetic creatures, with their painted hollow cheeks and eyes feverishly bright, who would go with any foreigner for the price of a piece of bread.

V

Meanwhile Rick had arrived, and he and Kurt set forth to investigate the activities of the National Socialist German Workingmen's Party. They found quickly that Heinrich Jung hadn't exaggerated the situation, for all Bavaria was in turmoil. The surrender to France hadn't had the expected effect of stopping the flight from the mark; "runaway inflation" ran over everything which tried to stop it, governments included. The distracted people were ready to hear any agitator with a plausible program, and the dingy headquarters of the Nazis were like a beehive at swarming time. Hundreds of young ex-soldiers with their swastika armbands were pouring in from near-by towns, saluting all over the place and being marched here and there.

It was the same odd combination of conspiracy and propaganda which the visitors had noted nearly a year ago. Nobody had the slightest hesitation about telling what they were all going to do: first take Munich, then march on Berlin. There was the same unwillingness to admit any imitation of Mussolini, but if you had read about the March on Rome you would hardly fail to recognize the pattern. The great war-leader General Ludendorff had publicly declared his adherence to the party's cause, so the success of its coming coup was assured. The extraordinarily bright blue eyes of Heinrich Jung shone with excitement as he whispered the most holy of secrets to a future musical genius and a representative of an English newspaper.

Heinrich's particular "hundred," as the Hitler groups were called, was going to march at seven o'clock the following morning. Heinrich couldn't tell where, because only the leaders knew, but Kurt and Rick might come along and see—it would be real history, said the youth. He used that phrase often, and it was evident that this thought had inspired him—he was going to be in history! In one nation after another, first Russia, then Hungary and Greece and Turkey and Italy, it had been shown that vigorous, determined men might seize power, and the followers of these men might become officials, persons of importance and of fame. It had been shown right here in Munich by the Reds; and now a new group was going to try it, with the newest of slogans, the most timely and potent: *Deutschland erwache!* Germany awake!

That was how it appeared to the visiting British journalist; but of course to twenty-year-old Heinrich Jung it meant the deliverance of Germany from the heel of the oppressor, the casting out of the money-changers from the temple, the setting free of honest German labor—the young Nazi's doctrines seemed as pink as his cheeks, and Rick laughed and said that the longer he talked the redder both became.

That evening there was a mass meeting in the same Bürgerbräukeller where they had heard Adi speak in January. This time it was a meeting of the Bavarian monarchists, who were also planning a revolt against Berlin. Heinrich Jung was very insistent that the visitors should attend this meeting—he practically told them that the Nazis meant to attempt some sort of coup; so the four friends went, and they saw plenty of history. Promptly on the second of eighty-thirty, Adolf Hitler burst into the hall, followed by steel-helmeted men, some of them pushing Maxim guns. Hitler rushed to the platform and took possession of it, delivering one of his wild tirades and telling the audience that the National Socialist regime had begun. At the point of his revolver he forced the monarchist leaders to pledge their allegiance to *his* kind of revolution, and to order their troops to obey him.

The meeting broke up in the wildest confusion. Apparently "history" consisted of parties of men rushing this way and that about the streets, so the visiting strangers went back to their hotel. They were out again before dawn, an ungodly procedure for two society ladies, but Beauty wouldn't let Kurt go without her, and Marie didn't think it "sporting" not to accompany Lanny's mother. When Kurt decided to walk alongside the "hundred," Beauty insisted upon walking with him; a fashionably gowned lady holding onto his arm would keep a sight-seeing stroll from becoming a military expedition. It appeared that other women of Munich had the very same idea, for many a young Nazi had a sweetheart hanging onto his swastika armband. Rick, being unable to march, followed the troop in a taxi, and Marie rode with him, glad of the protection of his journalist's credentials. Lanny and Zoltan were busy with their picture job.

VI

There wasn't much cheering, for apparently the working people on the streets at that hour didn't know what it was all about. The troop marched to the Capuchin convent, under whose five-foot walls great stores of rifles had been buried. All night the monks had held torches while the arms were being carried out and distributed to the storm troopers. Ammunition had been stored in the vaults of one of the city's great banks; a peculiar circumstance, in view of the party program concerning the money-changers. But nobody stopped to think about that, save only the skeptical Britisher; the eager young Nazis were busy getting their share of cartridges from the truck which suddenly put in appearance. Their guns were loaded, and then it was real war.

Off they marched, singing *Deutschland über Alles*, until they came to one of the city's bridges, where they halted, and there was an interminable wait. Nobody knew what it was for; presumably they were to hold the bridge against the enemy, but no enemy appeared, and making history was gradually discovered to be as tedious as making motion pictures. The four visiting strangers finally decided to repair to a near-by café for breakfast, and they gave a few marks to a street urchin to keep watch for them, promising him a still larger fortune if he would run to the café and advise them whenever the *Sturmabteilung* started to advance. One of the advantages of making history in a great city is that you can take a taxi and catch up with events.

They had an excellent meal, and sat for a long time over their cigarettes and coffee, agreeing that Lanny and Zoltan had been more sensible to stick to their picture job. But Kurt and Rick wouldn't quit and go home, and Beauty wouldn't desert Kurt, and Marie wouldn't desert Beauty. Presently Kurt and Rick got into an argument as to whether this Nazi movement was a plain "racket," or whether it had any ideas that might be fruitful for the Fatherland's future. Was Adolf Hitler Schicklgruber just a plain "nut," or was he an expression of the *Volk* spirit? Kurt insisted that for a people beaten and depressed as the Germans were it was important to have their courage and hopes restored, to be made to believe that they were a race with a world destiny. Rick replied that all this talk about racial superiority was "the bunk"; a half-cracked Englishman by the name of H. S. Chamberlain had put that bug into the Kaiser's ear—the Kaiser, half cracked himself, had circulated the book all over Germany, and it had spawned a whole library of rubbish, some of which this poor Schicklgruber creature had picked up.

Rick insisted that he knew just the type: you could hear a score of them ranting in Hyde Park any Sunday afternoon. One shouted that Britain was being bankrupted by the upkeep of the royal family, the next clamored that it was belief in God which was wrecking civilization; one would tell you that money must be abolished, and the next that Esperanto offered the only way of understanding among the peoples. Many of these poor devils slept in flophouses and old men's homes, exactly as Adi had done, wearing out their own vocal cords and the eardrums of their fellow inmates.

Kurt and Rick might have started a small civil war right there, but the urchin came rushing in to report that the *Sturmabteilung* was on the march. They paid him the promised fortune and took their taxi and followed. Kurt wanted to walk, perhaps to revive his enthusiasm for the Nazi cause; but Beauty wouldn't let him take a step without her hand in the crook of his arm. He couldn't raise the question of etiquette, for other women and girls were marching, each with her man. Would this become one of the war customs of the new Hitler Germany?

They were joined by thousands of other troopers, and with the *Hakenkreuz* banner at their head they marched out into the Marien-platz. Farther on was the Ludwigstrasse, and there, apparently to the surprise of the marchers, some forces of the *Reichswehr*, the regular army, were lined up. Then from behind the Feldherrnhalle came a body of the Bavarian state police; it looked as if the swastika bearers had been led into an ambush. As they continued to advance, orders rang out and shots were fired; a dozen or more of the Nazis fell, and the women began to scream and to scatter. Be sure there was no louder screamer, no quicker scatterer than Beauty Budd! She dragged Kurt with her, willy-nilly, dignity or no dignity; the taxi came speeding up, and in they hopped, and around one of the corners they went, the troops letting them pass unchallenged. And that was all they saw of the "Beerhall Putsch," the derisive name for the history that was made on those two days of November 1923. General Ludendorff was a prisoner, Adolf Hitler Schicklgruber was a fugitive with a dislocated shoulder, and Eric Vivian Pomeroy-Nielson was shut up in a room of the Vier Jahreszeiten Hotel, pounding out the story on his portable typewriter, to be cabled to a London newspaper.

VII

The visitors finished with their business and pleasure in Munich, and meanwhile they read that Herr Schicklgruber was in prison, and his movement outlawed under heavy penalties; they were glad to know that they would never again have to think about that danger-ous and most unpleasant "nut." Rick, explaining history to his Brit-ish public, wrote that people did not starve gladly, and that these events served notice that humane and rational elements in Britain and France must get together with those in Germany and find a way of reconcilement. The twenty-five-year-old social philosopher was planning a play in which these issues would be fought out among a group of characters. It was the "note" of the time, and even the French Nationalists were beginning to admit that the Ruhr technique hadn't proved a success.

Lanny celebrated his twenty-fourth birthday during this Munich visit. Zoltan asked Beauty's permission to give him a surprise party and invite several lovers of music and art whom he knew in the city. These were the "good Europeans," the sort of people whom the three musketeers of the arts had met in Hellerau before the war, when it had been possible to believe that the golden age of peace had come to Europe, that Orpheus with his lute was charming the furies of greed and hate so that they would no more torment mankind. What a change in ten years! Now many of the art lovers were dead, and others in mourning, or broken in health and spirits. If you invited them to a dinner party in a de luxe hotel, they would take out some ancient finery from a trunk and brush it and mend the motholes; they would come timidly, as if no longer sure how to behave. For a couple of those fabulous American dollars the most distinguished artists in Munich would be happy to sing and play for the gratification of a young Croesus, a young Fortunatus, a young Harun-al-Rashid.

The party moved on to Berlin, where there was another picture job to be done. This time Lanny guessed the values more closely; he was learning fast and gaining assurance. A portion of his mind would be set aside for a catalogue of art-works; in it would be several thousand names of painters, and the instant he heard a name and the date of a picture he would be able to say: "One thousand dollars," or "ten thousand," or "a hundred thousand." With lower figures it wasn't worth while to bother; but here was one of the temptations to which he would never be entirely immune—some poor devil of ability would be brought to his attention and he would have an urge to promote him, even though the commission on the sales wouldn't pay for the gasoline he used in traveling about.

But that didn't apply to the palace of a deposed nobleman in the suburbs of Berlin. Here were a dozen old masters, and Zoltan Kertezsi would decide their destiny in the manner of a hostess writing the place-cards for a dinner party. This Frans Hals should be in the Taft collection in Cincinnati, and that Sir Joshua belonged in the Huntington collection in southern California. Zoltan would "shoot a wire" and the sale would be made—those American millionaires like to do business in that swift yes-or-no way. Apparently they put a price on every minute of their time, and Lanny wondered what they did with any which they had left over. It must seem unbearably extravagant to go for a stroll or to look at anything so cheap as a flower. Zoltan said that that was the reason they had orchids.

Johannes Robin was delighted with what had been done. He was getting his money back in short order, and without earning the enmity of an aristocrat who had many powerful friends. He began to sing the praises of this Budd and Kertezsi outfit, and the pair received inquiries from other *Schieber* who wanted to put a part of their gains into something that could be rolled up into a small package and carried out of Germany quickly. One thing led to another, and Lanny could have spent all his time at this exciting new business.

But they must have some fun, too. Zoltan had brought his fiddle, and with two of these, a clarinet, and a piano they could play most any chamber music; they did so for hours on end. They even tackled the later quartets of Beethoven, and became lost in their mazes, and had to admit that they didn't know what the great master was driving at. Could it be that there was truth in what the critics of the time had said, that, being deaf, Beethoven no longer knew what he was writing? Or was he trying to say things so subtle that only a metaphysical mind could follow him? Lanny didn't know, and would have liked to ask Kurt; but the former artillery officer was firm in his refusal to visit the home of a Jewish speculator in marks, one who had so large a share in responsibility for the misfortunes of the Fatherland.

VIII

Kurt was staying with his brother; and Lanny was invited to a dinner party given by a group of young officers, Emil's friends. Lanny had met British army people and French, but this was his first acquaintance with Germans. He got the impression of men who took their profession much more seriously; they were highly trained technical men, like engineers. But that didn't make their conversation very interesting at a dinner party. All men "talk shop," but when your "shop" is killing other men, it is depressing to a lover of humanity. These officers were young in years, but old in tragic experience, and they had to drink too much wine before their tongues were loosened. They were interested in what Lanny and Kurt had to tell about events in Munich, and from their comments it was clear that they had little tolerance for Nazi lunacies; they were supporting the present republic as a stop-gap, but to a man they were convinced that the only permanent government for Germany must be a monarchy, and when the time came they meant to strike toward that goal.

During the Berlin visit Lanny and his mother laid siege to Kurt to persuade him to let them advance money for the publishing of his musical compositions. Here was the extraordinary situation, that for what Beauty would spend and did spend for a pair of dancing-slippers, all Kurt's compositions might be put into type by faithful German workmen who would be glad of a chance to earn their daily bread. Lanny's commission on the sale of a single mediocre painting would pay for paper and printing, and all Kurt's friends might have copies of half a dozen opera in first editions.

It was too great a temptation for any man who believed that his work had merit. Kurt gave way, upon the understanding that the money was to be a loan, to constitute a mortgage upon receipts for the rendition rights of the works. Lanny went with him to one of the old-established music houses, and a contract was signed, and Lanny wrote a check for a few of those pounds sterling which he had in one of the Berlin banks. Nothing he had ever done with money gave him more pleasure; and Beauty was even happier, for she knew that Kurt was at a serious crisis just then, and that attention paid to his music would be a powerful force to keep him at work. Beauty loved Kurt's music for one solid and practical reason —that it kept him shut up in her sanctuary, away from Schicklgrubers and Maxim guns!

IX

Christmas was near, so the party broke up. Beauty and Marie took the night train for Paris, the latter to return to her home, the former to spend a couple of days with Emily Chattersworth at Les Forêts and then to motor with her to the Riviera. Zoltan would have to travel between Berlin and Munich to oversee the selling and shipping of pictures—no simple matter in these times of disorder, when people did not starve gladly and any servant or employee might steal a painting and substitute an inferior one. Rick was returning to The Reaches, to write an article about inflation and its effects upon everyday life. After Christmas he was planning to bring his family to Bienvenu.

Lanny and Kurt traveled to Stubendorf, which had now become a sort of third home for a wandering young American. Once more the elderly horses toiled up the slope to the castle on the height; once more the sleighbells jingled and the family came running out; once more the hearts of two blond young Aryan widows went pit-a-pat at the sight of a super-eligible young American whose dark love secret would never be told to them. They sang the old Christmas songs, and some new ones which Lanny had picked up at the publishers'. They rejoiced at the news of Kurt's good fortune, and did their pathetic best to reward his benefactor and pupil—as they still thought of their guest. Once more the wise Herr Meissner discussed the affairs of Germany, and Lanny set down some of his opinions for Rick to use in his article.

In Upper Silesia were once prosperous families having art treasures they would gladly exchange for foreign money; Lanny traveled about and looked at them, and made notes as to prices expected. He learned that the Graf Stubendorf had a cousin in Vienna with a famous collection, and that this gentleman shared the hardships of his dismembered land. So, on their way home, Lanny and Kurt stopped for a couple of days in a city which had been famed as the home of wine, woman, and song, and which now had been sentenced to slow misery and decay. The beautiful blue Danube had turned a muddy yellow, the skies above it were gray and the people depressed, and pitiful in their faded finery.

The two friends looked at more pictures, and Lanny imparted some of the knowledge he had gained—but nothing about prices! He sent Kurt off to a concert while he discussed that delicate subject with an elderly aristocrat who seemed too tired to care what happened to his fortunes. Lanny made notes, and promised to do the best he could. He sent a complete schedule to Zoltan, and when he got to Bienvenu called in a stenographer and wrote letters to his growing list of prospective customers. Lanny figured that after deducting all the costs of the trip for himself and his friends he had cleared more than twenty thousand dollars—and he was only twenty-four years old!

So for the rest of his days he would have the comforting certainty of being able to have whatever he needed, and without asking any man's permission or being told what to do or say. The only thing that would make trouble for him was the trouble of all the people around him, of a world in torment whose cries came to him as if in a delirium. It seemed irrational to heed these cries, for there was nothing you could do about them; yet how could you help wishing that you could, and wondering if you couldn't? A strange plight for art lovers, who trained themselves to be receptive and then didn't dare use their faculties except upon imaginary things! Divide your mind in half, and build an emotion-tight compartment between the two; be sensitive to art and insensitive to life; learn to follow the example of that Russian countess who wept for the woes of the tenor in the opera while her coachman froze to death on the box outside!

19

Broad Is the Way

I

IT WAS to a greatly depressed France that the travelers came back. The franc had been going down all through the Ruhr invasion; reparations appeared to be mythical, and bonds that had been issued on them were losing value. Exaggerated amounts had been paid as restitution for war-damaged properties—it was a way of rewarding political supporters, not so different from what is called "graft" in the States. All the losses came back on those who had fixed incomes and salaries; the only gainers were speculators, and those fortunate few whose incomes were in dollars.

A delightful thing to find that you could get fifty percent more francs for your remittances from home! American visitors wrote or cabled about it, and steamers were crowded with refugees from Prohibition and Puritanism. Each year the boom on the Riviera became bigger and noisier; hotels and pensions were crowded, jazz-bands thumped all night, casinos were crowded with gamblers and dancers. The bathing-suits worn on the beaches became more and more scanty, until it seemed that nothing more could be spared. There was no longer any limit to anything; you did what you pleased, provided you had the price or could get it away from somebody else.

All the familiar figures came back every season: the kings playing tennis and baccarat, the maharajas playing polo or "chemmy," the Russian aristocrats running tearooms as a cover for pandering; the "beauty queens," the "lounge lizards," the "sugar daddies" with their "warm babies," the "hot mammas" with their "dancing boys" —the types were old, but the language was fresh from New York or Hollywood. The movie stars came, and walked like gods among an adoring population which had seen them magnified and transfigured upon the screen, and now stood to watch them, sleek and supple in tight bathing-suits, diving from the springboards below the great Hotel du Cap, or strolling on the Boulevard de la Croisette in costumes fit for a million-dollar superfeature.

Pick any famous name from the headlines of the newspapers, and it was a safe bet that you would meet him or her on the Côte d'Azur some time between January and March. The money they spent filled the purses of food and wine merchants, and the money they owned made the subject of awe-stricken gossip. If a giant hand could have come down on the Riviera and swept up a few hundred of them and put them through a financial squeezer, it would have collected most of the treasures of the earth. Cattle kings from the Argentine, wool kings from Australia, diamond kings from South Africa, copper kings from Montana—you had only to list the places where wealth was produced, and here were the owners of it.

Sir Basil Zaharoff, wearying of *la haute politique* and the financing of wars, had found himself a friendly little business, a toy to play with in his old age, a means of recouping his losses in Turkey; he had purchased for a round million pounds the stocks of the "Société Anonyme des Bains de Mer et du Cercle des Étrangers de Monaco," and was now its president and manager. The Knight Commander of the Bath had become yet another kind of bathing-master—but don't imagine that he went into the sea himself, or that he rented the privilege to others; no, the name of this company was a sixty-year-old camouflage for the most sumptuous and ornate gambling-palace in the world, so important that its locale was a separate nation all by itself, its owner a prince by right of purchase. The Monte Carlo casino had been done over and made more fashionable than ever. Previously you had been admitted free, but that was not according to the moral code of an old Greek trader; you now paid to get in, and paid still more before you got out—despite the fact that thousands of brains in Europe and America were concentrated on the devising of a "system" whereby they might beat the bank. Sir Basil himself might be observed taking his constitutional every afternoon, just as Lanny and his father had observed him ten years before; but he had a fixed rule never to go into the casino, and there was a story of a lady who had lost money and appealed to the great man to tell her how to avoid losing more. "Certainly, madame," he replied. "Do not gamble."

II

Ever more varied and strange were the forms which life took in this world of pleasure; and few were in better position to observe them than a young man with an agreeable smile, a well-filled purse, and a reputation for being able to dispose of works of art. It was astounding how many persons had inherited such works from their forefathers and cherished them as treasures without price; also how many schemes they devised to get introductions to Lanny Budd so that they might show him these possessions and sell ·them to him at almost any price. A Coromandel screen, a Japanese golden Kwannon—what means did Lanny have to know whether such things were genuine or not? He would never forget a sight which he had been taken to as a boy—a workshop in an obscure quarter of Florence where replicas of marble sculptures were made wholesale. The device, invented in America, consisted of half a dozen steel drills attached at intervals to a long rod, and caused to revolve by machinery. In front of each of these whirling drills a block of marble was fastened, and at one end of the rod an operator sat in front of the statue which was to be reproduced, a steel point attached to his end of the rod was passed over the model, and the other six drills moved in unison, eating away the marble from the other six blocks and gradually bringing into existence six replicas of the original. In other parts of this workshop the products were sprayed with chemicals and otherwise treated to make them "genuine old masters" for the American trade. *Garde à vous,* Lanny Budd —this art business is not all beer and skittles!

There was a young and dashing Rumanian countess who had fled from her country at the height of the war, bringing an old mother and a few art treasures in her automobile. She was pathetic, almost tearful over the plundering of her castle—she really had had one, and Lanny had been taught to respect genuine titles. The lady took him to her apartment and showed him an invaluable cloisonné vase —at least she called it that, and only with difficulty was she persuaded to suggest a value of a hundred thousand francs. Lanny said he didn't know anyone who bought vases, and he himself was not a dealer, he acted only as an agent for customers. The upshot was that the countess broke down and wept, admitting that she was in desperate financial straits. Perhaps Lanny might have been moved if she hadn't tried to spill the tears on him; he kept politely out of reach, and said that he would try to interest someone in the vase— with the result that the price came down ten thousand francs at a time, and in the end he paid two thousand for it, just to get away from a painful scene.

He packed the object carefully and shipped it to Zoltan, who was in Paris at the time, and in due course came a letter from his friend saying that it was a very lovely vase for anyone who wanted something to put flowers in, and if Lanny needed another to match it, Zoltan knew the shop in Paris where it could be bought for a hundred francs. Two thousand being then less than ninety dollars, it was a not too expensive lesson; but when the story was told to the family it was suggested that in future Lanny should take Jerry Pendleton or someone else when he inspected *objets d'art* in the apartments of strange ladies. Beauty made this suggestion, but Lanny had an idea that Marie had been taken into consultation!

III

Artists, also, began to take an interest in this well-connected youth. They all knew him because he was the stepson of Detaze and the nephew of Blackless—to say nothing of being the son of a pink-and-gold butterfly who had emerged from the chrysalis of an artists' model in Paris. Several who had painted her and fallen in love with her now lived on the Riviera or came there to paint, and when they heard about Lanny's good fortune they all brought their works and invited him to make such fortunes for them. It

got so that the servants were told that whenever anybody came to
the gates of Bienvenu with a portfolio, Lanny was absent for an
indefinite time. That didn't fit very well with a name meaning
"Welcome"; but how often it happens in this world that people are
not able to carry out their good intentions!

American painters came often to the Côte d'Azur; among them
the great John Sargent—a hard man to know, but Zoltan knew him
and gave Lanny a letter. Sargent was old, but still erect, a broad-
shouldered, handsome man with ruddy face and a small white
beard; he had painted portraits of the wealthy and great, and made
them noble-looking as they wished to be, but now he was weary of
them and desired no more of their wealth. One of the last had been
old John D. Rockefeller, who had paid him fifty thousand dollars
for a portrait, and the painter had given the money to the Red
Cross. Lanny brought him an offer from one of the richest ladies
in Cannes; he was free to name his own price, but he looked at a
photograph of her and remarked that he would as soon paint a bar
of soap.

Instead he said: "Come sketching with me." So Lanny, who had
loved this coast from childhood, took him to some little-known
beauty spots, and sat and observed Sargent making watercolor
sketches. One of the most interesting things in the world, to watch
a man of genius working in a frenzy of concentration and something
lovely growing under his hands. Lanny kept as still as a mouse,
answering only when he was spoken to, and after several such
expeditions the artist gave him sketches which might have been sold
for a thousand dollars.

All kinds of people on this lovely shore, and all kinds of art-
works coming into being! One day Lanny went with his mother
to lunch at the home of a divorcee from New York who had
brought a considerable fortune with her. On the walls of her
dining-room he saw four panels which hit him between the eyes.
They were painted on silk backed with wood, and he thought he
had never seen such a glory of color; peacocks and other great
tropical birds, magnificent stylized designs in purple and gold and
scarlet and black. Lanny couldn't eat for looking at them, and the

hostess said: "Oh, don't you know Dick Oxnard? He's spending the winter here."

Lanny listened to the story of a genius who came of one of the oldest and proudest New York families, and had inherited a fortune in his own right. He was divinely handsome, gay, a darling of the ladies; he was living here because of some scrape he had got into at home. "He's a bit wild," admitted the hostess, "but the most delightful company. You really ought to know him." Beauty, who watched over her darling so carefully where Reds and Rumanian countesses were concerned, saw nothing to worry about in a society painter, and later on the hostess went to the telephone and told Dick Oxnard about her friend. The answer was: "Send him to lunch tomorrow."

So, promptly at the appointed hour of one, Lanny's sport-car drove up in front of an elegant villa in one of the Riviera valleys. There didn't seem to be anybody around, and perhaps the bell was out of order; but the door was wide open, which seemed hospitable. Looking in, Lanny saw some of those gorgeous decorative panels and screens in the entrance hall, and as they were what he had come for, he ventured in. Presently along came an elderly Chinese servant in a white duck suit, grinning amiably. "Mornin'. You come blekfas'?"

"Lunch," replied the guest.

"Blekfas', lunch, allee same, maybe blunch. You go up, all light, allee same home." Nothing could have been more cordial; so Lanny went up the wide stairway, stopping half-way to look at a breath-taking design of a market girl of Tehuantepec wearing an elaborately embroidered dress and seated under a tree with an array of fruits piled up in great painted gourds. In the hallway above were several doors, all open, and Lanny didn't know which to go to; but he was in no hurry, for on the wall was a black Chinese dragon against a background of gold and scarlet flames. Lanny would have been just as well content if there hadn't been anybody at home in Dick Oxnard's villa.

IV

But the house was full, as it turned out. Through the open door of a large room the guest saw an enormous canopied bed with four posts of carved ebony and draperies of cloth of gold. It was such a bed as Marie Antoinette might have slept in; Lanny had never seen one so big in any castle. But even so, it was hardly big enough for the assortment of girls who were sleeping in it, and some of their arms and feet hung over the sides. They were in miscellaneous scanty costumes of as many hues as an Oxnard wall panel, and appeared to have draped themselves with unconscious art around the central figure of a man.

Lanny thought he might as well inspect this art along with all the rest. It was of the genre known as "still life," for the whole group were sound asleep, and their combined breathing was like the sound of a summer zephyr through a grove of pine trees. But suddenly Lanny gave a jump, for behind him the air was shattered by the most astounding racket. On the stair-landing was a great Chinese gong, and somebody must have been hitting it sideswipes with a hammer, for the crashes came rolling through the hall like breakers on a beach; they sped up and down and clashed with one another until it seemed there was nothing in the house but sound.

It caused one or two of the girls to open their eyes and stretch their arms. Finally the half-buried man came to life and, when he saw Lanny, sat up. "Hello!" he said, with no surprise. "You company?"

"Lanny Budd," said the visitor.

"Oh, good! Make yourself at home, Budd." The speaker deftly extricated himself from the tangle of girls, and slid over them to the floor. His costume consisted of a loincloth of green and silver, which had come from Ceylon, or Siam, or some such tropical land. He was a grand figure of a man, thirty or so, built like a statue of Hermes, with wavy golden hair and mustache of the same. Apparently this was the way he lived, and he made no apologies. He caught one of the girls by the toe and gave a firm pull, and she let out a shriek of pain; it must have been a familiar procedure, for all the others leaped into life and tumbled out of bed as if they had had an electric shock.

Some of them wore the costumes of Bali and some of Hawaii; others wore bathing-suits or birthday suits. They came streaming from other rooms—there were more than a score of beautiful young girls in the house, fair and stately ones from the north, and dark, languorous ones from the south. Lanny never did find out about them all, but he learned that several had followed the young god from America, and others had just drifted in and stayed. The doors of the villa were never locked, and coming and going were equally free and easy. The host who was so gay and hospitable would become angry upon the slightest whim, and then he was incredibly brutal to his attendant nymphs; he would address them in language which could not be indicated in print, and one who gave him displeasure would be propelled through the front door by the agency of the beautiful white foot of Hermes, messenger of the gods.

That came later. For the present all was gaiety. "These are the girls," said the painter; "help yourself." That was all the introduction required; apparently the girls liked the visitor's looks, for several attached themselves to him, told him their first names, and tried to sit in his lap at the first occasion.

The guest had come to lunch, but the host revealed that they had finished supper not long ago. Lanny said he would just as soon look at paintings, but the other declared that they were always ready to eat. The troop of nymphs came dancing and chattering into the dining-room, which had more of the vivid panels, this time of tropical fishes and long, waving sea-growths. The old Chinese brought in platters of scrambled eggs and buttered toast, and when he had distributed these he brought in half a dozen bottles of champagne and proceeded to open and fill glasses around the table. Fortunately it was a day of warm sunshine, and when you are young you can sit half naked and drink iced champagne for your morning pick-me-up.

There was another man present, an Englishman who was introduced as "Captain Abernethy, call him Neethy." It was he who had pounded on the gong in honor of Lanny's arrival. He too was fair, with brick-red, apoplectic cheeks; he was somewhat older than Oxnard, and apparently acted as his guardian, providing what little sanity there was in the establishment. But he hadn't always been like that, for presently Dick was telling with laughter how Abby had been in the cavalry, in the days when there was real cavalry, and while his brother officers were having a party in the mess-room he had ridden his horse through the door and sprung him over the table. Abby and Dick had been all over the world together, and in Mexico the cavalryman on a wager had leaped into the bullring and onto the back of the bull. He had stuck there, too. "But you know," said the host, "those greasers mobbed us; they took it as an insult to their bull!"

In one of the few moments of rationality during this visit Lanny expressed his admiration for the American's work, and asked him if he ever sold anything. Oxnard said that he hated to do so because it was such a bother; but if Lanny admired the things, he'd be happy to present him with one, for they cluttered up the place. Lanny said that he couldn't think of accepting such a favor. He said the same thing to a beautiful blond nymph who offered to accompany him to one of the bedrooms, and the result in both cases was the same. When he took his departure he found that a large black-and-gold tiger in a green-and-scarlet jungle had been deposited in his car; also he found a nymph—no painting, but a flesh-and-blood one dressed in a sports costume of knitted pink silk, waiting in the seat beside the driver's. She was determined to stay, and since Lanny was unwilling to use his foot, it took a lot of argument. He explained with all gentleness that he was devoted to a French lady and by no possibility to be won away from her. The blond darling, who couldn't have been more than eighteen years of age, wept gently on his shoulder, declaring that it was the dream of her life to find a man to be true to. Lanny said that he would have been delighted to be that man, had she not unfortunately waited so long before presenting herself.

V

Rick brought his family to Bienvenu, and he was in a more hopeful state of mind than Lanny could recall since the war. There had been a general election in Britain, the dreadful Tories were out, and the Empire had its first labor government. The Prime Minister was a

Socialist, a former schoolteacher from Scotland; a tall handsome man and an elegant orator. Ramsay MacDonald had taken a courageous stand against the war, and all forward-looking men now predicted a regime of peace and reconcilement. The German Foreign Minister, Stresemann, was also a reconciler, and all that was needed now was to get rid of the dull Poincaré. The French elections were due in May, and everybody agreed that the tide was running against the party which was responsible for the Ruhr fiasco and the *dégringolade* of the franc. The left forces were working out an agreement not to oppose one another's candidates, and Rick was as keen about it as if he had been a Frenchman. Lanny agreed with him, as he always did—but never a word about it in the presence of Marie!

The problem of reparations was at last being dealt with on a rational basis. A commission of experts was named to determine what Germany could actually pay—this after five years of efforts to compel her to pay what she couldn't. A Chicago banker was at the head of it, and this so-called Dawes Commission worked out an arrangement; by dint of scaling down the claims every few months—always amid cries of anguish from the French—they would gradually accomplish the purpose of letting Germany get on her feet.

When the Easter holidays drew near, Robbie was in London and intending to come to Paris; so Lanny drove Marie up, and once more in the drawing-room of the Château de Bruyne he listened to Denis and his father discussing the affairs of Europe; once more in his uncomfortable way he would begin wondering whether all the conclusions to which his English friend had brought him could be trusted after all. Was it really safe to let Germany get on her feet? Could you trust that thing in Berlin which called itself a "republic"? How long would it be before Hindenburg or somebody like him would come into power, and the old dreadful menace would be hanging over France?

Denis de Bruyne pointed out something which Lanny had heard in Germany, but of which the significance had not been made clear to him. All during the "mark swindle" the great German industries had been required to keep their workers employed and had received government credits for that purpose. They had set the workers to rebuilding and expanding plants; so now, having wiped out her debts both internal and external, the Germans were starting afresh with the most modern productive machinery in the world. What chance would the French stand in international trade, with their still-ruined factories, mills, and mines? It really seemed that the Germans were more capable than their foes. You could say, as Denis did, that it was because they were without moral or business scruples; that made you hate them more—but it didn't make your peril any less!

Denis had the idea that the United States ought to recognize this situation and put her moral and financial power behind France. But Robbie had to tell him the painful fact that this was out of the question; any American statesman who advocated it would be quickly retired to private life. This was a world in which you had to look out for yourself, and the very word "idealism" now gave Americans what they crudely called "a pain in the neck." Europe would have to find a method of paying her debts to America before she asked for any more favors.

VI

Fate had given Robbie Budd a new executive of his country. Poor old Harding had died, perhaps of a broken heart—anyhow, just in time to escape an avalanche of scandal which had been sliding down onto his head. The man who ruled in his stead was even more satisfactory to Robbie and his friends; the father described him as the oddest figure, the son of a country storekeeper, with exactly that sort of mind. Vermont, his home state, is a cold, mountainous country, where people work hard to wrest a living from a stony soil; they save every penny and hold onto it tightly, and keep their mouths shut concerning their own affairs. "Cautious Cal" was the name of the new President, and by the easy method of saying nothing he made it possible for the newspapers to build him into a "strong silent statesman." In reality, Robbie said, he liked to go down into the basement of the White House and keep track of the groceries that were being used. This suited Robbie and his big business friends, for he let them run the country and didn't meddle with what he didn't understand.

The master of money smiled when his son, the gentle idealist, talked about Ramsay MacDonald and the French Socialists with their dream of peace in Europe. Robbie revealed the one really significant fact: the munitions industry was coming back! All through the post-war depression Robbie had argued with his father against the entire making over of the Budd plants; Robbie's oldest brother, Lawford, had wanted to drop arms-making, but now, as usual, Robbie was proved to be right! Already he was picking up small orders for various sorts of arms; Dutch traders were buying them and smuggling them into Germany by the network of canals which ran into that country. Also France was making new armament loans to Poland, and to the Little Entente, a new coalition to hold off the Russians on the east and to attack Germany if she should attack France. "Just as soon as business picks up there's bound to be a boom," said Robbie; "and we shall get our share, believe me."

"But," argued the son, "what about those huge stocks that were left over after the war?"

The father smiled. "We have had engineers and technicians at work for five years, and so have Vickers, Schneider, everybody. We have a new machine gun that fires two hundred more rounds per minute than the old one, and reaches a thousand yards farther. The old guns will be all right for South America or China, but not for a modern war. The same thing will apply to grenades, fuses, bomb-sights; everything that America is going to use in the next war will have to be made new—and not far ahead of the war, either!"

VII

Lanny would absorb this information, direct from the fountain-head, and would be impressed by the authority of his masterful progenitor. Robbie Budd was acquiring weight, along with money, and it would be a long time before the sensitive and affectionate son would have courage to face him in a mental showdown. Lanny would drive the busy man of affairs into Paris, and then go wandering to look at new paintings at the dealers'; a temptation would assail him, and somehow he would be powerless to resist it—he had to go calling on that Red uncle of his! He would fool himself with the idea that it was to pick up gossip about painters and what they were doing, the boom in Detaze and what the dealers were saying about it—all that "shop" for which artists have just as much weakness as munitions men. But sooner or later one of Jesse's left-wing friends would drop in, or perhaps Jesse's *amie* to arrange lunch; the talk would turn to politics, and the forbidden "dangerous thoughts" would be flying about the room, hitting Lanny Budd in vital parts of his mental anatomy.

Again he would be struck by the curious point: how completely his revolutionary uncle and his reactionary father agreed as to the facts of the modern world. Both would say that it was money that made the mare go, and they would agree as to the road on which the mare was traveling and her rate of progress; they would even agree as to what lay over the next hill; their dispute began only beyond the far horizon's rim. Really, two such surveyors ought to have been able to combine forces and make their maps in common; Lanny, the great reconciler, had been able to bring Britain and France and Germany together in the same household, so why shouldn't he dream of bringing capitalism and Communism together?

Jesse Blackless was a man who had channeled his feelings in accordance with a set of social theories. According to his formula, the exploited workers were going to overthrow their oppressors and take control of the world and make it over into something much more rational. This being so, Jesse looked for all merit in the workers, and found it; he would sit all day in a barely furnished little room and paint a picture of some poor waif of the Paris streets, making a touching and pathetic portrait, and when the dealers weren't interested in it, he would understand that it was because their customers wanted pictures of rich and elegant things. When the painter went for a stroll in the parks and saw the children of the rich with their pretty clothes and their *bonnes* watching over them, he would have no use for these children, because what they had was taken from the poor child whom he had painted.

All problems that arose in conversation were disposed of by Uncle Jesse in the same way. All capitalists, all capitalist groups and nations, were seeking profits; they were like hogs rushing to a feeding-trough, trampling down everything that stood in their way. By the same formula, all Socialist politicians were "labor fakers," making promises to the people and selling them out to the big business interests. That included Ramsay MacDonald, in whom Rick placed such high hopes; it included Léon Blum and Jean Longuet, and the others who were now carrying on such a vigorous election campaign in France. Jesse Blackless described them as "yellow Socialists," and hated them for luring the workers away from their true goal of revolution. Lanny said: "Uncle Jesse, your mind is like a phonograph; I put the needle down, I push the lever, and I know exactly what you're going to say."

The painter was a good sport, and willing to take cracks as hard as he gave. "Maybe so," he replied; "but if a record is right, why change it?"

Lanny would go off and think about that. If it was true, as both Robbie and Jesse agreed, that competition for raw materials and markets was getting the world ready for another great war, it was certainly desirable that the common people of all nations should know about it and try to stop it. But what could they do? Uncle Jesse said that the capitalists would never give up to mere ballots. Was that true, or wasn't it? If they would, then obviously the wise thing was to use ballots; but if they wouldn't, you had to prepare other means. But it was possible to argue that the threat of using other means—that is to say, violence—would frighten the propertied classes, and lead them to use the violence first.

They had so used Mussolini and his blackshirts in Italy—that was one of the points on which Robbie Budd and his Red near brother-in-law were in their curious state of agreement. Fascism was capitalism's answer to the threat of Communism! But why make the threat, if you couldn't get any farther with it than that? A complicated world that Lanny Budd had been born into, and one must not blame him too much if he took a long time to decide by what road he wished to get out of it!

VIII

Zoltan Kertezsi came to Paris. He had sold more of the Berlin and Munich paintings, also he had been to Vienna and inspected those which Lanny had found, and had done some business with them. He presented an accounting and a large check, and said there would be more. If what he wanted was social life with Lanny and his friends, he had taken the right way to get it, for Marie invited him out to the château, and she and the boys listened for hours while he and Lanny played music and while they talked about art. Marie approved of "old masters" in the same way that Beauty Budd approved of Bach and Beethoven and Brahms; not knowing very much about them, but observing that they kept her *ami* out of mischief. Day after day she went with the two men to the *salon* in Paris, and to the Vente Drouot, and the various exhibitions of the dealers; she listened to their highly technical conversation, and when it dealt with prices, she considered it not a profanation but something very much to the point.

Zoltan was going to London to attend some of the sales. Why not come along? Marie had heard about London sales, and they sounded interesting. So Lanny put his two friends into his comfortable car— Zoltan in the back seat, leaning forward and talking away the whole time. He never got tired of telling stories about pictures and their painters and their prices. Lanny listened, and Marie never interrupted; it was education, as good as going to college—two kinds, in fact, an art school, and one of commerce and finance. When they stopped to eat, or to buy *essence*, Lanny would make note of things he wanted to remember. In this school one never knew at what moment the examinations might be held. Zoltan would say: "What do you think I should have got for an especially beautiful Ingres?"

London was always delightful in the spring; everybody and everything happy to come out of the fog and cold, and to discover that the sun still existed. It was the first time Marie had been there since love had awakened her heart; they walked on air together, and did those delightful things which people can do when they have money, and a bit of culture to help them enjoy it. They went through the

Tate Gallery, reveling in the Turners, and Lanny explained what his stepfather had taught him about "atmosphere." Zoltan told stories about various famous works. If one had been retouched, he knew it, and showed exactly how he knew it. He was bitter against leading dealers such as "Joe" Duveen, who would buy some old master that had become dim and proceed to "freshen it up"; this would double the price for the American trade, but the result was no longer an old master, and the fact that "Joe" had become "Sir Joseph" for his services to art didn't decrease the disapprobation of a Hungarian commoner.

Rick had brought his family back to The Reaches, and invited all three of the visitors for a week-end. Marie was shy about going to the home of a respectable English family in company with her lover, but Lanny assured her that these were "mod'n" people and proud of it; this *liaison* was now four years old, and surely that was enough for respectability. All three of them had an enjoyable time, and Sir Alfred told them about paintings in the neighborhood that might be bought. But Marie had to listen to plain talk on the subject of the French election results, for that was the English custom; you said what you thought, and if the other person didn't agree, he said what he thought. Strange how people could hold such opposite opinions; to Marie and her husband the victory of the left coalition threatened the end of France, while to everyone at The Reaches it was the beginning of a new and better era.

After the middle of May Zoltan had to return to Germany for more business; and just then he received a letter from one of his American clients who had taken up the notion that he must have cinquecento Italians for his collection. It happened that Sophie Timmons, ex-baroness, had just been visiting in Rome, and Lanny said she knew everybody, and he would get her to introduce Zoltan to some of the old Roman families. The dealer said it would be wise to act quickly, because there was talk of a tariff on art-works imported into the United States. There was already a law in Italy forbidding the exportation of art-works, but one got around this by the payment of what was called a *regalo*, a polite word for a bribe.

The upshot was that Zoltan asked Lanny if he would like to take a run into Italy when he got home, and if he could find anything worth while, Zoltan would come and look at it, and Lanny would get half of whatever he helped to earn. The prices would doubtless be high, and the reward according. Lanny asked Marie, and she said she would enjoy such a trip—but on one essential condition, that her escort wouldn't get himself mixed up in any more political affairs. Lanny had no hesitation in promising that, for he was in one of those moods which seized him whenever he had been listening to his reactionary father and his revolutionary uncle, and having his mind pulled and hauled between them. Away from all that!

IX

They went back to Paris and stayed for a day, because Marie wanted to leave some of her clothes and get others. Lanny went into the city, and in the Café de la Rotonde he ran into an American journalist whom he had come to know at some of the various conferences—there had been so many of them by now that they made rather a blur in one's mind. Lanny mentioned that he was going to Rome, and why, and the other suggested the names of persons who might know where old masters were hidden. Lanny in return passed on some of the funny stories his father had told him about "Cautious Cal," also some inside stuff about how the French Nationalists were taking their defeat at the polls.

Persons who possessed such information were very useful, so presently this journalist remarked: "By the way, I'm giving a dinner party for some of the French leftists this evening. I thought it would be a good thing to get them together informally, and let them iron out their differences while their stomachs are full and they feel good. Wouldn't you like to join us?" Lanny understood what would be the position of a young man of fashion at such a gathering; he would put on his glad rags and provide a couple of receptive ears into which each person of importance might pour whatever he pleased. Lanny had served acceptably at such affairs, and said he would be happy to come to this one.

In the far-off days before the war Lanny had met at one of Mrs.

Emily's lawn parties a tall and slender middle-aged Jew who was
then the dramatic critic of one of the Paris dailies; an art lover and
friend of poets, a lawyer who didn't practice very much, a rich
man's son who could afford to play, and did so in refined and delicate ways like Lanny himself. The American had forgotten him,
and if anyone had asked him if he had ever met Léon Blum he
would have said no. But here he was; impossible not to recognize
the rather full brown mustache, the high-pitched voice and manner
of an aesthete. Blum'had traveled far in the past ten years; after the
assassination of Jaurès he had become editor of the Socialist party's
newspaper and leader of its group in the Chamber of Deputies.
Lanny had been reading his scholarly and vigorous editorials, and
being convinced by them—up to the moment when he heard the
other side presented with equal cogency. Now Blum gave an eloquent talk, referring to the tragic years through which Europe had
passed and the hope that the new regimes of France and Britain
would get together *pour changer tout cela.*

Next to Lanny sat another lawyer-editor, a younger man, kind
and gracious. He had delicate, sharp features, a thin nose with pince-
nez, a light brown mustache, and rather unruly hair. This was Jean
Longuet, a grandson of Karl Marx; during the war he had had the
same kind of trouble as Ramsay MacDonald, for he was one of those
who stood by the program of the Socialist International. Lanny, who
had lived through all this in his mind, would have liked to talk
it out with this man, but a dinner party was hardly the place.

He mentioned that he was on his way to Italy, and they discussed
the tragedy which had befallen that country. As it happened,
Longuet had written an article on the recent Italian elections, which
the Fascists had carried by a reign of terror; this was to appear in
Le Populaire next morning, and Lanny promised to read it. The
Socialist deputies of Italy were in a desperate struggle against the
increasing tyranny, and Longuet said that Daniel in the lions' den
was nothing for courage compared to them, because Daniel had the
Lord to trust in, while Matteotti and his comrades had only the
moral sentiments of their half-strangled people. Said the lawyer-
editor: "There is something in each of us which makes us willing

to die rather than consent to evil. Whatever that is, it lifts us above the brutes and makes it possible to have hope for the human race." Lanny said that if that was Socialism, he was ready to enroll his name.

After which he went back to the Château de Bruyne, and didn't say much about the matter, knowing that, when it came to distinguishing among the various shades of Reds, Marie's eyesight was not very keen. Driving to Juan, they talked about pictures and the business in Rome; about the play Rick was writing and the music Kurt was publishing; about Marie's two boys and what they were doing and thinking; about their own love—in short, about anything in the world except the fact that Lanny liked to meet Socialist agitators and let them persuade him that the business system of France was all wrong, and that Marie's father and brothers and husband and their relatives and friends were collectively responsible for the drop of the franc and the piling up of debts and dangers for *la patrie!*

20

Roma Beata

I

LANNY and Marie stayed at Bienvenu for a couple of days, to rest and tell Beauty the gossip and hear what she had collected. Lanny had letters to read and to write; he had become quite a businessman, and would summon a secretary and say: "Take a letter," just as if he were the European representative of Budd Gunmakers. Sophie gave him letters to friends in Rome, and so did Emily Chattersworth and M. Rochambeau. These preparations made, they set out on the four- or five-hundred-mile journey to the Eternal City;

taking it in leisurely fashion and looking at both nature and art on the way.

The last time Lanny had made that journey had been ten years earlier, in company with old Mr. Hackabury, creator and proprietor of Bluebird Soap. So now this highly original character traveled along with them, and his amusing remarks were repeated to Marie. At San Remo they stopped off for a call on Lincoln Steffens, who now had a young wife and a baby, and was very proud of both. Stef had retired from politics for a while, in somewhat the same mood as Lanny. He had tried to change the world, and couldn't, so let's wait and see what the stubborn critter was going to do for itself!

When they came to the valley of the river Arno, they traveled up it to Florence and paid another call—this time on George D. Herron. He had moved to Italy because he couldn't endure to meet all the people who came to see him in Geneva—especially Germans—to ask how he had come to be so cruelly deceived about Woodrow Wilson! The father of the League of Nations had just died, broken in both body and spirit, and poor Herron was in much the same state; the two visitors agreed that he couldn't last much longer. A saddening thing to see what the world did to those idealistic souls who tried to improve it. A warning to Lanny, which his companion hinted at tactfully.

In Rome the "season" was just coming to its end, and hotels were still crowded; but there was always a "royal suite" or an "ambassador's suite" or something like that, which you could have if you were willing to pay; and of course it would pay to pay when you were there to make an impression upon the aristocracy. In such exclusive homes you didn't talk about money, but you had a secret code of a thousand small details whereby you made plain that you had it, and had always had it. Marie understood this code, but she didn't know how the old families of Rome would receive a French *amie;* since this was a business trip, she was quite willing to go and look at churches and tombs and paintings while her companion groped cautiously in the mazes of a world which had as many "circles" as it had periods in its architecture.

It wasn't going to be an easy matter finding four-hundred-year-old paintings and persuading their owners to sell at anything like reasonable prices. Lanny ought to have presented his various letters at once, before people went away to the seashore or the mountain lakes. But he had been deeply impressed by his talk with Longuet and the article he had read about the Italian Socialists; he knew that the new Parliament had just opened, and he could read enough Italian to learn from the newspapers that the country was in a political fever at the moment. Ever since the days of the Paris Peace Conference, Lanny had had a hankering to observe history from the inside, and he bethought himself who there was in Rome that might take him behind the scenes of this political show. The first thing he did after getting himself and his friend settled comfortably was to telephone to a newspaperman; taking the precaution to do this from the lobby of the hotel, so as not to worry his *amie*—so he told himself. She wanted to rest after the trip, and would wait until the cool of the evening before going out.

II

The man was Pietro Corsatti, American-born Italian correspondent of one of the New York newspapers; Lanny had met him at San Remo, and again at Genoa, and knew that he was open-minded and free-spoken. Lanny himself had something to offer, for he had just come from London and Paris, where he had talked with persons "in the know." He mentioned that he had recently dined with Blum and Longuet, and asked the journalist to have lunch with him. Corsatti said: "Sure thing. We'll have a fine time chewing the rag."

Corsatti had an olive complexion, sparkling black eyes, and wavy black hair; he was a Neapolitan, but also he was a New York boy. Funny thing, how one culture could be superposed upon another, and the stronger and more·recent would prevail. Corsatti spoke English with an East Side accent and the latest slang; he was completely American in his point of view, and looked upon this dead old town with pitying condescension. He revealed this to Lanny, but of course he kept it down in his contacts with the Italians, and mustn't let it show in his dispatches, because the censorship watched him like a hawk. Just recently they had "raised hell" with him for mentioning that Prime Minister Mussolini had appeared at some public function "in need of a second shave."

Lanny was a friend of Rick, of Stef, of Bill Bullitt, so he was an insider, a "right guy." He could be introduced to "the gang," he could be trusted with "the dope," and if in the course of his picture-hunting he should stumble upon any political "leads," he would not forget his friend. Seated over a bottle of good chianti in a little *trattoria* frequented by the foreign newspapermen, Corsatti proceeded to "spill the beans" about Italy and its upstart political movement. It appeared that the American newspapermen were divided about fifty-fifty on the subject of Mussolini; some thought he was a man of destiny, and others were equally sure that he was a "four-flusher," a "flat tire." Discussing him in a public place like this, you didn't use either his name or title; he was "Mr. Smith"—perhaps because that had been his father's occupation. Lanny's companion warned him that in this aged town there were as many spies as there were statues of saints, and one did not speak freely even in bed with one's mistress.

There had been a general election for members of Parliament in the previous month, and Mr. Smith's followers had won a majority. They had got it, Corsatti declared, by the most vicious repression; the opposition leaders had been beaten, and many of their followers killed; the police and the Fascist Militia, some of whom called themselves "Savages," had turned the election campaign into a farce. Mr. Smith had just made his appearance before the new Parliament, clad in a costume which the journalist said was suited to "a Gilbert and Sullivan Admiral of the Queen's Navee." In his speech he had remarked: "You of the opposition complain that you were restrained from holding free electoral meetings. What of that? Such meetings are of no avail, anyway."

The program was to have the Parliament validate these frauds, three hundred and twenty of them all in one lump. The "Verification Committee on Mandates" had put such a proposal before the Chamber, and it was to be debated that afternoon. "Longuet urged me to hear Matteotti," said the visitor. "Do you suppose he will speak?"

"He will unless they prevent him," replied the journalist, and Lanny asked: "Do you suppose I could get in?"

"I'll see if I can take you into the press gallery with me. Can you call yourself the correspondent of any paper?"

"I imagine Longuet would be glad if I'd send him a story."

"That wouldn't be so good—a Socialist paper. You don't want to put a label on yourself. But five lire will do a lot in Rome."

"Whatever you have to pay, it's on me," said the son of Budd Gunmakers.

"Too much would be no good," explained the other. "You'd frighten the attendant and excite suspicion."

III

They took a taxi to the Palazzo di Montecitorio with the obelisk in front of it, where the Chamber of Deputies meets. At the door the correspondent took his young friend by the arm, and said to the doorman: "*Il mio assistente.*" At the same time he slipped him five lire, and they went in, as Corsatti phrased it, "on a greased skidway." Lanny had a front seat to watch the making of history in a scene of bitter and furious strife.

Giacomo Matteotti was the Socialist party secretary and leader of its forces in the Parliament. He was then close to forty, but slender and youthful in appearance, with a sensitive, rather mournful face. Corsatti said that frequently he wore a frank, boyish smile, but he had no chance to show it that day. Lanny agreed with Longuet's remark that Daniel's stunt in the lions' den was easy compared to what this Italian idealist was doing. He didn't rave, or call names, but spoke in a quiet, firm voice, giving his people the facts as to what had been happening in their country during the past two years. Every promise to labor had been broken, while the inheritance taxes had been abolished at the behest of the rich. The financial statements of the nation had been deliberately falsified; there had been no reduction of expenditures, but on the contrary an orgy of stealing.

The intimate associates of the head of the state were smuggling arms into Yugoslavia, they were oil corruptionists, they were terrorists who had stolen an election by vicious cruelty and now presented themselves in the Chamber to have their crimes officially sanctified.

Such was the substance of Matteotti's speech. He was not content with vague charges; every time he made an assertion he went into details as to places, dates, and sums of money. Evidently he had been delving deeply, and he had a mass of papers before him, indicating that he was in position to go on for hours. The alleged criminals sat before him, and their reaction was the most appalling demonstration of mass fury that Lanny had ever heard. The Fascist deputies, about two-thirds of the Chamber, would leap to their feet, shake their clenched fists, and literally shriek with rage. Murder was in their aspect and murder in their cries; the frail orator blanched before this blast, but he did not yield, and as soon as he could be heard he went on with his implacable arraignment. What was spoken in this Chamber would become a matter of record, and sooner or later could be got to the people.

This continued for two hours—until it seemed that the Fascist regime was crumbling there before everyone's eyes. Mussolini's followers shouted insults and imprecations, and one of their orators rushed to the opposition side and bellowed into their faces: "*Masnada!*"—that is, band of scoundrels. Somehow—Lanny's eye wasn't quick enough to follow the events—a fight started, and in a twinkling it was a free-for-all, in which everybody jumped on anybody of whom he disapproved. That was the last that Lanny saw of the Italian *Parlamento*, for his friend whispered: "I have to get this story off!" and he went, his *assistente* following.

IV

Lanny mailed his letters of introduction and awaited replies. There were one or two which he might have presented informally, thus saving time, but the truth was, he had something else on his mind: he wanted to shake hands with Matteotti. He was on fire with admiration for a deed of splendid courage, and he wanted to say so. One doesn't meet a hero face to face every day of one's life.

"Sure, you can meet him," said Corsatti. "Just walk into his office. He's the party drudge, and everybody brings him their troubles and quarrels. He'll be there—if the *militi* haven't raided him in the meantime." So Lanny went to the Socialist headquarters, which weren't so different from those of the Nazis which he had visited in Munich.

Lanny had to learn the important lesson that heroes rarely look heroic, especially behind the scenes. The new Prime Minister of Italy had practiced thrusting out his jaw and swelling up his chest, and had created for himself the costume of an Admiral of the Queen's Navee, but this friend of the working classes had had no time or thought for histrionics. He sat at his desk with papers piled around him, looking like the overworked city editor of a newspaper close to the "deadline." People came and went, the telephone rang, and in a few minutes there was to be a conference of party leaders to determine whether they were to withdraw from the Chamber. But meanwhile the secretary could find time for a young American who had just come from Jean Longuet, and brought a copy of Longuet's recent article. Matteotti glanced at it, and asked if he could have a copy made, so that it could be reprinted in the party paper.

Lanny poured out what was in his heart. Behind his fervor of admiration was a feeling of guilt, because he too ought to have been a man of iron determination, instead of wobbling this way and that and changing his mind whenever he heard new arguments. This lion-hearted Italian had every excuse that Lanny had, for he was the son of a well-to-do landowner, he was a lawyer and a man of culture; doubtless he too loved music and art, and might have enjoyed time off for play. Heroes sound grand in the history books, but it's damned uncomfortable being one, and Lanny would be one in his fancy, but when it came to reality he just couldn't stand it.

Giacomo Matteotti of course didn't know all that. He saw a handsome, ardent youth, with the signs of money on him, and the flush of enthusiasm on his cheeks, the light of admiration in his eyes. Every now and then it happens that some generous soul among the privileged classes becomes touched in his conscience, and you have a convert, and a pair of purse-strings will be loosened to help a party which is always in debt, always facing some emergency. So the secretary took time off to explain the Italian situation to this scion of Budd Gunmakers.

Yes, it was a tragic crisis which the organized workers faced; they were completely unarmed, except for moral and intellectual weapons, and were confronted by enemies who had given themselves such names as "the Savages," "the Damned," and "the Desperadoes." With all their control of the government, they had been able to get a circulation of only 400,000 for their newspapers, while the opposition had ten times that. How long would men of violence permit that state of affairs to continue? How long would criminals allow the public exposure of their crimes? What might happen was terrible to contemplate; one woke in the small hours of the morning facing it, and could find no way of escape during the day.

Lanny mentioned his experience with Barbara Pugliese. "Poor soul!" exclaimed the Socialist. "I knew her well; we had many a conflict in party gatherings. One cannot help sympathizing with people who are driven to desperation by their sufferings, but it is a tragic blunder to brandish an empty gun. Now we face the consequences of the unwise tactics of these extremists; I have the agonizing task of urging our people to keep their hands down, to take their beatings, to die without resistance, if and whenever it pleases our foes to kill them. Such has been the destiny of the wage-slaves throughout the centuries, and the roll of our martyrs is far from complete."

Someone came to remind the secretary of the important conference. He shook hands with his visitor and said: "A little later, when this emergency has passed, will you do me the honor to come to my home and meet my devoted wife and children?" Lanny said that nothing would give him more pleasure.

"You understand," continued the other, "in the next few days I have to complete my unfinished speech. If they prevent my doing so, we must try to find some other way to get the facts to the outside world." He put into the visitor's hands a book which he had published, *A Year of Fascist Domination*, in which he had listed more than two thousand murders and other crimes of violence which Mussolini's partisans had committed. "We shall be glad of any help which you can give us in making these things known," said Matteotti, and Lanny promised to do what he could.

"Remember this, whatever happens," continued the other; "they cannot kill our cause. The workers will learn what we have tried to teach them, and there will be a new generation with more wisdom and courage than ours."

"Surely not more courage!" exclaimed Lanny, and added: "God help you!" He hadn't been able to make up his mind on the subject of God, but he had to say some word to this sorely tried soul.

V

The visitor went about his business of looking for sixteenth-century art. He studied the psychology of members of old Roman families, who had had these things in their palaces until they had grown tired of the sight of them; they didn't believe in the symbolism of the religious ones, and as for the worldly ones, they preferred flesh-and-blood beauties to painted; they preferred modern costumes, and thought how pleasant it would be to have a new motor-car and to pay their gambling debts. The lira was down to four cents, and the very word "dollar" had the power of magic. The only question was, how many could you get? Be wary, don't show too much interest, and try to figure out this good-looking, easy-going young aesthete. Was he a millionaire, or just bluffing, like the Americans in their well-known card game? Why wouldn't he come out and say what he was willing to pay, instead of insisting that you set a price—something which tore your soul in half, because no matter how much you got, you would think you should have asked twice as much.

Jerry Pendleton had told about a walking-trip which he and a friend had taken through Italy before the war. They had picked up half a dozen words of the language, among them *Quanta costa?*—how much? They would go into a country inn and eat, and when they were through they would spread out small coins on the table and say their phrase. The innkeeper would set aside what he thought he should have, and they would divide this into three parts and give him one of them. This was the normal difference between the price to an American and the price to a native, and the proprietor would grin and accept what was offered. Lanny had told this story to Zoltan, who said they would try it in their trading. Lanny would get a price on a painting, Zoltan would come and look at it, and, if it was genuine, he would bring one-third the amount in cash—always in lire, because they looked and sounded so much more!

Lanny put his mind on these affairs, because he had come to Rome for them, and he couldn't keep evading and deceiving Marie. But he had only half his mind on the work, while with the other half he read the newspapers and kept in touch with his friend Corsatti. In Mussolini's paper, the *Popolo d'Italia*, which Mussolini couldn't get the people of Italy to read in spite of being their Prime Minister, Lanny observed pretty broad hints of violence against the opposition. Said the head of the state: "Matteotti made a speech of an outrageously provocative nature which should deserve some more concrete reply than the epithet of *masnada* which Signor Giunta flung at him." Corsatti said that this was Mussolini's way. He would call for violence, he would give secret instructions for violence, and then when violence resulted, he would be shocked, and would say that he couldn't control the ardor of his followers.

The Socialist secretary spoke again in the Chamber, and came into direct conflict with the Prime Minister. Day after day this went on. Said the Socialist Gennari: "We are just out of prison, and we are ready to go back there for the sake of what we believe." Said Mussolini, amid shouts and uproar: "You would have got a charge of lead in your backs. We do not lack courage, as we will show you. There is still time and we shall show you sooner than you think."

Such debates provided exciting copy for foreign newspapermen, and Lanny would drop in at the little *trattoria* where they gathered;

Corsatti introduced him to "the bunch," and they would tell him the latest rumors and gossip. They were making wagers on the subject of the life-span of Giacomo Matteotti, and this seemed rather cold-blooded—but newspapermen have to live, and they are no good if they let themselves take sides on the issues which they have to report. The few Socialist papers in the United States couldn't afford the luxury of correspondents in Rome.

VI

For the afternoon of the tenth of June Lanny had an important engagement with the head of one of the leading princely houses of the Italian kingdom. He had already inspected several of this nobleman's valuable paintings, and now there was an intimation that prices might be discussed. If a deal was made it would be the biggest stroke of Lanny's art career, now in the second year. He was just finishing lunch with his *amie* when he was called to the telephone, and heard a voice, trembling, broken with anguished sobbing. It was the young wife of Giacomo Matteotti, and she was trying to say, in uncertain English, that her husband had been kidnaped from the Via Antonio Scialoja a few minutes ago and carried off by men in an automobile, and wouldn't Mr. Budd do what he could to save him? The horrified Lanny asked what he could do, and the distracted wife said to tell the newspapermen, to tell the outside world, there was nothing else that could restrain the cruel enemy but the opinion of Europe and America. "It is Dumini!" she cried, and repeated the name. "Dumini who was staying at the Hotel Dragoni—Giacomo knew that he had orders to do away with him. Oh, for the love of God!—" the voice broke off, the woman couldn't control her sobs.

Lanny hung up and rushed back into the dining-room to tell the dreadful news. "But, my dear Lanny!" cried Marie. "What have *you* to do with it?"

"I met him, and I must try to help him."

"But how, Lanny—for the love of God?" The same appeal as the wife had made. God would have to choose between them!

"I can't stop now!" Lanny exclaimed. "I must see the newspapermen, and find out what can be done."

"But your engagement!"

"I can't keep it. Phone the Prince for me and make my excuses—tell him I'm sick—anything."

"Lanny—I will go with you."

"No, please—stay here, and I'll phone you." He didn't wait for her consent, but darted out of the room. He didn't wait to get his car out of the garage, but hopped into a taxi and drove to the *trattoria* where he knew that Corsatti and the others would be, unless they had already got the news.

There were three of them, peacefully sipping their *vino rosso* and discussing the young American playboy who dabbled in art and politics, and did he really mean either? When he burst in among them they forgot both their wine and their ideas. "Jesus Christ, I've lost my bet!" exclaimed one, who had been betting on Matteotti's life-span.

They asked him a score of questions, most of which he couldn't answer; but one thing they got: Dumini! Oh, yes, they knew about him; one of the most notorious of Mussolini's associates. In the days before the March on Rome he had boxed the ears of a girl who wore a red carnation, the Socialist symbol, and when her mother and brother protested he had shot them both dead. "And it was he who kidnaped Mazzolani!" exclaimed Corsatti. "Carried him off in a car and forced him to drink castor oil."

"And Forni!" put in the others. That was a crime of the recent electoral campaign, the victim being a candidate for Parliament. It was what Mussolini had meant when he admitted that free electoral meetings had been prevented.

"What can we do?" asked Lanny, in anguish.

"Not much," replied Corsatti. "I'm afraid it's all up with your friend."

"What *we* have to do is to get the story," said one of the others. "If we let the outside world know, there will be repercussions, and that may do some good."

"But then it will be too late!"

"Probably so. It doesn't take long to club a man to death—especially if you shoot him first."

The correspondents had to hurry; it was all in a day's work for them, no matter what their private feelings. Lanny rode with Corsatti to the government office, where he would get the official handout on the story; the government would be in complete ignorance, of course, and would deplore the crime. Corsatti told his friend that, on the chance that Matteotti was still alive, Lanny might do some good by communicating with persons outside who enjoyed means of publicity. "Longuet, for example," he said. "Tell him what Matteotti said to you—the personal touches that will make a human interest story about a Socialist martyr."

VII

Lanny followed this course, because he couldn't think of anything else to do. After some delay he got Longuet on the long-distance phone, and poured out his grief and indignation. Then he went to the telegraph office and wrote a long dispatch to Rick; he was sure that Rick would attend to getting publicity for it. But the message was never sent, for as Lanny was about to hand it to the clerk, two men in the uniform of the Fascist Militia entered the office, looked at Lanny, asked his name, took the telegram away from him, and informed him that it would be necessary for him to accompany them to "headquarters."

It was the second time that this had happened to the son of Robbie Budd in his young life. During the Peace Conference in Paris it had been the *flics;* but French police agents were gentlemen and scholars compared to these self-styled *Disperati*, and Lanny had to think quickly. Was this a kidnaping, and was he to share the fate of Matteotti? If so, would it be better to make a fight for it here, in public? They were hard-looking guys, and had automatics in holsters at their waists; but at least he might attract attention, let people know what was happening.

"Where do you propose to take me?" he demanded, in his best Italian, which wasn't so good.

"To headquarters," was the reply.

"I am an American citizen." Technically it may not have been so, but they couldn't prove it.

"Tell that to the Generalissimo," was the answer.

"I demand the right to telephone to the American ambassador."

"You are to come without delay."

"I am a personal friend of the American ambassador." That too was a slight exaggeration, but he might get away with it. He was trying to get time to think.

"We have nothing to do with any of that."

"And if I refuse to go?"

"You won't refuse very long." The speaker moved his hand toward his holster, and Lanny decided that it would be useless to argue. He went to the street, with one of the men at either side, and he saw that they had an automobile, with a chauffeur in uniform. That reassured him slightly, and he got in and was driven quickly to the general headquarters of the National Militia. He had heard dreadful stories of things that went on in these places; his knees were weak and he had a hard time to keep his teeth from chattering. Inside him he didn't feel the tiniest bit of heroism, but he knew that he ought to behave as if he did. He tried to keep his face set and his head erect, as he had seen heroes do on the stage and screen.

They didn't take him to a cell, but directly to the office of the Generalissimo, whose name was Italo Balbo. Lanny, who had learned a lot about Fascist affairs in twelve days, knew that he was one of Mussolini's intimates, and had led the armed *squadre* in the March on Rome. He was the Ras of Ferrara—Ras was a word which they had taken from their Abyssinian foes, and meant a chieftain. Among the stories which Corsatti had told was of a letter this Balbo had written to the secretary of his home *fascio*, ordering that certain Socialists should be "bludgeoned, not to excess, but in style." The journalist had explained that *bastonatura in stile* was a technical Fascist phrase—let no one say they had not enriched the Italian language—meaning not to hit the victim over the skull, which might kill him, but to beat the lower part of the face and break the jaw-bone, which would lay him up for months. There was a special kind of blackjack, known as the *manganello*, made for this purpose.

VIII

Generalissimo Balbo was a stoutish, military-looking man with sharp black mustaches and a black beard trimmed to a point. In the room with him was another man in Fascist uniform, and a secretary with a notebook—all the apparatus of the *procès verbal*. The two *militi* gave the Fascist salute, and Lanny was marched up in front of the official's desk. The telegram was presented, and Balbo read it; then, fixing a pair of angry dark eyes upon the offender, he proceeded to shoot questions at him: his name, residence, and nationality; his father's name, residence, and occupation. Manufacturer of munitions might help, Lanny thought; but there was no change in the aggressive tone of the questioning.

"What is your business in Rome?" Lanny replied that he had come to arrange for the purchase of cinquecento art-works for an American collection.

"You called at the office of the Socialist party on May 31?"

"Ah!" thought the prisoner. That explained much! He answered, without hesitation: "I went to call on Signor Matteotti."

"What did you want to see him about?"

"I wanted to tell him that I had heard his speech in the Chamber, and how greatly I admired his courage."

"You are a Socialist?"

"I am not."

"Then why do you have so much admiration for a Socialist speech?"

"I admired a brave man speaking the truth."

"You feel quite sure that what Matteotti said was the truth?"

"Quite."

"What sources of information do you have about Italian affairs that you feel able to judge on such a subject?"

It was the sort of question for which Lanny's experience in Paris had prepared him, and his answer was prompt. "I shall make no statement regarding any source of information I may have."

"Oh, so that is your line!"

"That is my line."

"You may perhaps know that we have ways of persuading people to talk when we very much want to."

"You have no way of persuading me to talk about anyone but myself." Something strange was happening to the scion of Budd Gunmakers at that moment, something which surprised himself; a rush of feeling came up in him, telling him that he would stand anything these brutes might do to him—just for the satisfaction of not letting them have their way! Of course he couldn't know whether the inquisitor actually meant these threats or was just trying to frighten him; the need for determination was great in either case.

"You have consorted with certain newspapermen in Rome?"

"I have told you that I will answer no such questions."

"You know Pietro Corsatti?"

"Pardon me. I shall not speak again while you follow that line." There was a pause.

"You say you admire courage, young man. You think you have enough to go through with what we shall do to you?"

"I make formal demand as an American citizen to be permitted to communicate with my ambassador."

"You will not be permitted to communicate with anyone until you have answered my questions; and I warn you that if you don't answer them, you may never do any more communicating anywhere."

Lanny knew that Ambassador Child had recently returned to America; but he might serve in this crisis, even so. "I warn you that the former ambassador knows me personally, and it won't be very long before he will be inquiring as to my welfare."

"How do you come to know the former ambassador?"

"He was a guest of my father and myself at luncheon during the Genoa conference two years ago. It happens that my father

was a personal friend of the late President Harding, who appointed
Mr. Child to his post." Lanny thought he might as well pile it on;
because, while you can endure torture, there's no use doing it
unnecessarily. "It happens that my father is a leading backer of the
Republican party in the United States, and when the newspapermen
learn that his son is in the hands of the Italian authorities there will
certainly be vigorous action on the part of the Embassy."

Lanny had shot his bolt, and could only wait to find out if it had
come anywhere near the target. "Take this man out into the cor-
ridor and wait," said Balbo. "Watch him carefully."

IX

Lanny was seated on a bench with a stone wall to lean against,
and one of his captors on either side of him, not speaking. He
thought as hard as he could, and decided that the Generalissimo had
been trying to frighten him and that, having failed, he would now
do some telephoning. Having an abundance of time on his hands,
Lanny tried to imagine those telephone conversations. Would the
new ambassador know about Budd's? And what would he do?
Lanny knew that Mr. Child had been filling American magazines
with enraptured praise of Mussolini and his regime. Was the new
ambassador of the same opinion? Would he throw Lanny to the
Roman wolves? A far from pleasant thought!

For the second time Lanny was making use of his father's name
and influence to get himself out of a serious predicament. It was
humiliating, but how much chance would he have stood if he had
given his name as Blackless, nephew of a notorious Red agitator?
No, certainly Robbie would wish him to be a Budd in this crisis,
and to use the Budd name to the limit!

What was actually happening Lanny found out later on. Marie
hadn't stopped to telephone to the Prince, but had taken a taxi to
the American Embassy. The ambassador wasn't in, but she had
talked with the chargé d'affaires, who didn't need to be told that
there was a munitions firm known as Budd Gunmakers in Connecticut, or that Robert Budd was a backer of the Republican

party. Being a woman of the world, Marie knew how to present the case of an overemotional young art lover who had listened to an eloquent orator and been moved by an impulse of hero-worship. The chargé smiled and said that once upon a time he had been young himself. He promised that if Lanny got into any trouble owing to his too sympathetic nature, the Embassy would assure the Italian government that he was both well connected and harmless. The chargé hadn't heard the news about Matteotti; he said that it was unfortunate, but of course as a diplomatic official he was compelled to preserve an attitude of aloofness from Italian affairs.

So when Lanny was brought back into the office of Generalissimo Balbo there was no more "rough stuff." The official contented himself with saying: "Mr. Budd, the Italian government is under the necessity of requesting you to remove yourself from this country at once."

Said Lanny: "I am entirely willing to comply with that request."

"Where do you wish to go?"

"To my home on the French Riviera."

"There is a train this evening, and you will take it."

"You have perhaps overlooked the fact that I am motoring."

"Oh, you have a car?"

"I have. Also I have a friend with me."

"A lady friend, I believe?"

"*Sì.*" Lanny wondered if he was going to have to refuse to answer questions about Marie; but he didn't.

Said the Generalissimo of the National Militia: "You and your lady friend will start this afternoon. What is the size of your car?"

"It carries five passengers."

"These two *militi* will ride in the rear seat and see you over the border. You will not be permitted out of their sight until you are across."

"It is going to be rather crowded, because we have considerable luggage."

"You will have to find some way to strap the luggage on, or else have it forwarded. The men will ride with you."

"It wouldn't be possible for them to follow in a separate car?"

"I see no reason why the Italian government should be put to that expense."

"If that is the difficulty, you might permit me to pay the cost of an extra car."

The Generalissimo thought for a moment. Was he afraid that a fast driver might leave the *militi* behind? Anyhow, he answered, coldly: "The arrangement would not be satisfactory. You will take the men to the border in your car. And you will leave at once."

X

A third man in uniform drove Lanny and his two escorts to the garage where his car was stored. Lanny got it out and drove the two to the hotel, where they accompanied him upstairs. Marie was pacing the floor in an agony of fear, and when she saw him enter the room she had to sink into a chair to keep from fainting. When he explained the situation, she wasn't so much reassured; the sight of two dark and grim-faced men in uniform made it seem to her another Matteotti affair, and without saying what she was doing she rushed to the telephone to call the Embassy and explain the situation to the chargé. The latter told her that he had talked with the Generalissimo and received his assurance that no harm was intended to an indiscreet young American—they just wanted to get him out of the country before he made any more trouble for himself.

The hotel attendants carried the luggage down and it was stowed in one way or another. A great sensation in this de luxe establishment, a scandal that would be talked about under cover; but no one ventured to reveal curiosity in the presence of the two *militi*. This, Lanny came to understand, is a phenomenon of dictatorships; nobody stops to ask questions or even to stare; everybody has only one thought, to be somewhere else but where power is being manifested.

There were still two or three hours of daylight when the four set out on their strange drive. All the Embassy officials in the world couldn't give Marie complete assurance, and so long as those two partisans of despotism were in the car her heart would never beat a steady stroke. In Rome itself there was a certain amount of restraint upon the Fascists, there being embassies and newspaper correspondents from all over the world; but in the villages, in remote country districts, armed power had its ferocious way. The highway north which the two travelers had to take crossed many lonely wastes, and wound through mountain passes where an occasional peasant's hut or a shepherd watching his flock was all they saw. And soon it would be night!

X I

Fascismo had won its way as a revolutionary movement; it had sounded the slogans of the poor and dispossessed, promising them dominance over their oppressors. To be sure, it had been vague as to who these oppressors were, and still vaguer as to what was to be done to them; but the emotional content of the movement was subversive, its followers had marched and sung and shouted their joyful thirst for vengeance. These two soldiers were peasant lads who had been half starved and frozen in the trenches of the Adige, and had fled ignominiously from Caporetto; they had been forced to subservience all their lives—and now for the first time they enjoyed power over the most hated of all types, the idle rich foreigners who had helped to cheat Italy out of her war gains, and who dressed themselves in splendor and came into the country to lord it over the poor and live on the fat of the land.

Had anyone told this pair that they were at liberty to frighten these *stranieri* and teach them respect for the Blessed Virgin and the Pope, the ancient Roman *fasces* and the new Roman Empire? Or was it their own inspiration, their native folk humor, a spontaneous contribution to the evolution of *Fascismo?* No sooner had the car got beyond the suburbs of Roma Beata—blessed Rome—than they started telling each other what they thought of these two bloodsucking leeches, and what was going to happen to them before they escaped from the soil of *la patria.* They employed the most pungent words in their native dialect, and neither Marie nor Lanny understood them all, but the tone of venom was enough for the purpose.

The foreigners knew that they were being deliberately tormented; but how could they be sure whether words were to be translated into deeds? The safe-conduct they had received was purely oral, and there would be little possibility of appeal to authorities on the way.

Just one thing they could do, and that was to drive. Marie didn't know how, so it was up to Lanny. He would sit with his hands on the steering-wheel and his eyes fixed on the right-hand edge of the tortuous highway, guiding his car through all the different kinds of scenery there are in Italy, seeing nothing of it, but keeping his mind on the one essential task of putting five or six hundred kilometers behind him, one after another. Try not to listen to the "Savages," the "Damned," or the "Desperadoes," whichever they happened to be. Try to understand the poor devils, pity them as the victims of a perverted culture, products of forces which were forever beyond their capacity to comprehend. Apply the wise ancient maxim, to hate the sin and love the sinner!

Marie couldn't cling to his arm, for fear of interfering with his driving; she could only hold his coat edge, and whisper words of love and comfort. It would be all right; the ride would have its end, they would be safe at home. These poor fools had no real power over them, they could do nothing but talk. Marie whispered in English, on the chance that the poor fools might know some French, and of course she must do nothing to provoke them.

Not being able to get any reaction from the *stranieri*, the ingenious peasants bethought themselves of a new line of conversation. Those who live close to the soil, in intimate contact with animals, are well-informed concerning the processes of nature; they do not believe that babies are brought by storks, and when they discuss the facts of life they do not talk about the bees and the flowers. They knew that this insolent young *americano* was traveling with a beautiful *francese* who was not his wife, and they guessed what they did when they were alone in a bedroom; it entertained their imaginations, and they went into full details about it. Again Lanny and Marie did not know all the words, but they got the gist of it. The *francese* have a world-wide reputation for being sexually passionate; and perhaps it would be fun to stop the car in the course of the night and show her what real Italian *virilità* was like. Perhaps the *favorita francese* might like it so well that she would decide to return to Rome with them. What a joke upon the American millionaire—and surely the Generalissimo would promote them for such a feat!

Marie felt her escort trembling, and that made her tremble. She began a swift whispering, close to his ear, to keep him from hearing what the beasts were saying. "Lanny, don't speak to them! They are poor country louts. What they say means nothing. They dare not do me any harm, or you. It will soon be over, and we will be safe. Promise me that you won't answer them, no matter what they say! You broke one promise to me—don't break another! They want to provoke you, they would like a chance to beat you, perhaps to kill you. Promise me that you will not speak!"

"I promise," muttered Lanny. He knew that she was right. He would be the young philosopher, and observe human nature in the exercise of suddenly acquired power. He would reflect upon the state of a nation which trained its youth to hold such ideas as this pair revealed. It was something worth learning, it would help one to understand the future. These men were worse than the "Savages" they called themselves; they were barbarians armed with modern weapons, with science and its techniques, not merely industrial, but political and psychological. What would Italy be like if a generation of such men grew up and took possession of its affairs? What would become of history, of music and literature and art? What would they do to the rest of Europe?

XII

Lanny had one way to punish this pair; he discovered it with a sudden thrill of amusement. As the sun sank behind the hills and twilight settled upon the landscape, the spicy conversation gradually lost its charms. They came to a village, and there was an inn with lights, and an odor of roasting meats coming forth; but they drove by it without stopping; they passed through the village at the precisely lawful speed of fifteen kilometers per hour, so that no one could have any excuse for stopping them. When they were well outside, Lanny heard the first civil words he had heard from the lips of *Fascismo*. It was the Italian version of the familiar American slogan: "When do we eat?"

The deportee answered promptly, in the best Italian he could muster: "We do not eat; we drive."

Consternation in the back seat. "But, signor, it is necessary to eat!"

"The Generalissimo said nothing about eating. His order was that I should get out of Italy as quickly as possible. Shall I dare to disobey him?"

A long consultation on the part of *Fascismo*. It was carried on in low whispers, and Lanny could only try to imagine it. Would they consider putting a gun between his shoulders and ordering him to stop at the next *taverna*? Or would they reflect that on this basis they would have to pay for their own supper? Could it happen that a government sorely straitened for funds would fail to reimburse its servants for their meals? Would they reflect upon the reputation for lavishness enjoyed by American millionaires? And did they have in their language any equivalent of the American saying that molasses catches more flies than vinegar?

Perhaps so; for when the corporal of the guard raised his voice again, it had a sweetness equal to that of the thickest New Orleans "blackstrap." "Signor, if you will be so kind as to stop and let us eat, we will be *puliti* for the rest of the journey."

"Are the *militi* permitted to be *puliti?*" inquired Lanny, coldly.

"We will be *puliti*, Signor. *Onestamente!*"

So it was time for an American millionaire to show his better nature. "When we come to the next *taverna*, you may eat and I will pay." The whole atmosphere of the journey was changed by that one magical sentence.

They went into a little *albergo*, and the two "Savages" who had promised to be "polite" seated themselves at a separate table from the *damigella*. She wouldn't eat anything, just a cup of what was called coffee; Lanny ate a little, because he didn't want to feel weak; not too much, because he didn't want to feel sleepy. He told the *militi* to have what they pleased, including a bottle of wine, and he raised no question when the *conto* was presented. Lanny got a fresh load of gasoline, and as soon as they were in the country the two peasants fell asleep; they snored the whole night through, and Marie had nothing to worry about but the possibility that Lanny might doze at the steering-wheel.

He was determined to drive straight through. Soldiers had done such feats in wartime, and he would do one now; he felt safer in the car with these men than he would in any hotel room with a bed in it. He bade his *amie* to sleep, and she did so for a while, her head resting on his shoulder. But most of the time she watched the road, winding through the unending mountains of Italy, and if she saw the slightest sign of wandering of the car, she would whisper to Lanny to be sure he was awake.

XIII

They came out to the Riviera di Levante, and there was the familiar blue sea; also there was breakfast, with another bottle of wine for the *militi*. Still Lanny drove, haggard and in need of a shave, but silent and determined; the two Italians respected him now, a man of capacity as well as of millions. They had made a great mistake; if they had been *puliti* from the beginning he might have made them a fabulous present.

Here was familiar scenery; tunnels through the hills and glimpses of bright blue bays with little boats having red sails; cypress-covered promontories, gardens gay with flowers. But Lanny saw nothing of all that; he kept his eye on the right-hand edge of a winding high-way—fortunately the inside track, not the one close to the cliffs! Pretty soon it was Rapallo, and he thought of the Russians, two of whom had been shot to death in the interim. Then it was the crowded streets of Genoa, and the dark medieval building where the conference had been held, and the hotel which he had last seen while the body of the dying Barbara Pugliese lay in the car. After that it was not two *militi*, but one *sindicalista* who was being carried in great haste toward the French border.

Perhaps Lanny was growing a bit delirious, having sat for twenty-four hours at the steering-wheel of a car, with only two intermissions for food. His shoulders and arms ached, and a spot just above the first spinal process, where the motions of the car caused his head to sway, felt as if one of the Italians had put his Fascist dagger-point there and was pressing. But it was all right; they would soon be in France, and he wouldn't have to sit up any longer. He found himself repeating the *Mower's Song* of Andrew Lang: "Hush and be silent, for all things pass!"

At San Remo the party stopped for lunch, in the same little *trattoria* where Lanny and Rick had watched an obscure Italian editor, known as the Blessed Little Pouter Pigeon, devouring his *pasta*, and had seen his eyeballs nearly pop out with rage at the insults of a one-time Red crony. It amused Lanny to put his *amie* in that same seat, and then tell her about it—using, of course, the name of "Mr. Smith." What a sensation he could have caused if he had told the two guards! But he would speak no unnecessary word until he was out of the Fascist domain.

He drove to the border, and when the two men stepped out of the car, he thanked them for having been *puliti*, but offered them no tip, and turned his attention to the formalities of the French customs. The pair stood on their side of the line, watching mournfully; after the luggage and the passports had been inspected and the car was about to start on its way into France, the spokesman of the pair remarked, humbly: "We are poor men, Signor."

Lanny smiled his most amiable smile. "Your Signor Mussolini is going to remedy all that. Very soon you will be richer than we!"

21

The Course of True Love

I

WHAT had happened to Giacomo Matteotti? Lanny got all the newspapers he could find, and read their accounts of the affair. The Italian government had given out a statement to the effect that a passport to Austria had been issued to the Socialist deputy, and that he was probably on his way secretly to Vienna. Also the papers of that morning had a story about the son of a well-known American manufacturer of munitions who had been expelled from Rome for activities considered inimical to the government, and was believed to be motoring toward France, together with a woman companion, a Madame de Bruyne.

Of course that made it necessary for Lanny to phone at once to Beauty, to let her know that he was all right; also to send a cablegram to his father. The story had one unpleasant aspect, which he didn't realize until Marie called his attention to it—she had to be taken to a different hotel from the one at which he was planning to stop. He had involved her in a "scandal." Their love affair, which so far had been discreet and in all ways charming, was now a subject of publicity and gossip; therefore it had become something painful, dangerous, and morally wrong. If Marie had been a Red, or even a Pink, as Lanny appeared to have become, she might have been willing to brazen it out, to say that she was his lover and had been for the past four years—so what? But Marie was a conventional French lady; her friends would be shocked, her husband's family would be inexpressibly shocked, and therefore Marie herself was shocked.

In short, it was a sort of volcanic eruption in their love-life. When Lanny tried to argue with her about the matter, she exclaimed:

420

"There will be newspaper reporters looking for you. And what will you say?"

"I'll tell them about Matteotti, of course."

"But—are they to find me in the same hotel?"

There was nothing he could do to change the world's code of propriety, so he took her to one hotel in Menton and himself to another. It was a measure of the upheaval in his own soul that, instead of grieving over the grief he had caused his *amie*, the first thing he did in his room was to write out again the long telegram to Rick; then he wrote one to Zoltan, and after filing these he phoned to Longuet in Paris, telling him to pay no attention to the stories about Matteotti having fled to Vienna, there was not the slightest doubt that he had been abducted.

By that time the reporters had found the American deportee; they were supposed to be watching the border, but they hadn't thought he could arrive so quickly. He stopped only long enough to wash his face and shave off a two days' growth of beard before he invited them to his room. He talked to them about the dignity of soul of Giacomo Matteotti and the hideousness of the regime which Benito Mussolini had established in Italy. No, he was not a Socialist, he didn't know enough to say what he was, but he knew human decency when he met it, and he had learned what it was for a modern state to be seized by gangsters and used by them to pervert the mind and moral sense of mankind.

In short, it was a declaration of war against Italy; and this was a serious matter for Lanny, if not for Italy. It meant that he permanently removed from his list one of the great art repositories of Europe; also it meant that he branded himself with numbers of persons who might be or might have been his future customers. Many of these persons were like Marie de Bruyne: their eyesight wasn't good when it came to distinguishing among the various shades of red and pink. They had heard two things about Mussolini—that he had put down the labor agitators and was causing the trains in Italy to run on time; over their *apéritifs* or their teacups they would say: "We shall have to be finding someone like that in France before long."

II

Lanny took the long sleep which he had earned; and when he opened his eyes it was morning. His first thought was of Matteotti, and he rang for the newspapers; the boy who brought them to his room brought also a note from Marie. He tore it open and read:

CHÉRIE:

My heart is wrung by the decision which I have to take. I know that you have your ideas, and that you must and will follow them, and it is impossible for me to put chains upon you. Men have to choose their own lives, and it has been made plain to me what your choice is going to be. I am not blaming you in my heart; I am bowing my head to a blow of fate. It would be fatuous to hope that our love might continue under the circumstances. In any case it is impossible for me to travel with you now, so I am taking the night train for Paris. I am trusting to my husband's kindness not to deny me access to his home.

Be assured of my undying gratitude for the devotion you have shown me, and that my heart will always be with you. May God make it possible for you to find happiness in the course which you have chosen.

Your devoted

MARIE.

Lanny was shocked; but not so shocked that he could keep from turning to the newspapers to see what they reported from Rome. Matteotti was still missing, and the government still maintaining that he must have fled to Vienna; there was great excitement in Italy, rumors of uprisings against the regime and so on. The local papers reported the safe arrival of Lanny Budd in France, together with his companion Madame de Bruyne. They quoted the picturesque details regarding his expulsion and long drive, but they gave nothing of his denunciation of the government of a neighboring and friendly state. That sort of thing was left for *Le Populaire* and *L'Humanité* and the rest of the left-wing rabble; and of course anybody who was quoted by them was branded Red.

It was a sad and chastened playboy who drove home to his mother. She was prepared to supply him with a warm soft bosom to weep on, but he didn't make use of it; he was too busy getting the newspapers which came to Cannes on various trains from Paris and London and Rome, and writing long letters to Rick and Longuet and his Uncle Jesse. Lanny was haunted by the thought that Matteotti might still be alive, and that if there was enough clamor in the outside world the gangsters might be frightened into sparing his life. Hadn't Lanny promised the Socialist deputy to do what he could to make the truth known? It was very nearly a death-bed promise, not to be forgotten. He had a mass of facts which he had picked up from the conversation of the newspapermen, and he considered himself morally bound to get these facts published wherever possible. Of course, the more he did this, the more deeply he smeared his name and that of his father.

He had to write a long letter to Robbie, explaining and apologizing. He wrote to Zoltan, in the hope of excusing his bad conduct. He wrote a letter of apology to the noble gentleman in Rome with whom he had broken an engagement. To Zoltan he sent a list of the pictures he had found, with descriptions of them and his guess as to prices. Zoltan, a politically untainted person, could go to Rome at his convenience and take up the negotiations where Lanny had dropped them. To punish himself, Lanny said he wouldn't take any of the commission on these Roman sales. So would start another series of "Alphonse and Gaston acts" between the partners.

To his *amie* the young recreant wrote a love letter. He didn't try to justify his conduct, nor did he say any more regarding Matteotti. During the latter part of their long drive he had told her about the case, and had hoped that she was being sympathetic; now he realized that she had kept her thoughts to herself, in order not to excite or worry him while he was under such heavy strain. Whether she would ever forgive him for his broken promises he couldn't guess, but he wrote that he loved her, and pretty soon he would come and tell her so. "Meanwhile," he said, "remember that scandals have a way of blowing over. There are so many fresh ones for people to talk about."

III

The story of Giacomo Matteotti proved to be a long-drawn-out serial. The unfortunate deputy was never seen alive, and cries were heard in the Parlamento: "The government is an accomplice!" Mussolini had to drop his tale that his opponent had fled to Vienna, and stated in the Chamber that Matteotti had evidently been abducted, but that no one knew where he was. However, the car was traced by its license number, and the names of Dumini and four other criminals became known. Public clamor forced their arrest, and they were supposed to take their punishment like gentlemen, but they weren't that; three confessed that they had committed the crime at the order of Mussolini. Shivers of terror ran through the regime, and the uproar in the Chamber was such that for a few days it seemed possible that *Fascismo* might fall.

The five ruffians had taken their victim to a dense wood a few miles from Rome. They said that they might have spared his life if he had pleaded for it, but he had been "fresh." What he had said was: "You cannot kill my cause. My children will be proud of their father. The proletariat will bless my cause." So they had beaten him to death, mutilated his corpse, and left it unburied. His dying words had been: "Long live Socialism!"

Such were the stories which came out of Rome during the next couple of weeks. Later on the murderers escaped, except Dumini, who was sentenced to seven years' imprisonment. He served about two years and then they let him out. He was heard to remark: "If they gave me seven years they ought to have given the President thirty." So they arrested him again. He denied that by "the President" he had meant Mussolini, but the judges wouldn't believe him, and sentenced his bold tongue to fourteen months and twenty days additional.

All that took time; and Lanny had to manage somehow to go on living, and realize that he couldn't overthrow Fascism, but could only make life uncomfortable for himself and those who loved him. Ambassador Child, alias "Cradle," having resigned his post and returned to the United States, was using his prestige to tell the people of his country that Mussolini was about the greatest man of modern times. He wrote article after article in praise of the "empire builder's" achievements, and these were featured in a weekly magazine having two or three million circulation. What could the feeble voice of one obscure playboy accomplish in the face of such publicity? Lanny was spitting to windward.

"Take it easy, son!" wrote Robbie, patiently. "The world is a tough old nut, and uncounted millions of men have broken their teeth upon it." The father went on to point out that despotisms had existed upon the continent of Europe farther back than any archaeologist had been able to trace; and doubtless there had never yet been a tyrant who hadn't been able to provide moral sanctions satisfactory to himself. "They have built fortresses with thick walls," wrote the salesman of munitions; "and doubtless there have always been idealists butting their heads against those walls—but history hasn't found time to make up the roll of their names."

IV

Beauty had been very considerate of Marie de Bruyne during the past four years; they had made a tacit treaty of alliance; but all the same, there was treason in the mother's heart, and right now seemed to be her opportunity. Very subtly she began to hint to her darling that perhaps it wasn't such a bad thing that Marie had returned to her husband's home; that was where a woman of forty really belonged. Lanny had arrived at an age where he ought to begin to think seriously about his duties to society; it was time for him to look around and find some suitable girl whom he could marry. To save him as much trouble as possible, Beauty herself took up the search.

The Coast of Pleasure had not hitherto been a summer resort, but the "discovery" was being made, and there were a number of young females of property now sojourning in the neighborhood. Beauty put on her gladdest rags and went to parties, and asked such questions as mothers ask, for reasons which all mothers understand. In a few days she had the necessary information, and she gave a tennis party, inviting several darlings of fortune, who all came; for Lanny belonged to the sex which is not harmed by scandals, but on the contrary acquires a certain piquancy, a flavor of romance. Watching her son with hawk's eyes, Beauty saw that his attention seemed to be caught by one young thing of a delicious debutante age; one who enjoyed excellent financial prospects—not a great fortune, but a reasonable one—plus exceptional good looks and a lively disposition. With some encouragement from both mothers, Lanny invited her to go sailing the next day, and when Beauty saw them off across the Golfe Juan, she looked upon it as a major diplomatic triumph.

The young people knew what was being done to them, and took it gaily, playing with the idea of love in harmless delicate ways; making jokes, teasing each other, feeling each other out. It is one of the delights of being young; one of the ways of making a pleasure out of a duty. This girl wanted to fall in love, yet she didn't want to fall too much in love; she wanted to keep her pride, and the independence which her fortune gave her. But at the same time she wanted a thrilling and passionate lover; in short, she wanted a great deal for her money. She was conscious of the money, yet she knew that she mustn't be, because that would be vulgar. She wanted to be loved for herself alone; but it had been pointed out to her that this might be difficult to arrange in France. She had the idea that a youth who was able to make large sums of money by anything so easy as selling pictures wouldn't stoop to fortune-hunting; on the other hand she was frightened by the idea that maybe this would make him too independent, and too desirable to other women. She made little coquettish approaches, and then shrank away; she brought the conversation to a basis of intimacy, then with a quick turn changed it into a joke, and they were laughing at each other.

She was good company, and Lanny wouldn't have minded making love to her if circumstances had been different. What she did was to awaken in him vivid feelings which politics had driven from his mind for a while. He found himself thinking about Marie and wondering what she was doing. It was Marie he wanted in his arms, not any fluttering young thing who didn't understand him and perhaps might never trouble to. The upshot of the afternoon's sail was that he sent a telegram, saying: "*Je viens*," and packed a couple of bags, and kissed Beauty on each of her still-dimpled cheeks, and also in the soft warm neck which he told her was accumulating *embonpoint* once more. This outcome was a disappointment to the mother, but there was nothing she could do about it except beg him to drive carefully.

V

When he arrived in Paris he took the precaution to telephone Marie, who said she would rather come to the city to meet him. He named the hotel, and she came to his suite. She would never fail to be happy when she entered his presence. However, he saw that she was paler and thinner than when he had seen her last, and he had a pang of remorse. He had been cruel to her, he had hurt her more deeply than he could ever realize.

She said: "No, dear; you did nothing that you could help. It is fate that has put a hand between us. The gods are jealous, and they won't let such happiness as ours endure too long."

She didn't want to talk about the "scandal," the unhappiness of her family and her husband's; she knew that was all nonsense to him, and would be a bore. She said: "I am yours whenever you ask for me; but I can't travel with you any more. You must realize that."

"I realize it if you say so, dear. You don't want me to come to the château?"

"I don't think it fair to the boys, Lanny. They are bound to know about it."

"They have probably known for years. Why not be sensible and have it out with them?"

"I can't do it, Lanny. They are Denis's sons, and he has a right to say. After all, it is his home; and he has been very patient and tolerant."

It seemed to Lanny that nothing in the world could be more silly. Here were these big gangling fellows—Denis, *fils*, was now eighteen and Charlot seventeen; they were nearly as tall as Lanny, and their school companions had without doubt told them all there was to know about sex, and perhaps had taken them to those places which Paris has provided for youth to try experiments. But they were being brought up as good Catholic boys, and must believe that what they did was wicked; also that their mother was pure and good, and never did anything like that.

There was no use arguing about it. Marie settled the matter when she said that the home was not hers but her husband's. Lanny would have this hotel suite, and she would come there whenever he invited her. But their love would have to be "clandestine." Marie didn't want to meet any of Lanny's friends, because that would remind them—and her—of the fact that she was the woman who had been named in the newspapers as his traveling-companion. Anyhow, she didn't care for his friends, because they talked politics of the wrong kind, and she was an embarrassment, a wet blanket on the conversation. The only exception she made was Zoltan Kertezsi; he wasn't interested in politics, and he was discreet, a kind friend to Marie as well as a useful influence for her lover.

All right; Lanny would adjust himself to this new life. It had been pleasant sitting in the garden at the château reading a book; it would be equally pleasant sitting in the chairs in the Bois, at the price of a few sous which you paid to an old woman collector. There were any number of sidewalk cafés where you could find all the good things to eat that your fancy might suggest. There were theaters, concerts, and no end of pictures; Lanny could go on studying prices and carrying on his business correspondence. He could have a piano in his rooms, and get a fresh supply of music—yes, Paris could be delightful in summer.

Marie would stay with him two or three days, and then go home and stay with the boys. While the cat was away, the mouse would play—that is, the Lanny mouse would go off on a debauch of politics. He would pay a call on Longuet or Blum, and perhaps hear one of them make a speech. He would call on his Red uncle, whose "free" domestic arrangement was turning out successfully. He would meet Albert Rhys Williams, just back from Russia—the Soviet Union, they preferred to have you call it—with truly marvelous tales about progress in that vast land; they were actually managing to drill some oil wells without any help from Robbie Budd or Henri Deterding or Basil Zaharoff! Lanny would have lunch or dinner with George Slocombe or John Gunther, just returned from one of the capitals of Europe, and hear the latest developments in the world-wide struggle for oil and steel. Doing these things gave Lanny a tremendous sense of adventure; he would get quite drunk on dangerous thoughts—and when he had slept it off he would phone to his beloved and she would come to his arms again. She would guess that he had been misconducting himself, but she would ask him no questions and he would tell her no lies.

VI

Poincaré was out, and there was a new Premier of France, named Herriot. He was a "radical," a word which had its special meaning in that land. It didn't mean an enemy of the property system, as in the States; Uncle Jesse said it meant that France was no longer governed by the Comité des Forges, but by whatever miscellaneous capitalists had chosen to buy the politicians. Of course you couldn't take Uncle Jesse literally; he was just trying to find the worst things to say about the capitalist system. But Robbie Budd would come along and say practically the same things, and it was harder to disbelieve them both.

Anyhow, Herriot was a peace man; he wanted to get out of the Ruhr, and he wanted some way to make sure that Germany would pay her debts and stay disarmed as she had promised. He went over to London with his staff, and they had a series of discussions with the Ramsay MacDonald outfit; the statesmen were hurrying back and forth between London and Paris and Berlin, and it was in the air that big things were being planned. Rick wrote about it, and had high hopes of results. For the first time since the war there were statesmen thinking about the welfare of Europe as a whole; for the first time there was a prospect of real reconstruction for the tormented Continent. Once there was assurance of peace, it would be possible to think about a gradual evolution from the system of private industry to one in which the public welfare would be the end and goal. Rick wrote an article to this effect, and it sounded quite "radical," in the American, not the French, sense. Lanny thought it would please his Red uncle; but, alas, it appeared that no one could please that uncle except the uncle himself. When he read the article he said: "The tiger will agree to have his teeth extracted, one every year, and the extracting will be done by the lambs."

The London conference decided to refer the whole complex of problems to the League of Nations. Everybody had come to realize that the individual nations couldn't handle these matters, and the Entente Cordiale couldn't stand the strain of trying. Let all the nations agree to respect one another's territory, let all unite to punish any transgressor. The fifth meeting of the League Assembly was to take place in September, and Rick was going there to report developments. As soon as he heard this, Lanny began remembering what a pleasant time he and Marie had had in Geneva three years ago. Why couldn't they do it again? Alas for that dreadful, irretrievable thing called a "scandal"! Marie couldn't enjoy being in Geneva; she wasn't even sure that she could return to Bienvenu; not even under the chaperonage of Lanny's mother could the pair of besmirched lovers be made respectable again. Lanny tried to argue about it, but it did no good; he was butting his head against the social code of France.

VII

Every now and then the pair of lovers would have another threshing out of their problems. Marie kept fearing that she was neglecting her boys—even though the boys themselves preferred to be away from home with their boy companions. Also, she was well aware that Beauty didn't want her at Bienvenu. Beauty had been an angel, but in her heart she must hate the interloper. A devoted mother desired to find a proper wife for her son; and Marie, also a mother of sons, felt that Beauty was right, and even went so far as to say to Lanny that if her love for him were deep enough and strong enough, she would renounce him and help to find a proper wife for him.

The playboy never let himself be annoyed by the determination of all the ladies of his acquaintance to see him permanently paired off. He took it as a compliment, and amused himself exploring their ideas about his requirements. What did Marie think would be the proper sort of life-partner for him? She answered that it had become clear to her that Lanny would never be satisfied with a wife who wasn't interested in public questions, and who wouldn't travel with him to conferences and agree with what he thought about them.

"But I never can agree with myself!" objected the young social philosopher. "Don't you think I ought to make up my own mind before I make up my wife's?"

"I think I know pretty well what you believe," persisted the other. She wouldn't tell him what it was, because that might turn into an argument. "I think it's Englishwomen who take the sort of attitude that appeals to you."

"Well, I might go back to Rosemary," he said. He had told her all about that early love affair. But now Rosemary was the Countess of Sandhaven, and had three children—one worse than Marie!

She wouldn't let him turn it off with jokes. It was a real problem, which sooner or later they would have to face. If she had been a selfish woman she would have taken what she could get and let matters ride; but she was good—and that was why Lanny loved her, so the complication grew, and the more they struggled in the net the more they entangled themselves.

"What you are proposing is that I marry a Pink girl," said the wanton trifler. "I have met some of them, and they have indicated that they are willing."

He went into details. Recently he had attended a Socialist *réunion*, and had been introduced to the daughter of one of the speakers. "She isn't a bold new woman, as you might expect from a Pink, but a very simple old-fashioned girl, and I got the impression that she thought I was a romantic personality—on account of what happened in Italy, you know. It might be that she could easily be won. Do you think that would appeal to Beauty?"

Marie couldn't be sure whether he was spoofing or not, but she saw that he was determined to have her return to Bienvenu, whereas she wanted to stay with her aunt. Of course Beauty would have the last word to say about it, and Lanny had asked her to invite Marie, and Beauty hadn't yet done so. Now, smiling to himself, the rascal decided that he would use this old-fashioned Pink girl to settle the matter. He wrote his mother a long and quite serious letter about her, and of course threw Beauty into a panic. She was clinging to the hope that this stage of her son's development was a form of intellectual measles, which he would soon get over. But if he married into the Red movement, that would fix him forever; the designing creature would get him deeper into her toils—Beauty couldn't have said exactly what "toils" were, but they sounded terrible, and even a forty-year-old *amie* would be better. The anxious mother wrote Marie that she was the best influence Lanny had ever had in his life, and please to come and be their guest during the coming winter.

VIII

Marie wouldn't drive with Lanny to Geneva, but urged him to go by himself, and he decided to do so. He stopped off at the Château Les Forêts overnight and had a long talk with his wise friend Mrs. Emily, one of those talks which always left him clearer in his mind as to every subject they discussed. The châtelaine had many friends but few intimates; she said that she understood human nature too well, and it made one rather lonely. This woman of too great wealth presented to the world an aspect of proud serenity, but in the deeps of her heart she craved affection, and for the many years that she had known Lanny Budd she had watched him with maternal tenderness. She had never revealed this, other than by being always glad to see him and doing him any favor that she could. With the deftness of a woman of several worlds she would guide the conversation so as to bring into it anything that she thought he ought to know.

Either through Beauty or through Lanny himself she had shared the secrets of his love affairs, and had no fault to find with them. She thought that Lanny's present *amie* was doing him no harm, but much good. She had told Beauty that, and had something to do with the peace which had prevailed in the singular ménage on the Cap d'Antibes. She considered it much better for Lanny to earn money than to marry it; she could recall few cases where the latter process had done a man any good—and especially a young man. Many had wanted to marry Emily Chattersworth's money, but she hadn't thought it would do them any good!

Lanny told about his misadventure in Italy. Emily didn't think that men could change the world's economic system, which arose out of the excessive greed in their hearts; but that was an old-fashioned idea, perhaps, and she didn't urge it. She recognized it as something natural that a generous-minded young man should try to combat injustice; but she warned him as to the sad discovery he would make, that many of the people who pretended to be combating it were merely seeking advancement for themselves; they would use you all they could, and when they got power they would have no use for their old ideals or for those who had helped them to rise.

Lanny said: "I have observed that. Its name is Mussolini."

"I am sorry to say its name is legion," replied the other.

She talked about Isadora, who had gone to Russia with such high hopes three years ago. Doubtless she had expected too much; she always did. Russia was a place of starvation and dreadful suffering; a little handful of fanatics were finding that they had tried too much. "I don't know whether they are idealists or devils," said the châtelaine; "probably they are half and half."

Lanny cited what his Uncle Jesse kept insisting, that they were rebuilding the country out of their own flesh and blood; they were industrializing a modern state out of its own resources, the first time that had ever been done in history. All the other states had done it with foreign loans.

"That may be true," admitted the other. "But you can't expect that those who have money to lend will lend it for the abolishing of money-lending."

"Uncle Jesse calls that the class struggle," said Lanny, smiling. "He would say that you are a good economic determinist." Emily had never met Beauty's Red brother, but had heard about him; she was content to get her information second hand.

Anyhow, Isadora was having a hard time. She had danced and talked revolution, and had had thrilling receptions, but she had been unable to get what she needed for a school. She had fallen under the spell of a mad Russian poet who was trying to see how quickly he could drink himself to death. Just recently she had divorced him, and the government had arrested him for "hooliganism."

Emily showed Lanny some distracted, scrawling letters from the unhappy dancer. She wanted money, of course; she always had, and would so long as she lived. Emily had sent her a little, which ought to go a long way in Russia. "You are lucky," she said to a susceptible youth, "that you didn't get yourself involved. I suppose that is one of the things you owe to Marie."

IX

The Assembly of the League of Nations was the greatest international event that Lanny had witnessed since the Paris Peace Conference. Here were the diplomats of some fifty nations, many of them stirred by the belief that now, at last, they were going to do something for the peace of the world. Here were journalists, many with the idea that something big was going to happen and they were going to write the story of their lives. Here were the propagandists, the people with ideas, who chose this gathering as a pulpit from which to address the world. Here were the people with wrongs to be righted, lured by vain hopes. Here were observers, curiosity-seekers, tourists who preferred to look at live statesmen rather than at statues of dead ones. The old city of watchmakers and money-changers was crowded, and Lanny, the young prince with a private car, took his English friend to a hotel farther down the lake, and would drive him in every day to do his interviewing and drive him back again to write his stories. Lanny liked to sit in at interviews, and nothing pleased him more than to pay for the dinner of a diplomat.

The correspondents here were the "old bunch," whom the pair had met year after year. San Remo, Spa, London, Paris, Brussels,

Cannes, Genoa, Rapallo, Lausanne—it was like trying to remember the kings of England, which Rick had learned, or the presidents of the United States, which Lanny had never learned. These writing men remembered where they had been, and the statesmen they had interviewed, even the good things they had eaten; they would recall this or that event, what So-and-so had said, how Somebody had got drunk, the girl that Some Other had got mixed up with. Lanny found that his adventure in Rome had turned him into a personality; he had made the headlines, and was no longer a playboy. Men didn't have to agree with his ideas, they might tell him he was a "D.F." to imagine he could buck the Fascists, but all the same he had ideas and had stood up for them, so they respected him.

The young fellow, for his part, never tired of listening to men who traveled all over the world and had new stories every time you ran into them. He took a naïve attitude toward their wisdom; absorbed it gladly, and was puzzled when the wisdom of the next contradicted that of the former. Rick was tremendously impressed by Ramsay MacDonald; he was writing for a clientele to whom the Prime Minister of Labor was the banner-bearer of a new, revivifying force in British political life. Lanny accepted Rick's idea as a matter of course, and found it confusing to meet a correspondent for one of the Tory papers, and hear him declare that he had known Ramsay most of his life, and that there was as much substance to him as to a child's red balloon; Ramsay used fine phrases which he had no idea of relating to reality—his test for them was that they brought applause from the working-class audiences he had spent his life addressing.

The statesmen were working over a thing which was to be called the "Geneva Protocol." The real initiator of it was France, and its purpose was to enable her to back out of the Ruhr without too great admission of failure. Robbie wrote to his son that Marianne had got hold of a bull by the tail, a trying position for a lady; she wanted guarantees that the bull wouldn't turn around too quickly when she let go. According to the Protocol all the nations would agree to apply "sanctions" against any nation which attacked a neighbor; it was another effort to remedy the condition of which Clemenceau had

complained, those twenty million too many Germans in Europe. The
old Tiger, by the way, was still alive, in a little den he had made for
himself on the Vendée coast; every now and then some journalist
would travel there just for the fun of hearing him snarl at the statesmen who were throwing away the hard-won safety of *la belle
France.*

The Versailles treaty had set up a row of little states between
Russia and Germany, made out of territories taken from both those
countries. So long as the little states endured, France was comparatively safe; but who was going to protect them? France couldn't
do it alone, and the British navy couldn't get there. But British
money could arm them, and Zaharoff had the plants to make the
arms. Of course Robbie Budd didn't fail to point that out to his son,
and Lanny showed the letter to Rick. Was that what Herriot meant
when he clamored for "security" as well as "arbitration"? Mac-
Donald insisted that arbitration was enough, and he drew a picture
of "the League of Nations looked up to, not because its arm is
great but because its mind is calm and its nature just." Were those
samples of the phrases which the Prime Minister of Labor used because they brought applause, but which he didn't know how to re-
late to reality? Suppose somebody came along who wasn't either
calm or just, and didn't respect those qualities?

X

Zoltan Kertezsi had been to Rome, and stopped to see Lanny on
his way to London. He skipped about the world like that, and always
had something to report. He had sold a Moroni which Lanny had
found, and expected to sell a Lorenzo Lotto when he went to New
York later on. He had done more business in Berlin and Munich, and
had deposited to Lanny's bank account close to fifteen thousand
dollars. It was not merely having money grow on trees, it was having
it drop off into your pocket; in fact, this lively and intelligent money
opened your pocketbook and forced its way in. Zoltan wouldn't
listen to the nonsensical idea that Lanny hadn't earned his share in
Rome; if they started splitting hairs like that, they would have no

firm basis for co-operation. Lanny didn't know what he would do with all that money, but hoped that somebody would come along to suggest uses for it.

He and Zoltan were two men who knew how to enjoy life as they went along. Lanny took him driving along the shores of that incredibly blue lake. The tang of autumn was in the air and the leaves were falling from the plane trees which line the streets of the towns and villages; the sun shone dazzling bright, and the tops of the mountains glittered like scenes in a fairy-tale. Long after the sun had disappeared the snow-caps were changing from pale pink to lilac and then deep purple. Stop and watch them—for it's no good being so wrapped up in pictures that you can't enjoy the realities which the pictures attempt to portray!

They climbed to the Old Town of Geneva and looked at the ancient gray buildings and monuments; they went through the Musée d'Art together, and Zoltan said: "Why don't you hunt up some pictures here?"

"The Swiss made too much money out of the war," replied Lanny; but his friend said he'd find many German Swiss who had speculated in marks, and would be glad to get some cash.

So when Lanny was tired of hearing statesmen argue about the details of "sanctions" and who was to decide what an aggressor was, he would amuse himself looking for private art collections. Among his friends in Geneva was that Sidney Armstrong who had introduced him and Rick to the League more than three years ago. The young American had been promoted, and now was an important official, tremendously proud of his work in this crisis of history. He knew a lawyer in the city who was a lover of paintings, and for the cost of a luncheon Lanny got from this gentleman the names of several possessors of valuable works. Almost always a courteous note would gain permission to view one of these collections, and after that the tactful sounding out was a matter of routine. Before Lanny left Geneva he was able to send Zoltan a list, and when he got home he would add to his cardfile and send more descriptions and photographs to possible customers.

XI

Also, the day before Lanny took his departure he had an adventure. His *amie* had been talking about his finding a young woman who was sympathetic to his ideas, so Lanny could hardly be blamed for adding that idea to his others. It chanced that Armstrong had a secretary, an American woman a year or two older than Lanny—which wasn't as bad as being forty. She was quiet and unobtrusive, extremely well informed, refined in her manners—in short, everything that a secretary ought to be. Besides, she had qualities not so necessary to her profession—she was slender and graceful, had soft brown eyes and fluffy brown hair, and wore a cream-colored sweater of soft knitted stuff which set off her figure. When Lanny asked questions about people in Geneva who knew about art, it was Miss Sloane who looked up their addresses, and Armstrong remarked that Miss Sloane knew more about everything than he did, and what would he do without her? Which of course made Miss Sloane blush and made Lanny decide that she was an attractive young woman. He was always deciding about some one of them.

When he was ready to leave, he called on Armstrong to thank him and say good-by. The official was expected back shortly, so Lanny sat in his office, and as Miss Sloane happened to be there, he told her about the satisfactory outcome of his art researches. He discovered that she knew the Musée d'Art very well, but she had the impression that all great paintings were in such public places, and hadn't realized that great numbers were privately owned. She was disposed to find the buying and selling of them a highly romantic occupation.

She was going out to lunch. Of course it was accidental, their leaving the old League of Nations building at approximately the same moment. It was natural that he should ask if she was going to lunch, and then if he might invite her; it was natural for her to be taken aback, and to ask if she ought to let him. Lanny said: "Why not?" and she didn't seem to know any reason, so he took her. Because he was fastidious about his meals he drove to a good place, where they would be waited on in style. This would take time, and perhaps distract a secretary's mind; Lanny, who had been a secretary for six months, should have known better.

Miss Sloane had heard about his misadventure in Italy. Had she heard about the lady companion? If so, she didn't mention her. She said that the Italians were the least international-minded of any of the people who came to Geneva; the Fascists were intolerable. The attitude of many Italian men to women inspired an American girl with impulses toward murder; she didn't say what they did, but Lanny knew that they sometimes indicated their admiration by coming up in back of a woman on the street and giving her a large pinch on the behind. He said that he understood Miss Sloane's feelings.

In fact he found that he understood most everything about her. He talked about Matteotti, and didn't have to make apologies for his conduct; she didn't see how he could have done otherwise. He discovered himself to be a shining hero in the eyes of this fine young woman, and of course that is a pleasant sensation for any man, young or old. It transpired that she was able to discriminate clearly among the different shades of Red and Pink, and that these distinctions were important to her. She said: "We find the Socialists have the broadest viewpoint of any of the groups we have to deal with." By "we" she meant, not merely her employer and herself, but the secretariat of the League, which ran the League. In short, Janet Sloane took a broad view of herself and her activities, and Lanny could understand such an attitude, having taken it in the spring of 1919, when he had thought that he was remaking the world.

It is pleasant talking with someone from whom you don't have to conceal any of your thoughts. Marie had forfeited this position in Lanny's life; his mother and his father likewise had forfeited it—in fact, Eric Pomeroy-Nielson was the only friend with whom he felt free to speak with complete frankness. He told Miss Sloane about the struggle that was going on in his mind, the difficulty he had in being sure what he really believed. She said that was a credit to him, for the world was darned complicated right now, and it was better not to get set in a groove. This warmed Lanny's heart, and he talked a lot, and kept this young woman away from her work longer than he had any right to.

When he drove her back to her office he said how much he had enjoyed talking to her, and she remarked: "It's too bad you have to leave so soon." That certainly gave him an opening, and he said he wasn't leaving until morning, and did she have any engagement that evening? If not, might he take her for a drive and have supper at one of several pleasant places he knew? In the words of the old music-hall song, first she said she wouldn't, then she said she couldn't, then she answered, well, I'll see. She did.

XII

Lanny told this agreeable new friend to wear a warm coat, and he put a warm rug in the car, and drove her all the way around Lac Léman, a distance of some ninety miles; one doesn't undertake a drive like that unless one really means to get acquainted. They watched the sublime scenery through the changes of twilight and evening, and they became acquainted very quickly. They talked about nature and art and life—but not about love, because they didn't dare to.

What was appening became exquisitely apparent to both when they sat in a quiet niche in a café, with only a small table between them. Miss Sloane would lift her soft brown eyes to her companion's, and a flush would steal into her throat and over her cheeks, and she would have to drop her eyes, she just couldn't bear his glance; he knew it, and was afraid to look at her, because it embarrassed her so greatly, and he didn't want to be one of those Italians, staring into a woman's face. They would go on trying to eat their food, and to talk about the problems of Europe; but to hell with Europe!

It was something that had happened to Lanny more than a few times, and he didn't know what to do about it. There were just too many desirable women in the world, and one couldn't love them all. He had had enough experience to be sure that, regardless of what any woman might say, or even what she might believe, if she wanted a man she wanted him to herself and she wanted him all the time. Any temporary pleasure he might give her would be more than balanced by the pain she would suffer when he took his departure. Love 'em and leave 'em might be a good motto for callous hearts, but Lanny was kind, and really cared about the women he met, and so it was the very devil.

Right now was an especially distressing situation. He had labored for months to persuade Marie to come to Bienvenu. Now he had told her that he was coming for her, and she would be packing for the journey south. He had planned to drive all the next day and reach Paris late in the evening; Marie would be waiting at his hotel, and the blood would be in her throat and cheeks also, her arms would be warm for him. Now her image rose between him and Janet Sloane and made a blur between them.

No, he mustn't do it! He went on talking about the problems of war and peace, and when they went back to the car he wrapped her warmly, without adding the warmth of his arm. But it was hard to keep down his curiosity concerning her. Was she one of these modern women who took what they wanted? Most of the women of all nations who came to Europe didn't come because they meant to remain virgins. While she talked about the problems of "sanctions," and the deplorable consequences of American refusal to pledge support to any boycott—"It'll be exactly like breaking a strike!" she said —Lanny's mind would wander off on these sidepaths. He would be thinking: "I wonder if Beauty is right, and if I ought to find a wife. I wonder if this girl would make me a good wife. Perhaps I ought to stay and find out about her. How will I ever know if I run away from them?"

It was late when they arrived in front of the pension where she lived. There was no moon, and the street light was some distance away. Lanny got out, and took her hand to help her out, and her hand stayed in his; that was perhaps natural, since you shake hands with a friend when you part. He said: "I'm sorry I have to go." Then he should have gone, quickly. But he felt her hand trembling, and doubtless his was trembling. Suddenly he heard a faint whisper: "I want you to know, Lanny, I think you are the nicest man I have ever met."

"Oh, no!" he exclaimed; there was pain in her voice, and he didn't want to hurt her so much.

"Oh, yes!" she answered; and then: "Would you be willing to kiss me just once?"

Of course he couldn't say no. He took her in his arms, and it was one of those long kisses that don't want to end; the kind the Japanese censors cut out of the motion pictures that come to their country, and they put the pieces together and make one huge film of a great variety of Anglo-Saxon lips clinging to lips, and they show this to their friends with hilarious glee. Lanny still didn't know whether Janet was a virgin, but he knew if he had drawn her back to the car, she would have let him take her wherever he wished.

But close as they were together, the image of Marie was still between them. So Lanny said: "I'm sorry, dear. I wish I were free." That was enough, and she whispered a quick "Good-by" and fled to the door of her pension. Lanny stood by the car with his head bowed, mentally kicking himself. He would have been kicking himself whichever way that adventure had turned out.